This novel will be a special blessing for [...] comprehensive picture of the historical Jesus. The author [...] canonical Gospels, but expands it in a way that would make Marcus Borg smile. We will meet some familiar characters like John the Baptist and Judas Iscariot. But we will also meet and be captivated by some unforgettable personalities, as well, like the well-to-do Seti of Sepphoris and the charming and benevolent Lady Calpurnia of Alexandria, both of whom lay key roles in Maddox's delightful vision of the Jesus about whom we yearn to know so much more.

Dr. Tony M. Martin, Professor of Biblical Studies (Retired),
Mary-Hardin Baylor University, Belton, Texas

In his novel, *Jesus of Nazareth and the Kingdom of Weeds*, Robert Maddox gives us an imaginative, expansive and at times provocative representation of Jesus the man. Here, Jesus is obviously extraordinary, but has become so as he embraced both the joys and vicissitudes of life during a particularly turbulent and violent time in Jewish/Imperial Roman history. This two-volume novel is a vivid and poignant story of a man full of God who continues to compel millions to seek the purpose and meaning of what it is to be human.

Rev. Jill Johnson, Minister in Discernment,
United Church of Christ, Baltimore, Maryland

My Catholic grandmother and my Baptist grandfather shared very few doctrinal convictions. What they did share was the story of Jesus. With his telling of the Jesus story, Robert Maddox fashions an engaging narrative that both of my grandparents nurtured in me. Now, the author gifts us with this breathtaking view of that human story.

Dr. William B. Rogers, Professor of Religious Education (Retired),
Charlotte, North Carolina

The story of Jesus is perhaps the world's most influential story. But the gospels that tell us that story are limited. Glimpses. With this novel, Bob Maddox offers us insights, guesses and imaginative journeys into the full life of Jesus. With scholarship, history and lyricism Bob invites us to see a Jesus of flesh, blood, family, friends, pain, pathos and joy.

Rev. Dr. Timothy Tutt, Senior Minister,
Westmoreland Congregational United Church of Christ, Bethesda, Maryland

JESUS OF NAZARETH AND THE KINGDOM OF WEEDS

*a Novel*

Book Two

# The Kingdom of Weeds

## Robert L. Maddox

© 2020
Published in the United States by Nurturing Faith Inc., Macon GA,
www.nurturingfaith.net.

Nurturing Faith is the book publishing arm of Good Faith Media (goodfaithmedia.org).

Library of Congress Cataloging-in-Publication Data is available.

ISBN: 978-1-63528-114-9

All scripture quotations are free renderings by the author inspired by the
Revised Standard Version of scripture.

# Contents

# Foreword

I am heavily indebted to many scholars of the Jesus Seminar, especially Robert Funk, Marcus Borg, and Jon Dominic Crossan, as I wrote this book over the past twenty-five years. For most of my earlier professional life, I had hunches that Jesus of Nazareth had much to offer me that the Gospels omitted, but I did not know how to fill in those blanks. When I encountered the women and men of the Jesus Seminar and their compelling, respectful scholarship on the Jesus of history, I found the Jesus I was looking and longing for. These two volumes present an earnest and reverent attempt to use my tutored imagination to walk with Jesus of Nazareth, carefully and joyfully filling in some of the historic gaps that bring Jesus much more to life for me.

I am further grateful to Linda Maddox and Rev. Dr. Tim Tutt, who hung with me through the quarter century it took to write and rewrite this story. I am deeply indebted to Dr. Bill Rogers and Rev. Jill Johnson for over-the-top encouragement in this final effort. Words cannot convey my profound appreciation to Dr. Tony Martin, a friend of sixty years, a gifted New Testament scholar, for expert advice, line-by-line reading and careful editing. Tucker Ball and Ferew Haile are my IT gurus. Dr. John Pierce and Lex Horton of Nurturing Faith guided me in the publication that resulted in volumes one and two.

The anonymous authors of the four New Testament Gospels (from about 70 CE to maybe 100 CE) were not much interested in an extensive biography of Jesus. They wanted to celebrate what they regarded as Adonai's wondrous act of grace in sending Jesus into the world as Adonai's ultimate demonstration of love. Though the New Testament opens with the four Gospels, it is important to etch into the reader's mind that the Jesus movement had been in formation at least four decades when Mark's Gospel, the first one, made its way into a Jesus group in Galilee, Jesus's homeland. The Jesus movement as it unfolded, pointed to by Paul's letters (beginning in the 50s CE), created the Gospels, not the other way around.

The Gospels are magnificent, classic, world-shaping, reverent sketches of Jesus of Nazareth, who, to his followers, became the Christ. The Gospels have many tantalizing gaps in the story of the Jesus who lived, walked, and loved among family members, Galilean friends, and tyrannical religious and political systems. The Gospels are essentially memories of memories of a cadre of devoted followers of Jesus. That said, the four Gospels are all we have of the telling of the

Jesus of Nazareth story from about 4 BCE to about 30 CE. Through careful, reverent, well-researched twenty-first-century flights of informed imagination, I aim to fill in some of the historical blanks in the life of Jesus of Nazareth, this unique person, in the words of John Shelby Spong, "full of God."

Volume one imagines the Αρχή (beginning) of Jesus of Nazareth. Volume two trumpets the call of Jesus to serve his beloved kingdom of weeds. As the late Marcus Borg had a way of saying, "It may not have happened exactly this way, but it's true anyway." Meet Jesus again for the first time as he grew and served among God's beloved "weeds" in his own time.

# Chapter One

# The Voice of One

*A voice cries out: In the wilderness prepare the way of the Lord; make straight in the desert a highway for our God.*

News spread rapidly through Alexandria of Jesus's episode of walking out of the imperial stadium. As Julian had predicted, invitations to social events for Jesus and Calpurnia ended overnight. At first Calpurnia fumed, grieved, stormed in anger at Jesus. Soon, she began to laugh. "I have discovered something, Johanus," she confided to her chief steward with a broad, free smile on her beautiful face. "I do not need all those silly, wasteful dinners and receptions. I am not nearly so tired as before. I have time to do what I want without the constant rush to get ready for yet another dinner."

Jesus hardly noticed, and he certainly did not care.

—

"Jesus," the disheveled, travel-worn man at his door said evenly yet authoritatively, "It is time for you to come home."

Shocked, uncomprehending, blinking to see clearly who was speaking, he replied, "John? Is it you? John, my cousin! You are here?" His mind simply could not absorb what his eyes beheld. "What? Why? How?" Shaking off his stunned surprise, Jesus flung open the door. "It is you! Come in. Come in, please."

With no more inflection in his voice than he would have used if they had seen each other that morning rather than nearly ten years ago, John said tersely, "I will come in, and thank you. I have come to escort you back home. It is time."

A few minutes later, seated, with a cup of wine and some food, brushing aside Jesus's steady flow of questions, John said emphatically, "I suppose you have some loose ends to tie up before we can leave. That should take you only a few days at the most. I will wait."

"A few days!" Jesus blurted, pacing around the room in great consternation. "You have no idea what you're talking about. I have a hospital to run. Every day, I tend to scores of sick people. I have made many wonderful friends in Alexandria. I am in the midst of important studies dealing with a wide variety of illnesses. You expect me to just walk away from all this simply because you have come here on some harebrained notion that I ought to journey back home?"

Completely unruffled by Jesus's reaction, John took a drink from the cup, tore off a piece of bread, and said, looking at the food, "This is good. Better than I have had in a long time. You may miss it when you get home. And now, back to our departure. Close up your affairs as soon as possible. We have to be getting back."

"I know what this is all about," Jesus insisted, looking warily at John. "My mother and James have put you up to coming here and fetching me back home. That's it, isn't it?"

"I have not seen your family since Joseph died. I know nothing of them. When my mother died, we sent word to Mary. She wrote me a letter expressing her grief, but she did not come."

"John, Elizabeth died," his harsh tones immediately replaced by grief. "I am so sorry. She was a wonderful lady. Her death is a great loss to you."

"Yes," John said stiffly, guarding his emotions. "She was extraordinary. I miss her every day. The pain does not seem to go away. But we all must die. It's what we do while living that matters."

Jesus told Ebus of his cousin's arrival and stunning announcement. The physician—and, after the years they had shared, dear friend—looked thoughtfully at his brilliant colleague for a few moments, saying nothing. Then he continued, "Your cousin is right. It is time for you to go home. I have no idea why I say such a thing. The very idea of your leaving makes me want to weep and restrain you. Still, in my bones, I agree. It is time."

"You and John are both out of your heads," Jesus growled, pacing around the room like a caged animal. "I do not understand it. Not at all. I thought you were my friend," he fumed.

Calpurnia collapsed in a heap of angry tears. "Leave?" she moaned through her sobbing. "You cannot. It is impossible. Your cousin is insane. Ebus is jealous and wants all the fees for himself. He's glad to think of getting rid of you."

Erasistratus said, "Of course you have to go back home. You never came to stay. You are one of the most gifted physicians I have trained. The gods, if there be such, have richly endowed you. Go back to your homeland and make many people well. And those who cannot get well, help them find peace. I will miss you desperately."

His Excellency, Julian, governor of Egypt, sent for Jesus when he heard the news. "Listen, Jewish physician, if you want to stay here, I will make you court medicine man. You can go with me to Rome. I will make you rich and famous even though you say you care for neither. But you would be wasting your time in that swamp of humanity. Most of the people of Rome do not even deserve to live, much less have the benefit of someone like you."

After a moment's pause, he continued, "A word of warning. Pontius Pilate, the new governor of Judea, is not a good man. I have known him for many years. Stay out of his way. He craves everything you eschew. You would find him pitiable. He would find you dangerous."

Jesus declined Calpurnia's offer of a farewell banquet. He did gratefully accept her offer to gather his closest friends for a more intimate dinner. John refused to attend. John refused to do anything except stay in Jesus's apartment and wait for his cousin to conclude his Alexandrian life, and that not with the greatest measure of patience. He had no interest in seeing the city. He had no need to visit the great library. He would only say, "When the day of the Lord comes, all this will be of no value."

At the last service he attended at the Alexandrian synagogue, Caleb and a few other men who had come to be particularly fond of Jesus gathered around him. "Jesus, kneel before us. We want to pass a blessing to you."

He knelt while the men gathered around him in a circle, each touching him on his head, neck, shoulders, face while Caleb sang in Hebrew, *Bless the Lord, O my soul; and all that is within me, bless his holy name. Bless the Lord, O my soul, and forget not all his benefits. Who forgives your iniquities, who heals all your diseases, who redeems your life from destruction, who crowns you with loving kindness and tender mercies. Bless the Lord, all you ministers of his, that do his pleasure. Bless the Lord, all his works in all places of his dominion. Bless the Lord, O my soul.*

—

"No, John, we will not walk back to our homeland," Jesus declared emphatically. "I do not care if you crawled here on your knees; we will sail from Alexandria to Caesarea."

"I have no money for the fare," John snapped. "I never have money. Adonai has seen to it that I do not have any need for money."

"You need not become tainted this time either. I am already sufficiently corrupted by money to have more than enough for my fare and yours," Jesus answered lightly, an easy smile on his face.

"But I have never sailed on a ship. I will get sick."

"You probably will get sick. I accept your voice calling me home as the voice of Adonai, but he has not told me to walk those hundreds of miles when we can get on a ship and be home in only a few days."

The morning they left, Jesus's friends—young and old, rich and poor—gathered on the dock to bid him farewell and traveling safety. Each had a special Jesus memory. Many were people he had worked with to overcome illness, disease, and other life-threatening situations. To his amazement scholars and students from the library came, including Erasistratus, Alexandrinus, and Cabalium. Ebus and several from his house stood with tears streaming down their faces. Cleo was there with Johanus. Dinocrates and Aristarchus blessed him. Calpurnia did not come. He understood.

A mother and her daughter, a child five or six years old, caught Jesus's eye as they stood to one side of the group. It took him a minute to recognize the woman as the mother whose baby he had saved years ago when he first got started with Ebus. When her eyes met his, she lit up, waved at him, and held up the girl.

Over the heads of the crowd, motioning for her to stand still, Jesus dashed on board the ship, leaving others of his friends standing on the wharf in confusion. In a moment he returned and came to her.

"I never had a chance to thank you for helping me get out of jail," he whispered to her, reaching out to touch the little girl as he spoke.

"She's beautiful," he continued, looking back and forth between mother and child. "You are a wonderful mother. Keep it up."

The mother glowed. "Master," she answered, "when word got out in our part of the city that you were leaving, I just had to come say goodbye. My little girl and I would long be dead if you hadn't helped us. She knows all about you. We will always remember and love you."

"I have something for you," Jesus whispered, leaning down close to her face. In a way that no one else could detect, he slipped her a small purple velvet bag trimmed in cloth of gold braid.

"Do not open this now. When you get home, look at it, and then sell it. As shrewd as you are, it could bring enough money to last you and your daughter for a long time. Stay well. Serve others."

The mother blinked, felt the heavy, round, flat object inside the little bag, knelt before him, then stood and walked away, one hand in the pocket of her cloak, the other holding her little girl's hand.

At last, he had found a good use for that ridiculous gold medal from the governor.

As the ship eased away from the dock, Jesus's heart broke. He waved, saluted, called out over the rapidly widening distance. For all the world, he wanted to jump ship and swim back to these splendid people Adonai had allowed to cross his path. Now hoarse from shouting at his friends, exhausted from the ordeal, the people of the wharf becoming smaller and smaller, he dropped his tired body on a pile of ropes coiled on the deck and let the Egyptian experience wash over him. Again, tears of joy and parting flooded his eyes. Other passengers looked at him puzzled, asking themselves, "Who is this man who generates that much love and appreciation?"

John stood to one side, impassive throughout the entire leave-taking. He spoke to no one, and no one spoke to him. His austere appearance, the faraway look in his eye, his seeing but not seeing repelled any of Jesus's friends who might have warmed to him. Was he saying by his demeanor that they did not matter? Were they just so many human bodies taking up space on the earth? Were they such wretched sinners, so far off Adonai's mark that no hope existed for them? Or was he so insufferably lonely in the depths of his own soul that the evidence of those profound relationships between Jesus and the Egyptians conjured up such pain that he dared not let himself feel anything?

No sooner had the ship made it to the open sea than John, pasty-faced, perspiration popping out on his forehead, mewed to Jesus, "I am going to die."

For hours he writhed on the deck, heaving up nothing since he had long ago lost what food had been in his stomach.

"It's your fault," he groaned. "I wanted to walk!" And for the hundredth time he pulled his legs up against his body as convulsions shook him.

"John, I am sorry you are so sick. Believe me, it will pass. In all my medical books I found nothing that would relieve seasickness except the passage of some time."

By dawn the next day, John managed to struggle to his feet. At noon he could walk the deck, carefully clinging to the rail. By sundown he wanted something to eat. The third day, he began to enjoy the voyage, like countless others who, having found their sea legs, reveled in the beauty and power of the sea. The bright sun, scudding clouds, the screeching of the gulls that easily flew from the distant shore to the ship, the playful porpoises, the skittering flying fish all momentarily transported his monumentally complex spirit upward and outward to embrace the glory of the Adonai he served with such grim determination. He actually sang to himself, *The heavens declare the glory of God; and the firmament shows his handiwork. Day unto day utters speech, and night unto night shows knowledge. Let the words of my mouth and the meditation of my heart be acceptable in your sight, O Lord, my strength and my redeemer.*

Breaking into his cousin's reverie, Jesus said with some impatience, "John, I have tried to talk with you the entire time you've been in Egypt without much success. Now that we are out here on the sea with time on our hands, tell me what has happened in your life these years since you helped me get back home after my father's death."

"You have no need to know," John answered quietly, a note of finality in his voice that seemed to shut off all conversation.

"John, I must know."

Though he preached to scores of people every day, John still felt comfortable talking personally only to the spaces he and Adonai alone occupied. It took John many hours of halting speech before he got to the place where he was even willing to trust Jesus sufficiently to open his soul. At first in snippets and rivulets and ultimately in great swaths and cascading torrents, his story unfolded.

—

After accompanying Jesus home to Nazareth those years ago for him to tell his family of Joseph's death, he and Joses of Arimathea made the trip back home to Ain Karim without incident, even during the trek through Samaria. For a time John worked at odd jobs for neighbors. After some months of labor, with enough food and money on hand to supply his mother's simple needs for a time, he began to feel he must retreat into one of the region's uninhabited hideaways.

"John," Jesus asked while they talked into the night as the ship gently ploughed through the sea, "what do you do in those long spells alone? How do you eat? Where do you sleep?"

"I pray, mostly. I walk or sit or lie trying to think through my life, my own feelings about what Adonai wants me to do. What he would want me to say to the people when the time comes."

"What time?" Jesus wanted to know.

"God's time. It's a different time. But, Jesus, you know that. For years you lived by Adonai's time and not your own."

"I do not know that," Jesus asserted.

"Yes, you do," John replied irritably. "For as long as I have known you, you moved on Adonai's schedule, whether or not you admit it. Now the time has arrived for you to put everything together."

John continued his story.

"I could always find something to eat out in the hills. My years of wandering, of listening to roving bands of shepherds talk, of watching other men and women who, like myself, chose to spend many of their days and nights alone in the empty places taught me where to look for food. I never went hungry. Always, Adonai provided what I needed, just as he did our ancestors in their years in the Sinai wilderness. I slept where I was when I got sleepy."

"What did Adonai tell you?"

"It took me months, years to hear and discern his message to me," John said evenly.

"And do you now know?"

"Yes."

———

After one of John's especially long absences in the wild places, he returned to Ain Karim to find his mother ill. She had a bad cough. She looked emaciated. Her eyes were hollow, listless.

"Mother," he exclaimed fearfully, "you're feeling terrible. Did you give out of food or money while I was gone?"

"No, John. I simply became ill. Neighbors cared for me. I just could not get well, or so it seemed."

"I wish you had sent someone to find me," he replied, his voice choking.

"John, listen to me. I do not want to interfere with the conversations you and Adonai have. You must not interrupt your own search to take care of me. I will live or die either way in the hands of Adonai. I am not afraid," Elizabeth assured him.

Knowing he could not disappear into the emptiness for the foreseeable future in light of his mother's declining health, John intensified his labors in and around his village to provide for Elizabeth and himself. His heart was with his mother, his body in the work he performed, but his spirit was out there, wandering the hillsides, trying desperately to formulate his response to Adonai's call on his life.

Ever since he had reached maturity, the village leaders had pressured him to take his place in the priestly rotation for service at the Jerusalem temple. "It's your duty," they insisted. "You are of the tribe of Levi, of the family of Abiathar.

Besides, we have not had proper representation in Jerusalem since your father's lamented death."

He finally agreed. Elizabeth fully expected her son to come storming into the house any day during his first term furious, wounded, grieved at the perversion of the worship of the living Adonai he had witnessed at Jerusalem. To her surprise, relief, and no little confusion, he did not return home until his time was up.

"Mother," he admitted, "it was awful. The money, the money that changes hands. The cynicism with which most of the priests approach their work. They go through the motions for the pay they receive. They have no heart for what they do."

"Why did you stay? I honestly thought you would storm away in a rage."

"Believe me," he replied thoughtfully, "I came near many times until I would look into the faces of our people who were so earnest, so believing, so eager in their worship! They have such a powerful desire to be faithful in their devotion to Adonai. I did not have the heart to walk away. Maybe somewhere down in the middle of what we do at the temple, something honors Adonai and has meaning for the people. I will keep trying."

With the modest stipend he received from his temple duties, John could provide for his mother's simple needs, freeing him from having to pick up the odd jobs that sustained them during leaner times.

"John," she said a few days after he returned from Jerusalem, "you're getting restless. I can tell. I feel well enough. Go spend time in your wilderness. Come back soon. But wander with Adonai for a spell."

He and his mother understood each other so sufficiently that he did not put up a false front of hesitation. If she said he could and should go, he would.

"Thank you, Mother. I will leave at daybreak."

"Take some food with you," she insisted. "No need for you to forage the whole time."

"You keep the food," he insisted.

John headed south toward the Dead Sea, in the general direction of that colony of strange men, the Essenes who lived at Qumran. He had visited with them from time to time when he was younger. Before his father died, he considered becoming one of them. The austere life of discipline, hard work, sparse living, and constant prayer appealed to him. On the other hand, the prospect of living so close to other human beings day and night terrified him. When Zechariah died from his fall in the temple, John put aside any thoughts of becoming an Essene since that would have meant he could not care for his mother. Still, many of their ideas intrigued him, found resonance in his own soul. He was especially drawn to their revulsion of the temple system and their belief that Adonai would soon crush the priests, Romans, and all in Judaism who offended the divine sensibilities.

So rather than wandering in the wilderness this time, he decided he would invest the days his mother had given him in serious conversation with whoever among these otherworldly men would talk with him.

As he walked, he came upon a tree stump alive with bees. Using skills he had long ago learned from resourceful pilgrims like himself, he smoked the bees away from the hive long enough to glob several large combs dripping with honey into the skin bag he always carried. He would trade the honey with some of the Essenes for a few days' rations.

He wasted no time going to their settlement a short distance south of the oasis town of Jericho and a couple of miles inland from the Salt Sea, certainly one of the hottest places on earth. He braced himself for the ferocious heat.

Over the past several decades the Essenes lived in this dry, hot land, they had constructed many of their spartan dwellings at or below ground level, thus shielding their rooms from as much of the searing heat and scalding hot winds as possible. John remarked to himself that most of the men went down into their chambers in much the same way as the desert rodents darted into their burrows. He presented himself to one of the leaders and arranged to exchange his honey for some bread, dried fruit, a small bag of water, and a place in one of those underground warrens.

During the next few days, as he wandered freely in the settlement, baptisms caught his eye and surprisingly stirred his heart. Though he had watched their ritual baptisms in his other visits, the rite arrested him this time in a fresh way. Among some groups of Jews across the centuries, immersion baptism was part of the ritual by which a Gentile converted to Judaism. A person born into a Jewish family did not need initiatory baptism, though some of the larger homes of strict Jews did have baptistries inside. The array of purity codes called for frequent washing of the hands and other parts of the body; many natural-born Jews would have been insulted for anyone to suggest full baptism to them. Jews, as children of Abraham, were members of the faithful by virtue of their birth, and no amount of ritual baptism could make them any more connected to the family of Adonai.

For the Essenes, despite their Jewishness, baptism for ritual cleansing and testimony of their righteousness was part of what a faithful member of the community did. Scattered throughout the settlement, baptistries had been dug from the rocky earth then sealed with stone and mortar to hold water. On the basis of some inner, spiritual prompting, the men periodically submitted to the rite in the all-male community by stripping away their clothing, going down into the tank, and receiving baptism at the hands of one of the community's leaders. Since the pools were not that deep, and given the scarcity of water for any purpose, the devotee knelt on his knees while the celebrant pushed him forward, face down, into the sacred waters.

Perhaps the Spirit had moved among several of the men because John noticed that a dozen or more of the faithful were standing by several of the pools waiting their turn for their next baptism. Suddenly, grabbed by the sight, prompted by a profound inner need, John resolutely, with head bowed, took his place in one of the lines. When his turn came, he stripped away his shift and stepped into the small tank.

Startled, the celebrant looked at him and said, "You are not a member of the community. You cannot be baptized unless you choose to become one of us."

"Father," John answered the man softly, a pleading tone in his voice, "Adonai does not want me in your community. But if you do not baptize me, I think my life will end right here. Everything in me cries out for the cleansing that can come to me. I humbly beg you to baptize me."

Still hesitating, the man looked questioningly up into the face of one of the leaders of the Qumran village watching the proceedings prayerfully. The slightest nod signaled the leader's permission for the baptism to proceed.

After pronouncing the baptismal formula over John, the celebrant eased him down into the water. When he attempted to raise John, the young man resisted, keeping his head and face under the water for as long as he could, as though he did not want to reemerge into the world around him, as if these waters were washing away the spiritual and emotional debris of his twenty years of living. Anxious that this strange boy might actually drown in his pool, the celebrant gently raised John's head above the surface of the water.

Remaining in the pool on his knees, looking up in the white hot, brassy sky, John raised his arms heavenward and sang passionately in Hebrew, *Incline your ear, O Lord, and answer me, for I am poor and needy. Preserve my life, for I am devoted to you; save your servant who trusts in you. You are my God; be gracious to me, O Lord, for to you do I cry all the day long.*

When he stepped from the pool, John was trembling from head to toe, as if he were standing on a barren, snow-whipped hillside in the dead of winter. When he tried to walk, he stumbled. He looked around dazed, seeing but not seeing the startled Essenes who did not know what to make of this stranger and the holy ecstasy that had obviously laid hold of him.

"Come with me, but you might want to put on your shirt," the leader said, gently, an amused gleam in his eyes.

"Yes," John mumbled, pulling it over his head in one motion.

"We will talk," the leader said.

Stooping low, he made his way down into one of the chambers, this one apparently a bit larger than most of the others, motioning for John to follow. The comfortable gloom and the somewhat reduced temperature had no impact on the dazed John.

After offering John a drink of watered wine, the Essene leader began to speak softly, "Young man, suppose you try to tell me who you are. Why have you come here? And most specifically, what did the baptism mean to you?"

At first haltingly, then with more vigor, John succinctly told the man of his childhood and youth as the son of a devoted Jerusalem temple priest, of his father's death, of his solitary wanderings through the barren places of Judea and even up into Samaria. "I have come to Qumran before," John went on to explain. "Not with any regularity. Not with any real purpose. Qumran was just another place for me to visit as I explored the towns, hills, valleys, deserts of my homeland. When I have come, I have always paid close attention to the teachings that various members of your community would offer."

"Have you considered becoming one of us?" the Essene leader inquired.

"Of course. But when I have listened to my own heart, when I have compared your discipline with the way I feel compelled to live, I knew I could never stay put long enough to satisfy your demands. Living so close day in and day out to others, even those with whom I feel genuine connection, is simply more than I can endure."

"I see," said the wise man. "You have earnestly thought about us, I can tell. You have probably reached the right decision for yourself. We make no efforts to enlist brothers into the community. In fact, we make membership difficult as a way to ensure that only those Adonai sends our way become part of us."

Pausing to look more closely at John, the Essene leader went on, "And the baptism?"

"That was totally unexpected. In my previous visits to Qumran, I had seen your people receive baptism, sometimes going into the pool several times during the day. My studies of our Jewish ways have enabled me to understand ceremonial washing, especially baptism for Gentile converts to the faith. Frankly, I never paid much attention to the baptisms I had seen here before. If I thought about it at all, I would have told myself that is your way. Fine. It had no significance for me."

"And this time?" the mentor wanted to know.

"I saw nothing different about the way the baptism took place. As far as I know, you have a set way to do it each time. I suppose the baptizer was doing it in the prescribed manner. Suddenly, however, something seized me. I say it was the spirit of Adonai. I knew I had to be baptized if I were to draw another breath. I almost jumped into the pool."

"And now?" his inquisitor asked gently.

"And now? At this moment, all I can say is that baptism was right for me. It was something I had to do. I do not feel any more Jewish now than I did before the baptism. Still, I sense I have crossed some new spiritual line. The baptism, maybe the strong prompting by the Spirit, the very fact that I am at Qumran at this point in my life gives me the strongest impression that something of significance has happened to me, in me."

"I agree," his spiritual guide answered.

"What do I do now?" John asked, uncertainty mounting within him, an emotion that was always repugnant to him.

"I do not know," his mentor answered, studying the young, rugged, tanned face before him. "What I do know is you must wait before Adonai for a spell. If these new feelings inside you are from him, he will reveal it to you. I suggest you stay with us for a while. We have ways for inquirers to earn their keep while studying and praying. We can make our writings available to you. We have men well versed in Scripture who can walk with you through important texts that may help clarify your own call."

Calculating that his mother had sufficient food and money for a few weeks, knowing she would not be anxious about him, John decided to extend his time with the Essenes.

As the days in Qumran went by, reflecting on his own baptism and the sense of divine compulsion that prompted him to accept the rite, John gradually came to see the time with the Essenes as a turning point in his life, a rebirth of significance. The study, extended prayer, the prolonged conversations with

Essene Scripture scholars honed John's thinking about Adonai's intentions for the present and future.

The baptism, ah, the baptism! In ways he had never imagined possible, that experience provided John with a completely new identification with the common people who had neither the money nor the spiritual energy to keep all the onerous rules and regulations imposed by the religious authorities. It let him see that the poorest of the poor could come to Adonai through something like baptism. They did not have to break themselves with expensive pilgrimages to the temple and elaborate sacrifices. Anyone could be baptized, Jew and non-Jew alike.

As a result of those weeks with the Essenes, he looked with greater compassion on all men and women left outside the ranks of the faithful by the accident of their birth. To his amazement he began to see that the true people of Adonai were any who chose the way of devotion, justice, and compassion, regardless of their birth.

"When I came up out of the water, I felt that the heavens themselves were opening to me," he told his mother upon his return home. "Honestly, Mother, Adonai and I have had some stirring meetings during my wilderness wanderings. Never anything like that moment. I felt the very living presence of the Holy One right there."

John lingered with the Essenes. The leader, sensing a divine urgency in the young renegade, gradually released John from most of his menial labors, saying, "You must spend all the time you can, while you are here, reading and studying. We have many writings that are not available anywhere else in the land, actually subversive by the lights of temple authorities and Romans. Pour over them. Let the spirit of Adonai graft the wisdom of these writings onto your very soul; let their fire ignite your heart."

Among the many powerful if strange teachings gleaned from his hosts, he was powerfully moved by the Essene ideas regarding the end times and the coming Son of Man. These themes came from several portions of Holy Scripture, especially concepts drawn from the teachings of the book of Daniel. As interpreted by the Essenes, Daniel offered hope built around mysterious revelations that had emerged during the times of severe Jewish persecution under the Seleucid dynasty some 200 years previously. The Son of Man connected to and seemed to flow from visions of a deliverer in Isaiah and other prophets.

Equally, John was stirred by the Essene antipathy toward temple worship. The Essenes insisted that true believers did not have to sacrifice at the Jerusalem temple in order for their worship to be fully acceptable to Adonai.

"What I am reading fills in the blanks of the Scripture education my father led me through," John told his teacher and now soulmate as they sat out under the night sky after an especially exhausting and exciting day of laboring over the texts.

"Exactly," the man replied.

John continued, "You would get in serious trouble if the men in Jerusalem knew what you had out here."

"True," he agreed. "That's why we make several copies of everything. We discretely distribute copies of the writings to others of our communities around the region. What is not generally known, even among our people here, is that we seal yet more copies in large jars and hide them in caves up in the hills. Certain of our leaders know the locations of those caves. I do not. The idea, of course, is that in the event of trouble or a raid, the teachings Adonai has given us will not be lost."

Gradually, it became clear to John he would soon have to leave Qumran. "I cannot live this confined way," he explained again to his mentor. "Adonai is sending me in another direction."

He looked up into the far reaches of the night sky, then said pleadingly to his master, "May I return here from time to time if my life becomes too difficult?"

"John, you are always welcome. Come often. Stay as long as you choose," the mentor assured him.

———

Soon after John returned home from Qumran, Elizabeth died in her sleep. When John awoke, he saw her still form lying on the pallet, the bed covers unruffled, her soft, knowing eyes closed in death as though in gentle sleep.

John had known her death was imminent. He did not begrudge her passing. Still, grief overwhelmed him. Nothing he had ever known could have prepared him for the emptiness, the sadness, the suffocating loneliness that swept over him in waves in the weeks after she died. He realized he had lost his sounding board, his spiritual guide, and the best friend he had in the entire world.

A few days after the burial, he gathered up Elizabeth's belongings and gave them to her closest friend in the village. After a warm hug, she went back into her cottage, carrying the small bundle that represented the material remainder of Elizabeth's wonderful life.

Before dawn the next morning, John left the house and village. He took the handful of coins still remaining of the family's treasure, collected a simple necklace his mother often wore, a piece of the phylactery his father used in praying and placed them in a small, leather purse, looked fondly around the small house, thoughtfully touched the place where his mother last slept before joining his father in death, and walked away, not looking back. He would never return to the house nor to the village of his birth.

Jesus was never far from John's thoughts. Regularly in these past years since he and his cousin had parted company, John experienced assurances in his spirit that the unusual bond, the mystifying intersections between the two men had far-reaching significance. He had no doubt but that his own destiny and mission were intertwined with that of his Galilean relative. But he had neither seen nor heard from Jesus in a long time.

All in all, over those weeks of mourning, he redoubled his efforts to put the pieces of his experience together without much success. After a few weeks, for reasons he could not explain to himself, he felt persuaded to go to Bethlehem. He purposely gave Jerusalem a wide berth, feeling he simply could not bear the hypocrisy of the Holy City.

A gracefully aging Zipporah answered a knock at her door to see a man—young, she thought; vaguely familiar, gaunt, hollow-eyed, sagging under an emotional weight that threatened to bend him over. "John, is that you?" she asked hesitantly. She could not recall how long it had been since she had last seen this unpredictable son of her cousin Elizabeth.

Then, "John, it *is* you!" Now alarmed, "What has happened? You look terrible. Where did you come from?" looking imploringly into the face of her young kinsman.

"May I come in," he asked softly.

"Oh, yes, certainly. How silly of me to stand here staring, gabbing. Of course, please, do come in."

Within a few days, John began to feel better. The care, tenderness, and good food offered him by Zipporah, one of his last living relatives, revived body and soul.

She grieved with him in the death of Elizabeth. She listened with rapt attention as he related bits and pieces of his life and feelings since last they had seen each other before Joseph's death. As John talked, Zipporah perceived amazing depths in John, who had grown from prescient boy to charismatic man in the years since they had met.

"Zipporah," he said as they talked on and on, "what I saw happening at the temple during my rotations, short-lived though they were, only reinforced my conviction that our whole way of coming to Adonai is wrong, rotten to the core."

"John," she soon came to say, "the hand of Adonai is on you; the spiritual oil of holy anointing is being poured out on you. I think I knew that since you were a boy. The miseries and revelations you have endured for these years have refined you." Then, with a friendly gleam in her eyes, she teased, "You're not any nicer than before. You are certainly more focused." In all seriousness she allowed, "I have no idea what direction this will take for you. You are a man with a mission. I bless you. I do not envy you, but I bless you."

"Zipporah, I do not want a mission. I have no need for a mission," he complained honestly.

"Perhaps, John. But you've had one laid on you."

When they were not talking about his feelings, the sense of direction that beckoned, they talked about Jesus. "I did not know he had gone to Egypt. What possessed him to go traipsing off to that godless land? That must have been quite a decision for him and his family," John mused.

"According to the letters I get once or twice a year from Mary, it's been very hard on his family. For all her innate gentleness and love for Jesus, Mary is quite hurt and confused over what he did. It seems he just up and left without telling them goodbye. James, the second brother, is furious with him. Mary says he will hardly speak Jesus's name. Jesus should have stayed home and tended to his duties after Joseph died. Even though Jesus's patron sends money to the family regularly, accepting it from a non-believer galls James. It's unthinkable to me that Jesus would abandon his family like he did."

John replied, "I trust Jesus. He would not have made such a dramatic move without a strong word from Adonai." He looked away, then said quietly, "Jesus will be back. And probably sooner rather than later."

Zipporah did not comment. With no basis in fact, she knew with certainty that she had just received a word not from John but from Adonai.

In tiny Bethlehem, news of John's entry into the village spread in a matter of minutes. By sundown of his first day in town, neighbors began bringing food and drink. Knowing John's penchant for privacy, Zipporah did not divulge any of the details of his life and pilgrimage. When he felt better, she said to him,

"The villagers are buzzing with curiosity to know what has happened to you across the years. You have had experiences completely beyond everyone here."

As the Sabbath approached, Zipporah came to John as he sat out on a hillside reveling in the sunshine and fresh air. "Hannah, our synagogue ruler, has asked to speak with you, John, if you feel like it."

"A woman synagogue leader?" John commented. "We do not have too many of them."

"I know. She has such unusual spiritual insights, the men actually elected her," Zipporah replied.

"And what does this woman synagogue leader want to talk with me about?" he asked lightly.

"She wants to ask you to speak in the congregation this Sabbath. She feels the people of the village need to hear your story."

"Perhaps Hannah had better hear my whole story before she invites me to speak. Even then, I am not sure I can do what she asks. It may come as a surprise to you, Zipporah, but I've never spoken in public before. I might not have the words. I would embarrass you and the family of Jesus by my stumbling and bumbling."

"John," she smiled, "I readily admit I have not often understood what you are about. Still, embarrassment is the least of my worries."

Hannah observed all the protocols in approaching John, speaking to him outdoors in the presence of her husband and Zipporah. When John met her, he knew instantly why she had been elected. Though of average height and stature, attractive though not beautiful, she was both commanding and gentle, aware of her position of leadership in the town while, at the same time not taking herself seriously. In meeting John she was properly grave, fitting his station as a unique man from Adonai. From the crinkles around her eyes, however, John realized she laughed easily.

"Brother John," Hannah said without any attempt at conversational amenities, "I am persuaded you have much of importance from Adonai to talk about. We would be honored and most attentive if you would be our teacher this Sabbath."

"Hannah, as the ruler of the synagogue, you should know more accurately what I would say if I decide to speak. First, as I told Zipporah, I have never given a public sermon before. I've given many to rocks and trees and streams out in the desert. I've talked for hours on end with Essene fathers and many more learned men and women among our people. Still, I have never given a full sermon or lesson. I might make a mess of the speech."

"We have heard some very bad lessons from men who have given hundreds of speeches. No one's going to fret over your inexperience," she assured him, laughing warmly, enlivening her features and making her luminous brown eyes light up with joy and spirituality.

"Well, I warned you," he said easily. "If I decide to accept your gracious invitation, I will be compelled to give you what Adonai has given me. I am becoming convinced we are missing most of what Adonai has for us in worship. Temple authorities have convinced our people that they can worship, make sacrifices, actually please Adonai only by coming to the Jerusalem temple. That is not so." He paused for a moment to assess Hannah's action to his opening statement.

"Yes," she said, unfazed by his directness. "I understand. I have some of the same feelings. But go on."

Startled by her candor, John opened his heart to Hannah, who listened with rapt attention, feeding him a steady stream of questions that helped him further clarify his thinking as he spoke. Before they realized it, two hours had sped by as the two of them talked nonstop.

"John, you say to our people on the Sabbath what we have talked about, and I can promise you a thorough hearing. Not everyone will agree. Indeed, some will be mightily disturbed. You have this powerful word from Adonai that the people of Bethlehem must hear. I will be praying for you as you wait before Adonai in preparation."

Word of the guest teacher's anticipated lesson for Sabbath spread through the town with its usual speed. The town plaza, the place of assembly for Bethlehem's synagogue, was packed well before the appointed hour when the shofar was blown, announcing the beginning of the Sabbath service. After readings, prayers, and hymns, Hannah, without any fanfare, stood to welcome John as their guest teacher, saying, "I believe this man has the hand of Adonai on his life and the fire from the altar on his lips. We will hear him with open hearts."

John likewise wasted no time with niceties. "I have literally walked with Adonai most of my life out on the hillsides, in the valleys, in lanes of green trees, and beneath the scorching sun in the deserts. I have poured over our holy books. I have spent extended time with our Essene brothers at Qumran. My father, of blessed memory, was a priest of the order of Abiathar. He loved the temple and its worship with all his heart. It was he, out of his love for the temple, who first began to alert me that worship in that sacred place had begun to stray drastically. By the time he died as a result of a so-called accident within the temple precincts, he was sick at heart over the ways and abuses of the high priest and his top assistants. You have only to go to Jerusalem to see for yourself the gaudy, godless manner in which these men live. You and I and thousands of our fellow believers from around the country and the world are paying for that unholy extravagance."

A murmur of agreement moved through the assembly. John had already touched a sensitive nerve among the people.

"Adonai has begun to communicate with me that he will not long tolerate such desecration of true worship."

Someone from the edge of the crowd called out, "Amen! Tell us more."

Warming to his task, John began to speak more fervently. "Search the scriptures. You will see that in the days of the ancient prophets, when worship became corrupt, when poor people suffered at the hands of the powerful in order to pay dues and provide sacrifices in the sanctuary, Adonai came in judgment. Those same conditions are coming to bear at the temple. Why should we think Adonai will not once again visit us with his wrath!"

The gravity of this pronouncement fell on the assembly with such weight that no one dared to say a word. After a brief pause to catch his breath, John continued. "If temple worship is not pleasing to Adonai, what do we do? Do we go to the high priest and tell him of our concerns? If he and his counselors were honest men"—a gasp erupted involuntarily from the assembly at that indictment—"we as sons and daughters of Abraham could do just that. They are not honest. They would mock our complaints. We'd probably be thrown in jail as troublemakers."

"What do we do then, Brother John?" a young man from the center of the crowd asked earnestly.

Without hesitating, he declared, "We hear the word of the Lord that it is not necessary for us to worship at the temple."

"No!" several shouted, jumping to their feet, about to walk out in protest.

"You speak blasphemy," another yelled.

Instantly, Hannah was on her feet, motioning for the people to be quiet and urging, "Hear him out. What he says strikes a strong chord with me."

"All through our holy books we are taught that Adonai looks on the heart. He wants faithfulness from us. The place and precise manner of our worship are not nearly so important as our attitude. Listen to the words of the prophet

Micah: *With what shall I come before the Lord, and bow myself before Adonai on high?... He has told you what is good; and what does the Lord require of you but to do justice and to love kindness and to walk humbly with your God?* The Ten Words do not tell us where and how to come before Adonai—only that we are to come into his presence with nothing between ourselves and him. Our Shema that we love and recite from our mother's milk says, *Hear, O Israel: The Lord our Adonai is one Lord; and thou shalt love the Lord thy Adonai with all thine heart, and with all thy soul, and with all thy might.* Not a word about worshiping at the temple. Indeed, when those words were given to us by Moses, blessed be his memory, neither the tabernacle nor the temple even existed."

Sensing the mood of the crowd, realizing John had laid a very heavy word on the congregation, once again Hannah stood to her feet, this time to provide a respite for the inflamed emotions of the worshipers. "Brothers and sisters of Bethlehem, John has given us much to think about. I think it wise and best that we take a rest. We have not been here over long, but if your mind is like mine, we need some time to think through what he has said. Certainly, we have no need to reach any hasty conclusions."

Turning to John, she asked, "Can you stay with us for a while longer? I for one am eager to hear more. Maybe in the cool of the evening, those of us who choose may have you open your thinking to us even further. It's obvious you have given this matter careful thought and much prayer."

With a nod of his head, John agreed to remain with them.

The crowds grew. What he said also struck raw nerves with some. One night, a well-dressed man showed up and sat on the outer edges of the crowd, listening. At a break in John's teaching, he asked, "How do we know what you say is from Adonai? Maybe you're just trying to get everybody stirred up so you can start a fight. Maybe even loot the temple or something like that."

John replied, "You will just have to trust me, I suppose. I have no personal axes to grind. Believe me, I prefer to be out in the hills alone rather than sitting here with the likes of you who just want to cast confusion, to find something to complain about."

When the man made another biting remark, more under his breath than out loud, John unloaded on him, saying, "Listen, you're nothing but part of the generation of snakes who slide out from Jerusalem to bite those who want to find a better way." Standing even straighter, John pointed his finger at the man and cried out, "Go back into the hole with all the other vipers who are from the pits of hell!"

Everyone gasped at John's thunderous denunciation.

"You can't talk to me like that," the man shouted.

"I can, and I will," John blared back. "You have no desire to listen and learn. You only want to cause trouble, sow doubt. Leave us. Don't let me see you around here again."

Another night, a man interrupted John's teaching by yelling out, "Blasphemer!"

"What do you mean 'blasphemer'?" John demanded impatiently. "I am honestly trying to decide what Adonai wants of us. When you call me a blasphemer, you just stifle conversation, stop the flow. If that's all you have to say, I'd rather you go on home and go to bed."

So far, he had hardly mentioned his baptism. Soon, however, he felt it was time for him to tell the people of his personal experience at the Essene baptistry. "The man performing the rite on me had to lift my head up out of the water. I wanted to stay submerged. And when I came up out of that little tank of water," he said, his eyes flashing, "I felt that the heavens had opened up to me. I could have reached out and touched Adonai, so close to him did I feel."

When he went on to tell them that he was so caught up in the moment that he forgot to put his clothes back on, they roared in appreciative laughter, the first time any semblance of humor had been injected into the powerful conversations between him and the people. In fact, it was the first time John had laughed in months and months. "Zipporah," he said as they walked home that evening, "it felt so very good to laugh. I was not trying to be funny," he added as an afterthought.

Two nights later, a young man in the crowd pleaded, "John, please tell us more about this baptism. I knew about such practices as part of our religion, but I do not understand it at all."

After John recited the history of baptism in the Jewish faith, he said, "I have often thought on that experience. It seems to me that baptism points me to a new and fresh encounter with Adonai. It is not enough simply to be born a Jew. To become a true son or daughter of Abraham, we have to make a conscious commitment. I am no more or less a Jew now than I was before that unforgettable day at the baptistry. But I surely do feel much more connected with Adonai. Something of the utmost significance happened in my heart that day. The afterglow lingers to this day."

Hannah interjected, "John, many in our country will have difficulty with that idea. For generations we have heard that simply by virtue of our birth, we are children of Adonai."

"As indeed you are," he replied quickly. "All of us are children of Adonai, Jews and non-Jews alike. Baptism gave me a new sense of identification with our own history. But more, I felt a kinship with those not born as Jews but who still want to know and walk with Adonai." Then he thought further and said, "The waters washing over my body represented the washing away of my sins, a cleansing that can come only from Adonai. I think of the words from Isaiah when he said, *Though your sins be as scarlet, they shall be as white as snow; though they be red like crimson, they shall be as wool.*"

As he finished speaking, a palpable silence embraced the crowd of several dozen as they sat on the ground while the half-moon illuminated piles of clouds floating through the heavens. Then, ever so quietly, from the edge of the group, a young woman stood up and walked to where John leaned against a large rock. At first no one noticed her, but as she made her way through her family and friends as they sat on the ground, every eye strained through the blue night to see what she was about. When she came to John, she knelt before him, and with tears streaming down her face, she whispered, "Brother John, would you baptize me? I want to feel my sins washed away as you described. I long to feel close to Adonai like you do."

Shocked, John immediately lifted her up from her knees. "Me, baptize you?" he asked. Then, gaining his bearings, he answered gently, "Of course I will baptize you. Tomorrow we will find water, and I will be honored to baptize you."

Like a floodgate freshly opened, the young woman's request brought nearly everyone in the group to their feet, all saying in hushed chorus, "And me too, please." "And I, if you will." "Me also."

The next afternoon, a score or more villagers, Zipporah and Hannah included, gathered by the banks of a small brook, each dressed in a simple shift of the whitest material they possessed. The water was not deep enough to immerse the people fully, so John had them kneel, one by one, in the middle of the stream. After praying over them and whispering a baptismal confession the Essene had said over him, using a pitcher, he poured water from the stream over their bodies.

The reaction of the participants varied from quiet, joyful acceptance of their baptism to shouted praises and hallelujahs. John, most of all, was surprised by the number of people from Bethlehem who came to the stream for baptism and at their reactions.

Talking with Zipporah that evening, he shook his head in astonishment, "Never in my most far-flung imaginings did I anticipate what happened today. It will be interesting to see what happens in the lives of most of those who were baptized. Only as we live changed lives, repentant lives, does baptism or any other expression of faith have any long-lasting meaning."

"John, you will have to be patient with us," Zipporah counseled. "So much of what you are saying is very new. You've thought about this for years. We've had only a few weeks. As you stay and teach us more, we'll all have a better chance at developing along the lines you see."

He looked at her without saying anything for a moment, a look of puzzlement on his face, then said, "That's just it. I cannot stay here much longer. Some of you will have to pick up where I leave off."

Indignantly, Zipporah retorted, "Look, you cannot get this whole village stirred up and then just walk away, disappear on another of your desert treks. That's not fair. It's not wise. What you have begun will fall apart without more nurture."

Softening just a bit, he said, "Zipporah, listen, I am not going to leave tomorrow. Just soon. Besides, I have said about all I know, at least to this point in my own thinking. And I've baptized everyone in town who wanted it. You know I cannot long stay in one place. My calling is to be on the move with Adonai."

———

John nearly choked when he saw how many had come the next Sabbath. After more than an hour, he said, "I have spoken long enough today. I am tired. You and your families must find food and get some rest." And with that he hopped down off his rock.

From the back side of the crowd, someone cried out, "We want to be baptized." And the same chorus echoed through the worshipers, "Yes, we want baptism. Please baptize us!"

Warily, he looked at Hannah. She smiled back at him and said in a voice only he could hear, "John, Adonai has started something in you. You have your calling. You must answer."

For two hours on Sabbath afternoon, he baptized in the same stream where already scores had received the rite. When the last person had gone, he had to drag himself up from the creek bed, soaked to the skin himself, so exhausted he could hardly move. As yet another Sabbath approached, he said to Hannah, "I do not believe I can keep this up. No doubt the message from Adonai has caught on. I can teach, but I honestly do not believe I can stand the emotional and physical strain of more hours baptizing. Help me think of a solution."

She sat quietly for several minutes, then suggested, "Why not appoint some of us to help you? Explain to those who want to be baptized that it's not who pours the water. The attitude of their own heart makes the difference. You can stand by the stream to give your blessing and presence. Some of us who have been baptized can help."

"Do you think the people will accept the change? Will they feel good about their baptism at the hands of someone other than me?" hope rising in his voice.

"We will just have to find out."

Next Sabbath, when the plea for baptism went up from the crowd, John explained the new approach. To his satisfaction, the number of those seeking baptism did not diminish. John stood by the bank of the stream encouraging, supporting, touching, blessing while Hannah, Zipporah, Reuben, a synagogue leader, and several other men administered the rite to scores of men, women, and older children.

—

John left before dawn two days after more investigators from the high priest's office showed up at the Sabbath service to taunt him.

The night before he left, he told Zipporah, "I did not come here to cause trouble for the people of the village. Those temple snoops will be back. Maybe even bring a squad of guards with them. There'll be trouble. People will get hurt. It's time for me to leave."

Zipporah answered, "You may be right. It's time for you to leave but not to avoid trouble with the temple people or, for that matter, anyone else. It's evident to me that your time has come."

John grumbled, "Listen, I don't want a time."

"John, I tell you," she replied, ignoring his irritation, "it's another 'Day of the Lord' as the prophets have written. Hannah and I have talked. We think the time is ripe for Adonai to come in power and start his new kingdom. Evidently, you have a key role in this new day."

"Of course I am willing to do my part," he said, pacing around in the small room. "But why me?"

"Why Abraham? Why Jacob? Why Moses? Why any of the men and women Adonai has used across the centuries to do his work in a given time?

That's just the way it is. The great ones always shouted 'No' at first. No one in his right mind wants to go through all the agony of leadership. It is your calling. You cannot get away from it. You might as well accept it."

"And what do I do? Here in Bethlehem I had you and Hannah and others as links to the people. All I did was talk. Is that what I'm supposed to do now, just talk?"

"John," she retorted, "you talked and baptized. Scores responded. Perhaps that's what Adonai wants from you, talking and baptizing. I certainly do not know. But you will figure it out, of that I'm sure."

Putting up his hands in a good-natured way to fend off her torrent of words, he gave her one of his rare smiles and said, "I believe you. Calm down. Please!"

Her irritation gone as quickly as it had come, Zipporah said, "John, you ought to try those smiles more often. You're not half bad-looking when you smile." She beamed at him, giving him a big hug, ignoring his red face and discomfort at the warmth of her touch.

# Chapter Two

# The River

*Happy are those who are like trees planted by rivers of water, which yield their fruit in its season, and their leaves do not wither.*

As John left Bethlehem, Hannah asked him in her good-natured, blunt way, "Where will you go? You will need somewhere to work from. You cannot simply wander up and down in the deserts and have much of an impact."

"You still do not understand, Hannah," he answered irritably. "I have no desire to make an impact, as you say. What has happened here in Bethlehem is probably a one-time outpouring of the Spirit. And I most certainly do not need a place to live. I know all the caves and crannies for miles and miles between Jerusalem and the Jordan."

She chuckled knowingly. "Well, just in case something does begin to happen, I have a suggestion. My husband has a cousin named Lazarus, a man of some inherited means. He and his two sisters live in Bethany beyond the Jordan. Lazarus has long had poor health. His two sisters chose never to marry. The older one, Martha, is quite the take-charge woman. She's kept the family's merchant business going since their father's death many years ago. Mary takes care of Lazarus when he's down. They are good people and would let you stay with them if and when you need to."

"Stay here for a few days," the Qumran leader suggested. "Be quiet and still. You always hear the word of Adonai in the stillness. Your future will get clearer. No doubt about it."

Three days later, as John sat in the wise man's quarters reading more of the community's Scripture scrolls, a young novice came to him and said, "Brother John, you have visitors. They are waiting at the edge of our village."

"Visitors!" he exclaimed incredulously. "I never have visitors."

"You do now. About ten or twelve men would like to talk with you," he said emphatically. Hesitating a moment, he added with slight disdain in his voice, "A woman is also with them."

There they stood, a small cluster of men ranging in age from their late teens to middle age. He immediately recognized Reuben and the others from Bethlehem. In the middle of the band stood Hannah, a light in her eyes that warned John not to say a disparaging word to her or the men.

The leader ushered the newcomers and his guests into his quarters, provided something for them to drink, and said, "I will leave you alone. We do not normally have women in our settlement, but out of deference to John and as a token of hospitality, she too may come in. You may remain until sundown, at which time the woman must leave. Until that hour approaches, you are welcome."

"John," Reuben said tentatively, "we are here to help you answer Adonai's call on your life."

His words tumbling from his mouth, irritated that they had just appeared out of the air, John demanded, "Who sent you? What do you mean 'help me'? Who says I need help? And what's more, I have no idea what I am supposed to do."

Reuben answered smoothly, not put down by John's sharp tone, his confidence rising, "No one sent us; we sent ourselves. After you left Bethlehem, we kept talking and praying. We came to the conclusion that Adonai had started something new in you. And since we were the first to receive that new blessing, we decided he wanted us to be part of whatever it is you are undertaking."

"You know far more than I do," John snorted, but more gently, appreciative of the man's openness. Not through protesting, however, he said, "I have no money to sustain you. What about your families, your living?"

"We have some money," Reuben said. "Friends and family in Bethlehem, likewise touched by your ministry, will help our families as needs arise. So we are yours."

"And Hannah," looking at her for the first time, "why are you here? Do you too have this burning desire to be of assistance to me?"

"I do," she answered without hesitation. "You can try to send me away if you choose. I will linger at the edge of the crowds. My husband and I talked. He did not want me to leave, but he finally agreed. My children pleaded with me to stay with them. Other men and women in the village, even those who believe in you, thought I had lost my mind. I was determined to come. Here I am. So there." And she drew herself up in an attitude of quiet defiance.

Later in the afternoon, the Essene leader reluctantly said, "They can all stay here for a while, even the woman, though I will have much explaining to do to our men. She must keep out of sight. She will have to take care of herself as best she can. We will let them work for food. In good time, sooner rather than later, you will discern your next move."

Over the next few days, John and the band of followers, along with the leader and other scholars from the Qumran community, engaged in almost nonstop study, prayer, and talk.

"What is the overriding theme of what you feel Adonai is pointing you toward?" one of the brothers asked. "Try to tell me in a few words."

"Hmm," John thought. "Two words come to me: freedom and justice. They are powerful themes from our past. Abraham, Moses, and the prophets all sought freedom from oppression. These patriarchs labored to lead the people toward new measures of liberation. They all pleaded for justice from Jew to Jew, from Jews to others, and from others to us. We have known little of either justice or freedom."

The brother said, "And how are freedom and justice to be achieved?"

John surprised himself with his quick answer: "Repentance."

"And what is repentance in your view?" the brother wanted to know.

"Repentance is a confession of sin before Adonai and each other. More, it is a willingness to turn our hearts and energies toward Adonai. It is a determination to walk in a new direction," John answered vehemently, his eyes suddenly flashing with an inner fire they had not seen before.

Another Essene scholar explained, "John, I agree with you. Our people, however, have been taught by the priests that righteousness means keeping the rules of the temple accurately. Repentance, then, means correcting mistakes in observing the ritual or other purity laws. You're bringing something more powerful to the idea."

"Yes," he agreed somewhat defensively. "Still, I'm not inventing an idea. Just read our scriptures. Repentance has nothing to do with cutting the lamb's throat properly or bringing the right amount of grain to the temple."

"Oh, I concur, Brother John," the Essene leader said brightly. "I was merely pointing out that you are inviting even more criticism from the temple authorities with your reinterpretation of the word they cherish and use to keep the people in line."

He continued, following John's train of thought, "Freedom, liberation. When you talk about liberation, I think of crossing the water, the waters opening up, the power of Adonai to free us from slavery and oppression. In our history the connections between freedom, holy intervention, and new direction invariably involved bodies of water."

One of the young men from Bethlehem nervously stood to speak for the first time. "Sirs, I am anything but a scholar, but what you are saying makes sense. When John baptized me, parted the waters for me, my spirit took flight like I have never known before. I found a new freedom and liberation that I would like for everyone in our country to know."

"Yes, go on," John urged, new light beginning to flicker in his eyes.

Becoming more sure of himself, the young Bethlehemite said quickly, "Maybe Adonai is pointing you toward a ministry of preaching, teaching, and baptizing up and down the Jordan River. Everyone in our country connects the Jordan with the power of Adonai and freedom. He parted the river for Joshua, blessed be his memory, and our ancestors came into the promised land those many centuries ago."

Reuben joined immediately, saying, "And the river has many pools deep enough for you to baptize people completely. No pouring from pitchers like you had to do with us. And nearly everyone in our country is close enough to the river to come out and hear you if they wanted to."

"I don't understand any of this," John admitted, shaking his head in bewilderment.

"I accept what you are saying, though."

He nervously paced around the tiny, sweltering room and after a moment asked, "And how do we get this 'river ministry' started? Do I just go out and start talking?"

The Essene leader spoke up, his face lighting up with comprehension, "John, that's exactly what you do. With these people spreading the word, you should have little trouble getting people to hear you."

"Yes, that's it," several men echoed in chorus. "You just start talking. Leave the spreading of the word to us."

"And what's to keep the high priest and half the guards from the temple to come swooping out and toss us all in a bottomless jail like they have every other fuzzy-headed 'liberator' that's come along?" he asked with a twinkle in his eyes.

"We will cross that bridge when the time comes," Hannah insisted in a tone that brooked no more questions.

"But I am not a preacher," John insisted, making one more effort to put this entire affair behind him.

From the back corner of the room, another young man, perhaps the youngest of the group, who had said nothing, broke into a Hebrew chant: *Then I, Jeremiah said, Ah, Lord God, I cannot speak. I am but a boy. But the Lord said unto me, Say not I am a boy. For you shall go to all that I shall send you, and whatsoever I command you, you shall speak. Be not afraid of their faces; for I am with you to deliver you, says the Lord.*

"Let's get started," John said, grim resolution in his voice.

"Why so heavy, John?" the mentor asked.

"I do not want to sound heavy," John admitted. "If I sound heavy it is because this is not the way I had it planned. Crowds bother me. I prefer the solitude of the desert. But I believe you are all right. Let's get moving."

———

At first the people came one by one, then in small groups, and shortly by the score, gathering at John's preaching station near the ancient village of Bethany beyond Jordan, a few miles from Jericho, where the river flowed deep enough to allow full immersion. With growing effectiveness as a communicator of difficult ideas, undergirded by a force and fire of spirit that the preaching by the river seemed to ignite, John laid out his vision, itself constantly unfolding in those opening weeks of his effort.

Invariably, after each of John's sermons, delivered over a period of several hours, men, women, and older children cried out, "What must we do?"

Finding words from their ancient scriptures, from the ancient wisdom teachings that had flourished among the Jews in recent years, and from compassionate common sense, John instructed, "Do the right thing. For instance, if you have two coats, give one to a neighbor who has none. Share your food with those who have lost their farms and livelihood to the money lenders or the Romans," he exhorted. "And, most of all, act with love and justice toward one another. It is an abomination before Adonai when his own people treat each other cruelly."

As the weeks sped by, to John's surprise, public officials, tax and toll collectors, guards from the temple, even soldiers from the army of Herod Antipas and a few Romans began to trek out to his river camp near Jericho. Stricken in their consciences by his sermons, some revenue collectors presented themselves, asking him what they should do to relieve the burden of sin they felt.

He replied, "Take no more taxes than you may lawfully collect. Do not put greater hardships on your friends and family just because you can. Share your profits with the poor and dispossessed."

To repenting soldiers and temple guards he admonished, "Do your job. Keep the peace. Do not act in wanton violence. Do not bully the people. And stop complaining about your wages. You make more than most."

Nearly everyone who came to hear John sought baptism. The banks of the Jordan and the creeks that flowed into it were lined with people waiting quietly for baptism from dawn to dark. In fact, the whole scene was eerily quiet considering the large number of people who had gathered to hear John's preaching and to receive baptism.

When the phenomenon burst on the scene, John did all the baptizing himself. As the numbers grew, however, he could not keep up. As he had done at Bethlehem, he designated Hannah and some of the men who had come with her to assist him.

Within a few weeks, John had become a sensation throughout much of the region. Temple authorities and Roman military commanders, who at first dismissed him and his movement as just another minor irritant, began to take alarm.

Laudus, the commander of the Roman garrison, who met routinely with the high priest's first assistant, Izachus, said, "I'm getting anxious about that new preacher out at the Jordan. My reports are that hundreds every day are flocking out to him. Is he another madman trying to foment revolution?"

"The man's not organizing them into any sort of new community," the wily assistant assured the Roman commander. "He preaches, they get baptized, and then they come back home. It does not seem to be any sort of a movement."

During those same months, the high priest's comptroller of the temple treasury noted a gradual and then distinct drop in revenues. At first, he laid the downward trend off on bad crops or inclement weather. As the losses accelerated, everyone in the high priest's circle of closest advisers had to admit that John's preaching was taking its toll. "The local people are simply not coming to the temple like they used to."

Another one spoke up and said, "Those who do are not buying our clean animals. They show up for the worship services, the singing and ceremonies, but they are not making sacrifices."

Another cautioned, "We must move carefully. This man is extremely popular with the people of the towns and villages. He's put them on the alert that we may move against him. We would have a bloody uprising on our hands if we do anything hastily."

Months passed. John ranged up and down the Judean side of the Jordan, setting up camp at strategic spots along the river, determined by the access to the people and at the point where the meandering, often quite shallow stream itself was deep enough to accommodate immersions.

After a while John's inner circle began to bicker among themselves. As the new wore off, as homesickness among some set in, as the daily pressures of feeding themselves and John took their toll, friction hardly noticed at first began to surface.

Reuben managed to steer John away from the others late one afternoon when the crowds had dispersed for the day. John was so exhausted that he could hardly stand up, but he sensed that his Bethlehem friend had something of importance to say.

"John," Reuben began hesitantly, "some of your people have asked me to talk with you."

Immediately wary, John demanded, "What people? You say 'your' people. I have no people. I don't know what you're talking about."

This was not going to be easy, just as Hannah had warned him: "You know, those of us who have gathered in close support around you."

"I never asked you to gather around me. You came of your own accord. If you are here to tell me that some want to go home, they have my blessing. I'm grateful for their concern. But I never wanted to have a 'people,' and they can certainly go back to their families anytime they want to," he said over his shoulder as he nonchalantly wandered off in the brush, plopped down on the ground, and leaned up against an old olive tree.

"Wait, John," Reuben said cautiously, aware he was treading on shaky ground. "No one wants to go home. Just the opposite. They want to stay. It's just that we think we need to get organized."

"Organized!" John exploded in fury, jumping up from his olive tree. "Organized? What in the world do you think I've been preaching against for these months and months? What we do not need is another holy organization! Next thing you'll tell me that pushing and shoving is going on among 'my people' over who will be my 'second in command.'"

"That's what some of us were talking about. Certainly no one can take your place as the leader, the preacher. We do think we need someone who can take charge of all the details. Make assignments. Keep everything running smoothly."

Eyeing Reuben carefully in the twilight, John said, "Let me guess. You are the one to be my second in command?"

"Now just a minute, John. I never asked for such a position." He hesitated a moment before he continued, "Some of the people think I have the leadership necessary to do the job. And, if I may say so, I think I do have what it takes to see after the day-by-day matters."

"No! No! No! I admire you, Reuben. I am not out to start a party or group or community. That's not my calling. I have told you and the others all along that I am quite capable of caring for myself."

That ended the conversation about getting organized for a while.

A few weeks later, after more confusion among John's closest friends had arisen, he and Hannah were talking as the sun dipped below the horizon.

"Do you think I need someone like Reuben?" he blurted in the middle of their conversation.

"Yes, John. You do."

Reuben became the leader of the organization John had been determined never to bring into existence.

———

The numbers of those grew who streamed out to John's moving camps up and down the Jordan River. Also, anxiety about John intensified with the Jewish and Roman officials in Jerusalem who were forced to pay closer attention.

"My lord high priest," the first assistant counseled his master, "I have trusted informants in the crowds every day. John has yet to utter one seditious word against Rome or directly against your leadership. He never tells the people they do not have to come to the temple. He does say Adonai will accept their worship out by the river as well as in the precincts of the temple. That's hardly revolution."

"Is he still baptizing them and sending them home?" Caiaphas asked.

"By and large, yes, my lord. Maybe fifty men and women have collected around him. He teaches them each day, but he never says anything dangerous other than to rattle on about Adonai's new kingdom that's sure to come."

"And what does he mean by a new kingdom? Is he advocating a change in government?" the high priest wanted to know.

"Oh no," Izachus assured his master. "The new kingdom is some sort of divine intervention, the kind of ranting we've heard preached from all the wooly prophets for hundreds of years. A hard-headed Roman could interpret such noises as fomenting revolution, but no one who hears him has any notion that he is proposing the overthrow of either your or the Romans' rule."

"The Romans are getting nervous, nonetheless," the high priest declared anxiously. "They hate these gatherings that go on and on. At the slightest provocation they will tear into that crowd and slaughter any who get in the way. We must avoid that."

"I do have one more hand to play," the first assistant said slyly.

"And what might that be?"

"I have ways to get to one of John's closest confidants. If nothing else, maybe I can put pressure on my contact to persuade John to cross the Jordan, move further up north, into Antipas's territory. That will get him further away from us. If trouble does erupt, it will be on the head of Herod Antipas and not on yours."

"What are you waiting on? Make it happen," Caiaphas ordered the first assistant, the tension easing in his eyes a bit. "The Romans can still get to the prophet, but we can make it look like we had nothing to do with the clash if it does come."

"My lord, with all due respect," his first assistant said, "not *if* but *when* the clash comes."

A few days later, John and Reuben were talking as the crowds began to collect in the small, natural amphitheater that thousands of years of wind and rain had hollowed out from the hillside. "I never cease to be amazed," John said, shaking his eyes as the people poured into the arena. "I'll stand on that rock over there and say the same thing today as I did yesterday. They'll sit there listening as if I were Elijah or Isaiah. Then they'll wait half the day for baptism. What draws them?"

"Their souls are empty, John," Reuben said sympathetically. "What goes on in the temple and in most of the synagogues simply does not meet their spiritual needs. Adonai has raised you up to touch them and urge them toward righteous living."

"Will they keep coming, Reuben?" John said more to himself than to the man standing next to him.

"Probably. But that leads me to make a suggestion. We've not been across the river and up into Perea. Perhaps you should consider moving your camp up north. I am sure thousands from Galilee, Decapolis, and other regions would be just as inspired as the folks from here in Judea."

"But that's the territory of Herod Antipas," John observed, caution rising in his voice. "I don't trust him at all. At least around here I know some of the authorities."

"Listen, John, with your popularity, not even Herod Antipas would bother you. The people would rise up in rebellion against him."

"Don't be so naive, Reuben. He might have thought about it before he gave us trouble. But if he were sufficiently goaded, he'd not stop. Besides, he's got the Roman army on his side."

"Still, you should think of the needs of those up there that are every bit as great as the people around here," Reuben said with an earnestness that moved John to begin to take seriously what his adviser had said.

"I'll think about," John said as he moved toward the waiting crowd.

Within a few weeks John decided to move further up the river, where he preached and baptized without incident for three months to crowds every bit as large as those in his home territory. Caiaphas gave a sigh of relief to have John that much further away from Jerusalem.

John's movements had been duly noted by Herod Antipas, whose informants kept the ruler fully apprised of the prophet's activities. When nothing untoward occurred, the tetrarch, with much to occupy his mind, made no effort to interfere.

———

Weary now from more than a year's nonstop work, John arose well before dawn one morning and said to a sleepy Reuben, "I am leaving for a while. I will be back when I get back."

"But what will I tell the people who come out to hear you?" Reuben demanded, now fully awake.

"I don't care what you tell them. You can say I have disappeared. I had to leave and spend time alone with Adonai. I will be back, but I don't know when."

Irritated to the point of anger, Reuben demanded of John, "And what do we do while you are gone? Just sit around and twiddle our thumbs? You're the center of this thing. With you gone, the whole mission may come apart."

"You can go home if you want to," John snapped, anger meeting anger. "I never wanted to be the center of anything! And if the 'mission,' as you say, falls apart while I am gone, so be it. If I'm all there is to it, it'll fall apart anyway." While Reuben silently fumed, John disappeared into the predawn darkness.

John's spirit soared as he distanced himself from the small band of followers who had collected around him. He could almost reach out and touch the freedom of movement, of spirit, of connection with Adonai he felt as he strode confidently through the rocks and scrub and ravines that marked the stretches of uninhabited hills and valleys. Though John had never trekked these parts, still he felt at home. If he saw a village in the distance or a family of sheepherders on the horizon, he took a wide berth. He had had enough of people for a while, maybe a long while.

Days became weeks. He began to feel selfish that he was so exhilarated to be alone in the wilderness he loved so much. As he walked, sat, lay on his back gazing into the heavens, drank from tiny crystal clear springs, ate the foods the emptiness supplied in such abundance for those who knew how to harvest it, John's mind went over and over the powerful writings he had encountered at Qumran.

Two main themes began to surface all the more distinctly. One was the clear notion that Adonai was bringing a new kingdom. Only those who had repented and begun to practice the just and righteous life could live in this holy breakthrough. He'd been saying that all along, but kingdom preaching got muddied with everything else he was saying.

The other was the insistence on the one who would bring in that kingdom. Could this "coming one" be whom Isaiah of old talked about, the deliverer, the messiah? Some among the Jews longed for a deliverer. Most gave the notion no thought, so enmeshed were they in the struggles of everyday life. Certainly the temple authorities were not remotely interested in such an idea. Indeed, they would have been angered and threatened if such a one did appear. If the high priest and the Roman commanders had their way, anyone who came along even remotely resembling some sort of heaven-sent deliverer would not last long.

And what part did he have to play in these mysterious, heavenly movements? He hoped he would have no role to play. He had acted long enough on the public stage. It was time for him to recede, or so he fervently hoped.

———

John dreamed that someone far away was calling his name. He twisted restlessly in his sleep, but the voice persisted. It must be an angel, he thought, beneath the weight of the heavy sleep that enveloped him as he lay in the cave that sheltered him from the weather.

"John, where are you?" the voice came again.

It was not an angel. A human being with a voice he vaguely remembered was actually calling to him. But how? He was miles from any beaten path.

Now, fully awake, he sprang up from the pallet of leaves and moss he had made for himself.

"I am here," he responded loudly, emerging from the mouth of the shallow cave.

Within a matter of moments, a man came thrashing through the undergrowth toward him at a gait John recalled from his youth in Ain Karim.

"Joses, Joses of Arimathea? Can that really be you?" he hallooed into the early morning air.

"In the flesh, dear John," his friend answered with his usual jocular tone of voice, at the same time full of confidence laced with good humor.

"Everyone's been worried about you, friend of my youth," Joses hastened to say. "They feared that at best a wild animal had carried you off. At worst, you had fallen into the clutches of Antipas's wicked wife."

"I am well and safe. I must say, though, I am flabbergasted that you are here, that you found me. How? Who or what sent you looking for me?"

"It's really not so complicated, dear brother," his friend teased. "When I began to hear about this strange man preaching up and down the river, I did not pay much attention. Somebody's always out and about telling everyone else the world's coming to an end. Then when they called him John, I started to wonder. As your fame spread along with reports of the grumpy way you dealt with people who took themselves too seriously, I decided that had to be John from Ain Karim. So I decided to go and investigate. After all, it's not every day that one of my friends gets to be so famous that everybody in the whole country is talking about him. Better go and enjoy some of the reflected glory, I decided."

"But how did you get out here?"

"Wait, I'm coming to that. I went to the Jordan and started working my way north until I came upon the camp where a dozen or so of your closest followers milled about waiting for you to show up again. With nothing better to do back home, I decided to hang around for a few days so I could spend some time with you.

"When you did not come and did not come, Hannah and that fellow Reuben and I got worried. By the way, I'm not sure how much you can trust Reuben. I get bad feelings about him. But that's another story. Hannah's a jewel—smart, funny, tough, spiritual, and understands how the world works.

"Anyway, I asked different ones among your camp which way you had gone when you left for this latest holy trek of yours. Getting my bearings, talking with some old-timers in villages around your camp, I decided to go looking for you. So I followed my instincts."

"Lots of empty spaces," John opined.

"You are right. Frankly, when I did not find you in a couple days, I began to get nervous. That's when I started praying, sometimes out loud, that Adonai would give me some extra-special help. I kept searching. Back and forth. Up and down. And here I am."

John, in a gesture largely out of character for him, threw his arms around his lifelong friend and, with tears in his eyes, said, "Joses, among the things I've learned since last we talked is that I may have human endurance. I may have the call of Adonai on my life. But I've found out the hard way that I do need some people, at least the ones Adonai sends my way. Like you. At this time."

Swallowing a lump in his throat, Joses said, "We'd better get moving. We don't have time to sit around here and remember the good old days."

As they threaded their way back toward John's camp by the river, Joses pushed John, saying, "Tell me everything you've been doing since the last time we saw each other."

"Amazing," Joses kept saying as the story of John's explosive, unwanted notoriety unfolded.

"And what of Jesus?" Joses asked as they walked. "Whatever happened to him? Seems to me like you were particularly protective of him as we helped him get back to Nazareth after his father's death."

"He's in Egypt," John answered flatly.

"Egypt? What in the world is he doing in Egypt?"

"Studying to be a physician," John exclaimed, proceeding to tell Joses what he knew of Jesus's route from Galilee to the land of the pharaohs.

"When's he coming home?" Joses wanted to know.

"I don't know if he's coming home," John replied.

"Oh, he'll be back."

"And how do you know that?" John wanted to know. "Has Adonai sent you some sort of special message about Jesus?"

"No, not really. And I certainly do not know the man other than the time we had those few days with him. Those times were anything but good for him. Still, like I've never forgotten you, I've never forgotten him. There's something about both of you, apart and together, that makes me sit up and take notice."

"People are always saying things like that, Joses, and I don't know what they mean."

Joses said, "Just look at what kind of stir you have already generated. Everyone in the country is talking about you. And how many poor boys from Nazareth have ever been to Egypt for anything, much less to become a real physician?"

"What makes you think he'll give up the good life in Egypt to come back here and endure the priests and the Romans and the poverty?" John wanted to know.

"He's too much a Jew to stay there forever. Besides, he knows our needs. He'll be in Egypt as long as necessary, until something happens to bring him home, or until someone like you goes for him, friend John."

"And why, friend Joses, would Jesus listen to me or heed my advice?"

"Oh, John," Joses replied, "no one in their right mind would ever not listen to you about anything. You and Adonai are too thick for anyone ever to doubt that you speak for him."

"Strange that you should talk like this, Joses. I agree with you about Jesus. He is never far from my mind. For two or three years I had no idea where he was. Even then, I thought about him all the time. Now that I have learned he's in Egypt, it's almost like I could reach out and touch him. As more of this unbelievable work has settled around me, I have thought about Jesus constantly."

"What do you mean?" Joses asked.

John mused, "I hate being public. I live better out in the wilds shouting at whoever will listen about the coming day of Adonai. Jesus is the one who understands people. Besides, this whole thing is moving so fast, Adonai just has to send someone to put it together. Jesus is the one to do that. He'd better hurry, though. My time is limited."

"And where does Jesus figure in?"

John was thoughtful for several minutes as he limped along leaning on the staff Joses had made for him. "I have the growing feeling that he will be the actual point person for the new kingdom, the standard bearer. He just may well be the one Isaiah and the other prophets sang about."

"What does Jesus have to say about this place of honor you've bestowed on him?"

With another of his rare chuckles, John said, "Actually, he does not yet know of his place as leader."

"And what will he do as leader?"

"I'm not that far yet," John admitted. "The whole thing is still unfolding."

———

At the command of the adjutant to the Roman legate of Syria, the Third Legion assembled in full dress uniform on the parade ground that had been carved out of the middle of the ancient city of Damascus. As trumpets blared, Antonious, the emperor's man for the entire region of the eastern Mediterranean, strode to the raised platform. The troops, standing at attention—the morning sun dancing off their helmets, shields, and spear points—saluted this man they respected with the time-honored banging of their swords and spear shafts on their shields. For a moment the Roman received their homage, gave them the stiff-armed salute in return, then motioned for them to silence.

"Men of the Third Legion of Rome," he intoned, his strong voice carrying to the outer edges of the formation, "you have served your emperor with great distinction. You have conquered vast new regions, bringing millions of people under the rule of Rome."

Again, the rumbling of their noisy salute. "Now it is time that Rome expresses its deepest gratitude to you. As your twenty-year enlistment draws to a close, your emperor, the divine Tiberius Caesar, hereby decrees that each of you will have ten hectares of land in the country of your choice."

This time, a loud cheer went up from the entire legion. Land—that's what they wanted most of all. The vast majority of the troops came from Roman peasant families who owned no land. Ten hectares wasn't much, most of them thought, but still enough for a man to make a decent living and grow enough food to feed himself and his family.

The legate continued, "The emperor encourages you to remain in this part of the empire. For those who choose to homestead in the Syrian province, the emperor will bring your families from Italy to you, at his expense."

They let out a thunderous roar that could be heard throughout the city. That settled it for most of the veterans. Their homeland across the sea held very little for them. For the most part, parents were long dead. Even children sired during brief furloughs were getting up in years. The soldier and his wife, if he had one, could settle down and begin to make a life for themselves. If he had no wife—and many Roman soldiers had not married because of the demands of military service—with this much land he would have no trouble finding a good woman to spend the rest of her life with him.

—

The headman of the village of Shunem put out a call that everyone must assemble that afternoon an hour before sundown. "That's unheard of," one farmer said to his wife. "He knows we have to work every hour of daylight we possibly can. What is going on that we have to quit early and come to the town square?"

Amidst much grumbling, all the men and boys of Shunem were at the appointed place while the sun still stood an hour in the blue sky.

When the men saw the headman and a Roman centurion coming before them, an immediate hush fell across the entire group. Roman soldiers, though a ubiquitous presence in the country, rarely came to small villages like theirs. That was a bad sign.

"Men of Shunem," the headman called out, not daring to look any of them directly in the face. "The centurion here," and he motioned at the soldier standing beside him, dressed in full uniform, his helmet under his arm, signaling he was not there for battle unless circumstances dictated, "has some information for us. I'm afraid he does not have good news for many of you."

In heavily accented Greek, the Roman said, "It has come to our attention that many of you are farming lands that do not actually belong to you. We have researched the records and can find no sign of ownership."

For a long moment, no one said anything. Then a young farmer spoke, like the centurion, in halting Greek, his voice trembling yet firm, "That's not the way we do land in our country. I farm my land because my ancestors farmed it. No one ever questions it."

The Roman retorted, his voice rising in preparation for the conflict he knew was about to erupt, "That is not the way we do it in Rome. No deed, no proof of ownership, no land."

In chorus, several of the men shouted incredulously, "What do you mean? Are you saying this is not our land?"

"That's exactly right." He shifted his weight to lean toward them ever so slightly, sending an unmistakable air of defiance. "By decree of the Syrian legate, certain of your farms are forfeit for lack of proof of ownership. Your headman has the list. You will have thirty days to vacate the land. You can keep your houses if they are in your fields. You can keep your livestock. And just to show you that Rome is fair, you will receive compensation." With that he walked to the edge of the town, mounted the horse his aide was holding for him, and rode away.

The devastated men, taken completely by surprise, exploded. They yelled imprecations, shook their fists at the Roman, and would have made a run at him if soldiers had not held them back. "They can't do this to us," the men cried out.

After several minutes of pandemonium, the headman again held up his hands for quiet. "You say they cannot do this to us," he said. "Well, they just did. The centurion gave me the list of the farms the Romans are taking. They are going to pay something. My guess it is precious little."

Throughout the region, the scene in Shunem was duplicated again and again. Using a variety of ruses such as suspected disloyalty, nonpayment of loans that were suddenly called, as well as the fiction of no proof of ownership, a thousand families lost their land to Roman army veterans.

The high priest and the tetrarchs, Herod Antipas and Philip, made feeble protests that were completely overlooked for the half-hearted, cowardly efforts they actually were.

The agony of dispossession infected the entire region, especially in the areas around where John was preaching. Hunger and disease brought on by difficult social conditions were always a problem. Now, with a thousand already poor families tossed off their farms with no way to make a living, the specter of unimaginable human misery rose.

John and his close circle of advisers talked endlessly about ways to alleviate the suffering. As the crisis deepened, John urged those who came to the river to hear him preach, "Let no one in your village go hungry."

Hearing his word, the people responded from their meager supplies, helping feed those who had nothing.

Joses, by now an established member of John's inner circle, reminded the close-knit group after an especially difficult day, "Look, we're fighting a losing battle. We must do more than just talk the people into sharing food. Many will die from starvation if something's not done."

Frustrated beyond words, John agonized, "We must find someone who can help us help these people. But who? It will take a very special person."

And then, in a flash, both John and Joses said at the same time, "Jesus."

# Chapter Three

# The Weeds Cry Out

## His Twenty-sixth Year

*He has sent me to bring good news to the oppressed, to bind up the brokenhearted, to proclaim release to the prisoners.*

By the time the cousins disembarked from their ship at Caesarea, John had filled Jesus in on the details of the current crisis. As they made their way across the country to John's camp, they could see signs of the severe dislocation that had occurred.

John's camp was not where it had been when he left for Egypt. People who still lingered at the site said, "We heard they've set up in the area of Bethany beyond the Jordan, but we're not sure."

Next day, shortly after noon, the two men arrived at the new camp. Hannah and Reuben, along with more than two dozen of John's followers who had maintained themselves during his absence, rushed to greet him when they saw him topping a hill on his way down to the riverside camp they had set up. Amid prolonged hugging and hallelujahs, they expressed their elation at his safe return. John's usual reserve gave way briefly as he received their love and welcome. After a few minutes, he raised his hands, saying, "Wait, that's enough. It has been only a few weeks. You have done all the work while I was seeing the 'wonders' of Egypt."

Everyone laughed at his joke, most knowing him well enough to realize he had seen little of Egypt and probably enjoyed nothing of what he did indeed lay his eyes on.

Jesus stood at the fringes of this merry company assessing what he saw and felt. John, the reclusive wilderness man, had certainly generated strong feelings among this hearty band.

After a moment of celebration, John motioned for everyone to move away, sit down, and keep their hands off of him. The people stilled, and John beckoned for Jesus to come forward.

"I want you to meet my cousin, Jesus from Nazareth and, of late, from Alexandria in Egypt. When we have more time, I will tell you about him. From time to time in our years as relatives and friends, he's kept me busy keeping him out of trouble."

Jesus stepped forward, waved his hands in acknowledgment of the introduction, bowed, smiled, and said, "John has certainly stood in the breach for me and my family at several critical moments. I honor him as do you."

John went on, "You will discover when you know him better that Jesus has many extraordinary gifts from Adonai. For several years I have believed that he has a very special calling on his life. Indeed, the spirit of Adonai has all but transported me to Jesus's side more than once when he faced great danger. He has a large and holy responsibility before him. I cannot explain Adonai's purposes. I do, however, bow before the mystery of Adonai's endowment on Jesus."

Jesus, stunned, not expecting this kind of introduction, shifted uneasily. Not knowing how to respond, he just looked at John uncomprehendingly.

A hush fell over the group. Never had John spoken of anyone like this. All eyes moved back and forth between John and Jesus. Men and women, albeit unconsciously, began a process of trying to determine exactly who this new man among them was and what sort of relationship, if any, did they need to establish with him. Reuben especially felt vague uneasiness with Jesus's introduction into the circle. Friend or foe? Reuben wondered.

—

The grapevine quickly disseminated the news of John's return.

At dawn the next morning, the crowd began to gather by the river. Only this time, John felt a discernible difference in the people. Previously, a feeling of excitement, anticipation, joy coursed through the people. They had gathered for some grand news of a coming kingdom. Now an attitude of quiet desperation seemed to bind the people together. Something new and sinister completely beyond their control had descended on them. Out of the several hundred who quietly collected around John waiting for him to begin his teaching, only a score or so families had been directly hit by the latest wave of land expropriation, though everyone at the river knew someone who had been displaced. What's more, they understood the same fate could befall them just as swiftly and with no recourse whatsoever.

John began with some words of hope from the psalms: *He will command his angels concerning you to guard you in all your ways. On their hands they will bear you up, so that you will not dash your foot against a stone. Those who love me, I will deliver; I will protect those who know my name. When they call to me, I will answer them; I will be with them in trouble.*

He continued, "I know words from the psalms will not fill empty stomachs and make crops grow on land you no longer possess. I offer you today, however, hope that God's hand will fall heavily on those who oppress the poor. He will not forever tolerate the kind of injustice many of you have suffered in recent days. I wish I had an immediate answer to your problems. I do not. I do promise that I will stand with you in the name of Adonai, who unfailingly supports all his faithful people with his steadfast love."

Collecting his thoughts more precisely, John said, "Now, as never before, is the time we must come together to share what we have with those who have little or nothing. As long as anyone in your village has food to eat and a place to sleep at night, none of your brothers and sisters who have been tossed off their land should go completely lacking."

John fumed with fiery indignation at the gross injustice inflicted on the struggling people of his homeland. "Reach back into our history and let your ears and hearts burn at the searing denunciation of Elijah, Amos, and Hosea, who thundered over the gross mistreatment of the poor by the rich."

Catching his breath for a second, he shouted, "Those who have done this to you and your families are a brood of vipers. Blood drips from their hands. They are an abomination to all that's divine and noble about Adonai's creation. The Holy One will deal harshly with them. When his kingdom fully comes, they will be the first to be consumed in the fires of judgment."

Then he stared toward Jerusalem, raised his fist, and shouted, "The high priest and those who fawn before him who do nothing to right this wrong are an abomination of desolation. Just as surely as our enemies of the past desecrated Adonai's holy altars with forbidden sacrifices, these men desecrate the same altars with their arrogant indifference to the suffering of the people of Adonai."

His fury and burning words stunned the crowd. The close followers, including Jesus, caught their breath. Some of the people even began to glance toward the sky as if fires from heaven would fall any minute. Reuben noticeably flinched and looked around uneasily for anyone who might seem to be taking special note of John's message.

After another hour of preaching, John backed away, exhausted. Hannah invited any who wanted baptism to come toward the river. Jesus was amazed to see dozens and dozens silently make their way to the water. Several of John's band, following the routine they had established, moved purposefully toward the river, preparing to baptize those who came forward.

That evening, after a quick bath in the river just to wash away the sweat and grime of the day, John along with Jesus, Hannah, Reuben, and three of the close group settled down for conversation.

They talked in generalities for a while, and then Jesus asked with utmost seriousness, "What will happen to those families who've lost their land? How will they eat? Where will they find work?"

Without a moment's hesitation, John said, "Jesus, you are the one who is going to help them find a new way. Adonai has called you to make straight paths through this wilderness that has confounded the poor of our land."

Astounded, flabbergasted, Jesus blurted loudly enough to shatter the quiet of the evening, "What do you mean? I have no idea what to do with those people. Maybe if they got sick, I could help some of them. For them to find new lives—and that's what they've got to do—I have no idea, not the strangest notion!"

"Well," John said in his matter-of-fact manner, "it is yours to figure out. That's at least part of the reason why Adonai has raised you up, sent you to Egypt, and now has brought you back. When you get this problem addressed, a new one will crop up. You remember my friend Joses from Arimathea? He went with us to Nazareth after your father's death. He went to his home while I traveled to Egypt for you. He will return soon. He wants to help you. He and I have already discussed you and your part. For now, I'm going to sleep. The rest of you can talk a while if you want to. Goodnight." Within a few minutes he was sound asleep in the small tent someone had put up for him.

Jesus did not sleep well that night.

—

Jesus and Joses, upon the Arimathean's return to the camp, quickly renewed their acquaintance and discovered in each other ingredients of lasting friendship and partnership. Joses possessed the kind of hard-headed, practical, problem-solving knack Jesus came to rely on. In addition, he had a multitude of contacts and access to a fair amount of money to facilitate some of the initiatives Jesus had the intellect, persuasive powers of language, spiritual understanding, and creativity needed to think at the very edge of the presenting problem. Both were completely fearless.

"One of the aspects of this whole recovery enterprise we must keep in mind, Jesus," Joses said as they talked and talked, "is that we must do all we can to avoid attracting any attention to ourselves or to what we are doing. Any sign of active resistance against the Roman authorities and the retired soldiers who have taken the land and we are in big trouble. The Romans will not interfere with us if we find ways to help the people tossed off their land to make a new living. In fact, they'd like for everyone to be working, because that makes for more taxes. But the Roman army will not tolerate a moment's overt protest."

Jesus readily agreed. "You and I know that, but it will be another matter keeping frightened, angry farmers who feel they don't have anything to lose anyway from outright retaliation."

"It will take only a few crucifixions for them to get the message," Joses opined.

"I've seen those crucifixions. They and we must do all we can to avoid those crosses," Jesus said with a shudder. Horrible memories, never far away, yet again flooded his mind.

"Our first assignment," Joses told Jesus as they got down to specifics, "is food for those hardest hit. Hungry people cannot do much else but think about their stomachs."

By asking around among the people who came to hear John preach, Jesus and Joses concluded which areas seemed to be suffering the worst. When the two men visited those villages, they did indeed find rapidly deteriorating conditions. One dispossessed farmer after another said, "We're down to only a few pounds of grain to feed the family. What winter supplies we were able to put aside are gone."

After a brief time of exploration and investigation, Jesus and Joses decided to work at Shunem, the Judean village hardest hit in the region, a few miles north and west of John's present camp. Even though Jesus and Joses were not from that part of the country, the leaders of the village decided to respond, albeit cautiously, to the calls of the two men to meet and talk about their problems. As the first of many such gatherings got underway, Joses whispered to Jesus, "You do the talking. I'll be right by your side."

Like John when he began, Jesus did not regard himself as a public speaker, but the situation was too critical for him to quibble, so he immediately took the lead.

The people had no trouble listening to this man. Now in his late twenties, he was obviously in excellent physical condition, slightly taller than average, quite pleasing to look at, though not necessarily the stuff of Greek statues. Overriding all his physical attributes, however, was his obvious intelligence, the air of competence and confidence he conveyed, his grasp of the gravity of their problems, his willingness to become involved with them for the long run, and the obvious well-spring of faith in Adonai that animated him. From the very beginning of this frantic effort to stave off starvation and find solutions to critical human problems, people instinctively trusted Jesus. Joses, his friend with the warm and open nature, himself quick of mind and laughter, possessed a great deal of everyday common sense about how the world worked.

Jesus said to the men of Shunem, "With your help, we've calculated that your village has about one hundred twenty-five people—men, women, and children—in serious trouble with not enough to eat. Joses and I have some definite plans of how we can help several, if not all, the families gradually get back on their feet. We cannot feed them, though. If you will help feed these people, all of whom are your relatives and neighbors, we believe we can work on solutions with long-term possibilities."

The village headman spoke up and said, "We're willing to look for answers, Jesus. As far as food goes, we hardly have enough on hand to feed ourselves. If we start passing out what we've got put aside, we could all run short."

"I understand," Jesus assured him, "but consider your options. If you fail to help, then hunger, disease, and death will ravage your community. It seems to me that common sense, self-preservation, not to mention compassion, prompt you to take the chance. Put yourselves in their position. Hear the word of Adonai that comes to us from dozens of places from the scriptures saying, 'Love your neighbor as you love yourselves.'"

Joses spoke up. "Before we get in a panic, put down some hard numbers. How much food will it take to feed the most severely endangered people for a few weeks?"

Gradually, when the problems were reduced to facts and figures, the people in the village who had some reserves began to see they could share with their hard-pressed neighbors for a limited time. The crisis became more manageable bit by bit.

The dispossessed had to find new work. Jesus immediately set about determining what goods the dispossessed farmers could make locally and sell in Aenon, Salim, and other larger towns nearby. "I am a carpenter, actually a woodworker, by trade," he told them. "I can show you how to make tables, chairs, cabinets, bowls, and other household utensils. It looks to me like you could begin a selective cutting of olive trees that grow around here in great abundance and learn to make items you can sell or trade."

The former farmers groused, "Wait, Jesus, we know nothing about woodworking. We're farmers. That's all we know. Besides, you might have been a carpenter, but, frankly, that's work for tektons. We're men of the earth."

"Look," Jesus retorted with frank irritation, at the same time recalling the pain his grandfather endured after losing his land, "you need to understand that you're in no position to quibble. If you don't want to work, fine. What are you going to do? Your life as farmers is over. You have to find a new way to live."

Within a few weeks, under Jesus's tutelage, several of the farmers discovered they had good ability to craft marketable items from wood. At first, the rather crude bowls, platters, utensils, and other small pieces they fashioned did not sell well in the larger towns and cities. Soon though, as the men's abilities improved, sales picked up, bringing at least trickles of money. The dark moods in Shunem gradually begin to brighten.

Constantly, however, Jesus and Joses had to help the men deal with their wounded pride. "We've never worked for wages," they said sitting around campfires out from their village at night. "We've always looked down on those who worked for wages. It hurts very badly for us to be in that position now."

Jesus interjected, "Let's talk about what you are saying. I know that the common way to understand our lives is to think that plenty of food put aside for hard times, a few coins in the storebox, and everyone in the family well and happy is the sign of Adonai's favor."

The son of one of the farmers spoke up, "That's what I also thought."

"That's what most of us have thought," Jesus agreed. "But when you look back through our history, the special favor of Adonai is always on those who are having a hard time. Adonai sent Moses to our ancestors in Egypt not because they were enjoying the wealth of the land. No, he sent Moses to free our ancestors from slavery, oppression, hunger, illness."

"Does Adonai send hard times on his people so he can shower them with his favor?" a young voice piped up with a biting edge of sarcasm. "If he does, I'd prefer not to have so much favor."

Jesus had to laugh at the man's homespun humor. "No. Adonai does not put hard times on us. Hard times almost always come as a result of someone's disobedience to Adonai—our own or that of someone in a place of power or authority. What you are going through now is a direct result of greed and war. The Romans do not need to be in our country oppressing us."

A murmur of angry agreement rumbled through the group.

"Why don't we throw off the Romans?" another young man shouted out angrily.

"You had better have a lot more equipment and men than I see around here in Shunem if you try that one," Jesus replied lightly, still with the utmost seriousness.

"What do we do then while we are having a hard time? Just sit around and feel blessed of Adonai while our children starve and while Roman soldiers and their wives live on our land?" yet another man spoke up, this one a farmer of middle age whose grief was about to consume him.

"You do what we are doing," Jesus said with assurance. "You make the best of a bad situation. You do not do something silly or rash like trying to rise up against the Romans. You find ways to use the minds and abilities Adonai has given you to make a new life. Maybe you make new wine from the old vineyards, or maybe you plant a new vineyard on land out of sight of the Romans."

Evening talk sessions gradually became a regular feature of Jesus's days in Shunem. Villagers found in him an invigorating, commonsense grasp of the Jewish scriptures. He did not try to split hairs with them. While he avoided any attempt to set aside any of their historic teachings and ways, he began to put many of them in the context of their own times. "I know you are fiercely angry at the Romans who took your lands. Remember, though, those men served in difficult places for years and years. Some hardly saw their families for the twenty years they were in the army. The soldiers were doing their duty as they saw it. Now it's payday for them. Your own spiritual health calls for you to struggle to live with an attitude of understanding and mercy toward them even though you detest them. Hatred will make you sick in mind and body."

"You are asking a lot from us," one of the dispossessed farmers complained angrily.

"I'm not asking it from you," Jesus explained, feeling their pain. "You owe it to yourselves not to go crazy with anger and frustration. Use your feelings to help you make a difference."

"But what about the Romans? Who'll take care of them?" the young farmer asked Jesus, anger and desperation in his voice.

"You can be sure that Adonai will take care of them in his own good time," Jesus said with complete confidence. "The justice of Adonai never fails, for the Romans or the Jews."

After about six months of working in Shunem, with the economic and social situation somewhat stabilized, Jesus and Joses moved on up the Jordan River Valley a few more miles. Word had come to them that the area around the town of Amathus in Antipas's Perea had been as hard hit as Shunem.

News of their arrival preceded the two men, so they were met by a delegation of the community leaders.

"Welcome, Jesus and Joses," the headman said as the two of them approached the outer edge of the village. "We've heard of the work you did in Shunem. We hear that it's almost like a miracle. We hope you can do something like that with us. Over a hundred of our families in the outlying hills have been tossed off their land. We've already taken strong measures to provide food for them, but the supplies are running low for everyone. It's a big job feeding that many people."

Surprised by the welcome, Jesus and Joses nonetheless set about to see what could be done to point the Amathus farmers in new directions. "Why don't you put out the word for representatives from the dispossessed families to gather here in the town square within the next few days. In the meantime, Joses and I will be talking with others to get a better idea of what resources are available to enable these folks to make a living."

"We heard that you taught many of the men in Shunem how to work with wood. We have very little wood in this region. We certainly have nowhere enough to supply all the families with wood to make a living."

"I understand," Joses said. "Let me walk around for a couple days and see what I can see. Maybe I can spot something or a resource that you have overlooked because you live here."

By dark of their second day in Amathus, Jesus had to admit quietly to Joses, "So far, I've drawn a blank. Nothing seems available in enough quantity to make much of a difference."

"That's bad," Joses agreed. "We just have to keep looking. Maybe something will turn up. In the meantime, tomorrow we meet with the families. I wish we could have some positive words to give them. That surely would boost their morale."

More than fifty men greeted Jesus and Joses in the town square at dawn. Jesus had never seen a more dispirited, downcast, hopeless group of people. All life seemed to have drained out of them. The ravages of fear could be read on each face, young and old.

Jesus's efforts to cheer them up came to nothing. He and Joses told their stories of encouragement from Shunem. "But we don't have enough olive wood or cedar or oak trees around here to make fires, much less to start businesses," one of the men offered while the others nodded their heads in sullen agreement.

"What do you have?" Joses asked, looking anxiously into several of their faces. "Surely you've got more native resources around here than just ground to grow stuff in."

Until high noon, the two men talked, probed, asked questions, urged imaginative thinking on the farmers, all to no avail.

The headman from Amathus interrupted, saying, "We're tired and hungry and thirsty. Let's stop for a while. Eat a little something. Maybe we'll get an idea."

Just as the crowd began to disperse, a man from the fringes of the group called out, "I'd like to ask the Galilean to say a prayer for us. He's a man of spirit. Maybe Adonai will speak to him so he can talk to us."

Though he had been discussing his ideas of scriptures with people in the villages, Jesus hardly ever had led in any sort of public worship. He was no priest. Taking a deep breath, pausing to collect his thoughts, the lines of one of their psalms sprang to his mind, and he began to sing in Hebrew, *I will love thee, O Lord, my strength. The Lord is my rock and my fortress, my deliverer, my God, my strength, in whom I will trust. I will call upon the Lord who is worthy to be praised; so shall I be saved from my enemies. The sorrows of death compassed me, and the floods of ungodly men made me afraid. In my distress I called upon the Lord, and cried unto my God: he heard my voice out of his temple, and my cry came before him, even into his ears. He brought me forth also into a large place; he delivered me because he delighted in me. Therefore will I give thanks unto you, O Lord, and sing praises unto your name.*

To a loud and greatly heartened "Amen!" the men dispersed for what meager food they could find.

Jesus and Joses sat under a brush arbor munching on some bread and cheese. "This is unusually good bread and cheese," Joses said. "In fact, I've never tasted anything quite like it. You make them here?"

The headman spoke up and said, "We've always been noted for our bread and cheese. It seems there's something in the soil, or maybe the water, that gives products from both grain and livestock a special flavor."

His interest immediately sparked, Joses asked eagerly, "Have you ever tried to make bread and cheese in sufficient quantity to sell to other towns, even in Jerusalem or Tiberias?"

"No. Never thought about it. The men have been too busy farming to think much about making extra bread and cheese," the headman replied nonchalantly. When he saw Joses's face light up, he immediately asked, "What do you have in mind?"

"The Romans took the land. Did they take the livestock, especially goats from which you make this cheese?"

"For the most part, the Romans did not want to fool with the goats. Seems that these Romans came from a part of their native land that did not know anything about goats. We've got herds out over the hillsides, away from the farms, just roaming loose. No one's had enough energy to try to round them up."

"Why don't we talk about some of the farmers going into the cheese business?" Joses asked, his eyes now flashing.

"Making cheese is women's work," offered another man sitting by who had overheard the conversation.

"Hush, Mathias," the headman ordered. "When you're hungry, it doesn't matter who does the work. Just get it done so you can eat." Looking from Joses to Jesus, he said, "All right, maybe some can make cheese. But that will help only a few families, those who have some goats left."

"How much grain do you have stored up that you have grown around here?" Joses wanted to know next.

The headman hesitated a moment, lest he betray a village secret, then confessed sheepishly, "We actually had a very good crop last season, before the Romans took away the land. We grew a lot more grain than we need. Because the entire region had big harvests, we've not sold much. Yes, right now, we've got loads of grain."

Jesus was tempted to scold the headman for hoarding the grain from the hungry people. He resisted but did say, "Maybe we're on to something. These people can't forever make a living selling bread and cheese. They can do it until something else turns up. Joses, that's a good start."

The small group seated under the brush arbor were about to leave when a young woman appeared bearing a pitcher of water. "Would you men like to have a drink of water before you return?" she asked.

Jesus immediately spoke up, "Why, yes. Thank you. It's been a hot morning. I've done a lot of talking. I am very thirsty."

When she tipped the pitcher over to pour water into a cup, Jesus's eye fell on the graceful lines of the two utensils the young woman had in her hands. As he drank the cool water, he commented to the headman, "I have been to Egypt and back. I've rarely seen pottery so beautifully cast as this pitcher and cup. Did someone around here make them?"

"As a matter of fact, yes. Situated as we are, close to the Jordan, our village has always had access to a huge clay pit down by the river. Since anyone can remember, our women have turned out items like these. We've become quite good at making pottery."

Ever on the alert, Joses spoke up quickly, saying, "I'll ask about the pottery like I did the bread and cheese. Have you ever tried to make enough pottery to sell outside your village?"

"No. Never have. Never thought about it. Never had the time or the need." Then, looking for the first time at the pottery, he said to Jesus and Joses, "So you think we make good stuff, huh? Are you thinking maybe we could make it and sell it along with our bread and cheese?"

Jesus said to the men, "What you're doing here reminds me of a great story. A young woman was given a bushel of flour and told to make bread for a large party her master was hosting. The girl did not know much about cooking. She had certainly never tried to make bread for a big crowd. She took some of the flour and made a batch of dough. The bread was awful. When the girl began to cry over her bad bread, her mother said, 'Don't cry. Let me help. You've got to add yeast to the flour. Then it will rise and make wonderful bread.'

"'Oh, I didn't know about yeast,' the girl said. When she added just a small amount of yeast to the bushel of flour and let it rise overnight, she was able to bake a hundred loaves of bread for the master's party. And everyone raved what good her bread she had baked.

"What we're doing here is adding a different kind of yeast to the ordinary flour of your lives. With just a bit of care, new lives can rise as surely as the bread with yeast. Of course, bread and cheese and pottery will not make your lives new. An attitude of creative thinking, taking the second and third look, will make a big difference. That's really what Adonai's kingdom is about. It's the yeast that helps you make new and delicious lives."

—

After the two men had been trekking up and down the river valley for months, having only sporadic contact with John, Jesus said to Joses one day, "I am tired. We've been going day and night for months. Why don't we take a break and go find John, talk with him for a few days just to find out what's happening with him and catch our breath."

"Actually, Jesus," Joses replied, "I need to go home for a while. My father and brothers can take care of everything in my absence, but I ought to check up on everything. You go find John. Take what time you need. When I can get loose again, I will come find you."

"But how will you know where I am?" Jesus asked.

"Listen, with the way your fame as a miracle worker is spreading, I will not have too much trouble locating you."

———

"I have followed your progress up the river," John informed Jesus when they were reunited as they walked in the early evening. "From what I hear, you've been very helpful in pointing many of the hardest-hit farmers in new directions as well as helping hundreds and hundreds get a clearer view of the scriptures."

"It's been satisfying, if exhausting," Jesus answered. "I need to rest and think some more about Adonai's direction for me."

"I have an idea of where you can go to get real rest and all the good food you can possibly hold," John offered.

"And where might that heavenly place be?" Jesus wanted to know, his interest piqued.

"Across the river, at Bethany beyond the Jordan, I've become friends with a man named Lazarus and his two unmarried sisters. For people in these parts, they are fairly substantial. They have a comfortable house. Lazarus suffers from poor health. His two sisters, Mary and Martha, actually run the family business and take care of him. They have come to hear me, received baptism, and have become solid friends."

Jesus immediately found soulmates with the brother and his two sisters. They did indeed own a spacious house. Lazarus was lean, rather stooped, pale of complexion but robust of spirit. Mary, his sister, reminded Jesus of his own mother. She was slight, graceful, sensitive, hardworking, yet could take the time to watch the sunset. Martha, the eldest of the three, ran the household, the family business, and much of the town of Bethany beyond the Jordan. And no one seemed to take offense. Everyone felt secure when Martha was around, knowing she had every inch of her world under control, except, to her great and abiding distress, Lazarus's health.

For the first two days that Jesus accepted their hospitality, he hardly budged from his room. Indeed, he barely got out of bed. He had not realized just how tired he was. Martha cooked mountains of food served graciously by Mary.

By the third day, Jesus felt refreshed and ready to explore the region around Bethany beyond the Jordan and get better acquainted with his hosts. Since Lazarus's diminished health had prevented him from engaging in sustained manual labor for several years, he had spent countless hours studying the scriptures and liked nothing better than to explore them at great length with a person who was also well versed. He found a more than willing partner in Jesus.

Lazarus asked Jesus in one of their biblical gab sessions, "Have you paid much attention to the prophecies in the latter part of the book of Daniel?"

"No, I have to confess, I haven't," Jesus admitted. "They are, after all, not as ancient as our other scriptures. I've loved the stories of the exploits of Daniel and his three friends, but that's about as far as I have gone."

"You need to spend time examining the last half of the Daniel writings, Jesus. They describe God's plan to close down history through the work of the Son of Man."

"Close down history? A Son of Man?" Jesus mused. "I can understand Adonai's plan to send someone special to do his work in a given timeframe. He's frequently done that in our past. Abraham. Joseph. Moses. King David. And the rest. But close down history? That doesn't add up for me."

"It's right there in the writings. You have to puzzle it through, but it's there. That's what John preaches. He thinks Adonai is going to come sweeping in, wipe out the unrighteous ones, and set up a kingdom in which only those who have done justice and mercy in the eyes of Adonai will have a place."

"I'm not sure I agree with my cousin or, for that matter, Daniel on that one. I believe Adonai works within time. After all, that is where people live every day, in unfolding history. Nonetheless, I will spend more time with the book, especially if you think it's all that important."

After a moment of thoughtful silence, Jesus asked, "Let me change the subject a bit. Does John say you have to be baptized to have a place in Adonai's realm?"

"No. He does not say that," Lazarus exclaimed, sitting up in his seat, making a strong point he had made before to other critics of John. "In fact, he makes it plain that baptism is not necessary for living in closer favor with Adonai.

Frankly, I'm not completely sure what his baptism is all about, but it surely was thrilling for me to be baptized."

"My understanding of his baptism is that it is a personal experience, a moment that means different things to different people," Jesus said. "It's also a way to identify with all spiritually hungry people, Jews and others who desire to be part of Adonai."

"Have you been baptized?" Lazarus asked Jesus as they talked.

"No. I have not. Until coming here, talking with you, I have not given it much thought, to be honest. But I will now."

A few days later, as the two friends sat out in front of the house in comfortable chairs, a cushion for Lazarus to ease the strain on his bony frame, Jesus asked him, "What is your physical malady? I notice you are underweight, have little endurance, and have difficulty breathing from time to time. Have you talked with doctors about your illness?"

"Oh, Jesus, I have given up on doctors. I've long had poor health. One thing after another. Still, I get along fairly well. The doctors I have known are nothing more than charlatans."

Jesus did not comment.

The next morning at breakfast, Lazarus asked Jesus, "What did you study in Alexandria? We have not talked much about your time in Egypt. Tell me about it."

"Lazarus," Jesus said, leaning back comfortably in his chair, stretching his legs out in front of him, "you would not believe the vast store of knowledge in the Library of Alexandria. I read the philosophy of Plato and Aristotle. Plato and some of our wisdom teachers would get along wonderfully well. Aristotle, Alexander's teacher, tries to put all human experiences into a whole. He also has the disturbing notion that the world may be round."

"Did you concentrate on one special field of study?" Lazarus queried.

Jesus's face crinkled into a broad smile. "You might throw me out of your house when I tell you what I spent most of my time doing."

"Nothing would make me do that, I can assure you," Lazarus replied warmly.

"I studied medicine."

"You are a physician?" Lazarus demanded, amazed.

"Yes. I am, Lazarus," Jesus smiled.

"Why did you not tell me that sooner?" In all seriousness Lazarus wanted to know.

"Well, when I learned of your low opinion of physicians and your terrible experience with some Jewish practitioners, I just decided to keep that bit of information to myself," Jesus answered, half-joking, half-serious.

"You would not be like the 'healers' around here, I am sure," Lazarus assured Jesus.

"I do not know, Lazarus. My family and I have never sought the advice of a Jewish physician," Jesus said frankly. "My mother tended us when we got sick using what was at hand. Besides, we did not have anyone in Nazareth with any special healing skills. Certainly no one had any formal training. A few physicians lived in Sepphoris, but none of us in Nazareth could afford them. So we either got better or died, on our own, by the grace of Adonai."

"We have many sick people here," Lazarus said, waving his arms over his village.

"I know. It distresses me to see them. Some could be helped. Many cannot," Jesus answered ruefully.

"Why have you not offered your services?" Lazarus wanted to know.

"I felt it was more important to do the demanding task of helping the farmers find new lives. If the people found out I had medical training, they might want to go for short-term cures rather than for the long-range changes we were trying to bring about."

"I frankly do not think that is a good idea, Jesus," his friend replied bluntly. "If you have training, Adonai wants you to use it. He will take care of the short- and long-range issues that concern you."

Standing up abruptly, obviously stung by Lazarus's rebuke, Jesus said, "Lazarus, that's for me to decide."

Before he could walk away, Lazarus held up his hands, "Wait, Jesus," he said easily. "No need to get offended. That is my opinion. You and Adonai can work that out. I just think you ought to mull it over. So many of our people are sick. They need a man like you they can trust."

When the moment of anger had passed, Jesus sat down again.

"Now, young physician, suppose you tell me what you studied and what you did in the great and terrible country of the pharaohs."

Realizing he and Lazarus had crossed yet another important threshold in their friendship, and finding himself quite eager to talk about his years in Alexandria, an area of his life in which John had no interest, Jesus launched into a long conversation about the years in Egypt.

"Honestly, Lazarus, Adonai has put many cures to everyday illnesses right at our fingertips. The more imagination we use, the less superstitious we are and the better we will be able to deal with our aches and pains."

The two men talked into the evening.

When Lazarus began to twist around in his seat uncomfortably, Jesus stopped talking abruptly. "Oh, Lazarus, I have overtired you."

"Nonsense, Jesus. This has been one of the most stimulating conversations of my life. But I am tired. I will need to go inside, eat some of Martha's excellent cooking, and go to bed."

As the two of them were about to enter the house, Jesus placed a restraining hand on Lazarus's arm and said, "I do ask that you not tell of my medical training. I am just not quite ready for that next phase of my life to unfold.

—

No one was ever quite sure how Jesus's secret leaked. Within a few days, people from the village began coming to Lazarus's house, pleading for Jesus to help them with their own or family members' maladies. When Lazarus shrugged, Jesus patted his friend on the shoulder, looked suspiciously at the two sisters, rolled up his sleeves, and went to work.

Hours on end, day after day, Jesus saw the sick with Mary and Martha at his side. For the most part, he could do nothing for the people other than offer spiritual and emotional comfort. Broken bones that had not already begun to set, he could often set and splint. Conditions or lesions of the skin that many regarded as leprous, he could frequently treat with a variety of homemade salves that eased the lesion and freed the person from the blight of leprosy. Other skin sores he could lance, apply poultices, or otherwise offer suggestions for help if not cure. Always in such cases, he urged the people to go through the prescribed ritual religious cleansing so they could again be able to move with freedom in society. When he encountered a person with a severe internal problem, he could often give a diagnosis such as a diseased organ or invasive tumor, suggest medicines that might relieve the symptoms or reduce the pain, but he could do nothing to cure the problem, a fact that always caused him much emotional pain and frustration.

"If only I knew how to get inside people's bodies and get rid of the tumors without killing them, I could make a significant difference, but no one knows how to do such things. Maybe someday."

Despite his best efforts, sick people died every day.

Then he confronted a new phenomenon. Regularly during those opening days of his Bethany beyond the Jordan healing ministry, he encountered men, women, and children who appeared to be completely possessed by evil spiritual forces. Their symptoms ranged from foaming at the mouth, falling down in fits, screaming and running at other people, suffering from severe tics, battling imaginary enemies, hearing voices, and even cutting and tearing at themselves.

"It's amazing," he told Martha and Mary as they ate a late-night meal after the crowds had finally gone away. "I've never seen anything like this. In Nazareth we had a few people who apparently had serious spiritual problems. For the most part, they were harmless to themselves and to others. Their families did the best they could for the sick people. But to have so many coming has me seriously worried."

"Don't you think they are just demon-possessed?" Martha asked.

"I don't think so, at least not in all these instances. Why would demons jump on good, simple, poor people like these? I have a special problem with the idea that demons get inside little children. Now, I don't say that demons do not exist. They probably do. But I think we've got some bad human problems to deal with that make people sick in their heads."

Again, for the most part, Jesus could do nothing but bandage the wounds of those who hurt themselves when their spells threw them on the ground or flung them into household items or other objects that brought injuries. After a while, however, his skills at diagnosis began to come into play. In the night, as he lay utterly fatigued on his bed, still unable to fall asleep, Jesus would recall his conversations with Erasistratus and others at the Alexandria library about such conditions. These scholars of the human body had all but completely rejected the demons theory in favor of conditions that existed in the brain and body of the affected person.

The Alexandrian scholars had begun to formulate the idea that unremitting daily pressures could cause mental distress. Under Roman occupation the anxiety of dealing with desperate living conditions, illness in themselves or loved ones, indeed the whole gauntlet of problems could cause some of the wild or aberrant behavior.

With those conversations in mind, Jesus began to make serious inquiries of the disturbed people when they could talk lucidly. He made a point to talk with the family members who came with the afflicted. Not always, but often, the onset of their disorders could be traced to a dramatic change in the person's life, such as the death of a loved one, the loss of a farm, physical harm, injustice, or severe dislocation. As he thought through the number of mentally disturbed people, a new idea dawned on him. The dramatic and terrible upheavals the entire region had experienced with the Romans' takeover of the ancestral farms could have triggered a huge wave of severe, dramatic problems.

Working on that theory, he began talking more and more with the distressed people and their families. As he helped them understand what might have happened, when he could dispel the fear of demon possession, he began to see improvements in some of the people.

Jesus's reputation as one who could cast out demons soared one day soon after it became known that a remarkable healer was in their midst. The father of a young girl, about twelve years old, brought his daughter to Jesus.

"She has fits," he said. "She'll be talking just like anyone else. Then suddenly, with no warning, she'll start screaming, running around, falling on the ground. She's always hurting herself, getting cuts and bruises as she crashes into walls or gets into fights."

"And what do you do when she has one of those spells?" Jesus asked the father, looking carefully into the man's eyes, where he could see both love and anger.

"I've tried just about everything," he said.

"Tell me what you've tried," Jesus said.

"Holding her tight, but she's grown too big for that. Trying to tie her down, but she flails around so much. I've dashed a bucket of water on her. Lately, I'm ashamed to say, I've begun to slap her in the face when she goes into a spell. Someone told me that if I hit her, I just might knock the demon out of her."

Jesus thought a few moments, then said, "You and your daughter stay around here for a while. Let me see some other people. If she has one of her spells, I can be right here to observe what happens. Let's agree that if she goes into one of these things, you step back and let me try my hand. Is that all right with you?"

Early in the afternoon, dozens of people milled about in the small courtyard before Lazarus's house, talking, eating, pushing and pulling at one another to keep their places in the line. The man and his daughter stayed out of sight to avoid undue attention. Suddenly, the girl, with no warning, began to scream, "The demon is upon me!" She flailed around wildly, all the while yelling and screaming, a terrified look in her young eyes.

Jesus immediately stopped tending to a man who had a terrible sore on his foot and ran to the girl. For a moment he watched in fascinated horror. Then he began walking slowly toward her, talking quietly as he approached her. "My little sister," he said softly, repeatedly, "you are not in the grips of a demon. You have a sickness. But it's not a demon."

When his words seemed to make no difference—indeed her gyrations only grew worse—Jesus hesitated, looked anxiously at her father, then continued speaking softly, gently, to her: "You are sick. You do not have demons. You will be all right. Adonai has his hands of love on you. You are in his care."

Soon, his calm voice assuring her she had no demons started to have an effect. She began to calm down. Finally, she lay still on the ground, looking up into the sky, an expression of calm and quiet on her face. Motioning for her father to come toward them, Jesus said to him softly, "Now, very gently, help her get up from the ground."

Calling her by name, he took his daughter gently by the hand and said, "Here, let me help you up. You don't want to keep lying there in the dirt."

He smiled at her. For yet another moment she lay on the ground staring into his face. When he remained quietly by her side, she smiled and held out her hand to him.

The people in the yard had stood aside, hardly breathing. When they saw the change, they broke into a buzz, with some even applauding. Jesus instantly motioned for them to be still while the girl and her father collected themselves.

"Now," Jesus told father and daughter after a few more minutes, "I want you to stay around here for a few days. Let's see what happens if another spell comes."

Looking from father to daughter, Jesus said, "I do not know what causes you to fall down like you do. I can tell you for sure, you do not have a demon. Something is wrong in your head or body that causes this. But it's not an alien spirit. You can trust me to tell you the truth."

To the father Jesus said, "If she has another spell—and she probably will— go to her gently. Do not panic. Your harsh measures do not work. Try the gentler way, and pray for the best."

When nightfall came, Mary found the girl a place to sleep indoors with a neighbor. The father slept outside the cottage on a bedroll. About midday the next day, once again the young girl was cast into a fit with the same symptoms. This time, however, rather than Jesus going to her, he motioned for the father to approach his daughter, saying as he went, "It's all right. You do not have a demon. I am here. I will help you. I will not hurt you." Shortly, the thrashing and screaming eased, then stopped, and she soon got up from the ground with her father's assistance.

As father and daughter prepared to leave for their own village, the man said to Jesus in the hearing of several more in the courtyard, "You are a miracle worker. A great healer."

"No, my friend," Jesus replied, deeply moved by what he had seen. "I am not a miracle worker, at least not any more than you are. Adonai is the source of all the changes in your daughter. Love and understanding are the miracle workers. The love you have for your daughter and the care with which you tend to her in the future will provide hope and help, if not cure."

Then the father asked Jesus anxiously, "Will the spells continue?"

"Probably. We can pray they will become less frequent and violent. Remember, she is sick. She is not demon-possessed. Neither you nor your daughter need be afraid anymore. I hope you can convince other members of your family and your neighbors to stop being afraid of her and these spells. Who knows but that your own kind words will spill over into other parts of your village, making your very hard lives a bit better."

———

Jesus, surrounded by sick people, looked up, and there stood John.

"I decided to stay here for a while. I want to see what you're doing, and I needed a break," he said evenly. "I know you are in Lazarus's spare room. I will sleep outside, where I sleep most of the time anyway."

Mary and Martha greeted him warmly but did not try to persuade him to sleep inside the house even though they could have easily made room for him.

After an especially exhausting and frustrating day trying to offer healing for physical and emotional maladies, Jesus sought out John. "Let's go for a walk," Jesus said. "It'll be full dark before long, but I believe we can find our way out into the hills and back again."

"I can find our way back in the dark," John assured Jesus. "Have I ever taken you down a wrong path?"

"Maybe not wrong, but some have surely been rocky sometimes," Jesus replied laughing, trying unsuccessfully to draw out a smile from John.

They walked a few more minutes, and Jesus said, "I can hardly put one foot in front of the other." He sighed. "It's been a long and trying day. The area around Lazarus's house was full of people from early morning until almost sundown. I guess they would still be there if Martha had not come out of the house and shooed them all away. 'Sorry,' she said to everyone, 'if Jesus does not get some food in his body, he'll need a physician. Come back tomorrow.'"

"If she told me to leave, I would not give any backtalk," John said, and this time they had a good laugh.

Jesus immediately was very serious. "John, what is this whole thing about?"

"I have a strong impression we are where we are supposed to be, doing what Adonai intends. That's about all I can say for sure."

"You keep talking about the coming kingdom. Tell me more," Jesus asked, dropping down on the ground, leaning back against a squat tree.

John was quiet for a few minutes before speaking. Then he said, "Our sacred writings are full of teachings that Adonai will usher in his own special rule and reign, the Day of the Lord, some of our writers call it. In many scriptures, particularly in Ezekiel and Daniel, the prophets describe the new kingdom arriving on the heels of the judgment of Adonai against all unrighteousness and injustice. Adonai makes it clear to me the whole system is so thoroughly evil that only a clean break, a completely fresh beginning, will effect the change Adonai wants and what we need."

Jesus almost challenged John's declaration of clear revelation, thought better, then asked, "And what happens around here when the kingdom comes crashing in?"

"Obviously, the high priest and his crowd and the Romans and their armies will be wiped out. Adonai will destroy them. They will cease to be."

"And the rest of us?" Jesus wanted to know.

"Those who have turned to Adonai in repentance, who live with their neighbors in justice and righteousness, will be spared to become part of the new kingdom."

"And how will this kingdom be governed from the human standpoint?"

John, growing exasperated with the questioning, answered sharply, "This will be Adonai's kingdom. All those who remain will be so devoted to him that they will follow his ways as revealed in the scriptures. As Jeremiah said, the spirit of Adonai's laws and ways will be written on tablets of flesh, on our hearts."

"And what's to keep people from falling back into their old ways that brought this judgement of Adonai down on them in the first place?"

Now thoroughly agitated, John exploded in a voice that echoed through the night's hush, "Jesus, it will not happen. Adonai will remake the human heart by his power when the new kingdom comes."

"John, don't get angry. I am not trying to bait you. I really want to know what you think. You've been over this much more than I have. It will take me some time to come to my own conclusions. I will have to go back over many of the scriptures, especially the prophets, and see what they have to say to me."

"Fine," John said, more in control now. "You do that. And you will come to the same conclusion as I have."

With genuine warmth in his voice, coming from a reservoir of love for his cousin, increasingly understood as a prophet in the genre of Amos, Jeremiah, and others, Jesus said, "Perhaps. But for now, we had better go to bed. You'll have a riverbank full of seekers tomorrow. I will have a courtyard full of sick people."

———

Late one afternoon, some three weeks after their discussion about the coming kingdom, Lazarus's courtyard cleared of sick people earlier than usual. With a couple hours of daylight remaining, for no particular reason Jesus decided to visit John's riverside camp. He and his cousin had taken meals together since their last late-night talk, but had no extended time together. Maybe they could pursue their conversations further tonight.

A couple dozen people were still awaiting baptism when Jesus arrived at the riverbank, so he stood in quiet fascination as John, Hannah, Reuben, and others administered the rite. Again, he found himself puzzling over the meaning of John's baptism and especially applying it to himself. Why had Adonai chosen now to introduce baptism to those born into a Jewish family? What about this simple act had such a powerful draw for the people? What did they hope to gain from it? What sort of transformation occurred in their lives as a result of baptism?

After they had supper and rested for a while, enjoying easy conversation with each other and the circle of close friends, the two cousins again strolled off into the dusk.

"John," Jesus said after a few minutes of walking along not saying anything, "tell me again about your baptism. What happened? And why do think this is so important?"

Seated on the ground in the midst of a grove of ancient olive trees, with a full moon sending its shimmering, soft light through the branches, John said, "Jesus, it was one of the most important moments in my entire life. I had seen the Essenes baptizing and being baptized during other visits to their community. Out of the blue, it dawned on me: This simple act was what I needed to gather up the *new* that Adonai was impressing on me. While I had Abraham's blood flowing in my veins, for all my years I had walked with the living Adonai, I still felt unclean, unrepentant, as you say, 'unconnected,' with Adonai. Standing there in that ungodly heat by that little pool of water, the word of Adonai came to me as surely as I am sitting with you tonight: 'This is for you! By submitting yourself to this rite normally ascribed to those born outside the family of faith, you gain entrance not only into the family of faith, but you become part of the whole wide world that is stumbling toward some kind of reality with Adonai.'

"Jesus," he said quietly, tears now streaming down his cheeks, "if the Essene brother had refused me baptism, the angels of Adonai would have swooped in to bathe me in those sacred waters."

Then he told again of his teaching in Bethlehem and the spontaneous cry from the people for their own baptism.

"And, no, I don't think baptism is ultimately important of itself," he said to the night. "Water is water. Whether it's from Jordan River, a small creek, or from a pitcher poured over someone's head, it is surely not sacred. For me—and I believe for most who want baptism—baptism becomes their unique moment with Adonai, a witness to their passionate desire to be fully clean in his sight, and a way to feel myself part of his holy movement in the world."

"Will baptism have a permanent place in your new kingdom?" Jesus asked.

"I have no idea. Only time and the reality of the new kingdom will tell. As far as I am concerned, baptism can come or go according to the plan of Adonai."

"If I have not been baptized, will I have a place in the kingdom?"

"Jesus," John averred with decided exasperation in his voice, "let me say it one more time: Baptism has nothing to do with a place in the kingdom! Participation in the kingdom is a matter of the heart, of repentance, of justice, of living before Adonai. It would be a mistake for people to begin to equate something basically as simple as being dipped in the water with living a godly life in Adonai's new kingdom."

Then Jesus asked the question that had been more or less on his mind since his initial conversation with Lazarus these many weeks ago: "Should I be baptized?"

Without hesitation John answered, "Jesus, that is completely up to you. It seems to me that you, more than anyone I know, understand the ways of Adonai and practice them. You seem to have very little to repent. Adonai has abundantly blessed you. Since that first time we met years ago in Bethlehem, I have known yours is a calling of much greater significance than mine, maybe of anyone in our history as a person. When I am off the scene, you will continue. But baptism, that's your choice."

Jesus and John fell into a comfortable, contemplative silence for an extended time. Then Jesus said as much to the night as to John, "I want to be baptized."

"I would like that," John replied, his soul stirred.

"And I want it at your hands."

"Actually, you are the one who should be doing the baptizing, not me. But nothing would give me more pleasure than to assist you in your baptism."

"May we do it now? I do not want to wait. And I prefer not to make a public display of it. Tomorrow, the riverbanks will again be crowded."

"Now? Tonight?" John asked.

"If you will," Jesus said in hushed tones.

With the moon providing a holy light that both illuminated and enveloped the world of the river, its beams sparkling off the moving waters of the Jordan, with not a leaf stirring on the trees that lined the banks, John and Jesus approached the stream. Both men pulled off their shifts and silently waded into the water wearing only their loincloths. When they reached sufficient depth to make the immersion possible, they stopped. For a long moment Jesus silently stood looking up into the heavens at the brilliant moon and uncountable stars. John stood unmoving beside his cousin, his own eyes seeming to focus on some distant object, a faraway picture that only he could see. Feelings of sadness, loneliness, and exhilaration coursed through him.

After several minutes of complete silence and stillness, Jesus said, "I am ready."

Choosing not to pronounce a baptismal formula over him, John put his left hand on Jesus's back and his right hand over Jesus's folded arms and lowered him smoothly beneath the flowing stream and then brought him back up. Without a word, both men turned and sloshed back toward the moonlit bank. The event had lasted only brief minutes, but both would confess to each other later that they felt that time and eternity stood infinitely still for them that spectacularly beautiful night.

Walking back toward John's camp through some low bushes, saying nothing, their minds on the baptism and beyond, the two men were suddenly startled as a covey of quail they had accidentally disturbed jumped in the darkness and swooshed off in several directions into the blue-white night.

—

Jesus was too intent on tending the angry rashes on the arms of the woman seated in front of him to notice the sudden stir on the outer edges of the courtyard. When he looked up, a tall, square-jawed, blond Roman soldier was standing before him, the people having immediately cleared the way for him to get to Jesus. The young warrior, from his insignia a corporal, in stumbling Greek said, "You are the healer?"

"Yes, Corporal, I am," Jesus said easily in much smoother Greek, rising from the stool on which he had been sitting. "What can I do for you?"

"My centurion has sent me to bring you to him. He is commander of His Imperial Majesty's troops in Phasaelis."

"And what does the centurion want with me?" Jesus asked with no trace of alarm. "Have I broken any laws, caused a disturbance of some sort?"

"You are not to question the orders of Latvias," the corporal replied officiously. "You are to come with me, right now."

"Corporal, unless I am under arrest, I will find it quite impossible to leave with you right now. You can see that this yard is full of very sick people. They need me. Perhaps I can accompany you tomorrow," he replied, looking steadily but not arrogantly into the face of the Roman.

Flustered by the healer's unassailable demeanor, the young trooper was at a loss for words, completely unused to anyone, especially a peasant, defying his orders, particularly when he spoke for the centurion. "You do not understand. I have orders," he stumbled.

"Oh, I do understand orders, Corporal," Jesus answered with a smile. "I must say that I don't understand your orders. Mine, I understand. My orders are to remain here, at least for the rest of the day, and do what I can for these hard-pressed people."

"And who gave you your orders?" he demanded, some of his military bluster returning, trying to find his footing.

With a warm smile Jesus said, "It probably would not make any sense to you at all."

By now the Roman was in a genuine fidget. He sputtered in a jumble of halting Greek that Jesus could hardly decipher, "My commander's only child, a daughter, is very sick. He has tried every cure. He has heard you do miracles. He commands that you come and make his daughter well."

"Listen, Corporal, your centurion can command me to come, but only Adonai can make the child well. The idea that I am a miracle worker is not of my own doing. Others whom I have been fortunate enough to help have given me the title, one, I assure you, that is not accurate."

"At any rate," the soldier replied, "you must come." Again, he hesitated, his youthful face suddenly a study in quiet terror, then said, "If you do not, I will be in serious trouble."

Jesus answered with understanding, "I do not want you to get in trouble. Let me finish seeing these people in the courtyard, and I will then leave with you immediately. I have a special place in my heart for sick children, be they Roman or Jewish."

Before the soldier could protest further, Jesus sat back down on the stool and began dressing the woman's lesions. Though Jesus did not notice it, only as he sat down on the stool and resumed his ministrations did the large crowd breathe again, so fearful were they of an altercation that could occur between the Roman and their physician. Now the people added yet another epithet. They began to call him the *fearless* miracle worker. The ripple effect of his reputation gained fresh momentum.

Despite all of Jesus's efforts, the centurion's little girl died. By the time he reached her at the Roman headquarters at Phasaelis, the illness that had attacked her several days previously had left her still and all but lifeless. Her breathing was labored. She was drenched with perspiration because of the fever that burned within her. By putting his ear to her chest, Jesus could hear her lungs filling up with fluid. He sat her up, patted her gently on the back, hoping to enable her to cough up some phlegm that was drowning her, yet to no avail. All day and night, Jesus sat by her bedside, gently bathing her face with cool, damp cloths. He turned her from one side to the other to keep her lungs from filling too rapidly. During the last hours of her life, the centurion and his wife stood right outside the room and wept as they saw their only child slipping away from them.

Jesus whispered to her in his own native Aramaic, a language she did not comprehend, but the sounds and rhythms of which, conveyed by Jesus's reassuring voice, provided comfort and surcease. As she was about to breathe her last, Jesus motioned her distressed parents to gather around the bed.

Jesus softly said to them, "She is completely at peace. If she could speak, she would bid both of you a dear and loving farewell. She would say you have been wonderful parents and she doesn't want you to grieve over her too much."

The battle-hardened centurion, tears streaming down his face, looked at the slim form of his daughter, and without taking his eyes off her said to Jesus,

"Please tell her for us that we love her. We do not want her to be afraid. Tell her that even though she will not be with us, we will be with her. Our adoration will bear her up as she leaves us."

Jesus, by now on his knees beside the small bed, his head bowed, whispered softly into the child's ears. The flicker of a smile crossed her lips as she eased into death.

A few hours later, as the disconsolate parents prepared for the child's burial, Jesus placed his hands on the centurion's shoulder and said, "I regret that I could not help her. She was a beautiful little girl. My heart breaks for you."

"I, too, am sorry you could not save her life. Please, though, do not think you did not help her. Never did a child go into the next world with such peace and assurance. I can sense that you have wonderful gifts both as a healer and comforter. Should you be around when I start to die, I hope you will come to me."

After the burial, the centurion asked for Jesus to step into his room. "I am not a wealthy man, but I do have means. You would honor me greatly if you would take this bag of gold as an expression of my gratitude. You could probably help many of your people with this money."

"Thank you, Latvias," Jesus replied with gratitude. "I will not take your money. True, the needs of my people are great. We need what money cannot buy."

"And what might that be?" he inquired, listening to Jesus intently.

"Hundreds of farmers in the Jordan River Valley have lost their farms as the Roman military has expropriated them for your veterans. It is too much to expect those farms to be returned."

"Go on, Jesus," Latvias said, sympathetic with Jesus's words but unmoved.

"I ask that you persuade those veterans on our people's farms to look with kindness and understanding on these dispossessed people," Jesus requested. "Sometimes the soldiers and their families brutally mistreat those whose lands they took."

"I will do what I can," Latvias agreed. "Frankly, I had not tried to put myself in the places of the farmers. I can understand their grief and anger. I make no firm promises because many of those veterans are not under my control nor that of my commander. They are under Pontius Pilate, who, shall we say, is not known for his generosity of spirit."

Jesus went on, "My friends and I have worked long and hard with the farmers helping them find new ways to make a living. They are learning to make items of wood. They are baking bread and making a wonderful cheese. And they are producing pottery of very good quality."

"Yes," Latvias said, following Jesus's line of thought.

"If you could keep the Romans from disrupting their struggling businesses and if you could make efforts to purchase some of their goods for your troops, it would be of great benefit. Believe me, I would be more than repaid for a sad service I was only too glad to render," Jesus replied warmly but emphatically.

"Jesus, you have my word that I will do everything possible to help your people."

Standing at the door to the small villa Latvias and his wife occupied, the centurion told Jesus, "You know, of course, I could make you quite wealthy as a healer if you were to do your work from here in Phasaelis. We have no one with your skills and insights."

"You make a tempting offer, Latvias. I thank you. True, I cannot say with confidence what Adonai's way for me is right now, but I do not believe yours is that way. I value your confidence in me. I will call on you if the need arises."

As Jesus started to leave, Latvias said authoritatively, "I have troops waiting to escort you back to Bethany."

"Again," Jesus said, "I thank you, but only one or two will be enough. No need for that much trouble. Perhaps you could detail the young corporal and one more to go with me. I will enjoy their company and send them right back to you."

# Chapter Four

# Separation

*In the days of my trouble I seek the Lord; in the night my hand is stretched out without wearying.*

"I tell you," Levi, the temple comptroller, almost shouted at his superior, Izachus, the high priest's first assistant, "income continues to drop dramatically. We are not out of money, not even short of money. It's just that the people are simply not buying our animals and they are not paying their temple tax."

The two men were standing on one of the high marbled balconies overlooking the grand courtyard of the Gentiles, the largest open-air plaza in the vast complex of Herod's temple. Izachus swept his arms across the crowd mingling below and replied tartly, "You must be mistaken. Look at that horde of people. They are here in great numbers."

"No matter, my lord," Levi declared emphatically. "By actual count the crowd is considerably smaller. Those out there are mostly Jews from abroad. The locals are not here. And, besides, figures don't lie. By the thousands, the people from the region are staying away. And it is the fault of that crazy prophet, John, the one who's out at the river doing that ridiculous baptizing."

"That's hard to believe, Levi," Izachus answered skeptically. "For centuries the temple's been the center of worship. Does one man have the power to topple what our people have revered for all these years?"

"Not topple, cripple, yes, my lord," Levi assured Izachus. "Something should be done about him, and soon."

Later in the high priest's private chamber, one closely protected by the most trusted temple guards, both against intruders and to make sure the room was secure against eavesdroppers and spies, Izachus made his report to Caiaphas. This cunning, politically savvy man had managed to maintain control of the temple and its intricate economic and religious web of power for more than a dozen years.

"Levi has been telling us for some time now that the baptizer is hurting us. I suppose we thought he would be only a momentary irritant like so many others before him. He's proven to have staying power. At any rate, the man has got to go, and soon."

"Izachus, we cannot just up and arrest him," the high priest cautioned, his jowly face dark with worry. "A riot of monumental proportions could break out. Pilate and the Romans would tear into us in a blink. He's just waiting for us to make a major misstep so he can trounce on us anyway."

Caiaphas's once straight and well-toned body, now grown flabby, almost corpulent with too much indulgence and too little exercise, rose from the ornate thronelike chair and trudged around the large room, his hands clasped behind his back. "We must think of a way to accomplish our purposes without getting into trouble ourselves."

A few days later, Izachus unceremoniously came into the high priest's office and said, "My lord, I believe I have found us a way."

—

While John leaned back against his favorite olive tree, his legs stretched out in front of him, the soft sunset breeze gently brushing his face and the world around him, Reuben said easily but earnestly, "John, I've been thinking. It might be time for us to go further up the river again and maybe even cross into Decapolis. I've been getting word from your followers up there that many want to hear you and be baptized but they cannot afford to stop work and come down here."

Absently, John replied, "Reuben, how many times do I have to tell you that I do not have followers?"

"Call them what you will. We have been here for over a year. When we traveled up that way before, Adonai reaped a wonderful harvest."

Then Reuben, sensing that John was not paying attention to him, paused and said, "Well, at least think about it."

A few days later, John announced to his small band of assistants, "Reuben has suggested we go upriver again."

For some minutes the group talked among themselves before Hannah spoke up: "John, no doubt many there would like your witness. On the other hand, you could face danger primarily because no one ever knows what Herod Antipas might do. He is so unpredictable, especially since he took on his new wife."

The group was quiet for a minute. Then Reuben said, "True. You never know which way Antipas will jump. Still, do we neglect Adonai's people out of fear for Herod Antipas? Besides, John is far too well known and loved for Antipas to harm him."

"Listen," John interjected. "I'm not afraid of Antipas. When my time comes, it will come. I just don't want to make a foolish mistake."

"I think we ought to go. I've prayed about it, and I feel the Spirit leading us in that direction," Reuben said with conviction. "I really think we should do this."

Relenting, Hannah said with a shrug, "I have no strong feelings either way."

Perhaps it was the combination of being closer to Antipas's lavish city of Tiberias and the Greek-oriented towns of the Decapolis that John's preaching rose to new heat. At first his closest followers did not notice. Gradually, as his rhetoric became more reckless, they began to whisper among themselves.

Shortly, Hannah felt it necessary to talk with John even though Reuben did not seem unduly alarmed.

John said angrily, "Hannah, Adonai is offended at the way Antipas has spent money he has squeezed from the people. Everywhere you look, you see signs of extravagance while people go hungry. And take a look at life in the Greek cities. Did you ever see such godlessness, such total disregard for the ways of Adonai!"

"I agree, but, John, you are becoming harsh, even reckless. If you are not careful, you will attract the attention of Antipas and Herodias. They will get nervous, and who knows what can happen when they get that way," Hannah pleaded with him.

"I don't care about Herod Antipas or his so-called wife," he exclaimed so loudly that several people snapped their heads in his direction.

Now frightened, Hannah whispered, a note of near-panic in her voice, "Hush, John. You're asking for trouble. Keep your eyes and hearts on the needs of the people. You can do nothing about Antipas or the Greeks. Cool your anger, please."

In total disregard of her caution, however, his preaching about the coming kingdom only grew more inflamed. "I tell you," he yelled at the crowd of about two hundred the next day, "Adonai's soon going to come in fury and power and wipe out all this godlessness," he cried, waving his arms in the direction of Tiberias and the nearest Greek cities. "He will soon create his own kingdom of righteousness. Woe to those who go strutting around dressed in golden clothes while children die of starvation and disease!"

In desperation, Hannah sent for Jesus, who was still at the home of Lazarus doing his best to offer healing to the sick while also expanding his teaching ministry of opening the scriptures to the growing number who came to hear him.

Jesus arrived at John's camp unannounced mid-morning a few days after he had received Hannah's urgent message. Standing far to one side of the crowd where he could observe and not be noticed, he was startled when he saw John. Never one to pay attention to the care of his person, John now looked like a ragged beggar from the slums. His hair was unwashed and stringy. He had simply wrapped a length of rope around his waist to hold his shift in placed. His face was gaunt, his eyes hollow. Most unsettling to Jesus was the hysterical message John was delivering. In these few weeks, he had dramatically shifted his emphasis. John had always pointed toward the coming kingdom, yet he had concentrated on the present spiritual needs of the people. Now, to Jesus's dismay, he launched into a tirade about the kingdom's imminent, fiery, and vengeful explosion with hardly a word about the people's daily pain.

Even worse, he railed at Antipas, listing every known sin the ruler had committed in his long reign over Perea and Galilee.

When John finished, he greeted Jesus with indifference bordering on irritation. "I am glad to see you, cousin," John said, "but what brings you here? Did you get everyone in Bethany well?"

"No. Many are still sick. Frankly," he said, trying to sound light-hearted, "I heard you had decided to challenge Satan, Antipas and his new wife, the high priest, Greek civilization, and the entire Roman army. So I thought I should come and watch it happen."

Not at all amused or mollified, John answered him angrily, "Well, you heard right. And it's nothing to smile about. Adonai is coming with his axe— and soon."

Now realizing that indeed a dramatic change had occurred in John, Jesus made no further attempts at lame humor. "John, if what I heard from you today is an indication of what you're saying all the time, it may not be Adonai who comes with an axe."

John would not be restrained. Working in the swirling crosscurrents of Antipas's ostentation, Greek paganism, and the unremitting pain and suffering of the people had uncorked an even deeper reservoir of boiling righteous indignation within John. The prophet in him could not contain the fury. He could not focus his preaching. Day by day, he lashed out, his language becoming more and more incendiary.

Jesus and Hannah and the Bethlehemites grew increasingly alarmed as John's rhetoric became more inflamed—that is, all but Reuben, who, strangely, kept his distance. The preaching, however, struck a resonating chord among the Jews of Perea and the cities of the Decapolis, drawing to the river the largest crowds he had yet attracted. The Judean crowds had quietly drunk in John's preaching. The Perean throngs cheered and stomped their feet as he poured invective on the enemies of Adonai and his mistreated people.

One morning a few days after Jesus had arrived, Reuben unexpectedly announced, "I must leave for a few days. Word has come to me that my family needs me."

Startled, Hannah asked, "When did you hear from home? I did not see anyone from Bethlehem."

"You've been so busy trying to save John's hide, you did not notice. But I must go." With no further explanation, Reuben left the camp, headed south.

"That's very strange," Hannah remarked to Jesus. "I would have surely seen somebody from home. It's just as well, I suppose. For some time now, Reuben has not been with us. Maybe the strain has beat him down. He probably does need to go home. After all, we've been at this for nearly three years."

They could not see Reuben turn directly toward Jerusalem once he was completely away from the river camp.

When Jesus had been in John's camp for two weeks, he said to Hannah, "I have decided to leave you for a while. I have not been home in all these years. Other than sporadic letters between my family and me, we have not communicated since I left for Egypt. When I got back in the country, I wrote my mother. I invited her to come to Bethany beyond the Jordan, but she refused. Now that I am this close, only a few days' journey, I want to see them."

"I fear for John if you leave," she said, worry and grave anxiety on her face.

"Hannah," Jesus replied with resignation, "he's not paying any attention to you or me. That man has always lived according to his understanding of Adonai's purpose. Who am I to question what's going on in his life now?"

That afternoon, Jesus said to John, "I have talked with Hannah. Now I want you to know that I am leaving for a while. I have not seen my family in a terribly long time. I want to go home."

Taken back by Jesus's announcement, John fired back, "Go home? Go home? What do you mean go home? With Adonai about to do his mightiest work ever, you've decided to wander off to Nazareth! I cannot believe what I am hearing."

Now it was Jesus's turn to be surprised and angry. "Wait just a minute, John. I do not have your inside track to Adonai. He has not told me anything about the coming kingdom nor about its timetable. If the kingdom comes while I am gone, so be it."

Then, narrowing his eyes at Jesus, John said with finality, "If you leave me now, you have no part of the kingdom."

"John, if the kingdom does come, you will not be the one who determines who is in or out, who does or does not have a part, as you say," Jesus replied tartly.

Now, in a fury, jerking away, John screamed at his cousin, "Leave then! Go home! You don't care about the work anyway! I don't care if I ever see you again!"

Shaken, grieved, his heart heavy, greatly alarmed at John's display, Jesus called after him, "John, wait. Do not walk away like that. We must not leave each other this way." John did not slow down or look back.

# Chapter Five

# Home Again

*Filled with the power of the Spirit, Jesus returned to Galilee.*

With every step toward Nazareth, his anxieties mounted. Again, he put himself in their shoes. Of course they could not fathom what drove him to go to Egypt, especially for such a long time. Frankly, he admitted to himself, whereas he comprehended clearly the Egyptian impulse, he still had not fully sorted out his reluctance to go to Nazareth immediately upon landing at Caesarea. At the time he and John plunged into the maelstrom of human problems precipitated by the huge farm expropriation, getting right to work seemed the thing to do. In retrospect, he surmised, investing a few days in Nazareth first would have been better family politics. Still, the needs up and down the Jordan, around Jericho and Bethany beyond the Jordan were so critical! But maybe they were just as serious in Nazareth. At any rate, he had done what he felt was best. Or was it an attempt to put off as long as possible the intense pain his family might inflict on him and he on them?

Galilee was in full green. The hills sang to him from their rich splendor. Thousands of olive trees, cascading vineyards, acres of freshly tilled farms with tiny shoots already peeking through the rich earth made him wonder why he had ever left such a magnificent homeland. Egypt, in all its splendor, could not begin to compare with the lushness of the landscape that greeted him. His spirits soared. Surely his family, living amid such beauty, could not be too angry with him. It was going to be all right between them again, he was sure of it. Or was it?

Now that he was back home, what would he do with the rest of his life? He realized he had unique skills as a physician. A host of people whose health had been improved because of his ministrations demonstrated that fact. What's more, from the surprising response to the way he opened the scriptures, he undoubtedly had gifts as a teacher.

Quite apart from these abilities, his family would need him. He must restore himself with them. He would have to help them strengthen the family business. He owed them that much. It was long past the time when he should have married and had his own children. Maybe that's what lay before him in Nazareth, an ordered, ordinary life. Such prospects had heart-wrenching appeal to him, at least with a large portion of his thinking.

At the same time, he could not get away from the nagging thought that Adonai indeed had something completely different in store for him. Not better. What could be better than wife, children, his own home? Different, though. What? Spending his days as a healer? That was certainly a great need. Teaching? He reveled in both abilities.

His tumbling thoughts often turned to John. What had come over his cousin? Had the spirit of Adonai enveloped him? Or had the unremitting pain and confusion of the people, the gross injustice of a heartless system, the loneliness of his own life finally nudged John over the edge? Even as he created distance between himself and John, he felt all the more inextricably connected to him. Was he already in grave danger, in jail, dead? Almost nauseating anxieties for John waved over Jesus. A few times he had to stop, rest, drink from a spring just to settle his stomach and clear his head of worries about his beloved if impossible cousin.

As he came within a few miles of Nazareth, it seemed that he had been gone only a short time rather than seven years. Could it be that long? James had three children. Others of his brothers had recently married. Miriam, the older of the two girls, was also married. Did she also have a child by now? Probably. How had the years treated Mary? Would she still be pretty and vibrant as when he left? Would the years have bent her over? Topping a hill overlooking his village, for all the world he wanted to turn and run headlong back in the direction from which he had come.

Unaccustomed as they were to men coming into the village in the middle of the day, especially strangers, the women and children stopped what they were doing to stare at the man who strode into their midst with the distinct air of one who knew his way around. The better cut of his clothes communicated that here was a person with some means at his disposal. The authority and assurance that emanated from him created a flash of anxiety among the villagers. Had he come to cause them harm? Was he the harbinger of a new wave of oppressors? A few women thought they recognized him. But who was he? His hair, though cut somewhat in the Roman fashion, and bearing marked him as a Jew. Still, they could not quite place him. When he went straight to the house of Mary, recognition flooded over the women. This was Mary's son Jesus, come home!

The one who had abandoned his family to go off somewhere. What did it all mean, they pondered in wondering silence.

Mary, inside her house, going about her daily chores against the familiar background sounds of women talking and children chattering in the streets of her tiny neighborhood, suddenly stiffened when an unexpected quiet engulfed her. With senses honed by years of dealing with surprises, even terrors, she knew instantly that something outside had changed.

"Mother," Jesus said quietly, relief, eagerness, and uneasiness in his voice. His warm eyes conveyed his surging feelings of love, guilt, and joy at seeing his mother again after so many years.

Without turning around to face him, Mary's eyes closed, she gripped the tabletop to steady herself, took a quick breath she hoped he did not notice, then, with her back still toward him, said, "I'm making bread. Would you hand me that jar of flour? It's there, on the shelf, where it was when you left us."

If she had slapped him in the face, it would not have hurt any more than this. In a near trance of grief, Jesus got the jar off the shelf, took the three steps that put him squarely in front of his mother, and, without saying a word, handed it to her.

"Thank you," she said, her eyes fixed on the mixing bowl, her hands working automatically as they had for countless times at the bread-making task. "I've got to get this dough ready and in the oven. We will need it for the evening meal. Since the weather's good, I'm going to cook it in the oven outside. I still use the inside oven your father made for us before he..."

With that, she collapsed onto the floor, heaving with sobs, bobbing back and forth, her still slender arms tightly clasped around her trim body.

Instantly, Jesus was on the floor beside her. When he tried to hold her, she angrily pushed him away. "When I needed you to hold me," she whispered bitterly, "where were you? When everything was coming apart, where were you? In the night when I thought I would choke to death in loneliness and fear, you were nowhere to be found."

"Oh, Mother," Jesus wept.

Vehemently, she blurted, "Don't 'Oh, Mother' me you, you deserter! You abandoned us! Maybe you think you've been off serving Adonai in Egypt or wherever. But you've not. You forsook your first duty to him, to us, your own family."

Struggling desperately for composure, trying to get his bearings, groping for understanding, battling his own aggrieved feelings that made him want to lash back in anger, he answered, "I did what I felt I had to. That's all I can say. It was right for me."

"Right for you!" she fumed. "Well, I'm glad it was right for someone. It was terribly wrong for us!"

In frustration and grief, Jesus stood up and walked to the door.

"And where do you think you're going?" his mother demanded to know, still hunched down on the floor, tears coursing.

"It's plain I'm not welcome here," he said in a voice wracked with pain and agony.

"What do you propose to do? Leave us again?" she hissed with a bitterness he had never known from her.

"I have no idea what I'm going to do," he said vacantly.

"Well, you can begin by helping me up from this floor," she said petulantly as she reached her hand up toward him.

In his eagerness to help her, he tripped on a chair, knocked over the table, spilling the dough on the floor.

"Well, there goes dinner," she said.

"I have money. I will buy us bread for supper," he answered, sensing that maybe the worst of the storm perhaps was passing.

"Keep your money," she barked. "But if you will help me up and get out of the way, I might be able to make up a fresh batch."

"I'll do anything you say, Mother," he said, hope for reconciliation rising in his voice.

Mary, now for the first time since he walked into the house those minutes ago, looked him squarely in the face. "Let me tell you something, Jesus. You've been gone a long time. Much has happened while you were away. If you think you can walk back into our lives, tell us breathtaking stories of life in Egypt, toss us some money, and then go on about your merry way, you're badly mistaken. Do I make myself clear?"

"Quite," he said.

"Neither James nor I will ever fully understand why you left us," she said, her tone softening ever so slightly. "I, for one, will try to understand. In a way, knowing you like I do, I should not have been surprised. But," and again tears sprang to her eyes, "it's been so very hard."

He could resist holding her no longer. He put his arms around her, and this time she did not push him away. "I did what I felt I had to. I cannot apologize for that. I do grieve for the pain you've had to endure without me, maybe because of me."

With anger slowly giving way to gratitude, his mother said, "My son, my boy, I am glad you are home, at last."

Stepping back, she touched his face and said, "Jesus, it's really you. You've come back to us. I always knew you would. You would never just stay away, no matter how important your work, no matter how smart you had become."

"Mother," he said, now hugging her again, "I never intended to stay away so long. The thought of not coming back never entered my mind." Looking around the tiny house in which nothing had changed since he left, he said, "It seems like I've been gone forever and then only since yesterday."

"Jesus, you will have to bear with me," Mary said. "With all my soul, I am glad you are home. I hope you never leave again. But it'll take me some time to sort through all my bad feelings for what you did."

"I understand," he answered.

Then her motherly instincts came into play, and she asked eagerly, "Are you hungry? Have you had anything to eat today?" And before he could assure her he was not hungry, she began to put food before him.

"Wait, Mother," he chided easily. "No, I am not at all hungry. And yes, I have had food today. Besides, seeing you, being home again, is all the food I need for now." He eased her into a chair and said, "I want to see the family. I want to catch up on all the news. I know I have nieces and nephews I've never seen."

She reached out to him and said sternly, "Jesus, the family may not be so glad to see you, especially James."

"I understand their anger at my being gone, and for such a long time," he averred.

"It's more than that. You'd better hear it all from James since he's borne the brunt of it all," she cautioned. "And he's the angriest."

"Well, let's go to the shop. Let me talk with James and the others," Jesus said, rising from the chair and heading for the door.

"Wait, Jesus. That's just it. We have no shop. It's gone. That's the problem."

This was more than Jesus could comprehend. Seeing the pain and distress in his mother's eyes, he controlled himself and said, "Mother, where is James? I must see him."

"He and your other brothers have taken jobs in Sepphoris. When he lost the shop, Seti helped them find work in the city."

Jesus began to rock back and forth in dismay. "In Sepphoris? Working? Lost the shop? I've got to go to them right now, Mother. I would lose my mind if I waited around here for them to come home."

"Son," his mother said, tenderness now in her voice, "it has been very hard these last months. Though it is not your fault, your brothers will place much of the blame on you. Be ready."

He ran nearly all the way from Nazareth to Sepphoris. Where would he find his brothers? He would have to scour the city, but he would locate them and deal with whatever terrible problems had exploded in the life of his family. Jesus realized that Seti might know where they were, but he did not want to see his old friend under these circumstances if it could be avoided.

After probing and peering through the throngs, he rounded a corner and spied James and the others stripped to the waist, sweating profusely, silently, sullenly digging foundation ditches for some sort of new structure—probably, from the character of the neighborhood, a large house. The pain of seeing these skilled craftsmen who had built beautiful furniture for the finest houses in the city digging ditches was almost more than Jesus could bear.

Even before the men saw and recognized Jesus, without a word he had snatched off his outer garments, stripped to the waist like his brothers, grabbed up a shovel from a pile of tools by the site, and begun furiously to attack the hard soil.

Startled by the appearance of the stranger and the ferocity of his labors, the brothers said nothing for a moment, but kept digging. Then, sensing more than seeing, James paused to look intently into the face of the new man. With one motion, upon recognizing Jesus, James threw down his shovel, screamed wildly, and with hands flailing the air, leaped at his brother, grabbing for his throat.

—

The attack caught Jesus completely off guard, tumbled him on the rocky ground, and sent him reeling into the partially dug trench. "You traitor, you deserter, you high and mighty blasphemer," James screamed hysterically as he threw himself on top of his brother, pounding him mercilessly.

Recovered somewhat, Jesus scrambled to protect himself from James's furious assault, covering his face with his arms, trying to roll away from the pummeling, all the while resisting the temptation, reflexively now as he struggled for survival, to hit back at his crazed brother.

"James," Jesus gasped, laboring for breath, "stop! Please stop!"

Unrelenting, James, still slamming at Jesus, shouted through clenched teeth, "It's all your fault. You left us. And now everything is gone."

By then the other brothers, recognition of the stranger dawning on them, had run to the rolling, tumbling, bleeding, breathless men and began pulling them apart. "Stop it, both of you," the brothers cried. "You'll kill each other."

With both men struggling to their feet, James tried to lunge at Jesus, but Joses and Judas grabbed him. Covered in dirt and blood, struggling for breath, Jesus croaked, "James, I don't know what has happened. If I am to blame, I take responsibility."

"Hush," James spat, hatred, pent-up fury flashing from his eyes. "Nothing you can say will make a difference. We're ruined, and it's all your fault." Again, he would have grabbed Jesus if his brothers had not held him.

Leaning over, hands on his knees, still trying to restore even breathing, Jesus managed to say, "I saw Mother in Nazareth. She would not tell me what had gone so terribly wrong. Whatever it is, I will spend the rest of my life, if that's what it takes, making it right. I promise."

Before the brothers could get into a conversation, the foreman of the job came rushing up. "What in the world is going on here?" he demanded angrily. "You men have work to do. Settle your differences later. These ditches have got to be dug today. If you won't do it, I will surely find someone who will. Now," glancing at James and not even noticing that Jesus was not one of the hired laborers, the foreman ordered sternly, "get back to work. Right now!"

Under his breath, James said to Jesus, "We'll settle this later! For now, get away from us." James snatched up his shovel and began digging furiously, refusing to look at his brother.

"I'll stay and help anyway," Jesus said, glancing around at his stricken, confused, and pained younger brothers.

At sundown, work ceased. The brothers, without a word exchanged between them, splashed water from a barrel on their faces, pulled on their cloaks, and started toward the southern gate. Jesus, leading the way, kept his peace until they were well outside the city. As darkness fell across the Galilean hillsides, he abruptly spun around to face his brothers, held up his hands, and said quietly but with undeniable authority, "Now, tell me what great tragedy has befallen us."

James, still boiling with anger, exploded, "It's not *us*! You don't have a problem. You took yourself away from the family. You've got all your rich friends. We've got nothing," motioning toward the other brothers.

Joses spoke up, "James, it's no good blaming Jesus like you've done. Sure, we've all joined in with you. We might as well own up to the mess and see what can be done about it."

Infuriated at his younger brother's perceived capitulation, James yelled, "That's right. Go ahead. Take his side. If he'd stayed with us, all of this would not have happened."

"All of you," Jesus pleaded, "let's stop tossing blame around. You've got to give me the story."

James's resentment at Jesus's leaving had rapidly deepened into a consuming anger. Mary could not decide if James felt abandoned by his older brother, if he felt frustrated because he had to stay in Nazareth while Jesus went off for high adventure, or if he felt inadequate to run the business and lead the family, or some combination of the three. She often talked with her second son about his bitterness. In lucid moments he would admit that his feelings were misplaced and that they were destructive to him and to the family. Still, he could not shake them off.

With the steady rebuilding of Sepphoris after the rebel attack and fire, even though Jesus was gone, leaving them short-handed in the shop, James kept everything on track. The carpentry business was steady, providing dependable income for the entire family. James and his larger family even garnered some measure of security in the face of steady expropriation of farmland, saying, "Who would want a carpentry shop? We don't grow anything. We are the business." They would commiserate with others in their village who did see their ancestral farms taken over by Roman army veterans or repossessed to pay debts.

One day, a well-dressed man presented himself at James's shop, saying, "I am here representing the court of Lord Herod Antipas. He remembers the good work you did for him some years ago. On his behalf, I want to place a fairly large order with you. The tetrarch has friends in other parts of Galilee and even down in Samaria and over in Perea who are constructing large houses. They will buy from me all the furniture I can provide for them."

The broker spent several hours talking with James and the other brothers and Mary. He painted a glowing picture of steady business and handsome profits. James, in the absence of Jesus, talked the proposition over with the headman of the village and the ruler of the synagogue. They both agreed it sounded like a solid opportunity for the brothers' business.

"Have you verified this man's story with anyone? Maybe you should talk with Lord Seti about him. Though Egyptian, he knows everyone of importance in Galilee," suggested the headman.

"No, I have not checked him, but he seems well-placed. I will send word to Seti, asking him for his advice."

But James never got around to making inquiries from Seti.

"Here are the terms," the broker said. "You build to my specifications. I will give you a down-payment so you can purchase materials. You will have to work on a close margin at first until I can deliver the goods and collect for them. As soon as I am paid, I will pay you the price we agree on."

The production of the first order went smoothly. With the advance payment, James bought good wood and produced quality items. Upon completion of the order, the broker came to Nazareth with a string of small wagons and pack animals, loaded the shelves, trunks, cabinets, bowls, and other items and left. Within a few weeks he was back in Nazareth, settled with James, and then placed another order, this one even larger than the one before.

"With the money I have paid you, you should have enough to purchase materials without an advance," he suggested to James.

"If we work quickly and get a good turnaround on your payment to us, we can make it. It'll be close, but we can make it."

The two men struck a bargain.

James and the brothers worked from early morning until late evening six days a week to produce the order. At the agreed time, the broker came with his wagons and pack animals.

"And that's the last time we saw him," James said, his voice shaking with pain and rage. "We went looking for him but could not find him. We tried to make inquiry at the palace, but they only laughed at us. We suppose he sold the furniture and kept all the money."

"Couldn't you start again, even though you had practically no money?" Jesus asked, his own heart breaking for his family's anguish.

"No," said Joses. "So we could produce the order quickly, we used what money we had and then borrowed more funds from one of the Greek bankers in Sepphoris to buy the wood and other materials we needed."

"Oh no!" Jesus exclaimed, the fuller picture dawning on him. "You borrowed at high interest!"

"We did," James admitted.

"Why didn't you go to Seti? He would have helped. Besides, he kept giving you money to help make up for my absence."

"Frankly," Joses confessed, "we were ashamed. Our pride would not let us. He had been so helpful. We did not have the heart to let him know we had been duped."

Simon spoke for the first time: "Later, we learned the broker had actually tried to cheat Lord Seti out of money, but Seti caught on in time to stop him."

"In a last-ditch effort to save ourselves, we did go to Seti," James said, grief and anger still near the surface. "He got in touch with his friends in the region, hoping to learn something that would help us. He sent Albinus to business partners in Tiberias, Magdala, over in the Greek cities, in Jericho, all the way down to Jerusalem. Nothing. Seti guesses that the thief went over into Transjordan and sold our goods and then disappeared."

"I can guess the rest. When you could not pay the banker, he came and cleaned out the shop," Jesus surmised.

"Yes. He and his thugs took everything we had. Tools. Benches. Wood. Everything. And to make matters worse, we had to let him have the shop or he would have thrown one of us in debtor's prison. Now some of his people have opened their own carpentry business in our shop," James groaned, thoroughly chastened.

"I'm sorry," Jesus said ruefully. "I am very sorry. I let you down."

# Chapter Six

# Radical Solutions

*Mortals ate the bread of angels.*

Jesus decided not to see Seti for a while, though he knew his Egyptian mentor was already aware of his arrival back in Galilee, knowing the man had not reached his level of wealth and influence without a large intelligence network. Before he would allow himself the luxury of a long visit with Seti, Jesus realized he had much to sort through as he confronted his family's crisis. With James's concurrence, Jesus sent word to Seti to stop the payments he had been making to the family for these years.

"For the time being," Jesus told James early the next morning after his return, "we have to earn money to feed the family. I accumulated some money during my time in Egypt, enough to help until we can get better organized. I'll work with you in Sepphoris. At least we'll be together. Something will come to us; I am sure of that."

"Jesus," James retorted, "this is not your problem. I made the mess. I'll figure it out."

"Stop it, James," Jesus shot back impatiently. "That's nonsense. I am as responsible as you are."

During the walk to and from Sepphoris and at the brief breaks the foreman gave them, Jesus and his brothers talked, let their imaginations roam, and gradually began to carve out something of a new future for themselves.

They decided James would begin woodworking again. To make up for the loss of his income as a ditch digger, the other brothers would spend all the extra hours they could as laborers. With these new arrangements in mind, Jesus decided it was time to pay a visit to Seti.

"It is about time you came to see me," Seti cried when Jesus appeared at his door. "You've been back these past few weeks, and I have not seen you at all."

Jesus, likewise overjoyed to see his friend after such a long absence, replied, "A great deal has happened to my family in the past several months that has cast a dark cloud on my homecoming. I knew, of course, you would know I was

back. I counted on our friendship to deflect any irritation you might have felt
for me when I delayed calling on you."

"It is of no importance," Seti answered him warmly with a wave of his hand,
conveying the understanding on which Jesus had depended. "I am just so glad
to see you. And you are so tan and lean. The Galilean climate agrees with you."

For the first time, Jesus laughed. "I can assure you—I have not been exposed
to the Galilean climate by choice."

"I hope you have made plans for a very long visit," Seti said eagerly. "You
have much catching up to do. Thank you for your occasional letters, but they
cannot begin to give me the details I crave."

Into the evening, over a grand meal prepared by Asenath, joined later by
Albinus, Jesus talked and talked. At midnight Seti abruptly rose and sighed, "I
am fascinated. The half has not yet been told. The rest will have to wait until
tomorrow. I have to put my weary bones in bed. I hope you will plan to stay the
night with us. If need be, I can send word to your brothers."

"I will be pleased to stay the night with you, what's left of it. My brothers
know where I am, so no messenger is necessary," Jesus replied with a yawn.

Jesus slept soundly on a bed. As he drifted off to sleep, he mused: Could it
be that seven years had fled by since he had discovered the engaging comfort of
a bed compared with a pallet on the floor of his father's simple cottage!

"Jesus," Seti proposed carefully as they talked yet more during the morning
hours after breakfast, "you should do medicine. You can surely earn all the
money you need that way. Neither you nor your brothers would have to work
so hard."

The younger man replied thoughtfully, "I have not actually told my family
of my training and experience as a physician. Oh, they know I studied healing
arts in Alexandria. I wrote them about my training. They just have no idea of
the range of my studies and experience. I am reluctant to become known as a
healer. I want to find another way for the family to come back, one that all of
us can share in."

"What about the people of Nazareth and Sepphoris and the entire Galilee
who need your touch?" Seti gently demanded. "You are not going to let them
suffer needlessly because of misplaced family pride, are you? Sepphoris has a
few fairly reputable physicians, but for the most part, those who offer cures are
charlatans or incompetents or both. We have no one with your background."

"Seti, I understand what you are saying. I am hesitant to look like a big
brother rescuer to my family. Here is the super smart prodigal son come home

from the distant reaches of Egypt. He'll save us all. Furthermore, people get so unbelievably excited when someone like me comes along who can help them feel better. You wouldn't believe the stir I caused in Alexandria and then in Bethany beyond the Jordan when some of my commonsense medicine seemed to work miracles. I'm just not sure I want to go through that again."

"Listen to me, Jesus," Seti said, leaning forward, looking closely into Jesus's face. "If you have a gift, any gift, especially the ability to help people feel healthier and live richer lives, you have no choice but to use it. Your Adonai insists on it, if I may be so bold as to speak for him."

Without answering his friend, Jesus stood up. "Lord Seti, thank you for a memorable visit. Indeed, thank you for a memorable life. I must go. The ditches of Sepphoris clamor for my attention."

With the realization he had struck a raw nerve in Jesus, Seti rose also. "Should the gods call me to the grave today, you have more than made my life worthwhile, young Jesus. You and I both know that Adonai, Destiny, the gods—call it what you will—have only begun to work in your splendid life."

"Thank you, Seti, brother, father, friend, teacher." The two men embraced each other with the deepest measure of affection.

———

Over the next weeks, Jesus and the younger brothers trudged to Sepphoris each day while James remained in Nazareth doing odd carpentry jobs for villagers, turning out a few bowls as orders came in and as he could secure suitable wood. Still, times were hard, so business was slow.

"Jesus, this is moving at a snail's pace," James complained one night several weeks later as the two of them leaned against their favorite boulder out under the stars.

"I know it is. And scratching in the dirt of Sepphoris is no festival. But so far this seems the best way to get back on our feet," Jesus commented. "We'll have to stay at it for a while. Maybe before too long another of the brothers can start working with you."

A few days later, Jesus and the brothers arrived back in Nazareth just as the last daylight faded from the skies. Rather than finding the town nodding off for the night, however, people filled the narrow streets, talking in tight clusters.

"Mother," Jesus asked as he entered his mother's house, "what is going on? Everyone is in the streets."

"It's the headman, Hezekiah. He's fallen seriously ill. Talking out of his head. Having a hard time breathing. This morning, he was fine. At midday he came in from the fields feeling very bad. Now he's near death, or so it appears."

"I'd better go see him," Jesus said, more to himself than to Mary.

He made his way through the milling villagers to the cottage occupied by the headman and his wife. At first the people clustered at the doorway did not want to let Jesus through. Apparently they feared he was trying to take over their posts as town criers, ready to spread the news when the prominent man died, as they had all concluded that he would. But the air of authority that bore Jesus into their midst prompted them to move away so he could enter the house.

Hezekiah's wife and children, all grown, hovered near his pallet. From the dull glow of the tiny lamp that drove out some of the darkness, Jesus could see the sweat pouring from the man's pallid face and fever-wracked body. A few steps took him to the headman's side, where he knelt, looked into the wife's face, and said, "I am Jesus, Mary's son. I have some training in treating illness. I might be able to help if you will permit me to examine your husband."

She numbly nodded assent, hope overriding skepticism.

Jesus touched the headman's face and felt the fever that threatened to consume him. He placed his hand on the man's chest and could feel the lungs laboring for air, filling with alien fluids. Jesus had seen this kind of breathing sickness often in Alexandria and had some success in treating it with certain elixirs and by applying poultices to the chest and back. In the same instant he realized he had no medicines with him. Just as suddenly, it dawned on him that maybe Seti had some of what he needed.

To the headman's sons Jesus said, "Go bring my brother James here, immediately." This time without hesitation, one of the young men bolted for the door and went scampering to find Jesus's brother.

"Now," he said, "we must raise him gently into a sitting position. His lungs are filling up with fluids that will drown him."

With Jesus on one side and another of the sons on the other, they raised the man into a sitting position and held him there for a few minutes. Jesus rubbed his back in a circular, kneading motion. Then he did the same thing to the man's chest. His labored breathing became somewhat more normal. "Find something to prop him up. We want him to rest, but we also want to keep him sitting up as long as possible."

At that moment James burst into the room. "You must go to Sepphoris as quickly as you can to Seti's house," Jesus urged him. "Among his apothecaries he might have some medicines we can use that will possibly help our respected headman. Listen carefully, and I will tell you what I need." Jesus listed four medicines and other ingredients for James to secure from Seti. "We will pray Hezekiah can live until you return."

For the next four hours Jesus took the perilously sick man through several rotations of sitting up, gently rolling to one side then the other, and then lying down again. By constantly applying cool wet cloths to the man's head and torso, Jesus hoped to bring the fever down somewhat. Several times during the wait, he thought the man would die.

After what seemed like an eternity, James again burst into the room, panting and sweating from the run to and from Sepphoris. "Seti had three of the mixtures you asked for. When I told him how the headman looked and sounded, he also sent a substitute for the one he did not have and said it might help."

Jesus immediately began to dose the man with the liquids. He prepared a poultice for the man's chest. "Now we pray," Jesus said. "I will keep giving him the medicine and applying the poultices. He's very sick. It's in the hands of Adonai."

Daylight came, and Jesus could discern no real change in Hezekiah's condition. His wife and sons had dropped off into an exhausted sleep. Though Jesus was numb from fatigue, he forced himself to stay awake, fearing the man might die if he did not watch him constantly. While rubbing first the man's back and then his chest, making sure the poultice was firmly in place and fresh, Jesus began quietly to sing a hymn to the man: *You who live in the shelter of the Most High, who abide in the shadow of the Almighty, will say to the Lord, "My refuge and my fortress; my Adonai in whom I trust." For he will deliver you from the deadly pestilence; he will cover you with his pinions, and under his wings you will find refuge. You will not fear the terror of the night, or the arrow that flies by day, or the pestilence that stalks in darkness, or the destruction that wastes at noonday.* He sang the most familiar refrains again and again.

The gentle singing woke up first one son, then another, and then their mother. Without thinking, knowing the psalm like they knew their own names, they all joined in with Jesus until shortly the room was filled with the low hymning of the classic lines from Scripture. Those keeping vigil at the door, hearing the singing from within, thinking perhaps the man had died or perhaps this was part of the spell the healer was trying to cast likewise joined in the quiet singing. A passerby, not knowing the small drama that was unfolding in the house, might have thought he was in the midst of a chorus rehearsal.

All morning long, the singing continued with first one group, then another coming to the doorway replacing those who had to go to work or tend to chores. Jesus and the man's family remained in the tiny room, now growing stuffy from the warming sun. At noon, with the heat becoming uncomfortable, Jesus said, "Let's take him outside to a cool place. I believe his fever's down some. This room is getting too hot." As his sons lifted their father carefully, Jesus kept saying, "Easy now. Be careful."

By sundown it was apparent Hezekiah would live. He could speak, if weakly, and knew what was happening around him. He did not remember much of the previous day and night.

"Let's get him back inside now," Jesus said, as night came on. "The chill of the evening could be too much for him."

Feeling he could leave him, Jesus said to Hezekiah's wife, "I must now get some rest or I will be sick. You've seen me making and applying the poultices. Keep doing that. Every so often, help him sit up. Turn him carefully from one side to another. Help him sip all the water he will. Do not fret about food yet. He'll eat when he's hungry. If you see any change for the worst, do not hesitate a moment to come for me. And pray. If you want to, sing some more to him. I know the praying helps and the singing seems to bring strength and comfort to him."

"Thank you, Jesus," the man's wife said. Then she started to kneel before Jesus.

"Wait," he implored, alarmed, lifting her.

"You can thank me. More, you can thank Adonai. You have no cause to kneel to me. Just take care of your husband. This town needs him."

One of the sons said, "And, Jesus, this town needs you. Take care. Rest well."

Jesus was too tired to notice the hush that fell across the small crowd still lingering outside the headman's house as he walked wearily toward Mary's house and the sleep he so desperately needed.

The recovery of the headman, labeled miraculous by the villagers, catapulted Jesus to the pedestal he deplored. Overnight, he lost freedom of movement, privacy, the measure of solitude he craved. In short, his life was snatched away from him, and he labored under the loss. As he and his brothers left the town before dawn to walk to their work in Sepphoris, the people of Nazareth trailed along after them imploring Jesus to help them with their maladies. Within a few days, to his dismay, word of the headman's cure had traveled to Sepphoris so that the Jews of the city began to collect around the worksite asking Jesus to come see their sick loved ones or to offer advice on how to deal with the whole range of physical complaints that plagued the people. The Jews with some wealth then began offering Jesus money if he would work his magic on their behalf.

In irritation at the distractions Jesus was causing, the foreman fired him.

That night, the family had another of its frequent roundtable discussions. Jesus assured them, "I will find other work. I may have to work out in the hills tending sheep just to keep away from the crowds. This same thing happened to me in Alexandria and then again down south in Bethany beyond the Jordan. People need so much help. When families find someone with even a small amount of genuine knowledge, they become almost hysterical in their eagerness."

Joses spoke up and said, "Jesus, you are too smart to be out tending sheep. Something will turn up around here."

The brothers each had something to say. James had sat by uncharacteristically quiet. When the others had finished, he spoke up. "Listen, Adonai has shown us the way out of our family mess."

"What do you mean?" asked Mary, speaking herself for the first time.

"Why, it's obvious. Jesus has spent years in Egypt getting the best training in the world on how to help sick people. We saw what he can do the other day with the headman. Jesus tends to the sick. People pay what they can. We'll all work with Jesus. We don't have to worry anymore." He leaned back in his chair, waiting for the affirmation from his family he was sure would come.

To his dismay and rising anger, no one said anything. "Well, what do you think?" he demanded to know after a few seconds of silence. "Is that a great idea? A gift from on High!"

"Jesus must not use his training in that way," said Simon, the youngest of the brothers. "Yes, he can help sick people. But for us all to make money from his work, I don't like it. I'd rather keep digging ditches."

Others nodded in agreement.

Then Jesus spoke to James: "James, you are looking out for the best interests of the family. I know that. I love you for it. But Simon and the others are right; I cannot use my training in such a way. Adonai did not allow me to learn simply to go into the healing business. I will not accept pay for what I do. At least not pay in the ordinary sense. That the headman lived and that his family is grateful is pay enough for me."

Embarrassed, a deep sense of alienation from the family welling up inside of him, James jumped up from where he sat, glowered at his family, and shouted, "You're all ignorant, silly. Here we are working like animals for almost nothing. Along comes Jesus, who's probably the greatest physician in the entire district, and you refuse to make the most of it. I don't get it. Or maybe *you* don't get it. We've got a fortune in our midst. Money to be made not by hurting people, but by helping them. But no, you turn your backs." Swaying for a long moment, looking at his family in dismay, James shook his head and left.

When the brothers gathered the next morning for their trek into Sepphoris, James was not there. Two days of searching turned up no clues. James and his family had vanished.

Jesus concluded at sundown of the second day, "James does not intend for us to find him, Mother. When he cools down, I believe he'll come back or at least send us word where he is. In the meantime we've got to get back to work."

———

Now fired from his construction job, Jesus reluctantly accepted the role of healer, throngs of needy people thrust on him. So with sick people pressing on Jesus from dawn until dark, serious thought about James and his family receded. At night mother and son would pray for James's well-being, for his safe and soon return. Beyond that, they had no time to go looking for him. The brothers had to continue their work in Sepphoris despite the distractions. Mary and Jesus's sisters became his helpers in tending to the myriad of diseases and maladies that afflicted the Galileans. Within a few weeks of unremitting labor, everyone was exhausted to the point of collapse. Mary's face became etched with age lines. The family's children were on the brink of suffering neglect due to the unremitting demands on the adults.

"Something's gotta be done to organize this situation," Simon said one night as he and his brothers leaned against their boulder. "Jesus, you want to help all the people you can. You've got more ability and knowledge than anyone we've ever seen."

"Yes," Joses replied. "But let's admit it. Your work with the sick of the region is destroying our family. It's costing us our lives. People dog every step we take. Now they're even trying to get our children involved in pleading for you to come see their sick relatives."

Jesus wrung his hands in frustration. "I know. About the time I think I've taken care of everyone that's lined up at Mother's house, I look up and see another group coming. To make matters worse, I have nothing left with which to treat them. No medicines. No slaves. No potions. No bandages. Nothing! I've asked Seti for all I can and dare. He's not in the business to give away his medicines, though he's been more than generous. I've used every homegrown remedy I can concoct, but it's just not enough. I really don't know what to do." His head drooped in defeat.

When Jesus awoke the next Sabbath morning, he decided he would go into Sepphoris and talk with Seti. "Mother," he said when she stirred, "I am at my wit's end. I've decided to slip into Sepphoris this morning while the village is quiet and no one waiting to see me to talk with Seti."

Alarm flashed across Mary's face. "Jesus, it's Sabbath morning. You cannot walk that far without breaking our laws. Besides, people will talk. You're too well known just to stroll from here to the city without being recognized."

"I've thought about that," Jesus answered. "I'll wrap up in a cloak and hope no one recognizes me."

"But what about breaking one of the commandments against working on the Sabbath?" she asked, fear and anxiety in her voice.

"I doubt Adonai aims to punish me for going to talk with a friend about how better to care for Adonai's little ones," he replied, he hoped with sufficient assurance to ease his mother's concerns. Still, he started the trek on the Sabbath with some entrenched misgivings.

When Jesus appeared at Seti's door, the Egyptian's pleasure at seeing Jesus was blunted only by his own quick inquiry, "Jesus, it's good to see you. But what's wrong? Why have you walked from Nazareth on your Sabbath?"

"You and my mother," Jesus smiled as Seti stood back so Jesus could enter the house.

Talking with Seti, however, brought no easy solutions to his struggles as a healer. "Jesus, you are being consumed by your success. One way to put a check on all this is for you to begin making a charge. That will cut way down on the numbers who come to you. And the fees will enable you to buy more supplies."

"I don't want to do that. To charge goes against everything in me."

"I understand," Seti agreed. Then even more thoughtfully, "You can become an itinerant healer. Move around. Go from place to place. You will always have more than you can do, but it will be somewhat more difficult for everyone to find you, especially those who are not all that sick in the first place, that just want some special attention."

"I don't want to do that either, Seti" Jesus replied, shaking his head. "My mother has already lost one son and his family. For me to start roaming the countryside would only add to her distress. She's borne enough."

After several more hours talking, the broad outline of a plan began to emerge. "I will allow those who can to pay something for their treatment. Not to me. My brothers will provide food for me, and I live with my mother. The money we raise can go into a treasury we can use to buy supplies. A few fairly wealthy people I have helped offered to make contributions. I can begin allowing them to give so that more people can be served."

"You'll get some criticism, Jesus," Seti observed. "Despite your best efforts, some will say you are getting rich off the poor."

"I know. That's just a burden I will have to bear."

By the time Jesus got back to Nazareth after dark, the Sabbath had passed, but his trek to the city had not gone unnoticed. The town was buzzing with the news that Jesus had violated the Lord's day by walking to Sepphoris and, horror of horrors, eating with Seti the Gentile.

The issue of accepting some amount of payment from those who could afford to pay raised more than a few eyebrows. Mary and his sisters, as his helpers, found themselves in the unenviable position of explaining the new policy to those they perceived were capable of making a payment. "If you can afford to pay something, do so. Jesus will accept no money himself. All the money will go into a fund to help buy medicines for those many who can pay nothing."

He never refused treatment, even for those who could have paid but chose not to. The vast majority were only too willing to make contributions, fully understanding the need to keep money on hand to purchase essential supplies. Still, despite the good he did, naysayers nipped around the edges. For the most part, the gossip was regarded as just that. Still, the barbs stung.

A few weeks later, during a regular synagogue service, a man, a stranger, suddenly flung himself into the gathering, ranting and raving, falling down, writhing and twisting. Some of the men tried to hustle him away from the group, but he was too distraught. In the hubbub, Jesus rose from his place and knelt down beside the anguished man. Seeing Jesus looking intently at him only seemed to send the stranger into more tortured spasms.

"Get away from me," the man screamed in slurred speech, spit and foam erupting from between his clenched teeth. "You are from the devil," he mumbled loudly, "to torture me even more."

He ferociously jerked away from Jesus, upsetting several benches and sending worshipers scattering.

In the middle of the confusion, Rezin, father-in-law to Jesus's sister Miriam, who had been especially outspoken against Jesus of late, shouted out to others, "Get that sorry piece of human trash away from here. This is sacred ground. We must not have the demon-possessed interfering with the worship of our Adonai."

Without moving from the tortured man's side, Jesus said for all to hear, "This is a child of Adonai. No child of the Holy One is trash. He has an illness. If any should leave the place of Adonai, it is those who judge so harshly."

A gasp went through the assembly. Jesus had challenged the boisterous, opinionated villager. But more, in the same breath, Jesus vehemently struck at the notion of demon possession.

Not one to be put down so easily, the critic snapped back, "And since when does the magician trained in the strange ways of unclean Egypt know so much about demons? Maybe he's in league with some demons of his own."

That was too much for the rest of the worshipers. Nothing like that had ever happened in their assembly, not in any of their memories. It was terribly, unbelievably unsettling. In that moment all eyes turned toward the headman, the very person whom Jesus had brought back from the brink of the grave. Rising to the occasion, he lifted his arms and said above the tumult, "Brothers and sisters, we must calm ourselves. While this poor wretch flings himself around on the ground before us, we are foolish to engage in jabs at one another. Consider this service dismissed. Go home. Maybe Jesus can ease the distressed brother. We can talk more later. Now, go home. And let us pray for one another in these uncertain times."

Men and women made hasty exits, not wanting any further contact with the demons that possessed the stranger. The headman and a few other leaders of the synagogue, including Rezin, lingered to see what would happen.

At Jesus's quiet suggestion, Mary brought clean towels and a bowl of cool, clean water with which Jesus could wipe the sweat and filth from the man's face and arms. All the while, Jesus kept talking to the wretch, gently quoting scriptures and singing softly to him. Gradually, the stranger grew still. Finally, he closed his eyes in sleep. No one watching the drama unfold moved.

After a half hour or so, the man cautiously opened his eyes and looked into Jesus's face. "Where am I?" he asked. "Who are you? Are you an angel? Tell me I have died and been gathered to Father Abraham's bosom," he pleaded.

"My brother," Jesus said, "you have not died. You have had a very hard time for these past few hours. You are in Nazareth. You stumbled into our synagogue gathering. My name is Jesus. I am your friend."

"Did I have another of my falling-down fits?" he asked, tears now pouring from his eyes.

"Yes, you did," Jesus answered him. "You have had these before?"

Then, reaching up to Jesus, the man wept openly, "Oh yes. I have them all the time. I have driven my family away from me. Nothing can stop them when they come on me. Everyone calls me crazy, evil, possessed of the devil. Oh, Jesus, it's awful."

Now with tears in his own eyes, Jesus replied, "I wish I could tell you you'd never have another one. I cannot. I do not know what brings them on or what makes them go away. I do know that soft touches from people and gentle words from Adonai help. That's the very best I can do for you."

With heart-breaking earnestness in his voice, the stranger said, "People in my village say I have these spells because I have sinned against Adonai. I've never done anything bad enough in my life to deserve such torment. Tell me, is Adonai so very angry with me that he sends these fits on me?"

"Listen, I cannot tell you why you have these spells. I can tell you with all the confidence in the world that Adonai does not do this to you," Jesus answered with a new note of authority in his voice. "You are no more a sinner than the rest of us. For reasons I cannot explain, you are afflicted with these falling-down fits."

The eyes of the synagogue leaders were likewise wet with tears, all but those of one man who glowered in fury at Jesus and the man stretched out on the ground in their midst.

A few days after the tender episode at the synagogue gathering, a small group of young men and women appeared at Mary's house.

"We want to talk with Jesus," one of the men announced when Mary somewhat anxiously met them at the door.

When Jesus appeared at the door, his deep brown eyes sweeping the small cluster of people, many of whom he already knew, they instinctively moved back from him slightly, a sense of awe moving through the group. "Rabbi," the unofficial spokesman said, "we have a request of you."

Jesus replied, "You call me 'Rabbi.' No one has ever used that title on me. I am not a rabbi. Rather, I am one of you who wants to know and serve Adonai."

Nonplussed, collecting his courage, the spokesman went on, "To us, you have become a rabbi. You know much that has escaped us. That's what we'd like to talk with you about. We want you to spend time with us teaching us the scriptures as you understand them. We've heard you talk in synagogue. You've helped many people in our town. You've been given insights we'd like to know more about."

"Have you talked with the leaders of our synagogue about this?" Jesus inquired, fully aware of the incessant religious territorial squabbling that went on in every town in Galilee.

Another of the men spoke up, "The headman is my father. After what you did for him, he could hardly deny us this simple request."

"And what did he say specifically?" Jesus asked.

Hesitating briefly, the earnest young man replied, "He said you might run into some opposition from a few people in the village. He felt you seemed like the type of man who could handle that. As long as we do not try to become another synagogue, he did not see too many problems."

"So," Jesus said, a quick smile darting across his face, "Hezekiah was less than enthusiastic but did not say no?"

Shuffling somewhat uneasily, the headman's son answered, "I guess that's about the size of it. If we want to spend time with you, he will not actively oppose us. At the same time, he has not exactly blessed the arrangement."

Raising his eyes to take in everyone, Jesus said, "Are you willing to suffer the irritation of some of the elders in Nazareth, some of whom are your own fathers, in order for us to spend time together?"

With one voice, the men and women said, "Yes. We are willing."

At sundown concluding the next Sabbath, while light still lingered in the sky, Jesus and approximately twenty-five young families, a dozen or more adolescents, along with some children, settled into the area in the center of town normally used as a gathering place for the synagogue meeting. Jesus had spent much time in prayer, thinking about where to begin this teaching ministry, sensing that he was about to cross yet another bright red line in his life. After returning from Egypt, at Bethany beyond the Jordan he had taught crowds that increased until the hillsides would be covered with hundreds of men, women, and children. Somehow that previous experience seemed to him now different, incidental. By contrast, this invitation was intentional, direct, strategic, actually reaching beyond the small group of eager young disciples.

As the headman's son and his family prepared to join with their friends to listen to Jesus that first time, the young man said, "Papa, would you and Mother like to go with us? You've known Jesus all his life. He clearly saved your life when you were so sick. You might gain from his insights into the holy scriptures."

Of course his mother would not speak until his father had spoken. "No. We will not go. Several key men in the synagogue are uncomfortable with this whole plan. For the time being, I will remain on the sidelines. I prefer not to make bad feelings worse."

"I don't understand," the younger man said. "It's not like Jesus is from a far country. He's one of our own. What possible harm can he bring to any of us?"

Raising his hand to silence his son, the headman said, "When you are older you will see things more clearly."

Stung to the core by his son's sharp answer but knowing the young man was right in his assessment, the father did what fathers have always done to children who've suddenly become wise enough to challenge them legitimately: he got angry. "Leave my house, young man. Already, Jesus is causing divisions. That's the problem."

When Jesus sensed that most everyone who was coming had arrived, he motioned for them to be seated on the benches in the gathering area. As was their custom, the men settled on one side and the women on the other with the children sitting where they could on the benches or on the hard-packed ground.

"I have a friend, actually a relative, named John," Jesus began. "You may have heard of him. He's become quite well-known up and down the Jordan River further south in the regions east of Jerusalem. I respect and love him greatly. Adonai has called him to a unique and powerful ministry. John is challenging much that is traditional and time-honored in our ways of worshiping Adonai. What's more, John is leveling strong charges at the Romans and the temple authorities for their gross mistreatment of ordinary people like you and me. He's furious about injustice, indifference, and their almost total disregard for the true ways of Adonai that the rich and powerful demonstrate."

One of the men averred, "Jesus, I can understand his anger and frustration. What's he doing about the problems besides talking about them?"

"Let me answer your question this way. John does not see much if any hope for change. He's so pessimistic about the way things are these days that he believes our only hope is for Adonai to come with fire and thunder and literally overthrow all power structures. He has great power as a preacher, as he envisions the coming Day of the Lord pointed toward by our prophets from centuries gone by."

"Such a message must make the high priest, the Romans, and Herod Antipas nervous," another young man offered.

"You are right. I fear for John's safety. I've not heard from him since I left him several months ago to come home. As far as I know, he's still preaching," Jesus said, a heavy weight of concern in his voice.

"You left him?" still another of the men asked.

Jesus was silent for a few moments, collecting his thoughts. "Yes, I left him, for at least two reasons. One, I needed to come home. I had been gone for a long time. I did not know of my family's troubles with our business, but still I wanted to come home."

He looked away, sadness in his eyes. "The other reason is that I began to be more and more uncomfortable with John's approach. I completely agree with his perspective on the problems we face. I'm not sure his solution is the best, certainly not for me. I do not expect Adonai to come with fire and thunder and overturn all the people in power. My studies of the scriptures and my own sense of the ways of Adonai make me feel that we must work today, where we are, in our own time, with Adonai to bring about changes."

"That seems like the slow way," the headman's son offered.

"Maybe," Jesus agreed. "I have a different understanding of the ways of Adonai than John. Even though we've had some very bad times in our history, Adonai has never seemed to work like John predicts."

"What are you saying, then?" a young mother asked with everyone in the gathering quickly turning to this woman who dared to speak in the assembly.

Jesus did not hesitate nor seem to notice that a woman had spoken up. "I am saying that Adonai does intend to bring in a new kingdom, but as we understand kingdom. It will be in our midst. It will come as you and I do the work of Adonai, as we serve and love one another regularly."

"What about the future?" someone asked.

"I cannot predict the future. Anyone who says he can is stretching the truth. I have complete confidence that Adonai is in ultimate control of today and tomorrow. As we live for him today, our own future will take care of itself."

"What about the coming kingdom?" The questions were coming thick and fast.

Jesus said, "The kingdom is here now. I think the kingdom is also coming. It's once and future. Now and then."

"Give us a better word, a clearer idea," pleaded a young mother from the fringes of the crowd.

Again, Jesus grew silent, paced around in circles for a moment, thinking. "Maybe a better way to understand what I am saying is to try to grasp the *movement* of Adonai, the *process*, the *direction* of Adonai in the world. I believe, and the scriptures teach, that Adonai has a grand design for all of creation as well as a dream for you and me individually. He brings about that design in the midst of the everyday. We connect with his movement for ourselves one decision, one choice at a time."

Your whole approach is too slow for me," an eager young man declared. "I go for John's plan. I want Adonai to come, wipe out the entire Herodian family and the Romans, and even the high priest if that's what it takes."

A gasp went up from the crowd. The hot-blooded young man had spoken what could be readily interpreted as treason. If his words got passed around, they would all get in serious trouble.

Jesus let the murmur move through the crowd, and then he said in measured tones, "I understand your feelings. You have much company among our people, north and south. And it may happen as you wish. I think, however, the ways of Adonai are much more profound, deep, often almost imperceptible. They are sure, though sometimes it takes a while to gain an appreciation for what Adonai's actually up to."

"Tell us what you mean," another young woman asked, emboldened by her friends' courage to speak out.

"I've thought about this often," Jesus mused. "Maybe it's like the tiny mustard seed. You can hardly see a single seed with your eye. Yet when you plant the seed, it grows into a large plant. What's more, sometimes the mustard comes up in strange places.

"This kingdom of Adonai's is like that tiny mustard seed. The ways of Adonai and our cooperation with him may look small, innocuous. Given time and nurture, those tiny seeds grow up big. As you farmers readily know, mustard can sometimes be a bother. It can take over the whole garden if you're not careful. We may be starting sometime here that offers many benefits. It can also be threatening to the people who have always thought themselves in charge of Adonai's garden."

"Are we no more than tiny mustard seeds?" a bright-eyed father asked while balancing a little boy on his knees.

"We are mustard seeds," Jesus answered. "I don't understand us as 'no more than mustard seeds.' The potential of that tiny seed is quite astounding. Individually, we can accomplish much in the name of Adonai. As we combine our energy, love, courage, and vision, we can do even more."

"What are we supposed to do?" complained yet another young father. "I can hardly get my work done now. And I surely do have a tough time earning enough money and growing enough food to take care of my family, especially with all the taxes I have to pay."

Jesus thought for a long minute. "*Do?*" he said aloud to himself. "That's a good question. If we are trying to move with Adonai in his world, our world, what do we *do*? What ideas come to some of you?" Jesus asked, motioning to the group as a whole.

"We can try to fight the Romans and the temple priests," spoke up one of the unmarried men. "They are the enemy. We'll never have peace until they're gone."

Other men grunted in agreement.

"We can get rid of the foreign landlords and their overseers who've taken our farms," offered a tall, rangy farmer speaking from the outer edges of the group.

"Do you think any of those solutions will solve your problems?" asked Jesus quietly, understanding their anger and pain. "And what will you fight with? And how many of you fathers will die in the effort?"

"Adonai will help us beat these unbelievers who push his people down so mercilessly," a squarely built, thick-necked bull of a man shouted.

"I don't think so," answered Jesus with such authority that no one tried to offer a retort.

"Then what do we do?" another mother asked plaintively. "Do we simply trudge along through life with no hope, just living to die like our ancestors?"

"We have to find life and find it abundantly where we are," Jesus assured her. "And no, we are not born just to die. We have to open ourselves to Adonai's meaning for our lives today. He will take care of the future even if I doubt he will come sweeping down and help us beat the Romans in a pitched battle."

"Tell us, Master. What do we do?" several asked at the same time.

"First of all, we have to improve our daily lots in life. For those of you who work hard and still do not have enough to eat, we have to find better ways for you to feed yourselves and your families. We have to find subtle, nonviolent ways to reduce the amount of taxes we pay to the rulers. I think we start by resisting some of the more oppressive temple taxes. The Roman taxes will be harder to ignore. As bad as the temple enforcers are, the Romans are even more difficult."

"You are a healer," interjected a woman Jesus had known his entire life. "Maybe you could teach some of us so we could help overcome so much sickness in our families. What you did for the headman was remarkable. Yet you did not do anything I could not do if I had your knowledge."

"The teaching in the synagogue is often stale and dry," complained the headman's son. "It looks to me like the leaders ought to let you teach more often. And also let some of us who are coming along do our part to make the scriptures and synagogue worship more alive."

"Wait," Jesus said, smiling, holding up his hands. "You're laying out quite a program. I agree with all you are saying. We will have to make plans and get organized if we hope to accomplish anything at all."

By then it was fully dark. Children began to fret and wiggle. After a few more minutes of talk, Jesus said, "It is late. We have work to do tomorrow. Go home. Get some sleep. Ask Adonai to give us leadership so we will know how to help him do his mighty deeds among us."

The entire village of Nazareth came alive with talk. Hope gradually began to replace despair among the younger families. As young mothers did their chores, drew water, cooked, tended to babies, and washed clothes, they talked incessantly about the new ideas raised during their long evening with Jesus. Their husbands were no less animated, making plans, daydreaming, and scheming about new possibilities, pushing themselves even harder to come up with ways to improve their lives.

Jesus, using his abilities as a healer, concentrated his initial efforts on training the women in some medical basics, such as cleanliness, how to treat routine illnesses, what early symptoms to watch for, instructions on how to set simple broken bones, and what medicines were available from herbs and roots that grew in their area.

"Try not to be afraid of sick people," Jesus instructed them again and again. "Regardless of what you've always heard, sick people are not demon-possessed. True, some ailments are caused by bad behavior. But I do not believe that demons and evil spirits get inside our bodies and make us sick."

Every Sabbath evening, Jesus spent time with all who came, explaining to them his ideas about the movement of Adonai in the world. He used the everyday experiences of life with which they were familiar to open up the mysteries of the holy scriptures, the ancient wisdom of the Jewish people, and the overall commonsense way Adonai wanted them to live and serve. Within a short time the crowds had completely outgrown the synagogue gathering place, so Jesus moved outside the village to a sloping hillside. By standing at the foot of the hill and speaking up to the crowd, they could hear him better. If the crowd was especially large, he would stand more in the midst of them and turn from side to side as he talked. For two hours and more, well into the dark, scores of people from Nazareth and other villages came to learn from Jesus.

On an especially beautiful Sabbath evening, several weeks into the teaching effort, Jesus began by saying, "Tonight I want to tell you about an important part of my cousin John's teaching. As a sign or a symbol or a seal of a person's repentance and openness to new leadership from Adonai, John has initiated the practice of baptism."

"Baptism?" a young man seated near Jesus exclaimed loudly. "What's that? Never heard of it."

From another part of the crowd, a man with an accent that suggested he was from the more northern parts of Galilee offered, "I've heard of baptism. Isn't that the way people who were not born Jews can get accepted into the temple?"

For a few seconds the large crowd came alive with comments and questions about baptism, some having heard of the practice, others totally ignorant of it.

Jesus, smiling, waved them into silence. "You are not alone in your confusion. Most of us had never heard of baptism, or certainly knew next to nothing about it until John came along. Let me explain baptism and help you understand what John means when he urges people to receive it." For the next hour Jesus again led them through John's message about baptism.

When he paused, a man about halfway up the hillside stood and asked, "Master, you mean to say that thousands and thousands of our people in and around Jerusalem are being baptized? That must make the temple authorities and the Pharisees nervous."

Jesus laughed at the man's characterization, then said seriously, "You are right on both counts. For many people baptism has become the symbol, the seal, the sign of their new walk with Adonai. In fact, such a large number of people had become baptized and subsequently slowed down their temple attendance, or stopped going entirely, that the temple authorities sent out investigators. The people from the temple were not so much worried about baptism itself. What worried them was the loss of temple tithes and taxes. If ordinary Jews could come to Adonai directly through repentance and baptism, they felt they did not need the temple and animal sacrifices."

After more discussion, Jesus's brother Simon stood up and asked, "Jesus, were you baptized by John?"

Jesus remembered the wondrous night when John baptized him under the moonlight in the Jordan River. Looking away into the dusk, he began speaking in hushed tones that seemed to come from far away. "Yes, I was. It remains one of the singular moments of my life. As I came up from the waters, I have never felt so close to Adonai. It was that I could almost reach out and touch him. The moment will forever shape my life."

When pressed, Jesus described his baptism to the people who strained to hear his every word, sensing, if unconsciously, they were hearing something that would have far-reaching implications for themselves and perhaps beyond.

Then the scenes from Bethlehem and the Jordan River were repeated as one person after another stood to ask Jesus, "Will you baptize me?"

Within days scores of men, women, and older children had received baptism at the hands of Jesus. When the numbers grew too large for Jesus, Simon and Joses, his younger brothers, who had been baptized by Jesus, began to assist.

The people of the community who had chosen not to participate in Jesus's teaching sessions nonetheless flocked to the banks of the stream that ran alongside the village to watch the strange spectacle as their fellow Galileans waded into the running water and were baptized. A deep spiritual stirring coursed through Nazareth and nearby villages as the effects of Jesus's teaching, enhanced by baptism, began to take hold.

If, however, baptism stirred unabashed enthusiasm among the friends of Jesus, it engendered caution and skepticism among the elders and those who avoided Jesus's teaching as well as outright animosity among the few who had set themselves squarely against anything he had to say or do.

—

One day, about three months after Jesus had begun to teach, wild dogs carried off several baby lambs from the flock of one of the poorest families. Jesus readily joined the search party that went out into the hills looking for the scavengers, determined to find the dogs and hoping that maybe one or two of the lambs might still be alive. After trudging through the hills for hours, three of the men came upon the dogs' den. Braving the ferocity of the animals, they killed them with stones, short spears, and bows and arrows. In the course of the attack, one of the men was seriously wounded by the dogs. To everyone's delight, the group was able to save one of the lambs who, though injured, looked as though it would survive.

That Sabbath evening, Jesus began his teaching by saying, "Adonai is like those men who went out looking for the lost sheep. They risked their lives to find and save the little lambs. A man was hurt badly, though I believe he will get well. Why would grown men with wives and children risk so much to save a lamb? Because the well-being of the family who owned the sheep was at stake. If they lose their sheep, they lose the wherewithal to live.

"Duty, responsibility, and a strong sense of selfless love prompted us to go out looking for the sheep. That is Adonai's way. He is completely concerned about each of us. He sends us to each other to offer help, support, guidance, and, when necessary, deliverance itself. We have always had people who put their lives in danger for the good of others. From Abraham onward, Adonai has provided men and women who were actually messiahs for individuals, families, and even for the entire nation. We can have no higher calling than to risk and, if necessary, give our lives for other people."

—

The health of the people in and around Nazareth began to improve as the healing ways of Jesus became better known and more widely practiced. He consistently refused to let the people honor him, turning aside all efforts on their part to call him a worker of marvels.

As the villagers' health got better, as they found new spiritual liberation through Jesus's teaching and baptism, they, like their southern cousins, became less inclined to pay tithes and taxes to the temple as a way, obliquely, to buy Adonai's favor.

"Look," the villagers began to say to each other, "Adonai has sent us Jesus. He's doing wondrous things in our town and district. We have no need of the priests from Jerusalem and their fancy ways to get and keep Adonai's favor. Jesus says we already have the love of Adonai. We don't have to buy it." So a passive temple tax revolt gradually emerged, not by design, not as an overt protest to the injustice and lavish lifestyles of the high priest and his cohorts. Rather, common sense and well-being prompted the people of Nazareth to take a second look at their long unquestioned ways.

Some months later, the temple bureaucrats began to notice the drop in income from Nazareth and surrounding villages. "Someone must investigate," one bookkeeper told his superior. "Money from the area around Nazareth has slowed considerably."

The headman of Nazareth was both startled and baffled by the visit of
a temple tax collector. "Why have you come all the way from Jerusalem to
Nazareth? We always pay our dues to Adonai and to the temple. Of course,
many of us think the taxes are too high, yet I have heard of no one who is refusing to pay. In fact, our villagers are happier and healthier than they've been in
a long time."

"I do not know what the problem is," the official said in his most pompous
tones, "but figures speak for themselves. We are not getting much money from
here. My assignment from the high priest is to determine why, and I will stay
until I learn what's going on."

A few days later, after he had made himself thoroughly obnoxious to the
entire community, the tax collector accosted the headman after a synagogue
service at which Jesus had spoken briefly. Pulling the headman aside, he hissed,
"I have found the source of the problem."

"Oh, is that right?" the headman replied, trying to move away from the
despicable Jerusalem official.

"Yes."

Before the headman could get away, the tax collector pointed toward Jesus,
who was walking down the narrow lane toward his mother's house.

"He's the problem. He's the reason your people have chosen to dishonor
Adonai and not make their proper payments to the temple."

Incredulous, now giving the bureaucrat his full attention, the headman said,
"You are joking, of course. I've known Jesus all his life. He has done nothing but
try to help people make better lives for themselves. He loves the temple. You've
made a bad call. Besides, you've long overstayed your welcome in Nazareth. Go
somewhere else to stir up your mischief."

"That's just it. Don't you see? He's persuading the people they don't need the
temple. By helping them feel better with his Egyptian black magic, telling them
all that nonsense about demons not being the cause of sickness, fooling them
into thinking they can find better ways to make a living, telling them they can
know Adonai on their own without the temple, he's undercutting their faith in
Adonai. People who don't feel tied to the temple don't pay. No, sir. He's your
problem."

"Listen," the headman said, his anger rising, "he's not our problem. He's an
answer for us. He's pointed more of our people to a closer walk with Adonai
than all your priests in Jerusalem ever thought about. He may be your problem.

I assure you, he's not ours." Changing the subject, he added, "Now, please leave me alone. I'm hungry. I'm going to eat."

But the man grabbed the headman's sleeve and fairly shouted in his face, "You see, he's infected you too. What you just said is the very reason the people are not paying. Why, if many people were to begin listening to him and believing his nonsense, the whole temple enterprise would begin to crumble."

For a breathtaking moment the headman wanted to say, "With a man like Jesus around, who needs the temple?" He instantly checked himself, nodding, he hoped, in a way that conveyed wisdom and understanding, though his fleeting radical thought was indeed quite exhilarating.

When the temple tax collector began to spread his accusation through Nazareth, the majority of the people wanted to run him out of town. His charges, however, proved to be exactly the kind of grist Jesus's detractors were looking for. The naysayers began verbally to grind more viciously, especially Rezin, Jesus's sister Miriam's father-in-law.

"I don't understand," Mary puzzled to Jesus. "Why do some people like Rezin take such offense at you? Miriam and Azoc have tried to talk with him. When they explain, he orders them to silence, even ordering them to leave his house."

"Mother, it's all right. Fear and uncertainty play evil tricks on us," he said, shaking his head sadly. "I have an idea the men like Rezin, who are trying to give me grief, fear losing their bit of power over some of the people of the town. Rezin, as a shopkeeper, enjoys his small measure of respect. A sense of well-being gives people confidence to think and act on their own, enabling them to slide from under the control of the men who want to see the new energy and freedom among the younger families dissipate. The power struggle that's going on is not between themselves and me. It is within their own souls. The rest of us pay the price of their own lack of vision and courage."

"What are you going to do about their efforts to attack you?" his mother asked anxiously.

"Do about them? Nothing," Jesus answered calmly, though not without concern.

To the irritation of the temple investigators, the village leaders did not interfere with Jesus in his efforts to strengthen the lives of the common people. True, a few of the older men complained loudly, but even they refused to take any action against Jesus. In a few days the temple tax collector left the village in a huff.

—

Comparatively speaking, life was manageable in Nazareth. The weather had cooperated with farming. The livestock produced bountifully. The general health of the people held. The family of Mary reunited with James.

One day in early fall, James appeared at Mary's door. She had not been so overjoyed since Jesus had similarly showed up two years previously.

"I was foolish to leave like I did, Mother," her chastened second son confessed. "I was hurt and angry. I let myself blame Jesus for all our troubles, and then when he had a way for us to get out and refused, that was too much. I know now all my bad feelings were at myself. Running away in the middle of the night only made matters worse."

"Oh, James," Mary cried, "I have been so worried about you and your family. We sent out search parties, but they could find no trace of you. Jesus said you knew the hills too well to be found."

Calmed now, Mary asked him, "And what are you doing? How are you making a living? Where is your family?"

James reached out and hugged her again and answered lightly, "Rather than try to work as a carpenter, I decided to go to the wharves of Ptolemais and see what kind of work I could find there. My education got me a good job. I immediately hired on with a Phoenician merchant whose ships trade all around the Great Sea. I keep his financial books, bills of lading, oversee maintenance on the vessels, and whatever else comes along. Actually, he has made me his first assistant. My family is well and happy. We have a small house near the docks and warehouses. I am even earning enough money to pay for some tutoring for my children."

After a truly joyful reunion, James prepared to return to Ptolemais. He and Jesus walked out to their boulder for one last talk. "Mother tells me you are encountering stiff opposition from a few of the old heads in the village," James said thoughtfully, concern in his voice.

"Yes, it's true," Jesus agreed. "I'm not quite sure what to do about it either. I may even leave Nazareth and go elsewhere before real trouble erupts. I believe the people who truly want to do something about their lives now have the inner strength and sense of confidence to continue. The others will probably just rock along whether I stay or go. For sure, the opposition will not die down as long as I am here."

"Oh, Jesus, I hope you do not have to leave. The people here need you. Besides, it would be very hard on Mother," his brother said, genuine regret in his voice. "You can't do like I did, run away from trouble."

"Thanks for your concern, James. I will not be running away from trouble. I have the strong hunch I will only be exchanging trouble in one place for trouble in another. Strange as it might sound, when people who have been downtrodden begin to improve themselves, others who have prospered from that weakness get all the more grasping. That's what's happening here." Jesus shook his head at the vagaries of the human condition.

—

Jochobed, the only daughter of Rezin, his favorite child even over Azoc, his eldest son, went into labor, preparing to give birth to her third child. The previous two births had been extremely difficult, taxing the best abilities of the village midwives. They had urged the young mother to have no more children, yet here she was with her labor pains coming close and excruciatingly painful.

"The baby's breech," one of the midwives told the mother gravely. "We'll do all we can to turn the child. It will be hard. Try not to push so much until we can see what can be done."

When it became quickly apparent that mother and baby were in severe distress, the midwives said to Jochobed's husband, Asher, "We should send for Jesus. He's done wonders with others. Maybe he can here."

Jesus listened attentively to what the midwives told him. He secured permission from Asher to examine his wife, to feel her stomach, to get a clearer idea of the position of the baby.

After several minutes of unblinking concentration, moving his hands gently across the young mother's abdomen, Jesus said quietly to her and her husband, "Indeed, this is going to be very difficult. The women and I will keep working with you. We will also have to pray that Adonai will intervene."

After a full day of agonizing labor, Jochobed and the unborn child died. Jesus was stricken with grief. He reached out to the bereft husband and said, "I am so sorry. The women and I did everything we could to save your wife and baby. As hard as it is, we have to bow to the mystery of the purposes of Adonai."

"Jesus," Asher said, "I find no fault with you or the women. You did everything possible."

With Rezin it was another story. When he learned of his daughter's death, he became livid with rage. "It's Jesus's fault," he ranted and raved. "I knew from the minute he showed up here again after being off in demon-possessed Egypt, he would bring only trouble. He's got the people stirred up. He's got the high priest mad at us. And now he has killed my child, my beloved daughter!"

The man's entire family, the village headman, and friends tried to assuage his anger to no avail. He and some of his cronies became so crazed with fury that Jesus, Mary, and others in the village became seriously alarmed.

The leader of the synagogue came to Jesus on the day before Sabbath and said, "Maybe if you would speak in the synagogue on Sabbath, your words would have a calming effect on him and the few others in the village who are so set against you. Something's got to happen, and soon, or we are going to have big trouble."

Jesus was immediately uneasy with the suggestion. "Thanks for your concern and offer. Rarely, however, have I known mere words to turn away such awful anger as he and his friends have stirred up."

When the leader would not take no for an answer, Jesus consented.

On Sabbath the air in the synagogue was thick with anxiety and hope. The overwhelming majority of the people had come to love, even to adore, Jesus. He had wrought nothing short of the unbelievable in their town. They wanted the bitter conflict to go away. The vocal few, on the other hand, were out for blood. They entered the gathering with anger and darkness on their faces.

When it came time for Jesus to read, he stood and read from the Isaiah scroll: *The Spirit of the Lord Adonai is upon me. Adonai has anointed me to preach good tidings to the poor. He has sent me to bind up the brokenhearted, to proclaim liberty to the captives, and the opening of the prison to them that are bound. He has sent me to proclaim the present and coming year of the Lord, and the day of vengeance of our God, to comfort all that mourn. He has commissioned me to give beauty for ashes, the oil of joy for mourning, the garment of praise for the spirit of heaviness, that they might be called trees of righteousness, the planting of the Lord that he might be glorified.*

As was the custom, Jesus sat down and began to speak: "My good friends, people I have known all my life, you took my family and me in when we came here many years ago while I was still an infant. Nazareth is my home. During my years in Egypt, I would often lie awake at night remembering life here. Many of you would come to mind. I often prayed for you. You have been kind and generous to my mother and my brothers and sisters and now to their own families.

"Adonai sent me to Egypt for reasons that are not yet clear to me. I returned to a land in even greater turmoil than the one I left. Our rulers and the Romans are prospering greatly. We are more confined by circumstances. Despite the work of healing we've done here in Nazareth, sickness of mind and body are everywhere. All of this distresses me greatly.

"The needs that I found here in Nazareth have prompted me to use the gifts of healing I gained in Egypt. The painful problems of everyday life have made it necessary for many of us to use our imaginations as never before to make bad situations better.

"I turned to the words from Isaiah, blessed be his memory, because they get to the heart of what I have tried to do with and among you here. Many of us have found good tidings from the words of Adonai and even from each other. Broken hearts have been mended. Some of you, at least, are finding new freedom from the captivity that bound you even though you've not seen see the inside of a jail.

"These signs say to me that Adonai is breaking through in ways not seen before. I believe you, his special people, have a key responsibility in bringing about the new thing Adonai is trying to do.

"What's more, I am coming to believe that I will have a key responsibility in this new work. I do not have it straight in my mind as yet. My own spirit does seem to resonate with Adonai's spirit in such a way to lead me to say that much of this scripture is being fulfilled right here in Nazareth. We have just begun to see what Adonai has in store for us. We can love and labor together right here, and we will learn more of what the prophet meant when he spoke about the 'acceptable year of the Lord.'"

As Jesus spoke, a sense of awe, of holiness, of spiritual uniqueness hushed the people. They hardly breathed lest they miss anything he said to them. They dared not move lest the power of the moment evaporate. For many, this would be their own burning bush moment with Adonai. Their lives would forever be marked by Jesus's presence in the Nazareth synagogue that day.

A loud "No!" shattered the glory of the moment. Rezin, Jesus's chief protagonist, jumped to his feet, shouting, "It's bad enough for you to teach our children that they do not have to support the temple. You've forced many of them into baptism, an abominable ritual from who knows where. Now you've added blasphemy to your crimes. How dare you say the spirit of Adonai is upon you. It's not the spirit of Adonai that's on you. It's the spirit of Beelzebub!"

Cries of "Sit down!" and "Hush!" erupted throughout the gathering. As Jesus had feared, the full, pent-up fury of the storm broke. Emboldened by the man's tirade, others of his ilk likewise jumped to their feet, shaking their fists at Jesus.

One man from the outer edge of the group screamed out, "You ought to be stoned for your blasphemy."

"Yes, stone him!" a few others yelled.

The entire assembly erupted in angry imprecations. Shoving matches between erstwhile friends and neighbors broke out. All efforts to restore calm by the leader of the synagogue and the headman of the village were to no avail.

Mary alone saw Jesus walk out of the gathering place, agony and despair on his face. She immediately began to push her way through the heaving crowd toward her son.

—

"Seti," Jesus said to his great friend, "I wanted to come to you and open my heart to you. Strange, you an Egyptian, one who does not give allegiance to Adonai, has far more understanding of his ways than most of our own people, even those charged with leading our walk of faith."

"Your Adonai and my gods speak with the same tongue, Jesus. It is up to us to hear what the best of our traditions wants to say to us," Seti answered quietly but confidently.

"I am going to disappoint you, Seti," Jesus said, his luminous eyes now sparkling with tears.

"And how are you going to disappoint me, Jesus? Such is not possible."

"You wanted me to take over your business enterprises. That's why you sent me to Egypt in the first place. I will always be grateful. As you have probably guessed by now, running a business empire is not what Adonai has for me. I have wasted your money and hopes," Jesus said, his voice choking with emotion.

Seti reached out to touch Jesus's arm. "Wait, Jesus. You are the best part of this grand gift of life that has ever happened to me. The money I spent on you is far and above the best investment I ever made. Already, it has returned to me a hundredfold."

"But your business."

"Forget my business," Seti replied insistently. "When I am dead and gone, what you are doing will go on and on."

"Seti, that's just it. I am still not clear what I should be doing, what Adonai has in store for me. Here I am, thirty years old and still no clear idea of my calling," Jesus groaned.

"What did you come here to tell me, Jesus, besides that silly word about disappointing me?" the Egyptian asked.

"I came here to tell you that I am going to spend the immediate future among our small villages dealing with the poorest of the poor, the 'weeds in God's garden,' as one of our sages has written."

"Aha, Jesus," Seti replied with fresh comprehension. "Indeed, that is your calling. Your Adonai is sending you out among the weeds of the land, maybe of the world. Never has one had more capacity to make a difference among the most hard-pressed, downtrodden than you. Why, it's like King Croesus going out to give away his mountains of gold to those who have nothing."

Jesus blinked. "You share my feelings, my reach for Adonai's plan?"

"Completely, Jesus, completely. I could not do what you are about to do. I would be no good at it. You are the perfect one. My small part has been to help you get equipped for this wondrous, thankless work," Seti enthused.

The next morning, after another of Asenath's delicious breakfasts, the two men stood facing each other at the doorway of Seti's house.

As they embraced, Jesus said, "I will see you again soon. I will not be that far away from here."

"Jesus," Seti answered deliberately, "you will not be far from here. Probably, though, I will not see you again. At least not with these tired eyes. Like your ancient Father Abraham, you go to a new place, a new land. Because he left what he knew to journey to what he did not know, the world has never been the same. Something like that—no, even greater than that—lies before you."

When Jesus tried to protest, Seti shushed him. "Let me hug your neck one more time, Jesus of Nazareth, as you go to your kingdom of weeds."

# Chapter Seven

# New Frontiers

### His thirtieth year

*I will sing a new song to you, O God.*

Simon, Jesus's youngest brother, still unmarried, was determined to accompany Jesus as he left Nazareth despite Jesus's assurance that he could make it alone.

"No, Jesus," the brother said airily with a confidence that indicated growing strength for the young man, "you've got a knack for getting yourself in trouble. You'll need me around to take some of the blows that are sure to come."

As they started out at dawn two days after the ruckus in the synagogue, Simon asked with a smile, "By the way, big brother, where are we going?"

"To tell you the truth, I am not sure. I feel inclined to head east, toward the Lake of Galilee, toward the Jordan River."

Jesus pondered a moment before speaking. "My time with Adonai," he said in a way Simon had not heard before, "suggests to me that we stay out of the bigger cities. Not that people in Sepphoris and Tiberias and places like that do not need what we might be able to offer. It's just that the folks in the smaller towns and villages are so cut off. Besides, we'll attract less attention if we stick to the smaller places. The last thing I need right now is notoriety. A noisy reputation gets in the way of the work."

Simon had never been to the eastern section of Galilee. As a matter of fact, he had hardly been anywhere in his young life except the family's trip to Jerusalem, which he barely remembered, and Sepphoris for work.

Simon was taken with the beauty, the openness, the bounty of the hills and plains. What richness, he thought. In the next instant he realized how little of the fruits from these wonderful hills and valleys actually stayed with the people who labored from dawn to dark to produce them. A deep sadness waved over him, replacing the exultation at the beauty when he thought of this staggering loss to the people, his people, the stalwart Galileans.

Though they headed generally toward the Lake of Galilee, Jesus's inner map seemed to keep them wandering back and forth, stopping here and there to talk with farmers, craftsmen, artisans. The two men never lacked for food or shelter thanks to the hospitality of the villagers, made all the more generous because of Jesus's obvious attitude of caring, his willingness to listen to their problems, make suggestions, and subtly point them in new directions for their lives and occupations. Simon did notice, to his dismay, that if they stayed for more than a few days in a place, always some among the town and synagogue leaders began to get uncomfortable with Jesus. His brother seemed not to notice and probably would not have paid them any mind, so caught up was he in seeing how quickly a new sense of realistic hope could energize many of the people.

It soon dawned on Simon that his brother had great powers of perception, intuition, and a pervasive sensitivity with and for everyone he met. When Jesus engaged the people in extended conversation, invariably he would open to them his own thinking about the state of affairs and lead them into various parts of their Holy Scriptures that seemed to speak to their particular situations.

On numerous occasions during these days of meandering, Jesus employed his healing skills. He set the broken arm of a little girl who had tripped while running through a rocky field. He showed a mother how to make a chest poultice for her coughing baby that could relieve some of the infant's distress. About six weeks into the venture, they met a man on the road who frantically waved them away while he shouted, "Leprosy! Leprosy!" Jesus, ignoring his warnings, walked right up to him and said authoritatively, "Let me see your leprosy."

At first the man drew back, saying, "I am unclean. You will become unclean by talking to me."

"No, I will not become unclean simply by talking with you," Jesus said sharply, irritated not with the man, but rather with the system that held him captive. "That's nonsense. Now, let me see your spots."

Reluctantly, still pulling up the ragged sleeves of his cloak, the man revealed angry sores and flaking skin up and down his arms. Jesus looked closely, touching the lesions gently.

After several minutes examining the man, he said, "You do not have leprosy. You have a bad skin condition probably brought on because you have had a strong reaction to certain plants or even animals. What was your work before you began to break out?"

"I'd rather not say," the man replied, embarrassed.

"Look," Jesus said, "I'm not trying to pry into your life. But I might be able to help. Now tell me."

"I was a tanner." The man's face reddened with shame. "I know tanning is not an honorable business. When we lost our land, I had to do something, so the village tanner offered to teach me his trade, and I, well, I had to accept."

Brushing aside his apology, Jesus said, "Tanning is honorable work. Messy, but honorable. You are not condemned by Adonai because you are a tanner. I'm guessing your skin has reacted to some of the solutions you use in your work. If you stay away from tanning, find something else to do, I believe your skin irritations will shortly disappear."

Reflecting on what Jesus was saying, the man said, "You know, when I think about it, my arms do not sting and itch quite as much as they did when I had to leave home a few weeks ago." Hope sprang into his eyes. "Maybe you're right. Maybe I will be able to go home again. I can certainly find something else to do."

"Let me tell you about a salve you can make to smear on your arms that could speed up the healing." Jesus explained how to extract the juices from certain plants and how to mix the extract with herbs that were native to this part of Galilee. "Add this mixture to skimmed animal fats. Make up a small amount of this salve every few days. Don't make too much at a time because it seems to lose its potency rather quickly. Keep this salve on your arms. I've known it to work with other skin conditions similar to yours. With Adonai's blessing, it might help you."

"Are you a magician?" the man blurted, his fear momentarily overcoming his hope.

"No, I am not a magician. I do have some training in the healing arts. Basically, I am a man like yourself trying to live a life that honors Adonai and that is of benefit to people like you."

After a few more minutes of conversation, during which Jesus reminded the man to present himself to a priest for the proper rite of cleansing when the sores cleared up, the three pilgrims started to go their separate ways. "Where are you going?" the man asked.

"I don't have a particular destination," Jesus answered frankly. "My brother, Simon, and I are from Nazareth. Like Abraham of old, Adonai has set us on a journey without a clear trail before us. We are trusting him to give daily direction."

"I'm from Capernaum," the man said. "It's not very far from here. It's a nice town. Right on the shores of Galilee Lake. We'd surely like to have a man like you in our town. You make sense. And you don't seem like the sort of man who would try to cheat us by charging too much for your healing. Why don't you go with me?"

Jesus and Simon looked at each other, shrugged, nodded, and off they went. As they walked, Jesus said, "What's your name?"

"My name is John. My father is Zebedee. My family has lived in Capernaum on the shores of the Galilee Lake since anyone can remember. Some of my cousins are fishermen. My family had a farm until the Romans took it. My father now tries to make a living as a boat builder. I don't have a talent for building, so I had to find something else to do. That's when I got into tanning."

Jesus answered sympathetically, "I've heard your story hundreds and hundreds of times from Galilee south to Jerusalem and over into Bethany beyond the Jordan. Something like that happened to my father's family a long time ago. It completely changed our lives. I understand what you're talking about."

"We've whispered among ourselves," John of Capernaum said, "about trying to throw off the Romans, but we can't figure out how to do it."

Then, brightening, "Hey, maybe you could help us do that!"

"John, that's what some folks think. It just won't work. You and I both know the Romans will not tolerate any semblance of revolution for a minute."

With resignation John replied, "You're right. But many of us feel we've got to do something!"

"Together," Jesus encouraged, "together we might be able to come up with another 'something.' Going head to head with a Roman army is suicide. Besides, that's not Adonai's way."

John wanted to ask the rangy, handsome stranger why he could say with such assurance what was and was not Adonai's way. He decided to keep his thoughts to himself. Maybe I'll ask him later, John mused.

He swabbed his arms with the gooey salve. Within a few days John's skin did show marked improvement. Prohibited by custom and law from reentering Capernaum until he was completely clear of "leprosy," he kept the prescribed distance from the village. He did let his family know he had returned and, thanks to Jesus, was making progress toward restoration to a full life.

Almost from the moment Jesus and Simon reached the comparatively prosperous lakeside town of Capernaum, on the strength of John's recommendation and Jesus's obvious compassion and power, the community made them feel completely welcomed. A merchant of some means offered the two brothers a two-room cottage with a tiny courtyard connected to his own larger house. Thanks to frequent invitations to meals and the steady stream of dishes the women of the town prepared and brought by their house, the brothers never lacked for food or other basic necessities.

Soon the now-familiar pattern was repeated. John's cure from leprosy offered undeniable testimony of Jesus's healing gifts. Cautiously at first, then in rivulets, ultimately in torrents, the villagers, along with their families and friends from the surrounding districts, came to Jesus for treatment. Though many illnesses were beyond him, often Jesus was able to help. He encouraged the people to lay aside prejudices and superstitions that bound them to senseless rules of ritual cleanliness that often prevented them from touching sick people, much less becoming sufficiently involved to help them get well. Under his tutelage, dozens in the community learned commonsense ways to care for themselves. As he had done in Nazareth and other places, he trained a few men and women who showed particular aptitude in acquiring some basics in the healing arts. But like nothing else he did, episodes of bringing some relief to adults and children afflicted with falling-down sickness and fits ignited the people's imagination about Jesus. Despite his efforts to quell their runaway enthusiasm, within a few weeks of his arrival, the people of Capernaum were calling him a wonder worker. They reverently dubbed him a man from Adonai, a veritable son of the Holy One, who, with the touch of his hand, could heal all manner of sickness and cast out demons.

———

With John fully restored and constantly at his elbow, Jesus, now capably aided by Simon, labored with the sick from early morning until dark. John directed the crowds. Simon tended to minor physical problems using skills he had learned from his brother. Jesus dealt with the more serious situations. To the amazement of everyone, Jesus took no pay for what he did.

"I have no needs," he said again and again. "Adonai and the people of Capernaum have seen to that. If you have money or goods with which you might have paid me, give it to those who have nothing."

The almost complete appreciation for what he did was mitigated somewhat by the vocal few who objected to the way Jesus ministered to everyone who came to him—Jew, Syrian, Greek, and even the Romans. "He's not a faithful son of Abraham," the malcontents would mutter. Fortunately, hardly anyone in Capernaum paid them any attention.

A sharp rap at the cottage door brought Simon scurrying to see who was knocking so early in the morning.

Moments later, Simon went into the other room of the small house. "A Roman soldier is here to see you," he said nervously. "He says he has a message for you."

When Jesus presented himself at the door, the soldier announced respectfully, "Centurion Latvias invites you to dine with him this evening. You may also bring any others with you. May I tell him you will accept?"

"Latvias!" Jesus exclaimed with surprise and delight. "Could that be the same man who was stationed in Phasaelis a couple years ago?" Jesus asked.

"It is the same man. He was transferred to the Capernaum district only some days ago."

Jesus said eagerly, "By all means tell the centurion Latvias I will be honored to dine with him tonight. And I will bring one or two of my friends with me."

Jesus's acceptance of the invitation made everyone, John included, uncomfortable. "Jesus," he said cautiously, not wishing to offend his marvelous friend while feeling constrained to offer a word of caution, "you're risking the ire of many in the community by going to the centurion's house for dinner. We just don't do things like that. He may be an honorable man. But being at the table with him and others of his staff, that's going a long way, much further than anyone around here has ever gone."

Jesus smiled understandably. "John, sooner or later we've got to understand that we are all children of Adonai. Sure, we Jews may have a special place in his affection. At the same time, keep reminding yourself that not all the sheep are in one fold. Besides, I have a previous friendship with this man and his wife. He's Roman, a man of conscience, a man who, in his own way, reaches out for the ways of Adonai."

"Well, I, I just don't know," mumbled the son of Zebedee, laboring mightily with this completely new notion.

"Tell you what, John," Jesus said warmly, but still with an air of teasing, "just to show you that it's all right, you come with Simon and me to the centurion's dinner. I am sure he will be delighted to have you."

Now choking on his words, John sputtered, "What? Me, go with you to a Roman's house. My stomach would rebel. I would probably be thrown out of my father's house. No! I just can't."

John went to dinner with Jesus and Simon. The Roman thunder and light-ning did not strike him dead. To his amazement, Zebedee only grumbled, and his mother said nothing.

Upon arriving at the centurion's villa, Jesus, Simon, and John were met by Latvias himself. "Do come in," he said in his best Greek. Greeting Jesus specifically, he said, "When I heard of the stranger in town with wonderful healing skills who refused payment, I told myself that could only be the man who tended my daughter. The gods, or should I say, your Adonai, are good to have let my path cross yours again." Then he added, "The gods or Adonai have blessed us with another child, a son."

They enjoyed a stimulating evening of good food, wine, and conversation. Jesus and Latvias talked seriously about the complexities of life in Roman-occupied Palestine and engaged in reflective exchanges about the ways of Adonai for all people. As the cordial evening drew to a close, Jesus and his colleagues prepared to leave.

"Jesus," Latvias, standing in the doorway to his home, said with utmost seriousness, "stay out of trouble. As long as you are in my region, I will be ready to help you in ways that I can. You know, of course, I can tolerate no hint of an uprising."

"I understand, Your Excellency," Jesus answered gravely. "My ways may look and sound different, but they do not include any sort of armed conflict. Adonai works from within the human heart and human organizations."

The dinner stirred up the usual buzz of gossip in the town. For the most part, the talk evaporated quickly.

As the weeks in Capernaum passed, Jesus began to spend more and more time alone, often staying out all night under the stars. When John and Simon lectured him on the need for rest, he would say, cryptically, sometimes even irritably, "I get rest. Even when I do not sleep, I get rest. Besides, the days are uncertain for me. I must not spend too much time asleep. I am fine. Thanks for being concerned."

They also noticed that he could lie down on his cot in the tiny house and fall instantly asleep, not stirring for hours.

When Jesus had been in Capernaum for more than three months, Simon and John began to sense in him a growing restiveness, casting about, an anxiety for the next step. When they mentioned it to him, Jesus admitted, "You are right. I feel a strong ferment. I cannot explain it, though. Don't worry. Try not to fret too much. In his own way Adonai will let me know what to do next."

During evenings when Jesus would be out in the hills praying, Simon and John talked endlessly about this strange man, brother, and friend with whom their lives had become profoundly linked.

"He's not always been so mysterious," Simon averred. "He's been way ahead of me in his mind and in his grasp of the ways of Adonai. Until recently, I felt he had his feet on the ground. Now, I'm not so sure. Besides, I do not remember his spending so much time alone."

"Simon," John stated without equivocation, "he's the most amazing man I have ever known. I'd rather be around him than anyone. He makes me feel good. He makes me feel I can accomplish anything and everything. At the same time, I am awed by him, even afraid at times. It's not that he tries to put on airs. He's got a hold of something that's completely beyond me."

Late one afternoon, with the sun already below the hills that surrounded the magnificent lake that had nurtured the people who lived on its shores since time immemorial, Jesus was talking informally with a group of a dozen men and women. A short distance up the shore, three strapping men, bare to the waist, pushed their boat away from land and began to row out for a night of fishing.

—

Seeing them out of the corner of his eye, Jesus interrupted his teaching and asked, "Who are those men about to go out fishing?"

One of the villagers answered, "The biggest one is Simon, often called Cephas. Then there's Andrew, Cephas's younger brother. The other is Judas, a cousin."

Looking up into the gathering darkness with myriads of stars beginning to glow in the cloudless night sky, Jesus said, almost to himself, "They should not go out tonight. A storm's coming."

Everyone who lived around the lake knew that squalls could blow up in a matter of minutes. Since this was not the season for such weather and with hardly a breeze stirring, the people paid little attention to Jesus's concerns. Shaking off his own sense of foreboding, Jesus picked up his teachings where he had left off.

The people were so caught up in what Jesus was saying that they noticed neither the passing of time nor, at first, the strong breeze that abruptly began to whip at their clothing and toss the lake. Within a few seconds, however, the skies grew ominously dark. Instantly, a howling wind ripped across the water, churning the calm lake into a furious cauldron. Mothers and fathers grabbed

up their children and began to run for cover from the downpour. Others just
hunkered down under their cloaks to wait out the storm.

Jesus, oblivious to the thunder, lightning, and slashing rain drenching him,
sloshed toward the lake. When lightning flashes momentarily lit up the night,
he strained to see the men and their boat.

Nothing.

A native of Capernaum, seeing Jesus's concern over the fisherman, shouted
through the cacophony of the night, "Master, they'll be all right. Cephas is one
of the best men with nets and boats anywhere. Anyway, this'll blow out in a few
minutes."

The storm did not diminish. It only grew worse.

Soon others began to join Jesus on the shore, ignoring the torrential rain,
peering out across the waters now in an ocean-like frenzy. In great agitation an
older man suddenly appeared out of the darkness. Pacing frantically up and
down the muddy shore, wringing his hands, praying, pleading, he called out to
no one in particular, "Those are my boys out in the boat. The storm's lasting too
long. They'll be swamped!"

In the next moment Jesus waded offshore a few feet into the wildly tossing
waves that almost knocked him down. Through the sheets of rain, Simon darted
after his brother to prevent him from going into the water, only to have Jesus
vigorously push him away. To the astonishment of those who saw him in the
water, Jesus lifted his arms toward the furious skies and prayed fervently in a
voice that carried over the fury, "O, Adonai, calm this storm. You need those
men in the boat. Dear Abba, do not let them drown."

Later, a man who was near him at the shore that night reported, "After he
prayed, he just stood there in water up to his waist, waves beating on him, his
arms raised up to the heavens. By all that's holy, I swear that within a matter
of minutes, the wind died down, the rain slowed to a sprinkle, and before you
could turn around the skies cleared, the waters calmed as if nothing had ever
happened."

Others who had been on the shore that night would later say, "Jesus splashed
back up on the bank. He turned to Cephas's father and said, 'Your boys will be
home soon.' In half an hour or so, those of us on the shore cheered and clapped
as the boat emerged from the darkness making for the shore. You never saw men
any wetter, more worn out, nor any happier to put their feet on hard ground."

The next morning, as Jesus and Simon were about to begin the day's work,
Cephas appeared at the door of their cottage. "My father and others in the

village tell me you calmed the storm last night and saved our lives. We were
about to capsize when the storm stopped as fast as it started. I don't know how
you did it, but I want to thank you."

Jesus said, "You are Cephas, aren't you?" Not waiting for him to say anything,
Jesus continued, "Adonai calmed the storm. He did make it plain to me that he
has a purpose for you. It was not time for you to die."

Bemused, the big, tanned man demanded, "And what is it that Adonai has
for me to do?"

"I honestly do not know," Jesus answered frankly. "But you'll know in time,
in his time. Until then," he laughed, "you might be more careful when you go
out fishing."

A grand friendship was born that morning.

—

John shook Jesus awake at dawn a few days after the storm episode. "Jesus,"
he said breathlessly, poking his friend, "Jesus, you've got to get up! Quick!"

Jesus, who never slept past dawn, jumped up, rubbing his eyes, thinking he
must have grossly overslept. "Why, what? What's happening? Is somebody sick?
Has something bad happened during the night?"

"You've got to come outside, out to the edge of the town," John demanded,
already tossing Jesus's clothes at him. "Here," John said, "I've got a bowl of water
for you to wash your face. Smooth your hair. Wake up. Hurry." And with that
he was out of the door of the cottage, pacing around in the small courtyard,
impatiently waiting for Jesus.

Hearing John's clamor, Simon bounded from his cot, pulled on his clothes,
still not fully awake, ready to respond to whatever calamity had befallen them
during the night.

By now completely awake, Jesus trotted along behind John, with Simon on
their heels. "John, for goodness' sake, tell me what's going on!"

"You'll see," John called back over his shoulder as he ran through the town.

At the edge of the village, the three men topped a small hill. "There," John
exclaimed, spreading his arms open wide, "there's what has happened in the
night."

Jesus gasped. Simon gulped. Covering the sloping hills were three or
four hundred men, women, and children sitting, standing, lying on blankets,
leaning on rocks, or milling around, the very air filled with a palpable sense of
expectancy.

"Why are they here?" Jesus asked John in a hushed voice, his eyes and mind straining to take in the sight that stretched before him.

"Jesus, they've come to see you, to listen to you, to place their sick before you. The whole region is aflame with news of your power over the storm the other night. We hear that many more are headed this way," John said in a mixture of awe and exultation, looking back and forth from Jesus to the mass of people.

"John, you know I did not calm that storm," he insisted, frustration clearly in his voice. "Adonai did that. Adonai does the healing, not me." Running his fingers through his hair, gazing dumbfounded at the mass of humanity, he exclaimed, "This is unbelievable! What will I do with all these people? When I can't do what they want, they'll get angry at me, at Adonai. We'll have trouble. The Romans will come."

"I don't know what you plan to do," John replied, still looking back and forth between Jesus and the masses, quite surprised, a bit chagrined at Jesus's confusion and obvious uncertainty, "but it'd better be soon. These folks have walked all night. They've come from villages and towns throughout the district. Some are even Greeks from the Ten Cities on the other side of the lake."

Realizing John was right, with a silent and desperate prayer to Adonai, Jesus made his way through the huge crowd, chatting with men, nodding at the women, teasing some of the young people, even picking up some small children, until he stood in its center. Every eye was on him. Only a few babies in their mothers' arms whimpered.

"Dear friends," he began, speaking forcefully so they could hear him, "you've surprised me this morning. My colleagues told me that news of the calming of the storm has brought you here. I am no magician. Our Adonai is the power. The other night, while I stood in the water and prayed, he chose to send the storm away and save the fishermen for his own reasons. Along with many people on the shore being soaked by the rain, I was praying that Adonai would stay his power and bring back the men. I felt that Adonai has special purposes for the fishermen who were caught out in the storm. I simply asked Adonai to preserve them. He chose to honor my request."

A man near Jesus spoke up in a voice that carried over much of the crowd, "Master, we've not come just because of the storm. You have special words from Adonai we need to hear."

Another echoed, "Yes, and we also have heard you have awesome ability to help sick people get well, even cure leprosy. We have many sick among us. We want you to wave your hands over them."

"Friends," he implored, a brief panic welling up inside him, "I do not just wave my hands over sick people and they get well. Adonai has allowed me to gain considerable training as a healer. I can often help people with medicines and common sense. Not everyone gets well. Many die despite my best efforts. A few I thought would surely die got well. My brother and I can also give training to people among you who want to learn about healing."

"We accept what you're saying," another man said. "Still, you know more than anyone else in these parts. We'd like for you to do what you can for our sick relatives and friends."

His spirits began to lift at their common sense and reasonable expectations. He clearly said, "I will do all I can. My brother here," pointing to Simon, "and my friend John from Capernaum have worked with me here these months, learning a great deal about how to help sick people. Between us we'll do our very best to help."

He stopped a moment to catch his breath and collect his thoughts.

"I have a suggestion," he offered. "Why don't some of you take charge and help the three of us organize this large crowd? Help the sick people get to the center of the town. The three of us will go among them and try to decide what we can and cannot do. After we've tended to some of the most distressed, we can talk about what I believe Adonai is beginning to do in our land."

Villagers from Capernaum who initially came out just to stare at the crowd immediately sensed the myriad of needs before them. Capernaum boys and girls began to give the people water to drink. Capernaum women walked crying babies while Jesus tended to the infants' family members. Some of the older Capernaum men made it their business to chat with the strangers, generally trying to make these seekers feel welcome.

Women from the pilgrim crowd offered Jesus, Simon, and John small morsels of food, which the men declined. Until well into the afternoon, among scores of sick people, the three healers worked unceasingly.

John's mother, who was with the villagers, said to the three of them in her firm, motherly way, "Sit down. Eat and drink something. Doze a few minutes under the shade. Then you'll feel more like continuing. Believe me, these people are not going anywhere."

Jesus recognized her wisdom and complied, with John and Simon eagerly following suit. After a quick meal and a short nap, Jesus stood refreshed and said, "Now it's time we open ourselves to the healing wisdom of Adonai."

Waving his arms for attention, he jumped up on a small boulder, the better to be heard. "Our sacred writings reveal a startling secret that's not really a secret: Adonai loves us. Other faiths may preach gods who are out to give human beings a hard time. That's not the way of our Adonai. His overriding passion is that we love each other. With all the evil in the world, that may sound startling, but that's what he wants.

"What's more, he wants us to treat each other with justice. He's given us everything in the world we need to live and do well. He's given us a generous earth that can more than feed us. He's given us dependable seasons that come and go with amazing regularity, with, of course, some exceptions that throw us off some of the time. Still, we know all of creation is in the hands of the Holy One. Adonai's never the author of confusion, conflict, bloodshed. We human beings cause all that trouble for each other. Our greed, loss of focus, lack of love are the sources of all that's wrong in the world. Where terrible conditions exist, he will provide leadership to make them right."

For the next couple hours he gave them practical ways they could convert their difficulties into productive, positive ways to live. "Remember the scriptures that tell us to *be as gentle as doves and as crafty as serpents*," he urged them.

"Pray directly to Adonai. You don't have to go through the elaborate and costly rituals at the temple. While we all love the temple in Jerusalem, we know that Adonai is not part of much that goes on there.

"Do not attempt armed revolution against the Romans. Adonai will enable you to have a revolution in your own spirits so you can find his new life for you. I promise you it will be more abundant than you can imagine. It will not always be easy. In fact, because of resistance by those in power, his way will often be quite hard. Just know that when you place your lives in his hands, you will find the strength for that day."

Abruptly, it seemed, the sun dropped into the west. Jesus, almost in mid-sentence, looked up, startled. He had been talking for how long? He had no idea. He stopped speaking for a moment, looked at the hillside covered with people, opened his hands to them, and said apologetically, "I have talked too long. You've listened so very well. But now it's nearly dark, and you have journeys before you. You and your children will be hungry."

Motioning to Simon and John to come stand by him, he asked them imploringly but softly so only they could hear, "Can we feed these people? Many, particularly the children, will drop before they get back to their homes."

They both looked blank. After an awkward silence, John said, "Jesus, we don't have enough food in the entire town to feed this many people on short notice. You've got hundreds and hundreds out there. We've got no choice but to send them home, praying they can make it."

"Oh, I can't do that," Jesus anguished. "What will we do?" he asked as he unconsciously looked heavenward.

In the next moment they, along with dozens in the crowd, heard the tramping of many feet, the unmistakable clatter and clink of soldiers in battle gear. In fear, all semblances of quiet gone instantly, the crowd erupted with people everywhere shouting, "The Romans are coming. They're going to slaughter us."

Pandemonium swept through the crowd.

Then Jesus saw Latvias coming over the hill, a large contingent of torch-bearing troops behind him.

When the commander saw the fright among the crowd, he ran toward Jesus, shouting, "We come in peace! Tell the people to be still. We mean them no harm." He ordered the troops to halt where they were.

Gradually, Jesus and his comrades, aided now by several men from within the crowd itself, calmed the frightened people.

When order had been restored, the centurion explained to Jesus, "We heard about the large number of people out here. At first, this morning, we thought we might have an uprising on our hands. When my scouts told me you were here and what you were doing, I decided to stay away. As the day wore on and the crowd remained, I knew they would be hungry. From our own supplies we have brought bread and other food for them. We want to feed them and then send them on their way home. Even though they are peaceful, I never know what can trigger violence. Better to show them our concern than to run the risk of a fight. Besides, you've shown nothing but a generous spirit to my men and me."

On his signal, the soldiers fanned out among the crowd, distributing the food.

When all had received something to eat, the centurion said to Jesus, "Now do us all a favor," he motioned toward the crowd, "and send these people to their homes."

Before Jesus could thank the Roman, he and his soldiers were gone.

———

Jesus was showing a young boy how to turn a bowl on a lathe when he looked up to see a familiar man whom he had not seen for three years or more coming toward him. Instantly, his excitement at seeing Joses of Arimathea gave way to a rising sense of dread. Joses would not have come to Capernaum accidentally nor for a friendly visit.

Patting the boy on the shoulder, Jesus said, "Let's finish this later. An old friend is coming this way. He and I will need to talk. Will that be all right with you?"

Joses and Jesus greeted each other warmly, memories of many shared experiences flooding over them. After an exchange of pleasantries, Jesus said, "I could not be happier to see you. At the risk of sounding rude, though, I must ask why you have come. This is certainly not just a visit with an old friend."

"You are right, of course," Joses replied gravely, looking at Jesus hesitantly. "John is dead, executed by Herod Antipas a few days ago."

"Oh, Joses. Not John! Executed!"

Reeling from the news, Jesus turned and stumbled toward the shore of the lake, where he stood still for a long time, looking out across the gently lapping waters. After a while Joses saw him drop to his knees. With his head in his hands, Jesus wept like he had when his father, his other great friend, died.

When he had better control of himself, Jesus wanted to know, "Why? True, John preached a strong message. He'd never hurt a fly. You've got to tell me what happened."

"After you left, John's preaching became even more fiery," Joses explained. "He called down Adonai and all his angels on just about everyone in authority. Great numbers up and down the river continued to follow him. He and his companions from Bethlehem never stopped baptizing. By now, thousands of our people have received baptism, including myself," he said self-consciously.

"Soon, as you might expect, Herod Antipas and the high priest began to let it be known they were rapidly running out of patience with John. He grew extremely agitated at the way John seemed to draw the populace away from his rule. His constant attacks on the temple ways of worship got the high priest and his lackeys on high alert."

"But he was so popular. Did Herod and Caiaphas have no regard for the feelings of the people?" Jesus interjected.

"In the end it made no difference. John began to howl at Herod Antipas for marrying Herodias. She's actually his own niece. That's incest by strict Jewish standards. To make it worse, she's also the divorced wife of one of Antipas's half-brothers. Rumor has it that Herodias began to badger Herod to stifle John."

"That's a bad situation. Still, something must have finally snapped to prompt Antipas to go to such extreme measures," Jesus said.

"Despite all our efforts to hold him back, when Antipas and Herodias came to Bethany beyond the Jordan for a royal visit, John confronted them at the city gates. He called them adulterers, blasphemers, abominations of desolation, to remember but a few of the insults he laid on them. Within a couple days John had been arrested and clapped in prison at Machaerus. That was a few months ago. Different ones of us managed to get in to see him fairly often. As you can imagine, he hated being in prison. He had hardly been inside a house in years. Prison was suffocating."

"Go on," Jesus urged Joses.

"Before I finish the story, let me tell you a very important tale."

Joses stood up and paced a moment to compose himself.

"The last time I saw him, John asked, 'When have you seen Jesus?' I said it had been probably three or four years.

"Then John looked me squarely in the eyes and said, 'Whatever happens to me is of little importance. I know now my job was actually to get Jesus started. That's done. I want you to find him. Ask him if he is the one or if we should look for another. If I am still around, come back and give me his answer.'"

Once again, Jesus choked down his emotions. He looked away for several moments, thinking again of the irascible, gifted, powerful man of Adonai. He called up those heated debates while they were teenagers. He recoiled at Joseph's death while thanking Adonai for John's vision to rescue Jesus from the cross that killed his father. He grimaced yet smiled at the memory of John showing up at this house in Alexandria. Tears flowed down Jesus's face.

"Now he's gone!" Joses grieved, his own anger and hurt overtaking him in the moment of retelling. "During one of Herod's ridiculous, obscene, extravagant parties, they all got drunk, and as a lark, as entertainment, Herod ordered John beheaded. We hear they came parading into the banquet hall with his severed head on a silver platter."

"How awful! What a frightful waste. How heartless and capricious!" Jesus exploded in frustration, pounding a fist into the palm of the other hand.

"What happened then?" Jesus wanted to know, heavy lines of grief etching his face.

"Riots broke out all over the area. Antipas had to call in a few dozen Roman soldiers to quiet things down. A couple of the younger, more hot-headed men got themselves crucified for their part in the chaos," Joses said, shaking his head in dismay.

After a few more minutes venting their grief, Joses, in an effort to change the subject to something less traumatic, said with as much lightness as he could muster, "Anyway, Jesus, I've kept part of the bargain. I've found you, though it was not much of a task. Your fame has spread all the way down the Jordan River valley to Jerusalem, Bethany beyond the Jordan, and points in between. Your work goes before you."

At Jesus's insistence, Joses remained several days in Capernaum, meeting Simon, John, the centurion, and the brothers Cephas and Andrew.

When he finally had to leave, Joses embraced Jesus, stepped back, and asked, "Well, Jesus, are you the one, or do we look for another?"

"I'm not sure which 'one' John was asking about," Jesus replied with great care.

"If John were still alive," Joses said, "I would tell him what you are doing here, your healing, teaching, helping people find new lives even though their conditions are beyond difficult. I'd let him judge for himself. I have the strong hunch John would have decided he had found the One."

# Chapter Eight

# The Itinerant

*A wandering Aramean was my ancestor.*

Jesus and Cephas had begun to talk nearly every day in the aftermath of the storm episode. Fishing was both Cephas's business and passion, so he spent all the time he could out on the water or tending his nets and the two boats he and his family owned. Jesus made a point to be near the fisherman as he performed the endless landward tasks required by his profession, which meant they frequently talked while Cephas worked. The two men quickly developed an unusually strong, mutually reinforcing friendship despite, or perhaps building on, their dramatic differences in temperament. Jesus was turning increasingly into himself in his unfolding spiritual winnowing process. Cephas readily admitted to an almost complete lack of introspection. Still, the fisherman felt powerfully drawn to this inner-driven healer and teacher. Jesus found in the tanned, ruggedly good-looking, strong, compassionate Cephas the kind of man who would go the limits if the moment or the friendship demanded it.

Jesus had also come to appreciate Andrew, Cephas's younger brother. Jesus experienced in him a person of unstinting generosity, possessed of an all-embracing empathy, abetted by an abundance of common sense and innate ability to organize. Though he had always lived in the shadow of his older brother, no one who knew the two of them doubted Andrew's own strong personality. In fact, Andrew showed a much greater propensity to understand the nuances of Jesus's message about the present and future movement of Adonai than did his extrovert brother. Cephas wanted to go out and get the job done, whatever the job was. Andrew came to sense the subtleties of Jesus's task. Perhaps Jesus recognized in the two brothers two sides of an important coin. Andrew could envision and structure the task. Cephas had the energy and determination to carry out the assignment when he got it clearly in mind. It would take both of them, both types, Jesus concluded, to make much impact on the people.

Simon and John knew the day was coming, and probably soon, when Jesus would leave Capernaum. They talked about it often between themselves while waiting for the right opportunity to discuss the next direction with Jesus himself.

"The time will come when I will leave," he agreed one day as he and Simon talked. "That idea makes you uncomfortable?"

"Maybe not uncomfortable," Simon said. "I do not worry about personal comfort anymore. I wonder why it's necessary. You have people coming in droves from the entire region. You've earned the love and respect of everyone except a handful of the hard-headed locals. You've developed several able helpers with both of your parents who can expand your healing and teaching work. Why use up time and energy going to another place to start over again?"

"Simon, I'm not thinking of just going to another town and starting again," he explained, looking at his brother whom he had come to love quite beyond their family ties. "I'm thinking of going from one small town to another. Becoming an itinerant."

"You're what?" Simon asked incredulously. "Jesus, that would be a terrible waste. You know how people regard most of those vagabond preachers who roam from one place to another. The people don't trust them. They're just out for free food from gullible followers."

"I know what you're saying. Still, that is the way I am leaning," Jesus stated unequivocally. "I believe that's my next step."

Jesus hesitated a moment, took a deep breath, and asked, "Will you go with me?"

"How could you even ask!" his brother demanded, momentarily taken aback. "Of course I will go with you. I will go with you to the mountains, to the sea, even into the jaws of death if that's where you go." Then with a wry smile he said, "Can't say that such a roving life has a lot of charm for me. I like one house and one dry place to sleep. Make no mistake, though; I'm with you regardless."

Jesus grabbed his younger brother in a bear hug, saying, "Thank you, Simon. I will need you."

The next day, John made a point to draw Jesus aside. He stumbled a moment, kicked the rock at his foot, looked Jesus in the face, and said, "Look, Simon and I were talking. He told me you were thinking of leaving Capernaum, of roaming the countryside for a while." Then catching himself, "I hope that's not a family secret."

Smiling, Jesus said, "No, it's not a family secret."

"Well, I want to go with you." Hurrying on, he stammered eagerly, "I know the area. My family has relatives and friends everywhere. You know, I'd do anything you say. Carry your bundles, cook your meals, tend to the animals, whatever. But I would surely like to go with you."

Taken aback at his devotion, Jesus replied, "John, you can most surely go. You should know, though, that we will not have any bundles, no animals, no money. We're going out with only the clothes on our backs and our staffs. Adonai will supply our food. The foxes may have their lairs. We will have no regular place to lay our heads at night."

Surprised by Jesus's statement, the inconvenience, the discomfort of such meager living dawning on him, he paused, reflected briefly, then declared with a resolve that came from his own depths, "Master, that's all right with me. To be near you, to be part of what I've seen you do here will more than offset the poor food and hard ground. When do we leave?"

"Not right yet," Jesus answered him, placing his arm around the younger man's shoulder. "I too am ready. It seems that Adonai has not quite made up his mind."

A few days later, Jesus was by the lake when Cephas and his small crew of fishermen rowed their boat to the shore. Looking both tired and disgusted, Cephas nonetheless grinned when he saw Jesus sitting casually on the ground watching the timeless procedure of pulling the boat up on the bank, spreading out the nets on racks to dry, and setting onto the shore the baskets containing the day's catch.

"Hello, Jesus," Cephas hailed. "Can't find any sick people to make well?" he asked, teasing.

Jesus grinned at the big, free-spirited, open-hearted man. "Everyone in the whole district's well this afternoon, so I thought I'd come see what I can do for you. From the look on your face when you pulled in, it seems to me you need all the help you can get," Jesus observed with a grin.

"By the way," Jesus said, "how was the catch? Did you leave any fish in the whole lake?"

Cephas's face again darkened for a moment. "Hardly worth going out today," he complained. "Nothing. But that's the way it goes sometimes," the experienced fisherman admitted. "You got any wisdom on the fine art of fishing?"

"Not really," Jesus answered. "I've never been fishing. I've spent some time on the water sailing the coast of the Great Sea a couple times and going up and down the Nile. Even learned to swim in the river. Great fun. But I've never been out on your lake."

Instantly brightening, Cephas said, "Well, that's about to change, right now. Hang your cloak on that post," he said, pointing to one of the drying racks, "hitch up your drawers, and get ready to go fishing."

Again, Jesus laughed out loud. "You mean right now?"

"Let's go," Cephas ordered. Looking at his brother and cousin, he said, "Trusty crew, we're going out again. Let's teach this landlubber what it's like on our lake."

With a good-natured shrug, the two men sent the day's meager catch to the market for sale while it was still daylight, reloaded the gear in the boat, and shoved off.

Jesus loved the feeling of being on the lake. With the combination of rowing aided by the small sail, they were soon well out on the breast of the waters, the distant shore only a thin sliver in the fading light.

"Now," Cephas said when he had reached his favorite fishing area, "we'll give you a lesson on fishing." He proceeded to instruct Jesus in how to cast a net, wait for it to settle just right, then pull it back. "Let's see if you are as good a fisherman as you are healer."

For a couple hours they cast this way and that yet caught hardly anything. Finally, Jesus said, "Cephas, I'm tired. I didn't come along to work anyway. I just want a nice ride," he teased, settling down in the stern of the small craft to watch them labor in the light of the half-moon that had risen, giving the still lake a breathtaking, ephemeral beauty. For a while longer Jesus simply let the delight of the moment flood over him, filling his mind and soul with the wonders of Adonai's creation.

Still, the men's nets came back nearly empty.

Cephas said to Jesus, his big voice carrying across the waters, "Well, you've not brought us any luck. You do a pretty good job of healing, but you're a sorry fisherman," he boomed with laughter.

"I never told you I knew anything about fishing," Jesus answered, equally as lighthearted.

"Tell you what, Jesus," Cephas replied, "I'm going to try one more time. If nothing happens, we're going home. Wet tails but no fish."

"Go ahead," Jesus said. "I'll just lie here and watch you sweat."

Gathering the net in the time-honored way, Cephas took a deep breath and cast off to the port side of the boat. Instantly, everyone in the boat heard loud splashes as fish tumbled into Cephas's net.

"Quick!" he yelled. "You boys come help me! I'm about to be yanked into the lake!"

As a glorious dawn broke over the lake, Jesus worked alongside the fishermen, cleaning and preparing the astounding catch for the day's market. They had laughed and teased and jostled each other like boys. Fishing was cathartic for Jesus, a moment of fresh definition. He realized that he had not laughed, had fun, felt so free and unburdened in an unconscionably long time. It felt good in his body and spirit just to do the routine, almost mindless work of flailing fish with three close friends. Right then, for the moment at least, they needed nothing from him. They would have survived without a backward glance if they had again caught nothing. They enjoyed good fortune, the smile of Adonai on their enterprise. In every way the night had illuminated Jesus's soul to the wonders of Adonai, to the mysterious ways in which he chose to work. Jesus would long cherish the moonlit adventure on the lake.

Cephas, likewise, found something new in the moment. Given his lack of reflection, it took him a while to sort through his feelings and gain a measure of perspective on the successful expedition. In keeping with his nature, once having pulled his thoughts together, he began to talk. "Jesus, it was wonderful on the lake with you. I hope we can do it again soon. Even if we don't have a banner catch, I'd like to spend all the time I can with you."

Jesus appreciated Cephas's affirmation and dawning grasp of the new ways Adonai seemed to be opening. At the same time Jesus chose simply to remain quiet as his great friend's thoughts found words, something itself new for the fisherman.

"It's beginning to dawn on my dull brain," Cephas opined, "that Adonai is doing something very unusual, strange, important in you. I can't begin to put it all together. Everyone who's around you agrees; you have special standing with the Holy One. They just don't know what it means."

Jesus smiled and said, "Cephas, you've just moved inside my own head. I agree on both counts—something unusual and uncertainty about what it means and where it will go."

Cephas laid down his fish knife, looked at Jesus, and said, "The word's around town that you are planning to leave soon. To go on some sort of traveling preaching and healing mission."

"That's true," Jesus agreed.

"I wish you wouldn't go," Cephas said.

"I wish I didn't have to go," Jesus said with a sigh.

Several weeks passed with nothing more said about Jesus leaving Capernaum. One night as Jesus and Simon lay on their cots drifting off to sleep, Jesus said, almost casually, "It's getting close to the time when I must leave. You don't think much of my idea of moving around. That's what I've got to do, though, Simon."

Jesus was soon snoring gently.

Simon tossed until almost dawn.

—

"I want to go with you. No, I *must* go with you," Cephas declared in a tone that let Jesus know the fisherman had been thinking about this possibility for some time.

"But you have a family, a wife and children. A business. What will happen to them if you strike out across the countryside with me?" Jesus wanted to know, genuine concern in his voice.

"I've thought of that, of course," he allowed. "My parents will look after my wife and children. Andrew and our cousin Judas will keep fishing. Maybe I can come home every so often and catch another one of our big boatloads to help out."

Andrew and Judas both said they also wanted to accompany Jesus on his travels.

Surprised to learn that either one, much less both, wanted to go with him, Jesus told them, "You will have to work that out among yourselves. If you can both go, that's fine with me. If one needs to stay here and help with family responsibilities, that's for you to decide."

To Judas's dismay and obvious irritation, he was persuaded by the two brothers to remain in Capernaum.

"Judas," Andrew tried to console him, "I'll come back regularly and let you pick up with Jesus. You've just married. Your wife will have a baby soon. You need to stay here."

Not to be so easily deterred, Judas countered, saying, "She's got her family. Her parents. A house full of sisters to help with the baby. I really want to go. Something big is going to happen, and I want to be there. Anyway, I hate this little town. It's stifling. There's a whole world out there, and I want to see some of it. Jesus is going to make a big stir. I want to be in the middle of it."

When Jesus and his small band of helpers made their departure, Judas pulled Andrew aside and said vehemently, "Don't forget me. I'll do more than my part here. But come back soon and relieve me."

As Jesus and Simon left Capernaum at dawn, John and the brothers Cephas and Andrew accompanied them. Without intending to, Jesus had garnered a following.

Among themselves they had asked, "Where do we go first?"

If Jesus knew, he was not saying.

When Jesus began heading almost due north from Capernaum, Cephas, after a while, mustered the spunk to ask, "Jesus, are we by chance going to Chorazin? It looks like we're headed in that direction."

"Yes, that's right, Cephas. That seems where we ought to go for now. I don't know anything about the town. Since it's fairly close to Capernaum, I thought some of the villagers might have been down to find out what we were doing. With the possibility that some connections are already established, it seemed like a logical starting place," he explained, at the same time telling and asking Cephas.

"I don't want to question your judgment, Jesus," the fisherman replied carefully, trying to find his footing with the leader, especially during their first day. "But that's a tough place."

"Well, Cephas, let's just see what happens," Jesus answered, just a bit hard-headed himself, Cephas thought.

Jesus and his men walked into the village square at midday. The sight of five strangers appearing into the town with no bundles, no bags, just staffs and the clothes on their backs, sent a wave of uneasiness through the entire village. With most of the town's men out in the fields working, the women felt vulnerable.

It was not customary for a woman to speak to a strange man, especially with no other village men around. After a moment of awkward silence, one large, middle-aged woman put down her water jug. She covered the lower part of her face as her mother had taught her to do when meeting strangers, walked brusquely toward Jesus, the obvious leader, and asked defiantly, "And what are you able-bodied men doing here in the middle of the day? Why aren't you out working like all respectable men?"

Startled, Jesus nonetheless smiled and said, "My sister, we mean no one any harm. We are from Capernaum. Adonai has set us on a mission."

"I am not your sister. I am Huldah. My husband is the leader of the synagogue," she snapped back. "If it's any of your business, we're already faithful to Adonai and do not need the likes of you to tell us anything about him. Besides, from the way you talk, I can tell you're a foreigner. We don't need people from other parts to come snooping around here."

Cephas, angry at her rudeness, spoke up quickly, saying, "Woman, this is Jesus from Nazareth. He's a man of Adonai, sent by him to do mighty things for all of us, the people of Israel. In Capernaum he's healed the sick, taught many of our villagers how to make a better life, and opened the Holy Scriptures to us in ways none of us had ever known before. If you ask me, he can even calm storms, and he's the luckiest fishing buddy in the whole world."

Momentarily mollified when she recognized Cephas's native accent, she said, "Well, our men are working. I don't know what you want to do here, but you can't do it til they get home tonight. For now, we've got work to do."

After giving Jesus and his men one more disapproving scowl, she faced the village women who had collected silently and were listening to the tart exchange. "Now go on, all of you. Don't stand there gawking. You've seen beggars and shiftless do-gooders before. Go home."

"Welcome to Chorazin," Cephas said to Jesus, a broad, knowing grin on his face.

"It's early yet," Jesus answered defensively, irritation and frustration in his own voice.

Simon, John, and Andrew shifted a bit uneasily, saying to themselves, "This traveling ministry thing might not be such a good idea after all."

With the town square suddenly empty, Jesus and his friends did not quite know what to do with themselves. They realized the woman was at least partly in her rights to raise an alarm. They must have looked bizarre, even frightening coming into Chorazin in the middle of the day unannounced.

In the meantime these hearty young men had more on their minds than the angry reaction of the village's female bully. They were hungry and thirsty. When no one in the town had the decency to offer them anything to eat, Jesus's four companions, despite his insistence that they take no food, rather sheepishly began pulling small stashes of food from within their cloaks. John pulled out a lump of hard cheese and a small loaf of bread. Simon had brought dried figs along with a small pouch of parched grain. Andrew and Cephas produced a few small salted fish. They hesitated, looking at Jesus to see his reaction to their disobedience. He looked discouraged for a moment, then threw his head back laughing, saying loudly, "Boys, let's eat." All five of them unceremoniously plopped down on the curb of the well and began to devour their stash of food.

None dared ask Jesus what they would eat next, or when, since this was all the food they had brought with them. When he did not look concerned, they decided likewise to put aside their questions about their next meal.

After they had eaten, Jesus grew quiet. An hour or so later, while Andrew, Simon, and John napped, Jesus said to Cephas, who sat next to him, "It seems to me we ought to stay here until the men come in. I'll talk with the leader of the synagogue and try to determine if we need to stay around for a while."

Chorazin, like Nazareth and hundreds of other villages in Galilee, was tiny. The shabby mud brick and native stone houses stood bunched closely together, many sharing common walls, the houses opening onto a maze of courtyards and small alleys. Unlike Capernaum, which had a measure of attractiveness, situated as it was on the shores of the lake, Chorazin was brown, squat, cluttered, and obviously poor.

"They need a message of hope for the future," Andrew told Jesus. "We walked around a bit. We met fear and hostility on the faces of all we saw."

"But will they hear it?" pondered John.

"We'll soon find out," Jesus observed.

As the men returned from the fields toward sundown, it was apparent someone from the village had gone out and informed them of the presence of outsiders. Jesus went out to meet the men, trying to discern who the leaders were among the men as they trudged homeward, exhausted after a day of trying to extract a living from the fertile but resistant soil.

Jesus spoke first, ever so hesitantly, trying to get his bearings. "I am Jesus from Nazareth. My friends come mostly from Capernaum. We are here to offer Adonai's help and direction."

An older, wrinkled, yet dignified man stepped forward to meet Jesus. "I am Elihaz, the headman of the village. We welcome you and extend our meager hospitality to you," he said formally, caution bordering on anger unmistakable in his tone.

Cephas, standing some yards back from Jesus with his three companions, whispered to Simon, "Talk about the snows of Mt. Carmel; this is it." Simon had to look away quickly, lest the villagers see him giggle at Cephas's sarcasm.

"We've not come to intrude," Jesus assured him in the hearing of the men who had bunched in tightly, the better to understand what was happening. "In other places we've been able to offer healing to some of the sick. Adonai is bringing new and wonderful directions to many people in our land these days. We'd like the privilege of telling you what we have seen and heard."

Elihaz answered just as arrogantly as before, "We have sick people, but we take care of them ourselves. We have our own teachers, and I don't know that we need to listen to you."

Dashed as he had never been before, deflated, brought down, Jesus replied in a voice barely above a whisper, "I respect your judgment. We will leave immediately."

"Leave immediately and insult our hospitality!" the headman snapped angrily. "Chorazin will extend to you the courtesy of the ages. You will eat with us tonight. We will hear your message from Adonai. We will provide a place for you to sleep. Tomorrow you may leave. It will not be said of our town that we turned away strangers."

Later that evening, the meal completed, amid almost total silence, the leader of the synagogue stood and said with no feeling of warmth or expectation, "Now we will hear from Jesus. He says he has words from Adonai we need to hear."

The cluster of men sitting on the ground or leaning against the walls of the houses surrounding the courtyard where the Sabbath gathering of the synagogue took place listened indifferently to Jesus's words about the present and coming movement of Adonai in their midst that would bring all the faithful into a closer walk with the Holy One.

As Jesus began to explain that Adonai's love extended to all people, not just the house of Jacob, he could feel an uneasy stirring in the group.

"Adonai is concerned about everyone: Jew, Syrian, Phoenician, Egyptian, Greek, and Roman."

When he said *Roman*, a voice erupted from the darkness of the courtyard, "No, not the Romans. My Adonai hates Romans."

An angry undercurrent moved through the men.

When the leader of the synagogue stood and frowned at the men, they grew quiet. Coolly, he said to Jesus, "You may proceed."

The already strained session came to an abrupt end when Jesus began to explain that they needed to pay more attention to how they treated each other rather than simply to labor under the multitude of rules governing purity, strangers, and worship at the temple in Jerusalem.

"That's going too far, young man," a withered old farmer growled as, with effort, he rose to his feet.

"I am of the Pharisees. I'm born and bred here, but I'm trained in the ways of Adonai as a Pharisee. You are dead wrong on all those points. I'll see you driven out of town before I'll sit here and listen to one more blasphemous word from you. It's bad enough for you to dare say that our Adonai has any feeling for Romans. For you to question, to dare question, our sacred purity laws and to suggest we don't owe absolute allegiance to the temple is too much!" And he screeched again, "Too much!" With that the old man stalked out of the gathering with all the dignity his tired, frail body could muster. Immediately, everyone else rose and silently followed him.

As a parting diatribe, Elihaz said between his teeth, "Well, Jesus of Nazareth, I guess you know what Chorazin thinks of your wonderful word from Adonai! You sleep here tonight. No one will bother you. I cannot guarantee your safety past tomorrow's sunrise."

Well before first light the next morning, Jesus and his men were on their way out of Chorazin with Jesus still struggling under the weight of the rejection. "We could have done so much with them," he moaned.

The mood of the four companions did not match that of Jesus. They tried diligently not to let him know how glad they were to be out of the town, to have Chorazin at their backs. Because Jesus was so pained, they felt they should be distressed also, but they were young and energetic with a sense of high adventure too much on them to let one setback throw them completely off track.

With the village an hour or more behind them, while Jesus still struggled with the disappointment, Cephas spoke up, saying soberly, "Well, good friends," and he hesitated while they waited expectantly for the profound insight they were sure was about to be uttered, "I have only one thing to say. Adonai bless and strengthen Huldah's husband, whoever he might be. That man needs all the help from on high he can get."

Stunned for a moment at Cephas's irreverence, Jesus and the other three stopped in the middle of the road, looked at the fishermen, then all broke into laughter as mental images of Huldah and her husband came to mind.

When they had regained some measure of composure, Andrew said, "Look, we don't know what's out there." And he waved his arms in a wide arc. "But we'll have to be ready. More prepared than we were going into that place," pointing back toward Chorazin. "I've been thinking about a couple things. For one, we probably shouldn't go into a town in the middle of the day. Go in late in the afternoon as the men are coming home. No need to stir up folks' fears."

"That's a good idea," agreed Simon.

"And," Andrew went on, "maybe we should think about towns where we know somebody or have some history of friendly contact. To walk in cold like we did in Chorazin may be putting too much burden on ourselves and on the people of the village."

"Smart thinking, all the way around," Jesus agreed, gratitude effusing through him for the willingness of the men seriously to share his mission. "Let's sit down under the trees over there and make a plan. I'll try to listen carefully to Adonai, but I'll certainly try hard to listen to you four." Looking into each face fondly, he said, "It's no accident the five of us are together."

Their hastily devised strategy on the heels of the Chorazin disaster guided them on what became a six-month journey to the villages of Acchabare, Sepph, Bersabe, Ginnear, and other small, unremarkable communities more or less northwest of Capernaum. They drew heavily from lessons bitterly learned in Chorazin. They constantly grew in their collective understanding how better to do the work to which they believed Adonai had called them. Through their mutual commitment to each other, Jesus and his companions were able to experience the veritable hand of the Holy One on their lives. In not one town they subsequently visited did they meet the measure of hostility they encountered in Chorazin. Rather, everywhere they went, the five men were able to effect substantive changes.

Invariably, to his constant consternation, on every hand, though his reception was overwhelmingly favorable, Jesus encountered opposition from the strict purists, especially the Pharisees. These few objected to the way Jesus touched sick people. They did not like his loose attitude toward the rules and regulations governing worship. Most of all, his eagerness to eat with any who invited him drove the Pharisees to distraction.

Jesus chose never to fight back, electing rather to deal with their criticisms in a straightforward manner. Once, when Cephas got into a shoving match with one of the more persistent of these religious purists, Jesus irritably lectured him, "Cephas, that's no good! Think about it. These Pharisees genuinely love Adonai. They've gone to seed on a few of the narrower teachings of the scriptures and of our ways. They don't want to lose what they regard as essential. My words sound like a threat, though they really are not. Love these people. Deal with them. If necessary, pass them on by. But you just cannot hit them. Do I make myself clear?" He caught his breath, then said very evenly to his dear friend, "If you don't hear me, you cannot stay with me."

Stricken by Jesus's rebuke and utterly chagrined at the thought of having to leave, Cephas hung his head. "I promise. But they make me so mad!"

"They make me mad too. But to go at them, anger to anger, blindness to blindness, is just not the way."

—

The scope of their efforts expanded. To the degree that Jesus had initially conceptualized his calling, he envisioned traveling from village to village doing what he could for a few days at a time, then moving on. In fact, they often spent weeks in one village with the net effect that small groups of men and women were established throughout the region who simply appropriated Jesus's methods and teachings. When he journeyed to the next place, these local clusters took up where he left off.

Jesus's men had never known such satisfaction from work. Days flowed by. Always, the people clamored to see him, hear him, touch him. The four men with him, likewise, drew deep satisfaction from their rewarding if exhausting work. Never had they dreamed of meaning so much to anyone other than their own families. Now, every day, hundreds were present for healing, training, dreaming, and teaching.

After six months of this nonstop itinerant work, Cephas and the others, gradually at first, then more clearly, began to notice a distinct change in Jesus. He became increasingly compulsive, frantic, as if he were running a fiercely competitive race against an unseen, unremitting opponent. To the amazement of the tiny band, the response of the people to his healing and teaching increased dramatically. Delegations from neighboring towns constantly pleaded with Jesus to come their way. The needs of the people and their willing embrace of his message served to intensify his desperate efforts to comply with their requests. He ate and slept only fitfully. In every way it was obvious to all but himself that Jesus was becoming precariously stretched, emotionally and physically.

The frenetic pace all came to a head one day when the family of a dying girl, in their grief, furiously demanded Jesus perform another of his miracles and save their child. He became uncharacteristically angry and informed them in no uncertain terms that he was no miracle worker and could do nothing for their dear one.

Standing nearby, Cephas eased his friend away from the family and said, "Jesus, not long ago, you lectured me on the need to stay calm. Now it's my turn. You're about to lose control. You've got to have some rest. The four of us have been talking. We're taking you home to Capernaum for a short time. You're going to rest, fish, sleep, eat good food, and get yourself renewed. It's time. You've not stopped day and night for months."

Jesus snapped, "No, you listen to me. These people need me. In case you haven't caught on yet, Cephas, my time is short."

Cephas, stabbed by Jesus's sharp retort and grim prediction, reeled for a moment.

Jesus charged on, his fury unabated, "If you're tired, you go home!"

Cephas, recovered, grabbed Jesus by the arm in a vise grip. "No, that's not the way it's going to be. I heard John's mother tell you a long time ago, 'Rest awhile. The people will be here when you get back.' Jesus, we've only begun this work. We've got years ahead of us." Growing quiet, he released his friend's arm and said imploringly, "We love you. We don't want you to die before your time."

In that moment, never had Jesus loved any person more than he did the fisherman. "Cephas," relief and resignation suddenly in his voice, his face relaxing for the first time in weeks, "you win. I am terribly tired. We will go to Capernaum for a few days. All of us need to stop. I am selfish to push you four so hard. But understand this." He looked Cephas squarely in his strong face. "I do not feel that I've got years to get my job done. I'm not being morbid. It's simply that my time is far more limited than yours."

While Cephas was happy for Jesus's willingness to rest, he did look at his friend with a quizzical look. What did he mean about his time being limited? An uneasiness lodged itself in the pit of the big man's stomach that would become an unwelcome if familiar companion.

The Capernaum villagers enthusiastically welcomed Jesus and his friends home. They shouted and waved at him, the nearest to a hero ever to emerge in Capernaum.

From back in the crowds that lined the narrow streets, the village representatives of the Pharisees watched Capernaum's ecstasy with discomfort. Lackeys of the high priest made mental notes of the joyful welcome to report to Jerusalem. From a high hill that overlooked Capernaum, Latvias, the centurion, through narrowed eyes, ever on the alert for any signs of trouble, also anxiously studied the hoopla.

After a month's rest, Jesus and the men set out again, this time accompanied by Judas, his excitement boundless at the prospect of the adventure. He hardly paused to bid his wife and baby girl goodbye in his haste to join the small entourage as it headed out of Capernaum and journeyed in a southwesterly direction skirting the lake shore.

# Chapter Nine

# The Gathering Up

*Let us burst their bonds asunder, and cast their cords from us.*

After meandering for several weeks, stopping at first one tiny hamlet after another, Jesus and his companions came to the town of Magdala on the western shores of Galilee Lake, situated on the Tiberius highway, like Capernaum, a fishing and trading town. Since it was early in the afternoon, Jesus and his band stopped on the edge of the town, waiting until nearer sundown before entering.

At dusk Jesus and the five companions made their way into Magdala. They asked a fisherman on his way to the market with a basket of dried fish to point them to the headman or the leader of the synagogue.

"They're one and the same," the fisherman said. "His name is Aram. He owns that large warehouse down toward the shore." He pointed toward a clump of dumpy buildings that had obviously been built over a long period of time and haphazardly joined together.

Jesus approached the main door just as an older man, standing between two younger men, workers no doubt, was preparing to close and lock it for the evening. When he saw Jesus and his men approaching, the merchant looked up and said, "My lords, may I be of service to you? I am Aram and this," he motioned toward the warehouses, "is my establishment."

"We come as friends with a generous word from Adonai," Jesus said cordially yet with unmistakable authority.

"Pardon my interruption, friend," Aram interjected. "My business puts me in contact with people of many regions. You sound like you're from the area around Sepphoris, from Nazareth or another of the villages over to the west from here."

"As a matter of fact," Jesus replied, smiling incredulously, "I am from Nazareth."

"No, I do not connect you with Nazareth. Maybe Sepphoris?" queried Aram, now resolutely determined to make the connection he sought.

"My late father and my brothers and I have done much work for people in Sepphoris building furniture and other objects from wood," Jesus offered.

Then with a new light in his eyes, Aram asked, "By any chance do you know an Egyptian named Seti? He is a good friend with whom I have done business for several years."

"Seti is my dearest friend outside my own family," Jesus replied, warming up to Aram.

"Jesus. Now I have it. You are the precocious young man Seti has talked about when we would meet on occasion. In fact," he mused further, "some time ago, Seti sent Albinus asking me if I had any information about a charlatan who had beat your family out of a considerable sum of money. Am I on the right track?"

"My lord Aram, you are precisely on track. I am not sure about the 'precocious' tag, but I am that Jesus, and this is Simon, one of my brothers," Jesus assured him, his voice now full of wonder and surprise.

Recovering from his initial shock, the merchant reclaimed his manners and spluttered, "What a joy, an unexpected joy to meet you, Jesus. And your brother and friends." Then toning down, Aram said, "I'm babbling. Being unforgivably inhospitable. You and your friends must come to my house. My wife and daughter will be pleased to see you and would be honored to prepare a simple meal for you. You will come home with me, won't you?"

"We are many, Aram," Jesus demurred, going through the traditional motions of not appearing too eager to accept an invitation. "It would be too much of an intrusion."

"Nonsense," Aram replied. "You must accompany me."

Glancing at the faces of his young men, knowing they were hungry and tired, feeling their eagerness to settle down for the evening, Jesus said, "Thank you, Aram. We will go to your house."

"Welcome to my humble house," Aram announced when they were in the beautifully appointed courtyard. "I wish it were better suited to such distinguished guests. Be that as it may, what I do have is at your disposal," he declared with a cordial bow.

Following the timeless, unwritten rules of protocol, Jesus replied, "Quite to the contrary, Brother Aram, this is a lovely home. Adonai has been quite good to give you such a place. It is a testimony to your stewardship."

During these greetings, two women had appeared in the doorway of the main house. Knowing they were there because they were supposed to be there,

Aram said, without looking at either of them, "Permit me to present my wife and daughter."

"This is my wife, Abigail."

She bowed before the men.

"And this is my daughter, Mary."

She too bowed before the men.

"This is Jesus of Nazareth. He is a dear friend and protégé of Seti, the Egyptian from Sepphoris with whom I do business. Seti has talked with me about Jesus and his unusual abilities. Now Adonai has brought this same person to our doorstep," Aram declared, awe and respect already marking a deference toward Jesus.

Jesus responded naturally, gratefully to their welcome. He knew instantly he had found the camaraderie he would need to extend the work of Adonai in this town.

He also found and felt something else he had never known before: the unfamiliar, unsought stirring of love, yearning, even hunger for a woman. No, *this* woman standing before him. The powerful sensation startled, unnerved, unsettled him. For a moment he could not think. There she stood, surpassing all the Egyptian women who had surrounded him, younger than himself by three or four years, beautiful, slim, dark hair, smooth skin, proper in her manners, at the same time full of strength, resolve, courage and spirituality. His vision became maddeningly blurred.

As if on signal, breaking Jesus's spell, from the shadows a servant appeared with a pan of water and fresh towels for the men to wash away the dust of the day's travels. Mary, who gave no hint of noticing Jesus's wide-eyed appraisal, and Abigail placed wine and small cakes before them on a low table. "Please be comfortable while we prepare the meal," the women invited the men.

Both women ached to remain in the courtyard and listen to the conversation. Rather, duty called them to food preparation. They also knew that, later in the evening, Aram would tell them everything.

After more pleasant exchanges, Aram said, "Jesus, it is anything but coincidental that you have come to our town. Adonai has sent you here. I would be honored if you told me your plans."

With that invitation, Jesus, consciously shaking himself free of the rapturous vision of Mary, gave Aram a sketch of his relationship with Seti. With animation he related what that friendship had wrought in his life and the broad outline of what happened to and through him since returning home.

"Oh, Jesus, this is wondrous," Aram said enthusiastically, his eyes lighting up, unconsciously clapping his hands. "My own spirit has cried out for a deeper encounter with Adonai. Frankly, in our synagogue, even though I am the leader, we've grown stale. We seem to be doing the same thing over and over again without much meaning. You've certainly come along at the right time for many of us."

"Aram," Jesus said cautiously, "we've begun long-lasting work just about everywhere we've been. To my amazement and gratitude, at least a handful of people in almost every village we've visited have caught the vision and are building on what we started with them."

He pondered, then continued, "But not without a cost. Everywhere, we also run into people who oppose us."

A frown crossed Aram's strong, kind, wrinkled face. "Unfortunately, you will have the same experience here. We've got our share of folks who refuse to take a second look at anything. But if you are able to do for us what you say has been done in other places, my close friends and I will deal with the troublemakers."

With the blessing and support of Aram in his dual role as leader of the town and synagogue, Jesus and his comrades embarked on their most productive ministry thus far.

Within a short time, huge crowds were regularly collecting to hear Jesus open up the Holy Scriptures, hanging on to his every word for hours on end. As it dawned on the traditionalists that Jesus was actually pointing people toward personal relationships with Adonai, thus diminishing their dependency on the priestly and temple structures, the hardliners began to argue openly, even bitterly with him.

"Please hear me," Jesus said again and again. "Adonai has given us the temple for his glory and our good. It does not exist as an end itself. These are not my words. All the way through our scriptures, we are taught that Adonai calls for love and mercy and justice from us. He's not interested in huge sacrifices, 'rivers of oil,' as the prophet Micah has said. Worship at the temple should support us in our walk with Adonai. We are not called to support the temple, especially in the lavish, extravagant way the authorities demand."

Aram became nervous. "Jesus," he began often to say, "you're speaking the truth. I believe you. It's just that you're going to get in trouble. I can feel it coming. The men in Jerusalem have not paid much attention to you before. You keep up this kind of talk, no matter how much it comes from Adonai, and you will have them down on your head."

His alarm shook Jesus. "Aram, I really do not fear for myself. What will be will be. What bothers me is that I do not want to cause you and your family any harm. My friends and I will leave before we complicate your lives."

"By the same token, I am not worried about myself," Aram assured Jesus. "I have enough friends in high places to protect my family and me. But if the people in Jerusalem get really angry with you, I do not have the power to call them off."

"I appreciate that, Aram. I will be careful. My friends and I will not stay here one minute longer than you feel we should," he assured his now dear friend.

Talk of Jesus leaving sent chills over Mary, who had fallen hopelessly, desperately, instantly in love with this powerful man, at the same time transparent and opaque. She took every opportunity to be near him, to bring him food and drink, to wash his clothes and keep the cottage where the men stayed spotlessly clean. When he taught, she drank in every word, absorbing his message with every fiber in her body.

Jesus was, likewise, in love with Mary. At first he denied it to himself. Not used to thinking about his own personal feelings, his near total absorption with Mary left him confused. He watched her every move as she came and went. At times he became visibly distracted in his work just thinking about her. He longed to hold her in his arms and, maybe someday, more than that.

Cephas and the other men soon noticed the mutual affection between the two.

"Why isn't she married?" Judas asked Cephas one day as they worked. "A beautiful woman like her with her father's money, surely someone wanted to claim her."

"The story I get is that she was married for a short time," Cephas answered. "Her husband took a fever and was dead in a few days. They did not have children before he died. He had no unmarried brothers to marry her. So for several years now she's been a widow."

Cephas was quiet a moment, then went on to say, "Maybe Adonai has been saving Mary for Jesus. He's certainly smitten with her. When she's around, he hardly knows his name." Both men laughed, recalling their own youthful flirtations, actually not that many years ago.

"Why doesn't he just marry her?" asked Judas. "He certainly deserves a good woman. She couldn't travel with us. He could come back here and see her like we do occasionally with our wives back in Capernaum."

"It'd be fine with me. I frankly don't think, though, he'll take on a wife. A home and children just do not seem to be part of the plan for Jesus. But we'll see," Cephas mused.

They had been in Magdala three months when Simon called Jesus aside and said, "I'm feeling a need to go home for a while. You and mother have written back and forth, but we haven't seen any of the family for over two years. If it's all right with you, I'll go home for a few weeks, see how things are, and then come back."

"But what if we decide to leave? How will you find me?" asked Jesus anxiously. "Besides, I can hardly bear the idea that you would not be nearby."

Simon, appreciative of his brother's love, still was amused at the notion that Jesus could go anywhere these days and the whole countryside not know where he was. "Jesus, don't fret. I'll have no trouble finding you. I will be back very soon. I promise."

A few days later, Jesus was again teaching before a huge crowd of people. He moved around energetically among them as he talked, explaining in stories, parables, homespun humor, and abundant quotations from the Holy Scriptures the new ways of Adonai that were actually not all that new. The throng hardly moved as they listened to his clear, strong voice that had a remarkable way of carrying to the outer reaches of even the largest gathering.

From the back of the throng, someone called out, "Master, who will lead in your kingdom? Who will lay down the rules and regulations?"

Jesus looked at the questioner, thought a moment, leaned down and picked up a small child who had been toddling around at his feet, and replied, "Let me put it this way—unless you have your mind changed about power and place and become as open and trusting as this little child, you will have a hard time entering into the kingdom, much less have any responsibility in it. Whoever humbles himself as this little child, the same is the greatest in the kingdom. And what's more, whoever receives this child in my name is my true friend. Those, on the other hand, who offend one of these little ones who believe what I am saying would be better off to have a millstone hung around their necks and be cast into the depths of the sea."

He kept talking, listening to their questions, paying careful attention to those who were honest in their search, turning aside, even biting sharply at those who wanted to distract him and sow confusion among the earnest seekers. Finally, as the sun dipped below the horizon, he announced, "It's late. Let's all go home. We will meet again tomorrow and talk some more."

The crowd quickly, quietly dispersed, some to their homes in Magdala, others to begin the long walk to outlying villages, with a few deciding to camp on the hillside for the night to be ready the next day to listen again to the master's teaching. Jesus and Cephas started toward their cottage when a man in a finely cut cloak came to them and said, "Jesus of Nazareth, I am Boethus. We have met before, many years ago."

Startled but recognizing him immediately, Jesus smiled broadly and replied, "Yes, my lord. I recall. You were most helpful, and I am always grateful. What may I do for you now?"

"The Lord Herod Antipas was among the crowd today, disguised so no one would recognize him. He is waiting on the other side of the hill and wants to talk with you."

"What could I possibly have to say to the Lord Herod Antipas?" Jesus wanted to know, anger suddenly flaring, surprising even himself at its fury. "He killed my cousin, John. He has brought great harm to the people of his tetrarchy. No, I don't think I have anything worthwhile to say to him. And if I did, he would not like it."

The messenger sputtered, "Am I to understand that you are refusing to talk with your sovereign?"

"I talk with my sovereign all the time," Jesus replied somewhat cryptically, "but he does not reside in the palace at Tiberias. As for speaking with Herod Antipas, please thank him for me, but I will decline his invitation. At least for now. I do hope the time listening to the words from Adonai today proved helpful to him."

Without another word, he spun on his heel and strode briskly toward Magdala in the gathering dusk, a frightened, shaken Cephas scampering to catch up with him.

"He what!" exclaimed Aram when Cephas told him later that evening what had happened. "You mean he refused to talk with Herod Antipas! What was Jesus thinking? He's put himself in frightful danger."

Toward midnight, after he had been out in the cool, beautiful night thinking and praying, Jesus came to the cottage to find Aram pacing rapidly up and down in the courtyard of the house where he and his men were living.

"Jesus, we've got to talk," Aram said with great agitation. "Cephas told me what happened between you and Herod. You know I have complete confidence in you. I just don't understand what possessed you to spurn the tetrarch. You surely must have had some clear sign from Adonai."

"No, I did not have any thunder and lightning from on high," Jesus answered, trying to sound neither arrogant nor unduly alarmed. "I realized, Aram, in the moment, I had nothing to say to the man. You and I both know he only wanted to look at me like one does a freak of nature. He would not have listened to anything I have to say. Besides, he committed a grave injustice against all of us when he had John murdered as entertainment at a drunken party."

"Jesus, master, friend, I don't know where this is heading," Aram answered, consternation and confusion written all over his tired face, perspiration popping out on his forehead despite the chill of the night. "You have so much to give our people. I only hope rash acts like this do not cut short your efforts." Aram embraced Jesus warmly and returned home to twist and turn in his bed for what remained of the night.

Neither Cephas, John, Andrew, nor Judas slept much that night while listening for the heavy footfalls of soldiers coming to arrest them and Jesus. To their amazement, no one came. Antipas made no further move on Jesus. Whispering among themselves, the men decided Jesus had so thoroughly shaken the ruler with his refusal that he did not know how to respond without risking a major uprising.

—

One day at sunset, with the day's crowds sent home, Jesus appeared uninvited at Aram's house, nervously shuffling his feet, twisting his hands as he spoke, "My lord, Aram, I know it is not proper. I shouldn't even ask. Anyway, I ask your permission to spend some time with Mary, alone, here in your courtyard. I really do need to talk with her."

Surprised by the request, seeing Jesus's obvious nervousness, aware it was indeed against custom, Aram nevertheless said, "Of course, Jesus. If she wishes to see you, you certainly have my permission. Abigail and I will go to the back of the house so you may have your privacy."

In a few minutes Mary came to the door. Radiant in the dim glow from the lamps within the house, she hesitated, looked at Jesus with a mixture of anxiety and anticipation, and said softly, "My father says you wish to see me alone."

"Yes, Mary. If you would agree, I would like to sit with you in the courtyard. I want to—no, I need to—talk with you, if you will."

"Certainly, my lord. You honor me by your request." Her back straight, staring into the night, she stiffly yet expectantly sat down on a stone bench under a flowering vine.

"This is not easy for me to say, Mary. Please bear with me," he said haltingly, dropping down beside her.

She did not move, but she did look him squarely in the face.

"I must tell you, I have fallen deeply in love with you," he almost shouted, wringing his hands. "In my own mind I had hoped I would meet someone like you who would love me as I loved her. I've wanted a home and children with someone like you. Since meeting you, I realize how lonely I've been. Sounds crazy, doesn't it! People around me all the time, and still I'm lonely. You've changed that."

She sat still, not moving, hardly breathing. Though he was saying words she had longed to hear, words she had never dared dream he would utter to her, she did not think she liked the direction this conversation was taking. The tentativeness, the hesitation in his voice made her heart sink like a stone in her breast.

"First, I have to ask you, do you love me as I love you?" he asked imploringly, sounding for all the world like a young boy declaring his feelings to a girl for the first time.

For a long moment she said nothing, then, "Jesus, I have loved you from the moment you walked into the house. The man I married was gentle and kind, and I loved him. But never like I have come to love you. When my husband died, I decided I would not marry again unless someone like you came along. Without knowing your name, I longed for you. But I had resigned myself to a life alone."

Impulsively, shattering all rules of decorum, Jesus put his arms around her and pulled her close. Looking into her face, he touched her silk smooth skin. Then he kissed her. She slid her arms around him, eagerly returning his kiss.

Abruptly, he pulled away and stood up, pacing rapidly around the bench, running his fingers through his hair, pulling at his beard. Just as suddenly, he stopped pacing, looked at her, took a deep breath, then plunged ahead as if he were taking a bitter dose of medicine.

"Mary, I want to marry you. My soul, my body cry out to be your husband and for you to be my wife. At the same time—somehow it's clear to me—I cannot. Marriage and a home are not to be mine. It would be unbelievably unfair should I ask you to become my wife. I certainly have no clear picture of what lies ahead of me. I have the strong conviction that I face serious struggles before I can accomplish what Adonai has set out for me."

"Ah, Jesus," she replied, tears now flowing from her eyes, "with one part of my life, I want to argue with you, to persuade you that we can marry and that no matter what, I will be by your side. From the night you came to my father's house, I knew we would love each other. I think I also knew that's as far as we could ever go. We'd have no marriage, no home, no children. It tears me apart to agree with you, but you are right. We cannot get married." With that, she collapsed in deep sobs.

"Oh, Mary!" He knelt before her and laid his head in her lap. For several minutes, neither of them said anything as she stroked his hair and, through her tears, looked longingly at this splendid man whom she loved more than life.

Finally, she stopped crying. A measure of composure returned. She gazed up at the night sky for a long moment, gently raised his head so she could see his eyes in the starlight, caressed his face, and said, "Jesus, now listen to me. I know we cannot marry. I will not be separated from you. When you leave here, as soon you must, I will go with you. If I can find another woman to go with me, fine. That will add a measure of respectability. If no one wants to go, I will go anyway. You cannot make me do otherwise."

He started to protest, to tell her how impossible her choice was, how her presence might cast a shadow on the work, how difficult it would be on him for her to be in the group and still have to keep his distance from her. From the look on her face, the set of her jaw, he realized she had her mind made up and nothing he could say would make any difference. "Once we leave Magdala, our way may be very hard. Still, you are welcome to go."

—

"A woman going with us!" exploded Judas. "That's ridiculous. We'll look like tramps," he fumed. "What's gotten into Jesus? We've got serious business out there. It's no place or time for women. I object."

John replied in complete exasperation, "Judas, calm down. What's wrong with you? First of all, this is not your journey. It's Jesus's. He's never gone wrong before. I trust him. He loves her. He's decided they cannot marry. If they want to be together, let it be."

"I don't like it, not one little bit," he spat out.

"Listen carefully," John said, trying to placate the younger, far more impul- sive man. "You've worked hard with us. You've done just fine. But if you don't like his decision, you've got three choices. Tell him what you think. Keep your mouth shut. Or go home. So there."

In the end, Judas did not tell Jesus anything. He did keep his mouth shut, more or less. He did not go home. No need to cut his nose off to spite his face, he reasoned. Capernaum held nothing for him except a wife and a crying baby. Traveling around with Jesus, being at the center of such huge crowds, having people look up to him as part of Jesus's band was better than anything he had ever known before. He'd stay with it, at least for now.

—

At dawn, after another of his now-frequent late-night vigils out on the hillsides, Jesus called the men together and announced, "We're leaving Magdala. Let's wrap up what we're doing here. Andrew, you especially need to complete your work with the men who are learning new skills."

By now Cephas had grown bold enough with their visionary leader to ask, "Jesus, where do you think we are going next?"

He thought for a moment and answered, "All I know is we are heading more toward the south. We'll be leaving Galilee and Perea. We'll probably spend some time in Samaria and then move on toward Jerusalem. It'll be Passover soon. We just might celebrate the feast together in the Holy City," he said brightly.

"Samaria!" Judas groaned involuntarily.

Surprised by his outburst, Jesus replied with an edge, "Judas, do you have a problem with Samaritans?"

Put on the spot as he had never been before with the group, Judas swallowed hard, hung his head, and said quietly, "No, Jesus. It's just that I've never been there before, and, well, you know, Jews and Samaritans don't get along."

"Judas, do you know any Samaritans? Have you ever seen a Samaritan? Talked with someone from Samaria?" Jesus asked calmly, his flash of anger abated, feeling for Judas, whose prejudices merely reflected those of most of the people of Judea and Galilee.

"No, Jesus. No to all your questions," he said with a sigh. "If you go to Samaria, you can count on me to be right there with you," the young man said, flushed, thoroughly chagrined, and, underneath it all, angered by the gentle rebuke.

John and Andrew looked uneasily at each other at Judas's outbreak.

"Let me say," Jesus said earnestly, looking each one in the face as he began to speak, "if we've learned anything so far in our travels, it is that all people," and he made a wide, sweeping motion with his arms, "belong to Adonai. Our own people, the Samaritans, the Romans, the Syrians, and all the rest. I hope you've seen how Adonai's message and our service can tear down the ridiculous walls we've built up between ourselves."

Within a week, Jesus, the men, and now the two women, Mary and her cousin Leah, left Magdala. Aram and Abigail wept openly as they said goodbye to their daughter and Jesus. Mary tried to comfort them. "We'll not be that far away," she said cheerily. "It's not like you'll never see us again. Besides, Jesus has said you and any others from Magdala can come and work with us any time you choose."

"Do be careful," her father cautioned. "I love and trust Jesus, but he has a way of ignoring danger that scares me, badly."

"Papa," she said softly, hugging him yet again, "I will help him be more cautious. He certainly does not want rash acts to interfere with his work."

As she hugged him one more time, her father said in a voice barely above a whisper, "Mary, I want you to take this with you. You never know when you or Jesus will need something. Now, don't argue with me. Take it." He thrust a small leather bag heavy with money in her hands. Before she could protest, he turned quickly and went into the house, his head hung low.

She told no one, not even Jesus, of Aram's gift. Who knows, she told herself, when an emergency might come up. Along with the few items she had secreted away that women need when traveling, she tucked the bag in a deep pocket inside her dress beneath the cloak she wore.

When Jesus and his friends reached the low walls marking Magdala, they were shocked to be met by several dozen men, women, and children, some seventy or so in all, with their belongings loaded on their backs, heaped on carts, or, for those with some means, stacked on donkeys. Cephas ran ahead of the others in their band, stopped in front of them, planted his hands on his hips defiantly, and asked the group as a whole, "What are you doing here? Where are you going?"

One of the men stepped forward and said, "We heard Jesus was leaving. We don't care where he's going next. We've just decided to follow him no matter what."

Jesus caught up with Cephas in time to hear the man's intentions.

"You don't understand," Jesus pleaded. "The idea is not for you to go with me. You need to go to your homes and lead your families and friends to do among your own people what we've done here in Magdala and in other places."

"I know what you mean, Master," the spokesman said. "It's just that there's nothing for us at our homes, whether it's here in Magdala or in other villages. You've given us more hope than we've ever known. We'll take our chances with you."

Andrew spoke up and said, "But what will you eat? How will you make a living on the road? We take nothing with us. We don't carry food. We trust Adonai and the people we help to provide the basics for us. No community can take care of us all. Nor should we expect them to."

"We've talked about that," another man said, whose back was piled high with his family's meager treasures. "We don't expect you or the towns where we go to feed us. We've got some food with us. We'll do odd jobs to earn money or food. Besides, hunger's no stranger to any of us. It's all right. None of us will be a burden to you. We won't get in your way. Maybe we can be of help. If we can't make it, we'll go back to our villages and what's left of our lives there. For now, unless you tell us we cannot go, we're with you."

After several minutes of serious consultation among Jesus's companions in which a variety of opinions were voiced, Cephas, with a sigh of resignation, went to the pilgrims, saying, "We don't think it's a good idea for you to go with us. We do not know what waits for us. You should know Jesus plans to spend some time in Samaria. If the next portion of the trip is like what we've already known, we will be very busy and will not have time to watch out for you. Still," and he looked toward Jesus and the others for confirmation, "if you are determined to go, we will not stop you."

"We will follow Jesus," they said. Then, to the surprise of Jesus and his friends, that large group of earnest people spontaneously dropped to their knees while several of the men sang prayers and psalms asking Adonai's favor on their undertaking. *O God, when you went forth before your people, when you did march through the wilderness, the earth shook, the heavens also dropped. You did send plentiful rain whereby you sustained your people when they were weary. You sent your goodness to the poor. Armies of kings fled apace. Ascribe strength unto God; his excellence is over Israel, and his strength is in the clouds.*

At this display Jesus shook his head in wonder. What had he begun? Where was all this leading? He did not even know their next stop, much less the ultimate destination. Yet if this was the way of Adonai, he would walk in it.

———

Six or eight people could travel the busy roads and not attract any undue attention. Seventy or more was quite another story, one Boethus shortly reported to Herod Antipas. So this Jesus, this upstart who had spurned his demand for a conversation, was not just a starry-eyed preacher after all. Was he trying to stir up a rebellion against him or the Romans? What was it with this man of Nazareth and his fanatical cousin John that led them to think they could outsmart him? Was he not, after all, son of Herod the Fox? One more false move and Jesus would find himself warming John's old cell.

Bypassing Tiberias with the fervent prayer that Herod Antipas would not interfere with their southward march, Jesus and his swelling troupe made their way to Philoteria, a village at the southernmost tip of Galilee Lake where it empties into the Jordan River in its flow to the Salt Sea.

In this small town they met a cordial if not overwhelming reception. To the relief of Jesus, Cephas, and the others, the crowd of pilgrims trailing along proved no significant burden. The families still had enough food in their packs to sustain them, so they did not overwhelm the countryside. Because most of the pilgrims had already received Jesus's ministries, they were able to scatter through the outlying regions and perform invaluable services to the locals, even replicating some of Jesus's healing techniques. Several of the men and a few of the women had absorbed enough of Jesus's teaching so they were able to pass on to the people around Philoteria the heart of what he was saying. They all told their own stirring Jesus stories of how the man from Nazareth had touched and blessed them.

Mary and Leah worked right alongside the men doing whatever the moment or the day might require. The first time Mary bandaged the suppurating lesions of a woman nearly consumed with classic leprosy, she had to dart behind a bush to throw up. The leper and dozens more like her with every known illness, however, were so grateful that Mary soon overcame her squeamishness in the joy of service. By nightfall, she was so exhausted that she could drop to the ground and fall fast asleep. Well-prepared food and the amenities of home she had taken for granted soon released their hold on Mary and her cousin, so absorbed were they in Jesus's work. And she was near her beloved Jesus. When they could, they walked together in the coolness of the night, holding hands, away from any staring eyes, holding each other close, both yearning for more while simply counting themselves greatly blessed of Adonai to have this time together, such as it was.

As Jesus and his followers drew ever closer to Jerusalem, the political and religious center of Jewish conservatism, the defenders of the true faith marched regularly out to Jesus's gatherings in ever-growing numbers. Before too long,

Jesus could anticipate practically all their stabbing criticisms and had, of necessity, developed his stock answers. He came to the sad realization that these earnest though terribly narrow and unimaginative men had no intention to listen to Adonai's words no matter how he framed them. So Jesus decided to tolerate them as one did pesky mosquitoes.

From Philoteria, Jesus and his people moved to the northern reaches of ancient Samaria. Crossing the imaginary line between Galilee and Samaria sent shivers through Judas and several of the hundred or so followers of Jesus who had gradually collected around him in his southward trek. At the border, a few decided to turn back.

"We just cannot go into Samaria," one of the leaders of the ragtag band told Jesus. "I know it doesn't make any sense to you. It really doesn't to me. But all my life I've been told there's something bad about these folks. I can't get over it."

Jesus made a half-hearted attempt to reason with the man.

"Frankly, Cephas," he told the fisherman later, "I hate to say it, but I'm glad he went back."

Jesus realized how important their pilgrimage with him had become. At the same time, the crowd would make his life and ministry more difficult now that he had crossed into the regions ruled by the Roman Pontius Pilate, prefect of Judea. If Herod Antipas was bad, Pilate was unspeakable. At least Herod had some Jewish blood and sympathies in his veins. In his several years of rule, Pilate had demonstrated a total disregard for the welfare of the hundreds of thousands of Jews living in and around Jerusalem under his direct authority. Rumors flew back and forth on the grapevine that Tiberius, the Roman emperor since the death of Augustus, was going to recall his cruel governor, yet he remained in place.

—

"What is this, an invasion?" the headman of Beth Shan demanded of Jesus and Cephas when they halted at the outskirts of his village in northern Samaria. "What a motley crew of castoffs you've got following along after you! You cannot stay around here. Pilate will think it's a wild march on Jerusalem. He'll send in the troops and kill us all. No, you can't stay here. Get gone! Now!"

When Jesus and Cephas tried to explain their mission, the headman would not listen. With his hands over his ears, he yelled, "Ministry, you say! Looks to me like you've got an army of hungry Galileans who want free food. No. Either you move on, or we'll send for the Romans ourselves."

With a heavy heart Jesus said, "Cephas, we'll just have to go around this village. We cannot turn back. I feel very strongly that we need to go to Jerusalem."

"I won't argue with you, Jesus," Cephas agreed. "I do think it's time we sent the rest of the pilgrims home, though."

"Oh, Cephas," Jesus lamented, "I don't want to send them home. They really have nothing in Galilee. These are the most hard-pressed of our people. They've actually been little trouble. Think of a better way, please."

When even Mary urged Jesus to admit he had hit a wall in trying to keep the pilgrims with him, Jesus relented.

The next morning, Jesus called the entire crowd together. Cephas spoke first: "Listen, everyone. We've come to some difficult decisions. We're in strange territory. The Samaritans are not willing for all of you to remain in their land."

Jesus picked up the announcement, saying, "I feel I have to go on to Jerusalem. You cannot go with me. You will have to turn back. It grieves me to tell you, but that's the way it has to be."

The majority accepted his decision with tearful resignation and began making preparations to head back north, back somewhere, though most of them had no idea where they would go. The three men who had emerged as the unofficial leaders of the pilgrims told Jesus they understood the problem. "Being with you these past few weeks has been the best thing that's ever happened to us," one after the other told Jesus. "We know you've got a big job to do in Jerusalem. We're in the way. You've done the best you could for us. We believe we have the strength and savvy to make a life for ourselves even if it means starting our own village in a friendly part of Galilee."

One man in particular, Amos, who had shown unusual leadership ability despite his utter lack of education and knowledge of the larger world, said to Jesus, "You go on to Jerusalem. Show the powers there what you're made of. We'll be up here in the north somewhere when you come back. And that's a promise."

Jesus smiled, embraced the leaders and nearly all the rest of the pilgrims, and prayed Adonai's care and grace on them. When the moment of parting came, Amos called back over his shoulder to Jesus, "Remember, Master, you don't have to find us; we'll find you on your way back."

Jesus did not realize it, but six of the younger unmarried men chose not to return to Galilee. With no families to care for, unwilling openly to challenge Jesus's decision, they melted out of sight until the pilgrims disappeared into the north and Jesus and his men were out of sight to the south.

Nathaniel, the brightest and quickest of the six, who had chosen himself as their leader, said to the other five as they crept from their hiding place, 'We'll not let Jesus and the others know we're following him. We'll have to work our way south. And I mean totally work our way. No handouts. No stealing. That would dishonor the Master. You never know when he'll need us."

The others agreed, their stout young hearts racing at the thought of the adventure that surely lay before them. What Nathaniel envisioned for them, they each concluded, was even more exciting than simply wandering along with the large band of people.

Free of the crowd of earnest followers, Jesus's group made better time. Cephas and Mary noticed Jesus's inner tempo picked up the nearer they came to Jerusalem. He did not stay in any one place much more than a day, not giving his men time to build the sort of network they had developed in Galilee. Jesus's people neglected no one in need. They simply did not linger.

"Jesus," John asked him during a rest stop after several days of this relentless movement, "you seem to be in a rush. What's going on? We aren't going to spend time with these folks like we have in other places?"

"I feel a strange and powerful urgency to reach Jerusalem during the Passover season. I cannot describe it. Besides, the Samaritans do not have the same problems as the people of Galilee. They're not as desperate. Neither do they seem as willing to organize themselves or carry through like the Galileans. I'm not criticizing the Samaritans. It just seems to be a difference between the two groups."

Within a few days of this increased tempo, the small band arrived in sight of a village called Sychar. "I remember this place," Jesus said as they stopped at a well a short distance north of the town. "John, Joses of Arimathea, and I spent the night near here a long time ago."

For several minutes he was overtaken by his memories. The pain of his father's death and the senseless execution of John again swept over him. He had to control himself to keep from collapsing into a heap of grief.

Jesus's people, sensing but not knowing the source of his agony, left him alone until he seemed to have recovered. With supreme mental effort, he pulled himself back from the brink of despair. When he saw his friends huddled some yards away, anxiety and uncertainty written on their young faces, especially Mary, he reached out to them, explaining, "I'm sorry. This place has some powerful memories. I didn't mean to cause you concern. I'm all right." Further collecting himself, he suggested, "Why don't you men go into the town and get us some food. Mary, Leah, Cephas, and I will wait out here by the well."

Glad to have something to do that would break the spell of melancholia that seemed to have settled over Jesus, Andrew and the others gladly started walking toward the center of the town, one of the larger ones in Samaria.

Mary and Leah found a pleasant place on the ground under some trees near the well, settled down, and soon were napping. Jesus, seeing the women asleep, feeling a strong twinge of regret at their exhaustion, began to pace nervously around the small paved plaza surrounding the well, unable to staunch the flood of his painful memories or to get a clear focus on Adonai's direction for their lives as they neared Jerusalem.

A woman about Jesus's age seemed to appear at the well out of thin air, a water jug in hand. Jesus, along with Mary, who had roused up when he started his pacing, saw her in the same instant she saw them. Before she frantically pulled the veil over her face with trembling hands, they caught glimpses of terrible bruises and gashes on her cheeks, a swollen lip, and an eye as black as charcoal. The woman quickly turned away from the strangers and leaned over the edge of the well to draw water. As she did, the large jug fell from her shaking hands, crashed onto the curb, and shattered into a hundred pieces. With that, she burst into hysterical sobs and started running back toward the village.

"Wait," Mary called after her. "We'll help you find another jug. It's all right. It's only an old clay pot anyway."

Leah, stabbed awake by the crashing jug, sprang to her feet and ran after the woman who was, by now, swaying and stumbling from the confusion of her crying, or perhaps from the pain from her facial wounds made more excruciating by her running. Just as the woman fell sprawling in the middle of the roadway, Leah was at her side. Too late to prevent her from falling, Leah gently helped the distraught woman get up from the dusty road.

By then Mary had run to where the woman stood, still crying uncontrollably, straightening her clothes, smoothing her hair, and dabbing gingerly at her blackened eyes. From within her own cloak, Mary pulled a clean, soft cloth, offered it to the woman, put her arms around her shaking shoulders, and said, "My name is Mary. I'm from up in Magdala. This is my cousin, Leah. That man over there is our friend and teacher. His name is Jesus."

When the woman tried to jerk away, Mary kept her arms in place a bit more firmly and said, "I know you must feel awful about the water jug. We don't have another one or we would give it to you. If you are afraid to tell your husband or family about the pot, Leah and I will be glad to go with you and explain what happened."

Mary's sympathy seemed to irritate the woman. Though tears still flowed, she stopped shaking, stood tall, and shook her head proudly. Mary had to listen closely to understand her words through the unfamiliar Samaritan dialect. "I can take care of myself, thank you," she muttered, pride and anger in her eyes.

Leah, far less diplomatic than Mary, blurted, "From the looks of your face, you don't do a good job of taking care of yourself. You look awful. Somebody beat you up terribly."

"Be quiet, Leah," Mary shushed her irritably.

A sardonic smile played across the swollen lips, and the woman said, "Your cousin's right. I haven't done a very good job of taking care of myself. And, yes, someone beat me. You can see the results of his thorough work."

"Your husband? Your father?" Mary asked gently.

"Neither," the woman answered.

"My soul," Mary interjected, "who then?"

"My father's dead. Died working to pay off our family's debts," she answered in a matter-of-fact manner that told Mary this woman had lived a very hard life.

"The man who beat me up, he owns me."

Confused, chagrined, Mary exploded, "Owns you? You mean you're a slave!"

"Not a slave, exactly," she tried to explain. "In our country a person can be sold or traded to a creditor to help pay off a debt. I'm not a slave. I just can't leave this horrible man who paid money to my father until I can raise enough money to buy my liberty."

"That's a strange way to do things, seems to me," delightfully impertinent Leah retorted. "Besides, surely your father could have found a better way to work off his debts than to do such a thing to you."

Again, from Mary, "Hush, Leah. That's quite enough from you. We don't understand these ways because we're not from here."

"Well, strange or not, that's the way it is. And since I'll never have enough money to pay him off, I'm his to do with as he chooses. And, believe me, he chooses to do some bad things to me."

Mary, coming to understand the woman's great distress, said to her in a whisper, "I have some money." She pulled a coin from her pouch. "I will buy the broken jug. Tell the man I bought it." Before the woman could protest, Mary thrust a small coin in her hand.

Jesus, who had not said anything during the women's exchanges, spoke up and said, "The man who beat you is sick. He has an evil spirit that drives him. He doesn't know what to do with himself when this darkness comes over him, so he lashes out at you. You never know when it's coming, do you?"

Startled, even frightened by Jesus's pronouncement, the woman answered cautiously, tentatively, "Yes, I guess you are right. He can be fine one minute and the next minute he's in a rage. Anything in his way when it happens gets it. Me. The sheep. The colt. Dishes. You just never know, but how did you...?"

"If you will take me to this man," Jesus replied, not attempting to explain how he came to his insights about her tormentor, "maybe I can help him get rid of his darkness."

"You don't know what you are asking," she said, fear rising in her voice. "He's mean. He'll attack you like he did me, even worse if he thinks you're meddling."

"Perhaps. Maybe not. When you feel better, and if you are willing, let's go into town and meet this man," Jesus said calmly, yet with an air of authority that actually left little doubt that such a meeting would take place, and soon.

As Jesus, the woman, and the others started toward the town, Cephas told himself he would show this brute a thing or two if he laid a hand on Jesus, and frankly, he had to admit, he'd enjoy a good fight.

Jesus prayed as he walked.

The village grapevine had once again functioned efficiently. The man, big, rugged, red-faced, feet spread apart, hands on his hips, waited for them defiantly in the town's main square. Seeing Sarah, he roared, "Where have you been, out whoring around? Where's my jug? If you broke it or lost it, I'll take it out of your hide. And who is this foreign scum you've dragged along? Do they want a working over like you got?" he bellowed, laughing raucously, showing a mouthful of rotten teeth.

Villagers who had endured his wildness for years and knew he meant what he said drew back, getting out of the way while watching anxiously to see who would fall first before the man's fury.

Everyone except Jesus stopped in their tracks at the man's thundering. He kept walking straight toward the wild man.

"Boaz, be still," Jesus said softly, gazing into the man's wide eyes that saw everything and nothing.

The raging man stopped dead in his tracks. "Who are you?" he yelled at Jesus.

"It doesn't matter who I am," Jesus answered firmly, not letting his eyes wander.

"I don't know you," he roared. "How do you know my name?"

"Let's go to a quiet place and talk," Jesus invited, reaching out to touch Boaz's sleeve.

He shrunk back from Jesus's touch, jerking his arm away.

Here it comes, a villager who had known Boaz all his angry life thought. The stranger is about to get flattened.

Boaz, however, did not hit Jesus. He did retort, now in a more controlled tone, "I don't know you."

"I am no stranger to you," Jesus replied evenly.

Without another word Jesus began to walk toward a grove of olive trees he could see some distance from the village square.

For a long moment Boaz did not move, utter confusion written all over his face. He twisted, flung his arms in exasperation, popped the side of his head with the heel of his hand, looked at the villagers who, hardly breathing, watched this totally unexpected drama play out. Then, to everyone's amazement, Boaz slowly started walking toward the grove, his arms hanging limply by his sides. For reasons no one could discern, the town's angriest man had followed Jesus into the trees.

As dawn awakened the people of Sychar, Jesus and Boaz were seen going into the small cottage where he and the woman lived. Jesus and Boaz said nothing about the day and night they had spent in the olive grove. When the woman asked him why his hair was so wet, he said, "Jesus baptized me."

Thereafter, the people of Sychar kept waiting for Boaz's explosions. They did not come. On occasion he would get close to the brink of a tantrum if something seriously upset him. In those moments the people who knew him best would notice how he visibly struggled to hold himself in check. He would cross his arms across his chest. Perspiration poured from his face. Often, he turned, looking steadily at the grove of olive trees in the distance until the darkness passed from him. He never beat the woman again.

The Galileans decided to set up camp out near the well and spend a few days teaching. Boaz took his bedroll, stayed with them, said very little to anyone, not even Jesus, while hanging on to every word any of the group spoke.

Several months after Jesus's visit to Sychar, the villagers noticed the woman's absence. The townspeople dared not ask him her whereabouts. Finally, curiosity got the best of one of the oldest grandmothers in Sychar, who one day just hobbled up to Boaz and said bluntly, "Where is she? Did you kill her?"

"She went home." And that's all he would say about it.

—

Dust filled the air kicked up by hundreds of pilgrims coursing toward the Holy City and another Passover festival.

"Jesus! Jesus! Cephas! Wait! Stop!"

Over the cacophony of the cascading crowd, they heard the shouting and looked back to see Simon scampering his way through the crowds, not wanting to knock anyone down as he hurried, determined to catch up with his brother.

Within a few seconds Simon reached them. Panting for breath, he leaned over, his hands on his knees, perspiration pouring from his face, struggling for air. When he had caught his breath enough to talk, he blurted in short gasps, "We've been trying to catch up with you for several days. You're not letting any grass grow under your feet." He paused again so he could breathe better. "We missed you by a day in Sychar. A huge, rough-looking, yet gentle giant of a man gave us directions, saying you had spent some time in his village. Said you'd left the previous morning headed south toward Jerusalem."

"Simon," Jesus beamed, "it's so good to see you." He hugged his younger brother, clapping him on the back. "But I'm upset with you," Jesus teased. "You said you'd be right back. It's been weeks and weeks."

Jerusalem-bound pilgrims had to work their way around or through the knot of people who apparently had decided to have a family reunion in the middle of the road. Andrew took charge quickly. "Wait," he said hurriedly in his best manager's voice. "We're going to get trampled if we don't get off the road. Let's go over to that little grassy knoll," he suggested, pointing to a hillock a few dozen yards off the highway, "and let Jesus and his brother have a talk."

Without another word the Galileans moved sideways through the steady stream of southward-bound people. After a moment's hesitation during which he looked anxiously northward up the road, Simon joined the others as they edged toward the little hill.

Everyone except Simon dropped to the ground, some to sit, others to stretch out despite the lack of shade and the unseasonable warmth of the day.

"Simon," Mary said, "here, sit down by Jesus. I've got a water skin. You must be dying of thirst."

"Thanks, Mary." Though he said no more, Simon wondered what Mary was doing here. He drank the water. Rather than sitting down, however, he paced back and forth, straining to see the road. At first Jesus did not notice his behavior in his eagerness to ask questions about his family in Nazareth.

When Simon kept pacing, Cephas groused, "Simon, what on earth are you doing? You're making me nervous. Why don't you sit down!"

"I can't," he answered quickly, concern in his voice. "I have to watch the road."

Suddenly, Jesus's own senses came alive. Turning toward his brother, he asked, "What did you mean *we* had a hard time catching up with you. Who is with you?"

The brother held out his hands, palms up in a defensive gesture, and said, "Try not to get upset, Jesus." He gulped, then continued, "James and Mother are back there somewhere."

"James!" Jesus exclaimed. "James, my brother, our brother is with you? And Mother?" Then it was Jesus's turn to spring to his feet, standing on tiptoes to see the road.

Once again, Andrew interposed his wisdom. "Hold on, you two," he suggested, feeling anxious for them lest they miss seeing their family members. "If you're looking for someone, you'd better get down closer to the road. Unless they're wearing Joseph's many-colored coat or a mighty big hat, they could just walk by and you'd never see them in that mob of people."

The two brothers broke and ran to the roadside, getting as close as they could to the flow of humanity.

While they moved back and forth, straining to look at the passing faces, Jesus said, "You'd better tell me what's going on. Why is James with you? And Mother?"

"Wait a while on most of that, Jesus," Simon pleaded. "We'll have time after they get here."

"But why are they not with you? Why did you leave them? Why didn't you stay together?" Jesus demanded to know in a rush of worry.

"Hold on, big brother," Simon replied, irritation as well as amusement in his voice. "This morning, before daybreak, as we were starting out again, James turned his ankle on a rock. It's not broken. I know, I've had training in such things, in case you've forgotten."

"All right," Jesus answered, smiling, easing up on his younger brother. "So he hurt his ankle. I still want to know why you left without him and Mother."

"When he realized he would have to hobble along on a crutch we made from a tree limb, he made me speed ahead and find you."

"Jesus," Simon said tentatively, "about Mother?"

"What about Mother?" Jesus demanded fearfully.

"She's changed," he said painfully. "She had a terrible experience."

"What do you mean?" Jesus demanded, thoroughly alarmed.

"Please, let's wait until they get here. Let one telling suffice. She aged ten years in a few weeks, Jesus. You will be startled to see her. Wrinkles on her face. A limp in her walk. She's still got much of her spirit; it's just that her body took a real beating."

"Simon, that's so bad. I am so sorry," Jesus said, shaking his head in distress, struggling with feelings of guilt for not being with her in whatever it was that happened to her. "I'll be on the alert," Jesus assured him. "Thanks for telling me. Simon, thanks for bringing her with you."

"No thanks to me or James. She would have come if she had had to come alone. Jesus, she's still Mother, just a little bit less so."

The two brothers took up their vigil, pacing up and down the roadside, occasionally walking into the human tide. They took turns calling out James's name. Nothing.

Jesus ached to know what this was all about. Why did James come? And what terrible calamity had befallen his mother? He had to know. He decided, though, that Simon was right to wait to tell his stories until they were not so completely distracted.

It was nearing sundown when Simon shouted to Jesus even though he was standing right next to him, "There they are!" In the same breath he began shouting and waving to his brother, "James, James, over here! We're over here!"

Seeing both his brothers, a broad grin lit up James's face. Mary cried. The four of them embraced in the middle of the highway in their joy at seeing one another, ignoring the grumblers' complaints. "Here, put your arm around my shoulder," Simon said to his limping brother. "I'll help you through the crowd."

Simon was right about Mary. A trauma had exacted a fierce toll on his mother's body. His brother was also correct in saying her spirit was as bright as ever. What in the world?

Jesus retrieved their small traveling bundles, and the four of them moved out of the crowd.

Before joining the others at the clearing, James said, "You'll have to let me get off this foot for a minute. It's killing me." With a chuckle despite his pain, he nudged Jesus in the ribs and said, "What I need is one of your miracles."

Jesus, trying to laugh despite his grave concerns, joked, "I think I'm fresh out of miracles this afternoon, at least for bum ankles. I'll tell you what is a miracle, though: seeing you and Mother here. Never would I have thought that you'd be part of this throng in this place."

"What," James said lightheartedly, "let you and Simon have all this excitement by yourself? Not on your life!"

After a brief rest James said, "All right, help me up. Give me my crutch, and let's go meet these other people Simon has told me so much about."

Mary Magdala had spent her own anxious hours sharing Jesus's concern for his family. When she spotted the three brothers emerging from the crowd, she started running toward them, water skin in hand. By the time James was ready to move, Mary reached them but stopped short, suddenly not knowing what to do with herself. Besides, who was that elderly woman with them? She had to be Jesus's mother. Lovely. Older than she had expected. Obviously utterly exhausted.

Jesus, feeling both her relief and uneasiness, took Mary by the hand and said to his mother and brother, "This is Mary, daughter of Aram of Magdala. Adonai has graciously brought us together."

Simon, though he knew of Jesus's deep feelings for Mary, was nonetheless surprised to hear the devotion he expressed for her. Had they been married after he left Magdala?

James, seeing her beauty, her obvious love for his brother, sensing her compassion, bowed and said, "Simon told me of your parents, of your own commitment to Jesus's work. He neglected to tell me of your special feelings for one another."

Simon blurted, "That's because I didn't know all about this," motioning toward Jesus and Mary. Before he could check himself, he hurried on to ask, "Have you two gotten married? Did I miss the wedding?"

Jesus put his arm around his brother's shoulder and said, "Simon, no, you did not miss the wedding. We're frankly not sure there will be a wedding. And no," he went on to say before unseemly questions could pop up in his brothers' heads, "we are not living as man and wife. Much in our lives is on hold for now."

"It was my idea to come with Jesus," Mary quickly explained, looking at Jesus's family, especially his mother, conveying in one swoop the quiet determination that had driven her to take the unconventional step to accompany Jesus and her wariness at meeting his mother and brother. "We agreed marriage would not be best, as Jesus says, for now. I can accept that. Still, I did not want to be separated from him. I love him. I believe completely in what he's doing. So my cousin Leah and I have added ourselves to the list of Jesus's responsibilities."

"Ah, my lady," James spoke up, "from this brief word I have an idea you are one 'burden' my brother finds very light to bear."

By the time the five of them had met and gotten acquainted, Cephas had made the decision they should camp there for the night. Soon they had a small fire crackling.

The evening settled around them comfortably, reminding Jesus and James of a thousand such nights they had known as boys in Nazareth.

"Why did you decide to come, James?" Jesus asked.

# Chapter Ten

# Pontius Pilate and Herod Antipas

*Pride compasses them about as a chain; violence covers them as a garment.*

"But I do not want to go to Judea," Pontius Pilate railed at his agent who represented him in the court of the divine emperor Tiberius.

Lepidus the agent replied, exasperated with the well-born, brave, loyal, and impoverished knight, "You can just content yourself to go off on another campaign with the army, a jaunt you cannot afford. You've got to make some money, and soon. You'll be in worse trouble than you are now." Besides, Lepidus thought to himself, you've not paid me a penny of the money I've spent just trying to get your name before the emperor.

"There's no money in Judea. Just a bunch of crazy religious fanatics." Softening his tone, the solidly built, battle-hardened soldier, with no tender feelings for anyone in the world but his wife, said, "Look, I know I don't have much going for me. But I am blue-blooded—back to Romulus. We've just never made it to the upper ranks. Surely, though, Lepidus, you can do better for me than Judea."

Shifting in his seat, taking in a deep breath, looking straight at his frustrated client, "No, I cannot, my lord. Tiberius appreciates your service; he truly does. He knows he owes you a favor. It's just that he owes bigger fish in his pond bigger favors. I have it on the highest authority this is it. Take it or leave it." The agent gathered up his toga, rose, and started toward the door of the tiny room Pilate called his office in the respectable, if undistinguished, villa he shared with his wife Porcla in a decent neighborhood not far from Palatine Hill.

"Wait," Pilate pleaded, dropping into a chair at the desk, resignation in his voice. "I'll take it. You've done your best. I deserve more." He hung his head in despair. Then, shaking off his dejection as he had done countless times in battle, he looked up at Lepidus and said with new determination in his steady voice, "Maybe this will not be such a terrible assignment. Boring but bearable. I'll do like the rest of the prefects. Bleed the subjects for all I can get, then leave for a comfortable retirement somewhere away from the glare of publicity and the conniving of the court. After all, what of consequence can happen in that little hardscrabble province?"

———

Across the expanse of the Great Sea, a messenger from the emperor Tiberius was received in the court of Herod Antipas, tetrarch of Galilee and Perea, who yet managed to maintain control of his holdings for these twenty years since his father's unlamented death. That was itself an achievement of no little note in an era when the life of a provincial ruler was valued even less than that of a good slave. Dependable servants were hard to find and expensive to buy. Rulers were a dime a dozen and could be made and broken with the flick of the emperor's finger.

Amid due pomp the messenger presented himself to Herod and his wife; the striking, ambitious, icily cold Herodias, actually his niece and, until recently, the wife of one of the tetrarch's half-brothers.

"My lord Herod Antipas," the ambassador intoned, bowing to Herod, who was seated on a gilded throne, nodding with an ill-disguised sneer at Herodias, who stood by his side, "I have been commissioned by the divine Tiberius to inform you that Pontius Pilate, a highly decorated knight of noted military prowess, an esteemed friend of the emperor and of the people and senate of Rome, has been named prefect of Judea. His dominions are confined according to the lines on the map I bear for you. They do not, at any point, overlap the lands you and your brother, my lord Philip rule."

Of course, Herod Antipas had known for months Pilate was in line for the governorship, that he would probably get the position, that he would be a fierce and inept ruler. Still, Herod was pleased his standing in the Roman court was sufficiently strong that Tiberius would inform him in this official and personal manner. More to the point, he was relieved to know that Pilate's rule would not interfere with his own.

"Once again, the emperor Tiberius has shown his superior wisdom in his administration of the world the gods have entrusted to him," Antipas mouthed impiously and completely without feeling, saying what he was supposed to, knowing his words would soon be reported to His Imperial Majesty.

"My lord," the messenger went on after waiting an appropriate moment for the tetrarch to utter his scripted remarks, "there's more."

Antipas flinched. He did not want more.

"The emperor has declared that whereas Pontius Pilate has no authority to interfere with your administration on a day-by-day basis, he does have political and military power to act in the larger region for the best interests of the people of Rome in the case of extraordinary events."

This was bad news, bad news indeed, Herod realized. Other prefects had enjoyed similar power on paper. They had, however, shown the good sense to stay in their own backyards. Herod's Rome informants told him that Pilate was an intemperate and inveterate meddler. To add insult to injury, Herod's spies told him Pilate was deeply in debt and, therefore, would be looking for ways to rape the entire country in concerted efforts to stabilize his finances. No one's pocketbook would be safe once Pilate arrived.

Pushing aside his dread at the thought of having to deal with Pilate, Herod said again unctuously, "We understand and will cooperate fully with His Excellency."

*Change the unhappy subject as quickly as possible*, Herodias mentally communicated to her anxious husband. He got the message.

Preparing to rise from his throne, signaling the dismissal of the messenger, Antipas reminded the messenger, "You will let us know when his lordship plans to arrive. We will want to give him an appropriate welcome to our lands."

The messenger fidgeted, cleared his throat, giving his own signal that he yet had more news, unpleasant at that. "As a matter of fact, Your Excellency, Pilate will be landing at Caesarea within a few days. He sailed three weeks ago. You should prepare to leave immediately, today, to be on hand when he lands."

Herod Antipas exploded, "What do you mean leave today? Don't you know how busy I am? I cannot just pick up and go traipsing across miles and miles on such intolerably short notice! Besides, it's demeaning to my rank. We won't do it. And you can so inform your superiors. Pilate can come to see us when he gets here."

When Pontius Pilate, his wife, staff, and household landed at Caesarea, Herod and Herodias, Philip and his newest bride, Salome, were all on hand and properly caparisoned to greet the Roman prefect at the seashore with a commendable display of pageantry they had thrown together in a mere five days.

Pilate, the impoverished knight, felt and resented his lower station. Besides, he had done more for the empire in a month than these two sycophants had done in their entire lives. So rather than maneuvering to enlist the support of Herod and Philip to aid him in governing the volatile Jews, Pilate, to everyone's dismay, behaved like a complete prig before these fourth-generation royals and their courts.

The master of ceremonies introduced the three men to each other. By right of rank and birth, Antipas spoke first, followed by Philip. They did their best to offer cordial words to the Roman, realizing it was in their mutual interests for the two Herods to get along with the governor, offering their full assistance.

Pilate ignored their attempt at mutuality entirely in his hellbent determination to assert his superiority over the tetrarchs by virtue of his place as the direct representative of the emperor Tiberius. "Thank you, my lords," he replied coldly, "for your offer of assistance. I will, however, not be troubling you. The emperor has complete confidence in me to do the job. Should I need you, I will let you know." And that was it.

So Pilate was every bit as politically stupid as their informants had predicted. The two oft-estranged, perennially competing brothers rolled their eyes at each other in disbelief, instantaneously finding common cause in their visceral hatred of Pilate and an implacable determination to subvert his rule as often as possible.

Still, Pilate's arrogance, no matter how insufferable, was not enough to throw Herod and Philip off balance, at least not publicly. If arrogance was to be the name of the game, they could play as well, better than this dolt from Rome. Herod, completely ignoring Pilate's remarks, rose from his chair, looked over the heads of Pilate and his wife, and announced to the large assembly of honored guests, "We have a banquet prepared to which you are all invited." As he processed from the dais, glancing nonchalantly at the governor, he said, "And, yes, you two are invited if you care to join us." With that the tetrarchs swept away without a backward glance.

The master of ceremonies, fully aware that the welcoming ceremony had become a debacle of monumental proportions, quickly moved to salvage what he could. Bowing before the prefect and his wife, he said, "My lord and lady, if you will follow me, I will show you to the banquet hall."

They had no choice but to tag along behind Herod and Philip, now chatting amiably as if they had never had a crossword, completely ignoring Pilate. The tetrarchs got through the rest of the festivities without again speaking to Pilate or his wife. To the burning shame and fury of Pilate, hardly anyone else among the courtiers deigned to speak to him either, taking their cues from Antipas and Philip.

For Herod Antipas and Philip, less government was better than more. Pilate chose the opposite approach, motivated in no small measure by his desire to extract all the money possible from the Jews in his Judean region. He raised existing taxes and created new ones. Conscripting temple funds, he undertook the construction of a massive aqueduct for Jerusalem and other public building projects he could oversee. On their face the lavish efforts seemed worthwhile for the people. In reality they were inimical to priests and populace. He bullied contractors into undertaking the projects, extorted bribes and kickbacks from them, and paid himself exorbitant commissions for managing the construction. Any real or perceived breach of Rome's rules, most of which were contrived by Pilate, provided an excuse to bring in the soldiers. Large festivals like Passover in the spring and the Festival of Booths in the fall were potential holocausts. Thus, while the territories ruled by the brothers enjoyed relative tranquility and prosperity, Judea was in constant turmoil.

In a perverse way Pilate took his cue for governing from the Jewish temple authorities, the half-dozen men who controlled the temple and its vast wealth. To these temple aristocrats the welfare of the people was altogether incidental. At the center of this cabal, Annas and Caiaphas, father-in-law and son-in-law, kept a death grip on the high priesthood and the power the office conveyed. It was in the best interests of those among the power brokers not to question this arrangement. In years gone by unfortunate accidents mysteriously befell those who had the temerity to raise any objections. If taking the annual tithe from a peasant family brought great hardship, too bad. The blessed work of Adonai had to go on. Therefore, Pilate reasoned, if the people's religious leaders did not care for the masses, why should he? So he regularly vented his spleen on the hapless population, bullying them mercilessly, lashing them like slaves, and decorating crosses with them to a shameless degree.

He had been prefect for four bloody, tumultuous years ruling from Caesarea, the port city King Herod had dredged from the unforgiving Great Sea several years before he died. As yet another Jewish festival approached, one of Pilate's paid Jewish informants gained an audience with the governor. "My lord," he said, fawning before the prefect, playing to the Roman's vanity, hoping to garner a big fee for information of dubious veracity, "I have it on good authority that there might be serious trouble during this Succoth celebration."

Alarmed, Pilate demanded, "Who would be so stupid as to come up against me and the soldiers?"

"Who? Elements from several large and restless peasant families. According to their lights, they've been shabbily treated by the Romans and by the high priests. They are saying they'd rather die like men than to remain in bondage to you. Pardon me, my lord," he bowed again as Pilate bristled. "Those are not my words. That's what the rebels are saying."

"Well," the Roman commander said, smiling humorlessly, rubbing his hands together in gleeful anticipation of a good fight, "we'll just see about this."

After paying the charlatan a substantial fee, without bothering to check out the mole's story further, Pilate immediately called his officers together and said, "Put five hundred of your men on full alert. I have reliable reports of trouble. We must be ready."

The officers knew better than to ask any details. With Succoth approaching, however, it took no military genius to surmise the alleged unrest related to the festival. It must be serious, the officers said among themselves, for Pilate to call out so many troops.

A few days before the actual opening of the festival, Pilate gave the marching orders. "We go to Jerusalem," he informed the officers. Rather than hurrying to the Holy City, though, Pilate took his time, allowing a leisurely progress toward Jerusalem. At dinner that first evening, when one of the officers questioned the slow pace, Pilate answered him brusquely, "Don't you get it? I want the entire countryside to know we are moving in considerable numbers. Any potential rebels should think twice before causing trouble. No need to have a blood bath if we can avoid it."

When news of Pilate's advance reached the high priest's palace, he was completely thrown off balance, deeply alarmed. "Pilate's asking for trouble, serious trouble," Caiaphas warned several of his most trusted confidants. "When word gets out across the country of Pilate's march, every malcontent will come out of the woodwork spoiling for a fight. We must get word to him to reduce his numbers."

A personal representative from Caiaphas appeared at the Roman's large campaign pavilion and said, "My lord prefect, I see you have a very large contingency with you. My master, Caiaphas the high priest, asks you to please inform him why you come with such substantial numbers. The high priest fully expected you to be present to share the celebration. But to come with so many soldiers, my lord, he was simply wondering why."

Rather than tell the messenger of the intelligence he had received about a possible uprising, Pilate, with his usual arrogance and inordinate sensitivity to any semblance of second-guessing his authority, replied diffidently, "You tell your master that I know precisely what I am doing. He should tend to the Holy of Holies, and I will tend to the world as it is." Pilate turned to the aide at his side and said, nodding toward the messenger, "Give this man a meal and some wine before he starts back to Jerusalem." Without a fare-thee-well, Pilate walked away, leaving the high priest's representative standing there humiliated and furious at the Roman's condescension.

When told of Pilate's callousness, the high priest warned the commander of his own temple guards, "Get ready for the worse. I am afraid our governor has undergone a serious collapse of judgment. About all you can do is throw up a strong cordon around the temple itself and the palaces. If trouble comes, we'll just have to do our best to stay out of harm's way."

Pilate fully understood the Jews' unalterable opposition to the display of any representation, animal or human, feeling such emblems violated the sacred laws against making graven images. He had previously honored the taboo, covering the army's standards that depicted various forms inimical to the Jews' heightened sensitivity to such representations as the army entered Jerusalem or any other sacred precinct. This time, to prove some unfathomable point, he decided he would enter the city with standards uncovered for all to see. Rebels, priests, peasants impugned the might of eternal Rome at their own peril.

"My lord," a breathless servant informed the high priest, "the army is entering the city with standards uncovered."

"No!" Caiaphas screamed, jumping up from his elevated chair. "Pilate's lost his mind. Quick, man," the high priest ordered the servant, "get all our people to safety. The streets will run with blood."

The official report to Rome delivered six weeks later informed the emperor that an unforeseen uprising among the Jews in Jerusalem had resulted in a police action that cost the lives of three Roman soldiers. Some five hundred Jews, the report stated, had also been killed in the fighting and several more crucified as insurgents.

The high priest's own agents in Rome let it be known that two thousand Jews had died in that one day because Pilate broke all of Rome's rules guaranteeing the Jews' religious rights, proscripting the display of images in the Holy City. Fortunately for Pilate, when the news reached the palace in Rome, Tiberius was away at the Isle of Capri on yet another of his wild orgies. Sejanus, who ruled in his place, the ruthless commander of the elite Praetorian guard, though no friend of Pilate's, cared even less for the loss of two thousand fanatical Jews. "Good riddance," he told his aide. Tiberius was not informed of the massacre. He probably would not have cared either if he had been told.

When news of the massacre reached Herod Antipas and Philip, they hastily met to lay contingency plans in case the slaughter ignited passions in their own districts. When their domains remained quiet, the brothers relaxed and went back to their careless and indifferent governing.

High in the Galilean hills to the north, all was not quiet. Ezechias, son of the crucified Judas who had torched Sepphoris fifteen years previously, and grandson of the first Ezechias, who had been executed by Herod the King a half century previously, had been neither careless nor indifferent in his opposition to the Roman occupation of his country. In time, the young Ezechias had begun to make his own plans. To Eli, his cousin and closest collaborator, he confided, "We will get even with the Romans and the greedy Jews in Jerusalem who help them rape our land."

News of the slaughter in Jerusalem was the sign from heaven for which Ezechias had been waiting to launch his own liberation drive.

Eli knew he meant what he said. "Ezechias, I will help you. We can die only once. Let it be for Adonai and freedom. Tell me what you want me to do."

"First of all, cousin, do not talk to anyone about what we're doing. Gradually we will enlist men we can trust. One slip, one coward in our group, one informer and we're done for before we get started." They made a blood covenant.

Gradually, the cousins built an organization of men equally as bound by secrecy and blood to free their land from oppression, both political and religious. A battle plan evolved over the months.

"We will not go up against a city as my father did," Ezechias explained. "That's an invitation to disaster, though he and his band surely did a great deal of damage. We'll engage in underground warfare. We'll take up the tactic of the sicarii."

The dozen young men who huddled around the campfire that blustery night shuddered at the thought of becoming assassins. They were, after all, hardly out of boyhood, from solid peasant families, Galileans who had never hurt anyone. Now, to think of committing carefully planned political murders, often in broad daylight, sent shivers through them. If this is what it took to bring freedom, though, they would do it.

Over a period of months, primarily at night because they had to work during the day to provide for their families, the band of freedom fighters learned the terrible art of assassination from a Syrian Jew who had performed dozens of such murders. He showed where they must strike their victims to prevent them from crying out. "You must not miss. You have one chance. A miscalculation will cost you your life and will endanger your friends."

The assassin trained the men in how to conceal their long-bladed knives and schooled them in the sleight-of-hand technique of sliding their weapons from beneath their clothing in a fluid motion as they walked through the crowded streets while stalking their victims. Soon it was time, Ezechias declared, for them to begin their work. He, as leader, would go first.

"Sepphoris has a newly posted centurion. His name is Latvias. As Romans go, they say he's not bad. Since he's well-liked by many Jews, he might be less cautious in walking around the town alone. I'll find a way to study his habits. When the time is right, I'll strike," Ezechias announced, a twisted smile on his face.

Starting with a centurion is risky, some of the recruits thought. And quite brave, others concluded. No one questioned the leader. As he was about to leave for Sepphoris, they had a solemn moment when they laid their hands on his head as a blessing and commendation. "May Adonai go with you," each man intoned.

When Latvias's orders to relocate to Sepphoris had arrived, he and his wife dutifully moved even though they had established cordial friends among the Jews, Greeks, and others who lived in the northern and eastern districts around the Galilee Lake he patrolled. "It's the life of a soldier," he had told his friends as they feted him in a farewell banquet, highly unusual of itself, since normally Jews did not eat with non-Jews. As a final gesture, Latvias attended a synagogue service during which the congregation offered prayers for him and his wife, an altogether unprecedented accord from the occupied people for their military master.

It was as Ezechias had hoped. Feeling comfortable and accepted in his new post, Latvias began to go about alone when he was off duty. Veterans of the previous uprising cautioned him. "These Jews are crazy," one of his sergeants told him. "They'll act like your friend. Next thing you know, your house is on fire."

"I understand," Latvias assured his comrade. "I'll be careful. If I go about all the time with an armed escort, though, it sends bad messages about trust and peace."

The veteran snorted, "Trust and peace! Such doesn't exist around here."

Ezechias struck late one afternoon as Latvias strolled through one of the markets alone. Everyone knew who he was, but because he had become a familiar figure among them, no one gave him any undue attention. Though he wore light leather armor, it provided no substantial protection from a close-up attack such as Ezechias planned. The assassin closely observed his prey's movements as the centurion ambled from one vendor to another. He needed just the right situation to strike. He wanted to catch Latvias slightly off balance, alone, but in a group of people. In an instant, as the centurion strolled away from a stall, looking slightly distracted, several people happened to cluster around him, paying him no mind, yet providing exactly the cover Ezechias needed. With the flash of a fanged viper, Ezechias rammed his razor sharp, serrated blade up under Latvias's ribcage, piercing his heart before he could utter a sound, instantly killing the Roman. Like a wraith, Ezechias evaporated into the crowd, leaving his blade in the dead but still standing soldier. In the instant Latvias fell to the pavement, his life's blood puddling the street, Ezechias was gone.

Latvias's murder sent shivers through the entire population of Sepphoris and beyond. "Oh no," the people groaned, "not another uprising. Please. We've not recovered from the last mindless revolution."

The Romans reacted quickly to round up all suspects. Despite torture, however, and other tried and true methods of extracting information, no one knew anything about the assassination. The Syrian legate finally had to admit he had no clue as to the murderer.

"Maybe it was just random," he wrote his superiors in Rome. When several weeks passed and nothing else happened, everyone began to breathe easier.

Then a highly placed representative of the high priest, on an extended tour of Galilee for the leaders of the temple, met a similar fate as he left a gathering of the Jewish leaders of Sepphoris one evening. No clues. This time the assassin even managed to take his blade with him as he disappeared into the night.

A few weeks later, three drunken Roman soldiers were stealthily dispatched as they left a brothel in the Greek section of Sepphoris. A temple tax collector and his aide were murdered outside his home in one of the larger towns a few miles from Sepphoris. The tax money in their bags was not touched.

Murders began to occur throughout the region, always directed against the Romans, their collaborators, or men directly or indirectly connected with temple leadership. Intensive investigations turned up nothing.

"There's no pattern," the Roman legate groaned, "no way to protect ourselves. We cannot go around in armed squads all the time."

A climate of fear settled over the entire region. Wizened army veterans even began to wince as individual soldiers, army suppliers, even occasionally house servants of ranking members of the Roman military died at the hands of blade-wielding expert killers. The population worried that another rebellion would bring on them a firestorm of Roman retribution.

When more than thirty men had died with no arrests, Pilate decided to act, using his authority as designated peacekeeper for all of the province. The Syrian legate, his superior, had no foreknowledge of Pilate's incursion. Operating by stealth, Pilate later said, so not to alert the assassins, he put together a special unit of a hundred crack troops whom he personally led north. With forced night marches he and his soldiers were in Galilee before anyone knew they were on the move.

As he was preparing to leave, Pilate's wife asked him, "My lord, how do you expect to proceed? What do you hope to accomplish? The legate, the temple guards, Herod Antipas's people have not been able to find out who's doing the killings."

Her question made him angry, mainly because he had no answer. He just knew he had to do something quick and definitive; otherwise, his enemies in Jerusalem and Rome would never let him hear the end of it. After all, he was the emperor's man in the province. He would think of something.

When he and his men crossed over from Samaria into Galilee, he still had not come up with a plan. He was feeling desperate now. Here he was on a secret mission with a hundred of Rome's best soldiers and all their baggage and supplies going into a region he knew nothing about, blind as a bat as far as intelligence went, and because he wanted to sneak into the country, he could not enlist any natives to help him. The best help he had came from Melchi, a merchant from Cesarea he trusted who had lived in Sepphoris. Pilate forced Melchi to accompany him to the north.

"My lord," Melchi had pleaded, "you know I would do anything for you. But I know nothing about army matters. And it's been a long time since I lived in Galilee. Left when I was hardly out of boyhood."

"You can get us to Sepphoris, can't you?" demanded Pilate, already terribly out of sorts as he contemplated the bold and potentially disastrous course he had chosen.

"I can do that," Melchi assured Pilate, "but that's about all. You probably need to go into the hills beyond Sepphoris, and I am totally ignorant of that part of the region."

"You get me to Sepphoris. I'll decide then on my next move," Pilate blustered.

*Decide then on your next move?*, Melchi thought incredulously. What kind of commander goes off so clumsily? Melchi vowed to himself he would vanish from Pilate's sight as soon as he safely could. This expedition was headed for big trouble, and Melchi the merchant would have no part of it.

Without wanting to let his three officers know of his vacuous strategy while desperately needing to pick their brains, Pilate made it a point to have each of them ride alone with him for stretches of the march. To each one he said, "I've got some definite ideas on how to go about finding these rebels, but before I put my plans on the table, I wanted to get your thinking."

The officers knew exactly the game Pilate was playing, so they went along. The three of them had already been talking and had cobbled together the rudiments of a plan they thought might at least get them started. They also knew that if their plans did not become Pilate's, he would reject their ideas, and them, out of hand.

One of the officers said, "The killers have families and friends. From what I hear, it's pretty clear the families do not know if their people are among the killers. If the families will not talk, then we've got to get the killers to come to the families."

Another said, "Have you considered taking hostages in key Galilean villages? If you take enough from each town, you're bound to snare some family members of the murderers. We put out the word who we're holding of the men, women, and children. If the rebels don't start surrendering, we start executing the hostages. That's not a very clean way to fight a war, but these rebels are killers. They're killing indiscriminately. We can too."

By the time Pilate talked with the third officer, his plan was fully formed. Late that night as they camped for a few hours, Pilate called the officers aside and said, "I've come up with a plan. See what you think of it." He proceeded to unfold precisely the cruel strategy his officers had given to him piecemeal. They praised him effusively for his cunning, his brilliance, his courage in the face of a ruthless enemy.

Pilate refined the draconian plan. Relying for information on Melchi, now almost petrified with fear, Pilate selected a dozen villages surrounding Sepphoris as his initial targets. Without warning, Pilate's soldiers, divided into squads, sprang on the twelve towns simultaneously an hour before dawn, rampaged up and down the dark, quiet streets, grabbed sleeping people from sleep, and hauled them off screaming in horror. Within a few hours, scores of bruised, bloodied, terrified, bewildered, weeping Galileans had been herded into a square of scowling, spear-poised Roman soldiers who pushed and shoved the dazed people without any regard to age or sex. The few brave souls who dared ask the Romans why they were being held and what was going to happen to them got a slap, a kick, or a jab in the stomach with the butt of a spear.

By midday Pilate had sent word to each of the villages that their people were being held hostage until the assassins began to surrender. If the murderers did not show themselves within a day, Pilate would start his own round of executions. The Roman made it plain he did not care who among the captives died.

Within hours of the concentrated assault, word of Pilate's ultimatum had roared like a grassfire throughout the entire region. The headman from Nazareth, among the leaders from the villages that had been raided, not bothering with the niceties of protocol, declared indignantly to Pilate, "My lord, we don't know anything about the killers. If some of them live in our town, I know nothing about it, and I know everything that goes on here. You certainly cannot be serious that you are going to execute innocent men, much less women and children!"

"No, you listen, old man," Pilate roared back. "Unless you want to join these traitors, you'd better learn to control your tongue. You're talking to Rome! For now, I will not hold you responsible for your insolence. And, yes, that's exactly what I plan to do. Your rebels are killers, cowards to boot. Either they show themselves or these people begin to die. And, yes, by the way, tell your rebels my hostages get nothing to eat or drink until I have some killers in shackles."

Mary, sound asleep in her cottage, dreamed for an instant she heard loud noises and clomping boots on the brick-hard lanes of Nazareth. A moment later, she was snatched from sleep as the front door of the house was smashed from its hinges by the thudding kick of a huge Roman soldier. With shouted commands she could not understand, he viciously swept her up from her pallet and began dragging her stumbling and falling behind him, the ever-present stones on the streets tearing at her bare feet.

"What are you doing to me?" she screamed, trying with all her strength to escape the soldier.

He yelled something to her in his boorish tongue that she instantly judged must be a harsh warning for her to shut up and stop struggling. As he yanked her along, with her free hand she managed to pull her nightshift closely around her; otherwise, it would have fallen away and she would have been naked.

At the edge of the village, yelling men, weeping women, and screaming children were brutally herded together, falling, grabbing on to one another.

Then, on signal from one of the officers, the terrified hostages were hellishly driven like cattle away from the town. Soldiers who had experienced every possible nightmarish scene in their far-flung campaigns shoved and pushed the terrified people, totally unmoved by the human misery they were causing. Orders were orders.

Mary and the others from Nazareth had no choice but to keep moving. Instinct told them any who fell would not live to rise again.

Within a couple hours the human spoils of the Romans' morning labors had been collected on a small, treeless plain in the middle of nowhere. When Pilate's plan was made known to the hostages, they uttered not a word of protest. None wanted to die, but they would not forfeit their dignity to remonstrate with Beelzebub's agent.

As the day wore on, however, the suffering escalated to levels no one in their darkest nights of despair could have anticipated. Food, most of them, especially the adults, could do without, at least for a while. But no water! As the sun bore down with no shade to ease its cruelty, thirst became unbearable, particularly among the children, some of whom were quite young, hardly more than babies. They began to cry for water. Nothing. No response. Heartlessly, the calloused soldiers drank from water jugs in front of the hostages, often swishing out their mouths and derisively spitting the water on the ground right in front of the thirst-crazed Galileans.

Night brought some relief only because it was cooler. No rebels appeared. At noon the next day, one of Pilate's officers strode into the midst of the sagging, debilitated hostages, pointed to a man, and nodded at the soldier with drawn sword by his side. With one lightning-swift motion, the soldier's short sword swung with a swoosh through the still air, lobbing off the man's head. Blood spurted in every direction, drenching those hostages who happened to be standing close to Pilate's first victim.

As he turned to leave, the officer casually made it plain neither the body nor the severed head were to be touched. Anyone who dared would meet the same end.

Despite her age and intense agony, Mary moved around among some of the hostages, especially the eight or ten from Nazareth, offering them quiet words of comfort. "We are in the hands of Adonai," she assured everyone. *Though I walk in the valley of the shadow of death, I will fear no evil*, she rasped, quoting the psalm they all knew and clung to. *The rod and staff of Adonai comfort us*, the people would reply with great difficulty from their parched lips and dust-dry throats.

The next midday, another officer appeared in the midst of the hostages, followed by four soldiers armed with spears. This time, the entire crowd braced itself for the death of yet another of their fellow Galileans. To their unmitigated horror, the officer pointed to a girl, a boy, a young woman, and an older man. Before any could cry out, the soldiers had run them all through with their spears, deftly stabbing each one in the heart.

By dawn the third day, three of the oldest hostages lay dead from thirst and exposure. Additionally, the youngest captive, a little boy, lingered near death, lying listlessly in the arms of a woman from his village.

That noon, ten hostages were simultaneously garroted by expertly trained soldiers and their bodies left to decay along with the others that had collected around the compound, the stomach-turning smell of death heightening the madness of the diabolical escapade.

No rebels surrendered.

Mary, the leader of the synagogue in one of the villages, a boy of about fourteen, and a woman who identified herself as a mother leaned against each other all that night in a circle mumbling psalms, croaking out hymns and praying, not for deliverance but for courage and grace to die well and soon, if such was Adonai's will for them.

In the wee hours before dawn, they fell into a stupefied sleep, still leaning against one another so that none actually slumped to the ground. The synagogue leader had a dream in which he saw soldiers leaving. This was surely the presence of Adonai coming to him, the godly man told himself, as one does when having a pleasant dream. Then his happy dream was suddenly interrupted. Someone was pushing at him. When he managed to open his eyes, it was the boy. The man wanted to complain to the boy for disturbing his dream, but the boy was trying to say something. "What are you saying, boy?" the man managed to croak.

"Look, father," the boy said, using the term of highest respect for an elder. "The soldiers are gone." And they were. The troops, officers, bag, and baggage were nowhere to be seen.

"Be careful; it's a trick," a woman with age and wisdom whispered. Like the boy, she had seen the soldiers sneaking away in the night. "They want us to attempt to leave so they can slaughter us all," she warned. "Sit still."

No one moved until well past dawn when the full light revealed that indeed their evil captors had disappeared. One by one, the hostages struggled to their feet. A few of the younger men who found a new reserve of strength at the prospect of release cautiously stumbled around the area where they had been imprisoned by the human walls. "They are gone," the men reported. "No sign of a soldier. Adonai has delivered us. Hosanna! Alleluia!"

Mary's newfound friend, the leader of the synagogue, shakily stood to his feet, and said to the same young men, "See if you can find some help. Scatter to nearby villages. Tell the people the soldiers have gone. Most of all, bring us water. None of us can make it much longer without something to drink. And we've got to bury our brothers and sisters."

———

The moment Herod Antipas learned of Pilate's insane expedition, he mounted his fastest horse and, followed by a hastily assembled bodyguard, galloped toward Pilate's killing field. At the same time he dispatched Boethus to find the legate who was on an inspection tour of military readiness among the Greek cities of the Decapolis on the eastern side of Galilee Lake. "Find him, Boethus. Find him quickly. Tell him what we've learned. Pilate probably will not listen to me. He will listen to the legate. Pilate's stupidity will inflame the entire region, the whole country."

The hardest riding Antipas had ever done brought him thundering up to the outposts of Pilate's encampment soon after midnight that fourth night. With no pretense of ceremony, Herod loudly identified himself to the Roman perimeter guards who closed ranks to stop him.

"Get out of my way!" he screamed in Greek to the soldiers. "I am Herod Antipas, and I demand that you take me instantly to Pilate."

Pilate had been only napping in his tent as he agonized over what was quickly shaping up to be a blunder of enormous proportions. A dozen Galileans lay dead, rotting on the ground. More were near death from hunger and thirst. Not a killer had showed his face. Pilate knew he should withdraw, but he had not a clue how to bring it off without looking even more the fool.

Hearing the loud shouting outside his tent, he jumped up from his cot and started toward the entrance when Herod Antipas came bursting in, yelling, "Do you know what you've done? Do you! You've probably just incited the bloodiest uprising we've had in years! Your bungling will make the burning of Sepphoris look like a party if you don't stop this right now!"

Pilate drew himself up and shot back, "How dare you come crashing into my quarters like this. I'll have you arrested," he lamely blustered.

Herod squinted at the Roman and hissed, "Just try it. You lay one hand on me and your rule and life are history."

Pilate flinched. He had blundered badly, again.

"I've sent for the legate," Herod said, modulating his voice. "By the way, lord prefect," Herod asked him with biting sarcasm, "does the legate even know you are here? He certainly did not order this ill-conceived mad mission, did he?"

When Pilate said nothing, Herod answered his own question, "I thought as much. He'd know better than to drive these Galileans to the brink like this. Don't you know that every one of those hostages would have preferred death rather than see one rebel surrender. You have grossly underestimated the loyalty, or is it fanaticism, of these people."

"I made the decision," Pilate said defiantly, "and I stand by it. The assassins have got to be stopped."

"You made the decision, all right," Herod replied sarcastically, "and know, lord governor, you'd better unmake it, and quick!"

When both men calmed down, they worked out a cover story to help Pilate save some face, something like more pressing imperial business back in Caesarea had made it necessary to return in the middle of the night. Besides, the prefect had it on unimpeachable authority that in the face of the hostage-taking, the rebels had retreated in fear even further into the Galilean hills.

The legate wrote a scathing report to the emperor Tiberius, yet again urging him to recall Pontius Pilate. Before riding off for a morning of falconry, Sejanus absently read the legate's missive and tossed it in a box alongside Pilate's account of the episode.

While not ceasing entirely, the murders did abate.

—

Mary struggled back to Nazareth, her gently aging face suddenly lined with deep wrinkles, her beautiful eyes now lusterless, with sagging shoulders and a shuffling walk, forever changed by her foray into hell. A few days later, her son Joses disappeared. At first she did not worry over the absence of her son. Mary told his wife, "Joses will be back. He's always needed time alone to think when he gets upset. The trouble we've had with the Romans bothered him greatly."

"Mother Mary," the young woman replied, "it wasn't the Romans. It's what happened to you that nearly ate him up. But I didn't know how bad he felt." She hesitated a moment, then began to sob, "Oh, I hope nothing happened to him. What'll I do if he doesn't come back?"

Mary hugged her daughter-in-law and cooed reassuringly, "Now, now, Joses will be back. He'd never leave either one of us like that."

After about a week, Joses returned. He offered no explanation, and Mary did not ask for one. He's a grown man, she told herself. If he needs time alone every now and then, that's none of my affair.

A couple months later, Joses again disappeared. This time, he returned in three days.

He went back to work with his brothers and took up his duties as a husband and son, quiet, caring, good-natured as always. Mary thought she detected worry lines around his eyes, a slight nervousness when strangers happened to come through town. When nothing out of the way occurred, she chalked off her concerns as unwarranted. I've just been a bit anxious about his disappearance, she convinced herself.

The following Sabbath, after morning services, the villagers were talking about the latest murder, the assassination of Herod Antipas's chief steward. "What I heard in the city the other day was that the man always took a short walk before going to bed at night to help him sleep. He left his villa in Tiberias for his evening stroll. When he did not come back soon, his wife grew worried. They found him stabbed to death in a construction site for another one of Herod's fancy buildings, some kind of theater. He had money in his pockets, so it wasn't a robbery."

Everyone shuddered, praying the region would not have to deal with another round of political killings and their unspeakable consequences. Still, what's the death of one more flabby, highly paid toady for Herod! No one said anything. They just shook their heads.

At a family meal that evening when the murder was discussed, Joses did not enter into the conversation. He left early for his house, saying he was not feeling well.

—

"Joses is gone. We cannot find him," James explained to Jesus, irritation and deep concern in his voice. "He left soon after Simon got back home for his visit. He'd been restless for some time. Mother, of course, was the first to notice it. She tried to talk with him, but he assured her everything was fine."

"His wife, only sixteen, could not begin to deal with him," Simon added. "He told her nothing about his strange disappearances. If she pressed him, he only got angry with her. Stormed out of the house."

"I tried to talk with him," James said, "but got nowhere. He finally told me, 'Big brother, when I need your advice, I'll ask for it. Until then, just leave me alone.' So I did."

"Where do you think he is?" Jesus wanted to know. "And why have you come down here if he's missing in Galilee?"

"Are you ready for this?" James said to Jesus. "We think he's joined a band of rebels, maybe Ezechias and his crew. Honestly, there must be something in that family's blood that drives them to attempt such suicidal battles."

"I've been away too long," Jesus confessed. "I don't know anything about what's happening in our part of Galilee. You'll have to fill me in."

When James and Simon finished the harrowing story of the assassinations and Mary's imprisonment, Jesus was apoplectic, speechless with pain and rage. Turning to Mary, he said, "Oh, Mother, to think how they treated you! The agony and suffering you and the others endured hurts me so badly."

"I survived, Jesus. That's what matters," she tried to assure him, though the memory of the diabolical experience would never leave her.

He jumped up from the ground where they were sitting and began to pace around, trying to get a hold of himself. "And you think Joses and Ezechias are mixed up with these insane murders of Latvias, a fair and reasonable Roman, and the others?"

"We do," James replied with a sigh. "Terrorism like that has a way of finally leaking out. You can't do that much killing without someone involved sooner or later talking about it, or at least giving a hint."

Simon spoke up, "Joses, of course, has never breathed a word. The drift is, though, he's involved. It's crazy, but to some of the young hotheads in Nazareth, he's become the closest they have to a hero willing to stand up to those who beat us down. Now several of them want to go and join up with Ezechias and Joses if he's part of the gang."

Jesus looked at both his mother and brothers. "You believe Joses killed the steward?" Jesus asked in a low voice.

Their downcast eyes gave him his answer.

Jesus took a deep breath and sighed, "All right, he's with them. James, why have you come south with Simon? If Ezechias is holed up in the Galilean hills, why aren't you out looking for him? You know those hills better than anyone else."

Now it was James's turn to stand up and pace around despite his sprained ankle. "Rumor is they are not in the Galilean hills any longer."

"And where, might I ask, are they?" Jesus wanted to know.

"I think they are working their way toward Jerusalem," James informed his older brother. "Again, I don't have any hard evidence. That's the gossip from the hills. It's reliable gossip."

Jesus rubbed his hands through his hair, trying mightily to calm down before he asked his next question. "And what do they plan to do in Jerusalem?"

"We don't know, but you can be sure they're not here to celebrate Passover," Simon said grimly.

# Chapter Eleven

# New Birth

*Consider and hear me, O Lord my God; lighten my eyes lest I sleep the sleep of death.*

When Jesus and his small group were only a day away from Jerusalem, he announced to them, "I feel we should detour over to Bethany beyond the Jordan. I have some close friends there whom I've not seen in a long time. It's still several days before the festival. We'll have time."

Only Judas, inordinately eager for his first trip to Jerusalem, objected. During the past months he had learned to keep his complaints to himself, not an easy discipline for his self-centered, explosive nature. Now his disappointment overcame his caution, and he fumed, "Oh, Jesus. Don't go way down there. Let's get to Jerusalem. We don't know those people anyway."

"Hush, Judas," Andrew muttered fiercely under his breath. "How many times do I have to tell you this is not your journey."

Feeling Judas's anger, ignoring Andrew's remonstrance, Jesus spoke up, "Judas, I understand your excitement. I felt that way the first time I came a long time ago. If you want to, you can go on alone. I'll tell you where to meet us and approximately when."

Briefly, Judas considered that option, only to put it aside. "No, Jesus, I'll stay with you. Thanks for giving me the choice."

Walking eastward toward the Jordan, the group reached the banks of the river at sundown. For a long time Jesus stood watching the waters tumbling on their way to the Salt Sea, his mind overflowing with powerful memories. Jesus's mother, James, Mary, and the others kept their distance, not sure what Jesus was seeing and feeling, sensing that it was of the utmost importance to him. The sky reddened with a glorious sunset. One by one, his people silently drifted away to find places where they could rest. Only Mary remained nearby. Jesus shifted, stared into the distance, noticed for the first time since beginning his vigil that the sun had set. Glancing behind him, he realized that he and Mary were alone. He motioned for her to come stand beside him. He slipped his arm around her waist and said in hushed tones, "We are on holy ground, Mary. Up and down these banks my cousin John, of blessed memory, preached and baptized. Every day for months and months, people from the entire region flocked out here to listen and then be baptized. I've not been here in over three years. Like yesterday, though, I can see the people, feel their earnestness, experience their unbounded joy when they were baptized and celebrate the new life that flowed into them because of this experience with Adonai."

"It must have been wonderful," Mary exulted with him. "Being here with you, it comes alive for me also."

He looked at her adoringly. "Adonai is good to let me have this time with you. This river will teach you lessons about Adonai mere words could not accomplish. If you are not too tired, I'd like to walk you down a bit further along the bank and show you where John baptized me."

"Oh, Jesus, yes. Nothing would please me more," Mary answered, her eyes lighting up.

With a wave of his hand to Cephas and the others who had settled down a few dozen yards away from them, Jesus and Mary started picking their way carefully down the river, stepping over debris, hopping like children from one big rock to another, laughing quietly in the day's afterglow until they reached the spot.

"Let me tell you about my baptism," Jesus said. As they sat on a fallen tree, Jesus recounted the unforgettable night when John led him out into the moonlit river for the baptism. "I was transfixed, Mary. It was not the water; it was not John. Both were important backdrops to what transpired between Adonai and me. I have not been the same man. As I think back on the moment, it seems that the great ones of our past, Father Abraham, Moses, Elijah, and more, were there with me. I felt their energizing spirit and the blessings of Adonai resting on me."

"I believe I can feel what you felt," she said. "This is holy ground. Any time a man or woman meet Adonai in that way, it's the burning bush all over again."

She fell silent, listening to the waters of the river sing and dance in the darkness a few feet away from them.

When they had sat quietly for a long time, Mary looked at Jesus and whispered, "Would you baptize me in this sacred part of the river?"

He smiled and answered, "You'll get very wet."

"That's all right. I can slip my outer cloak off. It will not matter if my chemise gets wet."

"I would be honored to baptize you, my sister in the faith, my love in this life."

Hand in hand, they waded into the flowing waters. When they had reached a sufficient depth, they stopped. Jesus looked into her eyes, in which he could see the reflection of a universe of stars. Taking a deep breath, he sang in rich Hebrew, *Have mercy upon us, O God, according to your loving kindness, according to the multitude of your tender mercies, blot out our transgressions. Wash us thoroughly from our iniquities, and cleanse us from sin. Cast us not away from your presence, and take not your holy spirit from us.*

To Jesus's surprise and delight, Mary responded, likewise in lilting Hebrew, *O Lord, truly I am your servant, I am your handmaid. You have loosed my bonds. I will offer to you the sacrifices of thanksgiving and will call upon the name of the Lord.*

Jesus eased Mary gently under the rolling waters, quickly bringing her up out of the stream. "You are baptized, Mary. May you ever walk and live in the wondrous spirit of this moment. Whatever happens, we are bonded by the love of Adonai and by the power of this baptism."

Over a breakfast of fresh fish Cephas had caught in the river, Jesus related to them his memories of this part of the river. He did not tell them of Mary's experience the night before, reserving that cherished moment for the two of them alone. Mary could relate it when and if she chose.

As they finished eating, Jesus looked at them intently and said, "I cannot tell you what is going to happen in these next weeks. I have the strong impression from Adonai that we are about to sail through new, exciting, maybe turbulent waters. I will always be grateful that you have chosen to come this far with me."

"Master," Andrew said, using the term of respect with which they increasingly addressed Jesus, "I don't care what the future holds for any of us. The present with you and these friends," he motioned around the campfire, "is the greatest time of my life. As never before, Adonai has me in the palms of his hands. I can deal with whatever the future holds."

They were quiet for a few minutes, the only sound the ever-tumbling waters of the river.

James broke the silence. "I've come to know some of you only in these past few days," he said. "At the same time, I feel we've walked together forever. I pray that the future, whatever it brings, will enable us to do great work with Jesus, my brother, and with each other."

Looking a long moment at the river now sparkling in the early morning light, he continued, "As for me, I would like to be baptized in this river so important to our past, at the hands of my brother who, in a way I would have never imagined, has become a new way to Adonai for me."

"And me too," each of the others joined in a chorus. Except for Judas. If anyone would have noticed him, they would have seen a dark brown study on his face as if he were not at all sure what this was all about, as if he were not sure he wanted to get drawn into this maelstrom. Not willing to be a holdout against baptism and its plunge into an uncertain future, Judas trekked to the riverbank with the rest of them.

One by one, Jesus baptized them, including his mother. No one else stood on the riverbank to watch or record this ceremony. The high priest in Jerusalem, Pilate in Caesarea, Herod in Tiberias, the emperor in Rome, that day, each regarded what they were doing as crucial to the onward movement of human events. They were wrong. The joyful stirring of the waters of the River Jordan would prove to be history's most pregnant moment that morning.

Two more days' walk, punctuated with numerous stops to help distressed people along the route, brought them to Bethany beyond the Jordan. As he and his friends neared the town toward late afternoon, Jesus felt his excitement mounting at the prospect of seeing his cherished friends Mary, Martha, and Lazarus. The sisters would prepare a sumptuous meal for his band. He and Lazarus would have another of their invigorating conversations.

As he walked into the main part of the town, however, a pall seemed to hang in the air. Rounding a corner that led to his friends' comfortable house, he saw a somber crowd mingling in the courtyard that caused his heart to skip a beat. Something dreadful was going on.

Jesus broke and ran toward the house, calling out as he ran, "What's happened? I am a friend of these people. What's going on?"

A chorus of the villagers answered with one voice, "It's Lazarus. He's near death. He may already be dead. Oh, it's dreadful."

"Please let me through," Jesus urged.

"I know you!" a woman exclaimed. "You're Jesus. You were here some time ago and made many of our people well. Martha was saying this morning how much she wished you were here."

Shooing her grieving neighbors away from the door, she ordered, "Make way for Jesus. He's the healer. He'll make Lazarus well."

Instantly, people cleared a path for Jesus to go into the house. Martha looked at the door just as Jesus came through it. She fell at his feet, clutching his cloak, weeping, praising Adonai all in one breath, "Jesus, Jesus, thank Adonai you're here. Mary and I have been praying for days you would be led of Adonai to come. We would have sent for you but did not know where to find you."

"Martha," Jesus said, lifting her up, "I had no idea you needed me. A few days ago, I simply felt persuaded to come this way. I'm on my way to Jerusalem for Passover and decided to take a detour. What's wrong with Lazarus? The neighbors told me he was sick, maybe already gone."

"Three days ago, he did not get up for breakfast. At first Mary and I thought he might have decided to sleep a bit later, something he never did. For a while we did not go into his room. After about an hour, we became worried and went in. He was lying there, still as night, breathing, moving not a muscle. When we tried to rouse him, he did not respond. He's been like that since then."

"It seems he's had a stroke," Jesus said, more to himself than to Martha.

"Mary or I have been by his bed day and night. She's in there now," indicating the door that led into Lazarus's room.

"I will go in," Jesus said.

"Oh, do," Martha pleaded. "And wake him up, please. Dear Jesus, wake him up. We need him too badly to let him go."

After hugging a softly weeping Mary, Jesus knelt beside his good friend's bed. He took him by the hand, rubbed it gently, and said, "Lazarus, it's Jesus. I am here by your bedside."

Lazarus did not move. He gave no sign of recognition. Not even an eyelid flickered. His shallow breathing did not change.

"Mary," Jesus said, "would you mind leaving me alone with him? He may leave us. I would like some time with him."

Without a word Mary rose from the bedside chair, took one more backward glance at her beloved brother, and eased from the room, closing the door behind her.

Darkness fell. Mary and Martha met Jesus's friends. Neighbors gave them food and drink. As the hours passed, mothers with small children shuffled the youngsters off to bed. No one wanted to leave the courtyard. Hope and foreboding were woven together into an invisible tether that kept everyone tied to the vigil.

Well past midnight, Mary and Martha were suddenly roused from the fitful sleep into which they had fallen when Jesus quietly came out of Lazarus's room. Martha jumped to her feet and rushed to Jesus, saying, "Is he...?"

"Dead? No, Martha, he's not dead. He'd like a drink of cool water, though. He's very thirsty," Jesus answered, relief and joy in his voice.

Later, when no one else had fully mustered the courage to ask Jesus what had happened, Mary from Magdala, when they were alone, said, "Can you tell me about this wondrous event?"

"Mary, nothing happened in the way you suggest. I sat by his bed. I talked with him. I prayed. For long periods of time, I said nothing. I did not presume to suggest to Adonai what to do. If Lazarus was already at peace in the Father's house, far be it from me to ask that he be disturbed. If, on the other hand, the Holy One could rouse our friend and restore him to his family and friends for a while longer, we would be grateful."

"Everyone is saying you performed another of your miracles, Jesus," Mary said, her arm in his as they walked at sundown through the low hills outside the town. "It looks that way to me too."

"This is another example of the mind of our Adonai, Mary," he said. "Adonai's ways completely surpass our own. You and I have seen many signs and wonders from the Holy One. I, myself, on my own, did not do any of it, I assure you."

"Jesus, you've got to be more realistic," she said lightly, yet with the utmost seriousness. "Any way you want to say it, Adonai has used you as he has no one in these parts ever before. You've got insights, perceptions, a relationship with him that are completely beyond the rest of us."

"I will admit that I've been amazed at much of what's happened, especially in these past three years or so. You of all people must know it's not my doing. It's all the work of the Holy One. Maybe I have been in a unique position these days to be something of an aqueduct for his living water to flow through. If so, I am grateful and honored."

"Living water. What a wonderful picture, Jesus. That's what you have allowed to happen in your life. Adonai's living water has flowed through you to thousands of us," she said softly, hugging him even closer. "And you and I will be around to pour the water."

He looked far away for a moment, "It will happen, Mary, whether or not you or I are here to witness it."

Despite the close way she clung to him on that pleasantly warm afternoon, a sudden chill went through her as if she had been walking through frost.

Jesus made one sustained effort to explain to the people of Bethany beyond the Jordan that he had done no miracle, that Adonai simply decided Lazarus's nap had lasted long enough and woke him. The people would have none of it. Far and wide, the news traveled of the wonders Jesus had wrought. They recalled and expanded on the work of healing he had done in their region those years previously. Within hours the courtyard was full of sick people.

Early in the evening of the third day after Lazarus's recovery, Jesus and Cephas played a quick game of stickball with some of the village boys. A dignified, well-dressed man approached the playing field and stood there watching the spirited contest. From the skillful, passionate way Jesus handled himself on the field, the man could immediately tell that the Galilean was a veteran of this game.

After half an hour or so, Cephas threw up his hands and gasped, "I quit! I'm bushed. You young boys and that big boy," he thumbed affectionately toward Jesus, "can outplay me. I've got to rest. Bring me some water, somebody, please."

As Jesus smilingly wiped his sweating face and arms with a cloth, the man moved forward and said, "You are a man of many talents, Jesus of Nazareth. You teach with the wisdom of Solomon, heal with the skill of Asclepius, and play ball with the skill of Mercury."

Jesus's eyes sparkled with the man's warm words. "You are gracious in your comments."

Looking intently at Jesus, brushing aside accepted civilities, the man said, "My name is Nicodemus. I am from Jerusalem. I have been friends with Lazarus and his sisters for many years. They've spoken of you often since they first met you. When word reached me that you were again visiting with them, I made a point to come over here."

"I am pleased to meet you, Nicodemus," Jesus said. "I sense that you are a man of broad learning and a gentle spirit. How may I be of assistance to you?"

"It would be my pleasure to talk with you for a while tonight, if possible. With the festival coming in Jerusalem, I must get back tomorrow," Nicodemus explained with the bearing of one who usually has his requests granted summarily.

"If you will give me time to freshen up a bit from the game, I would be honored to spend all the time you choose," Jesus replied, his curiosity aroused.

Bathed, in a fresh, easy-fitting shirt that came to his knees, loaned him by Lazarus, seated on chairs in the garden, a plate of fruit and cakes on a small table between them, Nicodemus, again in his brusque manner, began, "I have only met you. I am convinced that you are the most unusual person I have ever met, Jesus of Nazareth. Indeed, Adonai has endowed you with more gifts than one sees in ten ordinary men."

Jesus accepted the compliment without comment.

Nicodemus continued, "Several of my colleagues in Jerusalem and I have been watching your movements over the last few months. You make us uneasy. You seem to have no axe to grind. You seem to have no other agenda than to communicate Adonai in his richness to the people."

"And that makes you uncomfortable?" Jesus queried, a smile on his face.

"Everyone with a following has an agenda. That's just the way it works. Unfailingly, they are out to advance themselves or some cause," Nicodemus insisted.

"I do have an agenda, as you say," Jesus replied. "It is indeed what you have described, and well put, I may say."

"What else do you want?"

"Nothing. Absolutely nothing. And I certainly do not want anything you or the other temple leaders of Jerusalem can offer. Neither am I attempting to upset or challenge anyone of your group," Jesus assured him.

"How did you know I am among the temple leadership?" Nicodemus asked, caught off-guard by Jesus's observation.

"That takes no soothsayer. The way you dress, your manner of speech, the attitude of authority are complete giveaways," Jesus answered.

"It's that obvious?" Nicodemus replied, a smile now playing on his face for the first time.

"Yes," Jesus replied easily.

"Many of your station would be intimidated by my rank," Nicodemus offered.

"Perhaps," Jesus answered, narrowing his eyes thoughtfully. "I am appreciative of your responsibility. I do not disparage your leadership. Still, we are both sons of the Holy One. You have some measure of power over me. You do not, however, have ultimate power over me. Only Adonai has that honor. So why should I feel bothered by your rank?"

Jesus munched on a cake, crossed his legs comfortably, and said, "But, my lord, you did not come this far to banter with me. Why don't you tell me what's on your mind?"

"'Cut to the chase,' as the hunters say," Nicodemus averred.

"Yes."

"What animates you, Jesus of Nazareth?" he asked quietly yet with almost breathless urgency. "What you did with Lazarus is nothing short of an act of the Holy One. How do you do these things?"

"Let's get it straight, Nicodemus." Sitting up straight in his chair, Jesus said insistently, "I did not do these things, as you say. Adonai does them. Gifts, you say I have. I accept that. Those gifts I have surrendered completely to him. My ability as a healer has come on the basis of years of training in Alexandria, made possible by the generosity of an Egyptian whose vision of humanity supersedes that possessed by most of us Jews. The teaching you mention comes from our Holy Scriptures and from the common sense that Adonai has given all of us."

"That's not enough," Nicodemus protested, leaning forward in his chair. "You've got more than all you enumerated. You're more than the sum of your parts. Where does it come from, and where is it going?"

Jesus did not answer for a long moment, then said, "Nicodemus, all that I am is from Adonai. For most of my life, especially in these last few years, I have felt his hand on my shoulder to encourage me in a process that simply seeks to connect people like you with the Holy One at the deepest, most significant level of their lives. What you see me doing are outgrowths of that sense of connection."

"How can a person like me become connected with the Holy One in ways you describe?" the temple leader asked, his breath coming now in nervous gasps. "Jesus, my greatest desire has been to relate to Adonai as you describe, as you seem to have achieved."

"Nicodemus, it's like you have to be born again. You have to become as a child before the Holy One. You have to unlearn and relearn much about life. Like a child, you have to trust the Father to provide what you need. And you have to love other people with an active love like you love yourself, maybe even more than you love yourself."

"What you describe, Jesus, is enormously expensive for a man like myself, in my position," Nicodemus answered with sadness.

"Maybe in the short run, Nicodemus. In the long run, however, the cost is inconsequential."

"I will have to think on this further," Nicodemus said, rising from his seat.

"No, Nicodemus, you do not have to think anymore," Jesus replied, keeping his seat while looking with penetrating vision into the patrician face before him. "You know exactly what I am talking about. You have to decide if you will do what you know."

"I must go," Nicodemus answered, obviously changing the subject. "Thank you for the time. I hope we meet again."

"We will," Jesus answered. "I assure you we will meet again."

# Chapter Twelve

# Jerusalem

*O deliver not the soul of your turtledove unto the multitude of the wicked.*

Jesus and his friends climbed the rising road from Bethany beyond the Jordan and Jericho on their way to Jerusalem. James put his arm around his mother, giving her extra support as she gasped with the exertion of the long climb. The excitement the group, as faithful Jews, would normally feel as they approached their Holy City was blunted by Jesus's increasingly somber mood, darkening, it seemed, the nearer they got to Jerusalem.

Cephas, Simon, and James made attempts to cheer him up with no success. Finally, James motioned for Mary to move in beside Jesus, hoping to draw him out.

"Jesus," she asked anxiously, "what's bothering you? We're worried about you. You have hardly said a word all morning. Are you ill? Have you had a word from Adonai that has depressed you?"

With an agitation she rarely saw in him, he exploded, "Mary, surely you can see what I see. It's enough to depress us all."

Glancing nervously around for soldiers or robbers, looking into the sky for signs of bad weather, she said, "Jesus, I guess I don't see what you see. Help me, please."

"All these people. Just look at them." He flung his arms wide, embracing the milling throng that ebbed and flowed around them. "Old, young, confused, most unspeakably poor, sick. Just look at them, Mary! Where are they going?"

Before she could answer, he furiously exclaimed, "To Jerusalem! And what's there? I will tell you. Nothing! Nothing that can do anything about their terrible conditions!"

"But, Jesus, Jerusalem is our Holy City. The City of David. Mount Zion. The place where the Holy One has revealed himself countless times," she answered with profound consternation. "They can meet Adonai in the temple. That's why they are all going to Jerusalem."

"Can they meet Adonai in Jerusalem, Mary? Really meet him. You've been there this time of year. Thousands pushing and shoving. Screaming and yelling at each other. Bartering. Bargaining. Is that what Adonai wants to take place in his sanctuary?"

"Oh, Jesus," she pleaded, anxiety in her eyes, "of course you are right. But what's to be done? This has gone on a long time."

"What Adonai has called me to do and be is what's to be done about it," he said emphatically, with a certainty she had never heard or felt from him.

His declaration utterly silenced Mary. She did comprehend, at some level within her own being, that he had just made an announcement akin to anything declared by any of Israel's great prophets. True, she had no idea what he meant specifically. Yet she knew in her soul that the man she loved and revered had delivered an utterance of magnitude that would reverberate beyond this moment along with Moses from his mountain. For much of the rest of the morning, she said nothing more to him.

Still walking, still ascending, at high noon Jesus and his band rounded a curve that took them to the top of a hill many called the Mount of Olives overlooking Jerusalem. Abruptly, Jesus stopped. In front and below them running north and south stretched the shallow Kidron Valley, rising up to meet the city's walls. Hard on that eastern stretch of the walls stood Mount Zion, topped by Herod's temple. Beyond the temple sprawled the warren-like city chopped into a thousand pieces by its maze of narrow, winding streets.

And people!

By the thousands they walked, scurried, milled, pushed, shoved, stumbled. Talk from thousands of throats in scores of languages converged to create a constant undertow of noise.

Every eye in the little group was on Jesus. They hardly breathed. Without saying a word, totally oblivious to his friends and the throngs that swirled past him, Jesus held out his arms toward the city, looked up into the sky, and mumbled something no one could understand. Standing still for a long moment, he suddenly crumpled to the ground as though squashed by a giant hand. Instinctively, Mary started toward him, only to be restrained by James with an almost imperceptible shake of his head and gentle touch to her sleeve. Hunched down in the middle of the road, Jesus sobbed, silently, uncontrollably.

When he regained control of himself, Cephas, who was standing closest to him, heard him utter under his breath, "O Jerusalem, my people, why don't you open yourself to the ways of Adonai? You need not suffer like you have and will.

You have ignored the great ones of the past. Will you never accept the love of Adonai and walk in his path?"

The depth and pain of Jesus's lament tore at Cephas, causing him to likewise double over in agony as if stabbed in the ribs by a knife.

Jesus was not through speaking.

He said, "And now, are you about to destroy yet more of Adonai's messengers and, this time, yourselves in the process?"

James, Mary, and John would later puzzle over what happened next. It seemed that a light, an ephemeral aura, briefly enveloped their friend and teacher as he slumped down on his knees atop the hill overlooking the City of David. As quickly as it had come, the vision, the mirage, the epiphany, whatever it was, was gone.

Cephas, beyond himself, exploded, "Jesus, what are you doing? You're about to rip me apart! Let's get away from here. Go back home to Galilee, Capernaum, anywhere but here! Nothing but bad can come of this!"

Before Jesus could respond, Cephas grabbed him under his arms and pulled him up from the ground. "You're too good for all of us. People like you don't last long on this rotten earth. Come on, let's get you to a safe place. You can keep on doing the work of Adonai. People need you. Let's flee! This city stinks of corruption and death. We don't belong here."

Startled, snatched from within himself, Jesus looked like a man coming out of a trance, a coma, struggling to get his bearings, find his footing. He looked blankly into Cephas's open, honest face. Gradually coming back from where he had been, Jesus stared at the city, turned his head northward toward Galilee, toward home. For a fleeting instant, an ineffable longing seemed to tug at him. Just as quickly, he shook loose from Cephas's grip, straightened his clothes, and said firmly, "Cephas, you don't know what you're saying. I may be going home but not to Galilee."

When Jesus looked at his friends, he was surprised to see how shaken, how confused they appeared. Consciously putting off the ache, the pathos, the yearning that had momentarily overwhelmed him, physically shaking himself, he said, now brightly, with obvious effort, "Come on, let's go into the city. I'll be all right."

His dramatic change of mood caught them by surprise. Nonetheless, happy for the transformation, they all eagerly complied.

Though the throng of pilgrims threatened to swallow up Jesus's small entourage as they approached Jerusalem, the pulsating excitement of the roiling scene immediately gripped Jesus and his friends. By the time they reached the Water Gate, the melancholia of the hilltop had given way to untethered joy.

"Jesus, Jesus," a chorus of men's voices called out over the noise of the crowd.

"We knew you'd come!" one of them shouted joyfully.

"Who, what...?" Jesus stammered, his mind rushing to place these men who knew him. "Why, it's Nathaniel and the other Galileans we sent home weeks ago!"

Cephas came trotting over to the small cluster of excited men. "We thought you went home, you rascals." With high-spirited laughter he grabbed them in a bear hug. "But how did you find us here?"

Nathaniel spoke up sheepishly, "We've been shadowing you from a distance. When you went across the Jordan, we decided to hang back. We figured, though, when you decided to go to Jerusalem for the festival, you'd come this way, so we've been waiting and watching, and here you are."

"You certainly fooled me," Jesus replied, delighted to see the young men who had risked much to keep up with him. "Well," he said enthusiastically, reaching out to include them, "let's all go into Jerusalem and see what Adonai has in store for us."

Heedless of the throngs around them, Jesus and his friends laughed, sang, and clapped their hands. The men patted each other on the back, welcoming one another to the Holy City with traditional greetings. Joining in the joy of the new moment, Mary and Leah swirled their skirts and waved their head coverings in the crisp sunshine. Though quite exhausted by the ascent and the strain of Jesus's behavior, his mother put on her best face, not wishing to dampen the exhilaration of the rest of them with her fatigue.

One of the Galileans chanted, *Clap your hands, all you peoples, shout to Adonai with songs of joy. For our Lord is awesome, a great king over all the earth.* Bowing with an exaggerated flourish toward Jesus, he chanted, *He is king over the nations, he sits on his holy throne.*

Another Galilean picked up the theme, singing, *My heart overflows with a goodly theme, I address myself to the king.* He too dipped jubilantly toward Jesus. *Your throne endures forever and ever.*

A third young man, now nearly beside himself with the ecstasy of the moment, shouted out in Jesus's direction, *Blessed is the one who comes in the name of the Lord. You are my God, and I will give thanks to you. You are my God, I will honor you.*

As the exuberance of the moment grew, Cephas snatched off his outer cloak and, with fanfare, spread it like a royal cape on the roadway for Jesus to walk on. Embarrassed at this show of deference and affection, Jesus, for an instant, thought to halt Cephas's demonstration, reconsidered, saw his friend's gesture as the good-natured display of love that it was, and boldly, with an air of understated ceremony, trod across the garment. Spontaneously, in response to Cephas's action, Andrew and Simon likewise tossed their cloaks before Jesus.

Now thoroughly embarrassed by their display, Jesus, with a broad smile on his face, held up his hand and said, "Enough of that. Keep your coats on. Don't get them dirty in the grime. Besides, you'll need them in the cool nights. I thank you for your affection. I love you too."

A boy of about eight or nine years, standing with his mother by the side of the street watching the scene, turned to her and asked, "Mother, who is that man?"

She replied, "I don't know, but I surely do like his looks. Don't you? He's the kind of man I'd like to have nearby if I needed help."

"Why did his friends let him walk on their coats?" the child wanted to know.

"That's a way of showing respect and love," she replied gently, keeping her eyes on the mini-processional unfolding before them.

"Can I let him walk on my coat?" the boy asked brightly.

"Why don't you keep your coat on. You can go and speak to him if you want to. Ask him his name. Tell him yours."

"Will he be nice to me?" the child asked his mother, now looking into her face for assurance.

"I am sure he will. He looks like a very nice man."

Without any further hesitation the boy walked confidently up to Jesus and said, "Kind sir, my mother said I could talk to you. She said I could ask you your name and tell you mine. I wanted to let you walk on my coat, but she didn't think that was a good idea."

Jesus beamed at the child. Kneeling down so he could be on eye level, he said, "My name is Jesus. I live in Galilee. Now tell me your name."

"My name is Saul. I'm from Tarsus."

"You're a long way from home, young Saul," Jesus said warmly.

"Yes, I know," Saul replied with a confidence and maturity beyond his young years that immediately intrigued Jesus. "My parents are going to leave me here in school to study the Holy Scriptures. I'm scared about being alone, but my father says it is Adonai's will. My father tells me everything will be all right. I hope so. But I'm still scared about being left here by myself."

"Saul, I agree with your father. You will be fine."

As Jesus started to stand up, the boy fixed his eyes on Jesus's face inquiringly and asked, "Are you Adonai?"

Startled, smiling, Jesus replied, "You see beyond your years, young Saul. I am a man in whom Adonai lives." Moving quickly to catch up with his friends, Jesus said, glancing back at the boy, "Maybe we'll meet again later in our travels for Adonai. I would like that. Would you?"

His intelligent, brown eyes flashing in the morning light, Saul answered, waving to Jesus, "Yes, my lord, I would like that too."

The group now through the gate, coursing into the crowded city, Judas spoke up for the first time: "I'm ready to go to the temple. I've never been. Let's go, please!"

The Galileans, again in chorus, said, "Yes, let's do that. We've not been there before either."

James, with an eye on his exhausted mother, cautioned, "I think Mother and I will wait until later to get into that mob. She's tired from our climb up the hills this morning."

"Oh, James," she said, "I'm fine. If the others want to go, I can make it."

With nothing else said, the band started toward the nearest stairway to the temple mount. As they started to climb, Mary stumbled, her breathing labored, perspiration popping out on her forehead.

Mary Magdala and Leah rushed to her side, saying to Jesus, "Your mother must rest. Tell us where to meet you later, and we will get her out of the crowd."

"Look," Jesus averred, "I don't have any need to rush to the temple. Let's leave the city for now, regroup, rest, and plunge into the temple ceremonies later."

"I want to go now," Judas said, petulantly. "You tell me where to meet you, and I will be there. All my life I've wanted to come here. I'm sorry your mother is not well. But I don't want to wait."

Andrew and John fumed at Judas. Jesus held up his hand to silence their protests. "Judas, if you insist on staying here, I can tell you approximately where to meet us. I have not been to Jerusalem in many years and the place may have changed. If you get separated from us, that's something you'll have to deal with."

He described the hillside outside the walls on the north side of the city where he hoped to make camp. "We'll be there at least until tomorrow midday," he told Judas. "After that, I don't know what we'll be doing. We do need to find a good place inside the walls to have our own Passover supper. You'd better make sure to join us no later than tomorrow morning or we'll get separated."

"I'll be there," Judas assured Jesus.

As Judas turned to leave, accompanied by four of the Galileans, Jesus took him by the elbow, looked into his eyes for a long moment, and said, "Judas, be careful. And wise."

Jesus led them to the same place he and his family had used on their previous trip from Nazareth to the Passover those years before. Thanks to the generosity of Martha, Mary, Lazarus, and others in Bethany beyond the Jordan, they had enough food to last several days.

"We'll camp here for the night," Jesus said after looking over the site. "Judas and the others can find us. In the meantime we can decide on our next moves."

"Do you have any specific plans for our stay here in Jerusalem?" Mary asked Jesus. "I get the feeling you anticipate something."

"I say again, I do not know what to expect," Jesus answered. "I have the impression that Adonai has plans for us in the next few days. I have no idea what they are. We'll have to wait."

Cephas spoke up, joking yet serious, "Just waiting is not something I like to do."

"I know, Cephas," Jesus answered with understanding. "Maybe this is a time when you will get a lesson in patience."

As the afternoon wore on, Jesus talked further with his friends about the temple and what it represented to him. "Of course, the structure is magnificent. Herod has given us one of the most gorgeous structures in the empire. My mind does go to the scriptures that recall the building of Solomon's temple a long time ago. Adonai said, in effect, to the king, 'You can build this house if you want to. I'll tell you how to build it. Just remember, you will never confine me in that house or any other.'"

Cephas said in his blunt way, "Frankly, I'm proud of the temple. Makes me glad to be a Jew."

"It is beautiful, Cephas," Jesus said. "Make no mistake, though. Adonai wants something different from us. More heart. More compassion. More justice. This temple and the system it supports know nothing of spirit, or concern, or fair play."

"What's going to happen?" John wanted to know.

"I believe the entire institution will eventually collapse of its own weight," Jesus explained, that faraway look in his eyes they had begun to see more often.

"Do you mean the building will fall down? Or that we will find another way to worship?' Mary asked, fear rising in her voice.

"Who knows," Jesus answered. "Maybe both. The whole thing's decayed to the core. I don't see how it can last."

Jesus had spoken with such complete authority that the group fell silent. In the years to come, each would remember his pronouncement made on top of the small knoll just outside the city's Tadi Gate.

In that moment of reverie, realizing he, again, was about to cast gloom again over the group, Jesus shrugged, stood, smiled, and said, "Let's not get down under. We're not here to change the world. We're here to celebrate. Let's talk about where we can have our Passover. Any of you have any friends or relatives in town or in one of the villages where we might get together? We've got a few more days, but we do need to be deciding."

Leah spoke up, glad to make a contribution to the group: "Jesus, I have an uncle on my mother's side of the family who has a small house inside the city. His wife is dead, and he has no children. He might let us use his second-floor room."

"That's a good idea, Leah," Jesus agreed. "Can you find his house? Some of us can go with you."

Leah assured him eagerly, "Oh, yes. He's my favorite uncle. I've been to his house many times."

Within a few hours, it was arranged. They would have their dinner at the home of Mark, Leah's uncle. Andrew, who went with Leah to see Mark, reported to Jesus and Cephas, "He's glad for us to use his second-floor room. 'Funny,' Mark said, 'I just felt that something special was going to happen to me during this Passover. Your coming to me was that special thing.'"

"We'll have to get the food together," Jesus said.

"Mark said it would be his honor to prepare everything for us," Andrew told Jesus and the others. "Since he lives alone, he has the time to do it and wanted to. I agreed. I hope that's all right with you, Jesus."

"That's fine," Jesus said. "Very generous of Mark to go to that much trouble and expense."

After the group had eaten their evening meal that night around a small campfire, Mary and Jesus, hand in hand, took the starlight stroll that had become a regular part of their life together. As they looked at the city off in the distance, aglow with a thousand lamps still pulsing from a long day of unceasing activity in the name of Adonai, Mary said, "I am glad we are here in this gentle darkness rather than in the noise and glare of Jerusalem. Jerusalem is both great and terrible. Looking at it tonight, I draw comfort knowing it's been here for such a long time and will be after we are gone. Still, I fear what can happen to any of us within its walls."

"Mary," Jesus said, a smile in his voice, "how philosophical you are tonight. It is a great place, full of history and hope, at the same time short-sighted and despairing, all wrapped in one. We don't have to fear it, at least tonight. We are together. Adonai is all around us. We'll never move away from him, whatever happens."

Mary halted, looked at him, and implored, "Jesus, what's before us? You must have some idea of Adonai's plans. You and Adonai are too close for you not to have some notion."

Again, he smiled, then grew serious. "I have some intimations. All I can say is that we are here on appointment from the Holy One. I feel events are moving over which we will have no power. The comfort I get is that nothing can move beyond Adonai's control."

"What's your part in this?" she asked, her voice laced with anxiety and calm at the same time.

"I get the impression that I will be both at the center and at the edge," he said. "Does that make any sense to you? I am more than a bit player. I am not simply being swept along mindlessly. At the same time, Adonai is in charge. If I do what he wants, my part will be accomplished."

"What does he want?" she asked.

"I really do not know."

"Jesus, I love you. I do not want anything bad to happen to you."

"And I love you. And I assure you, I don't want anything bad to happen to me either." He enfolded her in his arms and held the embrace for long moments, their spirits mingling even more intimately while, at the same time, taking flight to realms far beyond themselves.

———

"Papa," his young son Eli said, "I've got a lamb all picked out for us to take to the temple. He's perfect like you said he should be. I hate to see him sacrificed. I'll miss him. I just know Adonai will be pleased. Maybe he'll bless us real good." He held the wiggling little animal up to his father for inspection.

Looking the lamb over thoroughly for any flaws or anomalies, the boy's father said after a few minutes, "He looks good to me. Let's hope the priests accept him. The little fellow certainly comes from a loving and giving heart." His young son swelled with pride while the father looked on adoringly.

Jediael, a priest who lived near Jericho, in Jerusalem for his priestly service rotation as one of the men in charge of examining all sacrifices for acceptability, had not had a good day.

To his assistant he complained after several hours standing on his feet, "I can't take much more of this." He spread his arms out over the milling crowds, saying, "From early morning these people, these pilgrims, by the hundreds and hundreds, have pushed and shoved, whined and wheedled to have their animal sacrifices inspected to see if they are acceptable to Adonai."

Swaying a bit from the heat and pressure of the crowd, he lamented, "And when I turn one down, you'd think they'd be glad. But no, they just yell and carry on all the worse. I am about ready to jump off the edge of the mount!"

He had not slept well the night before. He missed his place back home. As he was about to begin work soon after dawn, that sniveling toady from the temple treasurer's office had sidled up to and said, "Brother, Jediael, uhm, err," and he snorted a bit, swallowing globs of phlegm that always seemed to be in his long, skinny throat, "His lordship suggests, that's right, only suggests, mind you, that, er, uhm, you pay special attention to all homegrown animals today. We would not, er, uhm, want to displease our glorious Adonai with tainted sacrifices." He peered into the priest's eyes and said, "I am sure you understand."

The priest knew the message actually meant no homegrown animals would pass muster that day. Someone's coffers must be running low, he surmised, with a mixture of anger and resignation. It always galled him when it was strongly suggested that he sanction only temple-approved animal sacrifices. In his younger days he had resisted the suggestions, frequently blessing homegrown sacrifices free from any obvious flaws. To his dismay he soon learned those in charge had definite ways to punish the independently minded and reward those who went along. When he received shit cleanup duty for three rotations running and then was short-changed on his stipend to boot, he caught on. After all, he began to tell himself, those in authority probably did have better eyes than his to decide which sacrifices would and would not please Adonai.

The day was three-fourths gone, he noted with relief, when a peasant family came up next in line. A boy of about nine or ten years held a wiggling, pure white lamb in his arms while his parents and two other children, a boy, somewhat older, and a girl, slightly younger, clustered around the lad.

"Father," the boy with the lamb bubbled to the priest, his eyes sparkling with excitement, if tinged ever so slightly with grief. "This is our best lamb. He's white as snow. My papa says that's the way they're supposed to look. We've checked him all over, and my papa and the leader of our synagogue didn't find anything wrong with him. We want to offer him to Adonai." The lad proudly held up the little animal for the priest to inspect.

Taking the lamb, the priest laid it on the examining table. What a perfect little animal, Jediael told himself. With deft fingers he felt the lamb at all the ritually important points. There's nothing wrong with this animal, he said to himself, and was about to pronounce it pure when he spied the treasury bureaucrat scowling at him from a few yards away with a strong warning look in his own eyes.

Taking a deep breath, Jediael said, "This is a nice animal. I have to say, though, the hoof on his back left foot is not perfect. Sacrifices to Adonai have to be perfect in every way. He's not acceptable." Handing the lamb back to the little boy, now devastated, the priest called out, "Next."

"Wait just a minute," the boy's father said, mustering all the respect he could. "Let's look at those hooves. All four are exactly matched. He's without any blemish. And our boy here has raised him for sacrifice. Please don't turn him down." Looking at his dismayed family, the farmer said, "Besides, we don't have money to buy a new lamb, and we've come a long way."

Though the farmer's words stabbed the priest, he ignored the remonstrances, saying loudly again, "Next!"

The boy started to cry. The father got in the priest's face, insisting, "Now listen here, you've got to take another look!"

With a subtle nod of his head toward the armed guard at his elbow, the treasury official signaled for the soldier to intervene. Thrusting himself through the crowd with his shield as the wedge, the guard brusquely confronted the farmer, saying, "What's the trouble here?" Glowering at the family, he demanded, "You folks causing trouble?"

"No, they are not causing any trouble," declared a tall man who came striding authoritatively toward the small cluster of people, his short-sleeved, knee-length, tan-colored tunic revealing a lean frame, his long dark brown hair tied back behind his head, his face dark with ill-concealed anger.

"No," he said again, now standing between the priest and his soldier and the confused, aggrieved family. "I saw the whole thing. This boy," and he put his hand on the lad's shoulder, "was bringing his most prized possession, this flawless lamb, for sacrifice. The priest," and now he fixed his gaze on the profoundly disconcerted man, "on signal from that temple money man over there," and he pointed toward the leering bureaucrat who was taking in the simmering confrontation from a safe distance, "refused the animal as flawed in some strange way, it seems to me, to make this poor family buy an animal from the temple merchants."

"Now see here," Jediael said defensively.

"No," Jesus said, "you see here," his voice quickly rising. "This family is not causing the trouble. You, along with that money man and this bully of a soldier, you're the trouble!"

"I don't have to take that kind of talk from the likes of you," the temple guard retorted heatedly, making what he intended to be a subtle motion to draw his sword. By the moment his hand reached the weapon's hilt, however, strong arms from behind him clamped him in a vice grip.

"We'll have no bloodshed today," the huge fisherman said quietly into the ears of the stunned and now wiggling soldier. "Trooper, just move away when I let you go and we won't have any trouble. And in case you haven't figured it out, I have some good-sized friends scattered around in the crowd who can take you along with a dozen or so of your buddies if you do not behave."

Cowed by the strength of the grip, now looking around anxiously, the soldier stopped his struggling, persuading Cephas to let him go. Immediately, he slunk off into the throng.

"Now," Jesus said to the priest, "suppose you take another look at this pretty little lamb. Maybe you were a bit hasty in declaring him unfit. Is that all right with you?"

Numbly, the chagrined priest nodded yes, giving the boy the chit he needed to verify the animal's fitness for sacrifice.

"Thank you," Jesus said. Taking a closer look at the priest, he said, "You are not a bad man. You've let the pressures get to you. If you will, you can repent of your faithlessness and again be an effective servant of Adonai."

For a second Jesus scanned the magnificent complex, then said to the priest, "You know, Jediael—that is your name, isn't it?—what you did today to that poor family, and who knows how many more, is the root problem with this whole temple system. If you and the other priests keep up these unjust practices, you will destroy this place. In fact, it will fall of its own weight, stone upon stone."

Before the priest could reply, the vanquished guard, along with three of his comrades, short battle swords drawn, came crashing through the crowd, knocking one and all aside, the temple bureaucrat at their rear pointing toward Jesus, saying in a hissing voice, "He's the one. Get him! He's stirring up trouble. He's even threatened to destroy our beloved temple, stone by stone. Get him!"

Again, out of nowhere, it seemed, strong arms grabbed the rushing soldiers, stopping them instantly in their tracks with Cephas saying now loudly to the soldiers, "No one's going to harm you. The fight's over. Go on about your business and no will get hurt, all right?"

Retreating to an even safer distance, the bureaucrat shouted out shrilly to the soldiers, "Don't you dare let these troublemakers get away with this! I'll see to it that all of you lose your jobs and go to jail if you don't do your duty!"

Humiliated at allowing themselves to be restrained by unarmed peasants and threatened with severe punishment, the four guards simultaneously began a fierce struggle to free themselves. In the fracas that exploded, that entire section of the Court of the Gentiles compound was wrecked. Money from the overturned bankers' tables flew everywhere. Animals and birds approved for sacrifice broke loose from their pens, scampering off bleating, howling, and fluttering in every direction. Men, women, and children rushed to get out of the way while cheering the plight of the despised temple guards.

When Jesus, distraught at the fight, raised his arms in an attempt to quell the disturbance, Cephas, who had loosed the soldier he was holding, grabbed Jesus by his sleeve, saying forcefully, "Let's get out of here! We'll be in trouble."

"This is wrong!" Jesus exclaimed over the noise, attempting to pull away from Cephas. "Adonai's temple is supposed to be a place of prayer and worship!"

Cephas hurriedly dragged Jesus away from the ever-spreading violence. Blending into the tussling, churning crowd of several hundred, Cephas, with surprising good humor and airy confidence, said, "You're right, Jesus. But for now this is war. We've gotta get out of here before all hell breaks loose."

"But the people," Jesus protested.

"They'll have to take care of themselves," Cephas called out to him as the two men, followed by the Galileans who were scurrying along behind, started scampering down the grand staircase that would take them away from the uproar.

—

"That Jesus fellow, the one from up in Galilee, the one we've been watching for over a year, he's the one started the whole thing," the temple money man whined to his superior. "I had everything under control until he and his stupid Galileans butted in."

"We'll have to report this to the captain of the temple," the superior said to his subordinate nervously. "He's given us strict orders to put up with no nonsense. If this Jesus or any of his people show their faces around the temple again, they'll have a lot to answer for."

—

"My lord," Menna, the high priest's adjutant, said to Caiaphas, "it's time we began the processional to the temple. The people are waiting expectantly."

"Where are we to meet Pilate?" the high priest wanted to know. "He is accompanying me to the temple ceremony, isn't he?"

"Yes, my lord, high priest," the adjutant replied, "he is going. Reluctantly, of course. Meeting us at the bridge. It would appear that after so many years, he would finally grasp the political importance of these events, even if he cares nothing for the religious significance."

"Ah, Menna, it would seem by now, after these years, that you would understand just how politically stupid the man actually is," Caiaphas said nonchalantly as he adjusted the tall mitre on his head while looking at his reflection in the finely polished brass mirror. Turning to his aide, he said, "How do I look?"

"Splendid, my lord, truly splendid. You will convey the wonder and power of Adonai by your very bearing and vestments," he said eagerly to the master whom he had served for fifteen tumultuous years. *Despite your ever-growing paunch*, the servant noted to himself. *Too much of the good life, my lord.*

Caiaphas loved to dress up and welcomed every high holy season so he could retrieve the appropriate vestments from the clutches of Pilate, who held them hostage against misbehavior on the part of himself or any of his close associates. Caparisoned in the magnificent garments, the high priest could do that at which he was exceedingly adept, strut. Dignity, officiousness, solemnity, holiness fairly oozed from his pores on great occasions. He could recite the prayers and psalms flawlessly in rolling, mellifluous tones. With precise timbre and inflection he chanted the calls and response that sent the heart of every devoted Jew present aflutter.

The high priest knew that from the moment his servant opened the door of his private apartment shortly after dawn until he closed it that night, he was centerstage. The feeling of exhilaration, the roar of the adoring crowd, the fawning of the hosts of priests before him made all the scheming and conniving he and father-in-law Annas did to hold power more than worthwhile. Preening in the predawn light, he cared not a whit for any of the humans strewn in his path. With the sun now just rising over the greening hills of Jerusalem, he could hardly wait to get started. The timing, though, had to be perfect, calibrated by astrologers who spent most of their nights studying the heavens. Those bleary-eyed men would tell him the exact moment when he should begin. He dared not take a step without their nod.

Pilate, in his house across the city, squirmed. He hated, deplored, loathed these tiresome ceremonies. While still in Rome, he had contrived to miss every official religious extravaganza he could without incurring the ire of the emperor or powerful senators. He surely did not have any patience with the mumbo jumbo of the Jewish priests. If their Adonai was so powerful, why had his followers spent the last thousand or so years paying tribute to first one, then another foreign power?

"Why should I go through this nonsense three or four times a year?" he fumed to his wife.

Porcla, always the long-suffering wife, was nonetheless bone weary of his complaining. Every time he started this litany, she responded with her own, "It's your duty, Pontius. It's your job. It's why we live in two big houses and have servants and soldiers at our beck and call. For you to back out would insult the Jews. Probably cause another riot. None of us can stand another one of them. So," she said, patting his arm with as much affection as she could manage a weak smile, "go. Do not complain. Stand still when you're supposed to. Get up and sit down on cue. When you come home tonight, a good supper, a hot bath, and I," she whispered, she hoped coquettishly, "will be waiting for you."

Grousing, somewhat mollified by her promises, he left the large house that served as his official residence when in Jerusalem.

He and Caiaphas would rendezvous at the entrance to the soaring viaduct over the Upper City's stretch of the Tyropoeon Valley. From that point onward they would process together across the bridge through the Grand Arch onto the expansive plaza of the Court of the Gentiles. As much as Pilate despised the ceremonies, the Roman grudgingly admitted that Herod had outshone most of the imperial world with the temple and its surrounding grandeur that adorned the small Jerusalem hill.

Custom dictated, as a show of humility, that Caiaphas had to walk the entire distance from his palace in the northern section of the Upper City to the temple, something under a mile. But what a walk, he told himself!

As trumpets blared, leading a splendidly uniformed honor guard, the captain of the temple, officially second in command of the entire Jewish religious establishment, preceded the high priest. As they processed, the throngs that lined the way cheered, waved palm fronds, and tossed their cloaks on the cobblestoned street for Caiaphas and his entourage to walk on. Flower petals, showering from upper-story windows, fluttered to the pavement like colorful, fragrant snow. Fathers lifted their youngsters into the air for a glimpse of the nation's spiritual leader, who, other than at these sacred occasions, was rarely seen in public. The lines of temple guards, their arms interlocked, leaned against the surging pilgrims who longed to touch the high priest or fall at his feet. Marshals walking closely by Caiaphas would have preferred even tighter crowd control, but the high priest derived far too much pleasure from the adulation to allow the troops to stifle all the spontaneous displays.

As the representative of the emperor, Pilate rode his horse to the rendezvous point and dismounted. Thanks to careful choreography on the part of both the temple and imperial planners, the two men and their parties arrived at the rendezvous at precisely the same moment.

Protocol demanded that both men acknowledge each other at the same moment since neither would recognize the other as supreme.

"My lord, the high priest," Pilate said in Greek, nodding his head at Caiaphas. "Your Excellency, Pontius Pilate," Caiaphas said at the same moment, likewise in Greek.

With no other word called for, the two men turned and stepped off together, walking with all the dignity and bearing they could evoke toward the bridge leading them to the royal archway into the temple's spacious Court of the Gentiles. Once in the temple precincts, Caiaphas would preside over this festival, a glorious prelude to the Passover itself that would occur two days hence.

The pavement at the entrance of the bridge narrowed a few feet, forcing a bit of shuffling on the part of the official parties to accommodate the more restricted passage. The planners had anticipated this slight alteration in the cadence, tutoring their respective masters on the best way to maneuver the change without losing the beat of the march. Since no pilgrims were allowed on the viaduct because of its narrow gauge, always, as such processionals unfolded, a small knot of well-wishers collected on both sides of the roadway at the entrance onto the bridge.

In the moment of transition, as Pilate and Caiaphas readjusted themselves for the walk across the bridge, four young men, who a second ago had palm fronds in their hands, nodded at each other. Before the bodyguards could react, the four men whipped daggers from within their cloaks and lunged at the rulers with the furies of hell bent on a suicidal mission of vengeful assassination. Pilate, trained as a soldier to sense any untoward activity, caught the sudden movement out of the corner of his eye and instantly jerked away from his two attackers. Caiaphas, burdened with his heavy vestments, unused to defending himself from any assault, froze. Fortuitously, the same brocaded garments that slowed his reaction saved his life. He felt a blade tear at his side, but the layers of clothing deflected the worst of the stab. In a flash, temple and Roman guards fell on the four young men and began viciously hacking at them. In the wild confusion and shouting, three other men stationed among the bystanders rushed into the fight, distracting the guards just enough for one of the assassins to get away, wounded but alive. Quickly determining that their other three comrades were dead on the spot, the intervening threesome likewise fled into the crowd.

Pilate screamed at his men, "After them! Catch those murderers! Someone will pay for this carelessness!" Temple police and Roman soldiers rushed into the crowd, knocking pilgrims aside to no avail. The three backups melted into the hundreds of well-wishers.

In the next instant, seeing the high priest lying on the pavement, Pilate groaned, not actually caring about the priest, worried how this frenzied incident would reflect on him at the imperial court, "Oh no! Not the high priest!"

Then, to his vast relief, he saw Caiaphas moving.

"What's the condition of the high priest?" now all solicitude, he demanded of the captain of the temple.

"He's wounded! I don't know how badly," he answered, kneeling by the fallen priest, grave concern in his voice. "We've got to get some of these clothes off him," he said. Looking up from where he knelt, he called to Caiaphas's chief aide who had rushed to the scene. "Menna, remove some of the vestments," he roared. "We've got to see how badly his lordship is hurt."

Caiaphas, raising himself on one elbow, said, despite a grimace of pain, "I'm not hurt badly. I think it's only a flesh wound. Here," he said to his aide, "unbutton this surplice. I think then we can lift the outer cloaks and you can see what's happening. I do not want the blood to blemish the vestments. They are far more important than I am."

In a few seconds it was apparent, to everyone's relief, that indeed the high priest's wound was not serious. The temple physician, always nearby during big events, quickly applied some salve and wrapped a swaddling bandage around the high priest's body. "Give him some wine," the doctor ordered. "He needs the fluids as well as the boost from the wine itself."

Within a few minutes, the high priest could sit up. After yet another brief time, he said, "If some of you will help me to my feet, I believe I can stand and walk."

Despite their remonstrances, Caiaphas rose to his feet, stood swaying a moment, then said, "I can proceed. We must not keep the people waiting. We are already overdue. The omens will have passed. We will not be able to make the celebration if we do not hurry." Then, sternly, "I do not want a word of this episode to leak! Do you hear me?" he demanded, looking into the faces of all his servants.

"That will not be easy to accomplish, my lord," the captain said, "considering the large crowd of pilgrims who witnessed the whole sordid episode."

Ignoring the captain, the high priest said through clenched teeth, "Let's get moving. My side is beginning to hurt. I need to get through the ceremony before the pain gets too bad."

Pilate vowed vehemently, "We will find out who's behind this insane attempt." Glowering at the three slaughtered assassins sprawled on the ground, he said, "For sure they will not be any help. But this was too well planned for it not to be the work of some fanatical cabal, maybe even that crazy bunch of Galileans."

———

News of the assassination attempts roared through the city. Pilate and the captain of the temple immediately ordered a systematic roundup of all possible culprits. Torture of the more likely perpetrators revealed nothing.

"None of the people on our list know anything," the captain told the officer Pilate had put in charge of the investigation.

"Pilate is convinced it was the work of the Galileans," the officer said. "True, the other murders were done by stealth and this attempt was wide open. It has the markings of their kind of daring insanity."

"We have hardly any way to track them down," the captain answered, shaking his head. "Besides, there must be thousands of Galileans in town for the festival.

"We'll keep checking," the officer said. "Sooner or later, someone will talk or come forward. The whole episode was too sordid, too juicy for everyone involved to keep quiet about it."

Several hours of intensive investigation produced nothing. The captain told his chief aide, "We must get to the bottom of this soon or we'll lose our chance. If Pilate is right and this was the work of Galileans, they'll be slipping out of town when the crowds begin to disperse."

"My lord," his aide said, "there's one angle we've not explored. The man who escaped was wounded—badly from what I saw. If he has not already died—a real possibility—he will not be able to travel any time soon."

"You're right," the captain answered thoughtfully, rubbing his chin as he spoke. "If he should try to leave, we just might be able to spot a man needing special assistance to get around. Post extra guards at the gates, especially on the north side of the city. Detain any man who appears wounded. That might net us something."

Toward sundown, as the captain briefed the still-dazed high priest, Annas, and three other advisers on the lack of progress on the investigation, one of them, a treasury officer, said, "What about the Galilean preacher who stirred up trouble in the temple. Anything on him? Would he try something like this?"

Annas, oldest and canniest of the group, always the one who had stayed abreast of notable Jews outside Judea, replied authoritatively, "I've had my eye on the Nazarene for some time now. He's been busy. He's certainly no friend of ours. He and his cousin John, who caused us so much grief until Antipas had him executed, have long worked against the temple. Still, I don't believe he's involved in this. Murder is not his way. He's just not violent. The strongest thing he's done is that episode at the Court of the Gentiles, and from what I've been told, the fracas arose when his friends and the guards got in a shoving match."

"But you would not rule him out?" another of the advisers asked.

Annas thought a moment and replied, "I never rule anyone out. People do strange things. Even stranger things when they believe Adonai talks to them in a special way."

The temple treasurer said, "My people tell me he's still in town. If I had been at the center of a fight like he was, I'd be gone. He's still here."

"Who is with him?" asked the captain, his interest in Jesus aroused.

"I'm not sure," the treasurer answered. "It's not a big crowd or I would have been notified. My people are always on the alert for big gatherings. He does have some women with him, I'm told. Who they are, I do not know."

"Find out more about him," Caiaphas ordered, speaking for the first time as he sat up on the couch where he had been resting. "Determine who's with him. See if anyone in his group could become our friend."

After a moment's reflection, Annas offered eagerly, "You know, Jesus has gained quite a reputation as a healer. Done some pretty remarkable things, I'm told. Rumors are that he actually studied medicine in Egypt for a while. If—and it's a big if, I admit—the assassins are Galileans and if one is injured, this man just might have been called in to dress the wounds."

Standing up abruptly, the captain said, "My lords, if you will excuse me, I think I'd better get right on this. Even if Jesus had nothing directly to do with the attempt, he might know who is involved."

As he started to leave the room, Caiaphas held up a cautioning hand, "Now, Captain, move carefully. We don't know what kind of following the man has. The town's full of Galileans. If you make a hasty move, you could have a huge riot on your hands."

"I understand, my lord, high priest," the captain replied as he reached the door.

"How will you find him, Captain?" Annas asked quietly.

"Be assured, my lord, I will find him," the captain said confidently as he exited the room. "No one of any prominence can hide from me. Besides, he suspects nothing and so is out in the open."

———

Jesus and the group, in the early evening chill, had huddled around a crackling campfire to eat their meal. Suddenly, from the descending darkness, four temple troopers and an officer appeared amid much clatter and clinking.

"We want to speak to the Galilean named Jesus," the officer said loudly, causing a stir among everyone within earshot.

Immediately, Jesus stood up to face the officer, saying calmly, "I am Jesus from Nazareth."

"I am from the captain of the temple," the officer declared.

"Welcome to our campsite," Jesus said cordially. "We extend our greetings to you. We hope His Excellency, the captain, is well."

Slightly thrown off by Jesus's unruffled manner, the officer said, "You've no doubt heard of the cowardly attempt on the lives of the high priest and Pontius Pilate."

"Yes, we have. We thank Adonai that the attack did not succeed. Such violence is not the way of Adonai or of ours," Jesus replied without equivocation.

"You maintain, then," the soldier said, "you know nothing of the attack. Is that correct?"

Genuinely surprised, Jesus replied without wavering, "You have my word, neither my friends nor I have any knowledge whatsoever of the attack. We learned of it through the grapevine like everyone else in Jerusalem." Pausing for a moment, Jesus said, "May I ask why you are questioning me?"

"We have our reasons," the officer replied officiously, belying the fact that he had no idea why he had been sent to question this cool-headed Galilean about the attempted murders.

"You may tell the captain of the temple and your other superiors that we know nothing. We pray for the high priest's full and rapid recovery. We adhere to the Scripture's command that no one should lay a hand on the high priest as Adonai's elect. Please tell him that should you have occasion to talk with him."

As the contingent of temple guards began marching off into the dusk, the officer stopped, glanced at the bewildered Galileans gaping at him, and said, "I am authorized to say it will be worthwhile to any who come forward with information on this crime."

"We will be happy to cooperate," Jesus answered, "and we want no reward."

"What was that all about?" Cephas asked Jesus.

"You know as much as I do," Jesus answered, his brow now furrowed with worry. "They have some reason for questioning me," he said.

"Could it be that trouble in the Court of the Gentiles?" Mary asked.

"Maybe," Jesus answered thoughtfully. "I think, though, there's more."

Andrew warned, "You know the entire temple and Roman operation is fanning out over the entire city trying to find out who made the attack."

"But why us?" Jesus's mother asked.

"Yes, Mother," James offered, "of all the Galileans in Jerusalem, why single us out?"

"Jesus's fame has caught up with him," Simon explained. "Anytime someone becomes as well known as Jesus, the rulers began to watch him extra closely."

"I have an idea their questioning is connected with the Galilean killers," John said to Jesus. "After what your mother and the others from Galilee endured with Pilate's botched roundup, you can just put it down he's still smarting. He wants to give all Galileans a hard time. And you, Jesus, as the most famous Galilean of our time, are a natural target."

"We'll have to be very careful," Cephas warned.

———

Jesus was roused from a deep sleep by the slight touch of a man's hand. Before he could speak, the man placed his hand gently over Jesus's mouth and motioned for him to follow silently. Cephas, asleep right by Jesus's side, ever on the alert to aide his friend, was immediately awake. When Jesus rose to slip away into the darkness, Cephas was right behind him. Though Jesus made a feeble attempt to motion Cephas to go back to sleep, not knowing what was about to happen, he was glad to have the fisherman nearby. Padding silently after the messenger, Jesus and Cephas looked around at their sleeping friends, hoping none were stirring. All seemed to be asleep. In the darkness they could not see Judas raise his head ever so slightly, watching their hunched forms slip away from the encampment.

With pilgrims by the scores scattered everywhere on the ground under the stars wrapped in blankets or sleeping in small tents, the three men said nothing until they were well away from all the campsites.

Huddled behind a large clump of boulders, the messenger said in a voice so low Jesus and Cephas had to strain to hear him, "I am Joda. There's been some trouble."

Recognizing his Galilean speech, realizing the messenger knew where to find him among the throng of pilgrims, Jesus was immediately anxious. "What sort of trouble?" he demanded, trying to keep his voice down despite his agitation.

"It's your brother, Joses. He's been hurt," Joda said.

"Where is Joses?" Jesus hissed, his worst fears realized.

"He's in the city. I'll take you to him."

"How do we get in?" Cephas whispered. "The gates are closed."

"I know a way," Joda said.

Jesus stifled the plethora of questions that tumbled through his mind.

"Let's go to my brother," he said.

Within half an hour, after a route neither Jesus nor Cephas could ever hope to replicate, they were at the door to a hovel in one of the more disreputable sections of the ancient city. After a quiet, coded knock, the door opened. The smoky light of a small lamp enabled them to see the huddled form of a man lying on a pallet, shaking, twisting, pouring sweat.

Without a word, Jesus knelt down beside the form, pulled back the blanket, eased him over on his back, and peered into the face of his brother.

"Let me see your wound, Joses," Jesus said resolutely.

Joses tried to shake his head. "No, Jesus," he rasped, "you don't need to be involved in this. I wanted you only to know I was hurt."

"Hush. With you hurt, I'm in it. Now, let me see the injury."

Jesus reeled when he saw the slashes. If Joses were to live, these wicked injuries needed immediate attention.

"Joses, listen," Jesus said. "I'll have to stitch these cuts. Even then, I am not sure you'll make it."

"Jesus," his brother pleaded, "go. For the sake of all of us, leave now."

"For the sake of all of us, I will stay," his brother said in a way that left no more room for argument.

Casting his eyes around in the tiny house, he said, "Does anyone have a needle and thread?"

From a dark corner, a woman spoke up and said, "Yes, Master, I do."

"I will need some wine," Jesus said to whoever wanted to respond to him from the darkness.

"Here," a voice replied, handing him a jug that felt about half full.

"This is going to hurt very badly, Joses. I don't have time for you to get drunk on the wine. Drink some of it to help replace the loss of blood. I am going to wash away what I can of the grime around the injuries. It will sting like nothing you've known before."

"Do it," Joses said quietly, turning his head away.

As easily as he could, Jesus swished some of the liquid on the gaping knife cuts. Joses jerked, bit his lip until it bled, but did not cry out. With a clean cloth handed to him from the darkness, Jesus wiped away the wine, dabbed at the now freshly bleeding gashes, and prepared to start stitching.

"There's nothing to do but bear this, Joses. Seti has some creams that help deaden the pain for stitching, but he's not here. When you cannot stand it anymore, tell me, and I will stop. We've got to close these wounds or terrible infection will set in. Are you ready?"

For an hour, Jesus stitched, paused periodically to let his brother catch his breath and for the pain to subside somewhat, then began again. No one in the cottage said a word throughout the ordeal. After Jesus had done what he could with each of the several stab wounds, he again swished the wine over the lesions and covered them with cloths.

Dawn's light began to seep through the one tiny window on the street-side of the house. Jesus leaned back, stretched his arms, shook his head, and said, "Now it's in the hands of Adonai. The next couple days will tell the tale," he said.

Despite the pain, Joses fell asleep, exhausted.

Arriving back at their encampment, Jesus said only, "Cephas and I got word in the night that a man needed me, so we went. We must pray for him today."

Everyone yearned to know the details, but none asked. Jesus's mother, with one look at his face, knew instinctively it involved her son Joses.

—

At midday, Jesus sidled up to Cephas and said under his breath, "I think we'd better go back into the city."

"I'm with you," Cephas said.

Making a lame excuse, the two men left the group and headed for the city. It took some effort on their part to find the house where Joses lay, but after correcting a few wrong turns, they came to the tiny cottage. At the door stood a large man, his arms across his chest, a sturdy cudgel leaning against the house's wall. Neither Jesus nor Cephas had seen him before. When the two men stopped at the house, the big man reached for his staff and said in a Galilean-accented voice, "You have no business here. Move along."

Cephas, always ready to defend Jesus's prerogatives, said brusquely, "And you don't know what you're talking about. Now suppose you get out of the way and let us in."

Unfazed by Cephas's manner, the guard replied defiantly, "I was told to let no one pass. That means both of you."

Laughing at the two men, Jesus said, "If you two roosters will quit strutting around each other, it will help."

To the guard he said, "Tell them Jesus is outside."

Blinking, the guard said hastily, "You're Jesus? *The* Jesus?"

"I'm Jesus. I'm not sure I am *the* Jesus you're talking about."

Now looking furtively around to make sure no one else could overhear, the guard asked, "You're Joses's brother?"

"Yes."

In the next moment, Jesus was kneeling beside his brother. "How are you feeling, Joses?" Jesus asked.

"Better," he answered, hardly above a whisper. "I'm still alive, so that's progress," he said with a wan smile.

After gingerly examining the wounds, Jesus leaned back on his haunches, looked at Cephas, then said to his brother, "Joses, I don't see any sign of severe infection. You're not well, by any means, but you just might make it."

"When can I leave?" Joses wanted to know. "I want to go home."

Patting him on the shoulder, Jesus answered, "I'm afraid you're several days away from being able to move from this house, much less make a long trip. Might as well content yourself to stay here."

"Are they looking for me?" Joses asked softly, looking around anxiously in the dark room.

Jesus and Cephas both gasped and glanced nervously at each other. Then Jesus said, "I don't know what you're talking about, Joses."

"And don't want to," Cephas interjected, a bit too loudly to suit Jesus.

"And, no, as far as I know," Jesus said, "no one's looking for you. If they are, they'll have a hard time getting by Goliath at the front door." And he laughed gently, as much as anything to relieve the palpable tension that had suddenly filled the tiny house.

"Jesus," Cephas said emphatically, "we better go."

Kneeling close to Joses one more time, Jesus whispered in his ear, "I will see you tomorrow. Let's pray no one is looking for you. *Let the steadfast mercy of Adonai be upon you.*"

Joses responded weakly with a smile, *I sought the Lord, and he answered me, and delivered me from all my fears.*

Cephas joined the spontaneous litany: *The angel of the Lord encamps around those who fear him, and delivers them.*

Clasping hands, the three men whispered, *Amen! Selah!*

—

Early in the afternoon, Judas grew almost manically restless. He had been sitting around in the encampment for most of three days with no activity. The mystique of the officer's inquiry had kept him stirred up for several hours. Now that agitation had worn off.

Abruptly, he jumped up from the ground where he had been sitting and said to everyone and no one, "I'm going for a walk. Just sitting around is about to get to me."

To his irritation, no one said anything to him either way. Leah had the decency to at least wave to him, but hers was the only attention he received.

As he neared the city, he veered and began trekking the outside perimeter of the walls, all together three or four miles, he calculated. It felt good to walk, to be on his own, out from under the increasingly oppressive control of Jesus, Cephas, and the rest. What did they know? He was the one who had the curiosity, the courage, the verve to do something with his life. The rest of them could truck around after Jesus if they wanted, but not him. He had seen just enough of the world to stir his wanderlust. He had no money, though. What an aggravating problem. And there was the problem of his wife and baby back home. If only he had some money of his own, he could strike out, see the world, make even more money with his cunning. Soon, he'd return home rich and famous, sweep up his wife and child, and go away again to a beautiful place away from that grubby little town of Capernaum. Maybe Rome. Or Alexandria. Or Antioch. If only he were not so poor!

It was nearly dark when Judas strolled back into the camp. To his dismay, only Leah and some of those tag-along Galileans were seated around the campfire. "Where is everybody?" he irritably demanded of Leah.

"About an hour ago, Jesus called out the names of several of them: his mother, Mary, Cephas, James, and the others. He asked me and the Galileans to excuse them while they talked. It bothered me to be left out. But it's all right."

Furious, Judas said, "I tell you, it's not all right with me. I've been with this thing from the beginning. To just go off without me makes me furious! Which way did they go?"

"Off to the north somewhere," she said absently. "Cephas told me to tell you if you got back just to wait here for them."

"It's that way, is it? Just dump me off with the likes of you and these stupid clodhoppers. I'll not take that lying down!" he shouted as he stalked off toward the north.

Leah and the Galileans quizzically looked in his direction for a few minutes, then, with conscious effort, turned back toward the campfire and began chatting inanely about the events of the day.

—

When Jesus, Mary, Cephas, his mother, Simon, John, and Andrew had walked a couple miles north of their camp and away from other pilgrims, Jesus stopped and looked at his friends. "Sit down, please. We've got to talk."

What did he have on his mind? His tone was ominous. None wanted to hear. No one dared miss a word.

Jesus sat down on a rock while the others leaned up against tree trunks, knelt, squatted, or settled onto a softer spot on the ground.

"I have some grave anxieties about what's happened here in Jerusalem that I must keep to myself," he began, looking thoughtfully into each face in the circle as twilight began to encroach. "If my fears are borne out, and if you were privy to my suspicions, we could all be in serious trouble. Events are closing in around me that may prove terribly dangerous."

Mary Magdala sprang up, her voice trembling, pleading, "Jesus, what are you talking about?"

Jesus looked at her adoringly, cautiously. "Mary, you will have to trust me. I hope I am wrong. If I am right, you need to listen very closely to me."

"You're making me nervous again," blurted Cephas. "You know we don't like to hear you talk like this."

"Cephas, I don't like to talk like this either. But it's necessary." Taking a deep breath, Jesus went on, "Whatever happens, I don't want you to be sad. Not too long anyway." And he gave them a smile.

"We can each count it a great privilege to have spent this time together. To the limits of our abilities, we have sought to make real the words of our revered Isaiah when he sang, *The spirit of Adonai is upon us because the Lord has anointed us to bring good news to the oppressed, to bind up the brokenhearted, to proclaim liberty to the captives, and release to the prisoners.* We have proclaimed the time of the Lord's favor, the day of judgment from Adonai and comfort to all who mourn."

Now standing up, he clasped his hands behind his back, swayed a moment, then continued, "On the basis of the measure of faithfulness you have shown in the work of Adonai with me, you can create a new future built on justice and true peace. Whatever happens to me, you will go on. You are all Galileans. Our homeland is only a tiny part of the world, but that's not important. In Adonai's good time you will venture far beyond the boundaries of our country. You will travel to new worlds of religion, tradition, nationhood, even of our Jewish culture. The entire world will be yours to influence with Adonai's new ways.

"I need to warn you," he cautioned, opening his hands in a way he had of including everyone in what he wanted to say. "As you have learned from our own experiences, not everyone will welcome you or receive what you offer. When your fresh ways threaten entrenched power, you will face opposition, maybe even harsh persecution. Throughout our history, when preachers and prophets challenged the evil ways of our own leaders, those in control maligned, imprisoned, and even killed the people of Adonai. You and I can expect no less."

Searching for words, Jesus continued, "You might ask, 'What are we to do to keep alive, to extend what we've begun?' The answer is that you will simply persist. You will touch people, all kinds of people, knowing everyone belongs to Adonai. Contrary to what you have been taught, no one is unclean. No human condition is unclean. In touching people you will help them come to the abundance of life. You will feed people, try to help them get well from their diseases, and enable them to find new ways to enrich their lives. Empty stomachs, hurting bodies, and idle hands have a hard time celebrating good news.

"Beyond the troubled living conditions of your brothers and sisters—remember, everyone is your brother and sister—you will learn to deal with the sweeping issues of the human spirit. You've seen me try to assist distressed people with falling-down sickness. You will do even better with those conditions. In fact, consider all the wonders we have seen come to pass, and know that you and those who come after you will certainly surpass all of these."

For several minutes he said nothing. The group hardly breathed. "Our scriptures point to a 'Suffering Servant.' I've thought a lot about that. Maybe I am, maybe we are, something like that. Isaiah does not paint a very flattering picture of that figure. Our own scholars have long debated exactly who or what the prophet had in mind. Lately, I've begun to identify with that figure from a long time ago. Maybe Adonai has ordained that you and I celebrate and suffer for our fellow Jews in ways we can neither imagine nor comprehend. Maybe," he caught his breath, "maybe we are being singled out to celebrate and suffer for everyone, Jew and non-Jew. Maybe Adonai is going to use us to create a new human family gathered around the idea of Adonai as loving Father of us all."

The tiny band caught its collective breath yet did not move.

Fully dark now, they could not see his eyes misting over. They could feel his passion when he urged, "If you remember nothing else about me, when your days are bright or your nights long, know that I have loved you. With all my heart, soul, and mind, I have loved you. You understand the commandments our father Moses gave us. I give you a new commandment, not to replace the Ten. Rather, to gather them up. 'Love one another.' As the Father has loved me, as I have loved you, love one another. Love these here tonight and hereafter, everyone you meet, even those who mistreat you."

Now pacing nervously, his words flooded, "The hour grows late, not only tonight, but in Adonai's way of measuring. Thick clouds are gathering. I may have to leave you."

"No," cried Simon, his voice choking, "you cannot. You must not!"

"It's all right, Simon. We've not talked much about what's out there." He motioned toward the heavens. "Let me tell you what I'm thinking. We all go away. We all die. What's different now is if I go away, at some point I will gather all of you to myself. Where I am, there you will be also. It's like I go home to the Father's house. It is a large house with more than enough room to provide everlasting living space for you and the entire world. While you continue working here, I'll be there getting ready for you."

Andrew, the practical one, full of pain, implored, "Master, we don't know what you're talking about! We surely don't know where you are going, nor do we know how to follow you there."

Jesus looked lovingly into Andrew's shadowed face. He let his eyes again move from one to another in the circle, their faces opaque in the failing light, yet distinct to his mind's eye. He assured them, "I am our way to the Father. Or, let me say it like this, the ways in which I, we, have served and loved our hurting people are the paths to the Father. You keep doing and feeling and ministering like we've been doing. In his good time, in this life or beyond, you will come to the Father."

Mary Magdala pleaded, her voice aching with grief and confusion, "What's going to happen to you?"

"Mary," he answered her warmly, appreciatively, "I tell you honestly, I don't know. Maybe nothing, at least for now. These are evil times. Human life is cheap to those in power. If I have become sufficiently troubling to either the temple or Roman rulers, they will not hesitate to get rid of me."

"We will never let that happen," Cephas cried out from the now almost complete darkness, jumping up to stand tall by Jesus. "I will lay down my life if necessary to protect you from all harm."

"Cephas, thank you. You have the best of intentions," Jesus responded quietly with profound gratitude. "Beware, though. If the threats against me become dire enough, even you might cave in."

"No, Master, no!" he wept, wringing his hands, now pacing frantically in a circle around Jesus.

"Cephas, it is no matter," Jesus said, reaching out to calm him. "Upon you and these others here, and those who will gather around you, Adonai will build his future place in the world."

His voice choked with tears, James said, "Jesus, my brother, now my master, what will we do without you, if and when the time comes? We've just begun to understand Adonai's new ways, We've barely begun to grasp the meaning of our own scriptures as you have opened them to us. Now you are talking of going away. Say it, of dying! We will collapse without you."

"No, James, you will not collapse," Jesus promised. "Understand, James, even if I go away, I will never leave you. Adonai will make it possible for me to be with you, always, for as long as the world lasts. I will be like a grain of wheat that is sown in the field. That lone grain dies to itself to give birth to a full stalk of life-giving abundance. In due time you and I will understand more clearly what I am sensing for myself and for you."

In the electricity of the moment, his mother rose from the rock where she had been sitting, steadied herself for a moment, slowly walked to him, put her arms around him, and said softly, "Jesus, there's much about you I have never understood, beginning with your birth. And neither did your honored father. Nor do I now. Of this I am sure: You were born for such a time as this. As you speak, my mother's heart shatters into a thousand pieces. As one who has always walked with the Holy One, what you say tonight finally brings me a measure of understanding." Taking a deep breath, looking again into his eyes, she whispered, "Do what you must."

"Mother, all of you," Jesus said, struggling for composure, "if I go, when I go, Adonai will provide you with a continuing presence. The very breath that brought this vast world and its heavens into being will be and abide with you forever. Open your minds, and the Spirit will come. You will never be alone."

A hush akin to the silence before that stupendous instant of creation enveloped the small band. They sat still, waiting, waiting, waiting for they knew not what.

Judas exploded into the silence. From out of the night, he came storming into the midst of the circle, shouting, "I've found you! You tried to get away from me. Go off and hide! That's not fair. Leah told me to wait in camp. No way! I wasn't going to let you get away with ignoring me again!"

Startled and angry, Jesus snapped, "Judas, be quiet! No one has tried to leave you out. If anything, your attitude cuts you off. Besides, you were not in camp. I was not sure where we would go. That's why we said for you to remain there. You are part of us."

"It won't do," he shouted angrily, his voice carrying through the cool, clear night. "From the very beginning all of you have tried to cut me out. Cephas and Andrew, my own cousins, did not want me to come in the first place. This is the final insult."

Balling his fists at them, stalking away into the darkness, he yelled, "I can't and won't take it anymore. I'm leaving, and a curse on all of you!"

Andrew sprang up to block him, but Jesus raised his hand. "It's all in the hands of Adonai."

It was noon the following day before Judas returned to their encampment, an air of cockiness about him, a veneer of confidence mixed with fidgety uneasiness. As if he had rehearsed it, upon returning to the group, he went straight to Jesus and said apologetically yet with the slightest edge of impertinence, "Look, I am sorry for my bad behavior last night. I was upset. I was tired. I did feel left out. I know better now that I've calmed down. I went too far."

Jesus looked at him closely, started to say one thing, changed his mind, and said instead, "Judas, it's all right. Welcome back. I'll be more careful to make sure you know what's going on."

"Thank you," Judas answered as he walked away, unrolled his pallet, lay down on it, and fell sound asleep, his hand securely around the small bag of coins in his pocket.

# Chapter Thirteen

# Tetelestai

*Into your hands I commit my spirit; you have redeemed me, O Lord, faithful God.*

In the early afternoon Andrew said to Jesus and the others, "It's getting time for us to make our preparations for Passover. Someone needs to go to the temple, buy us a lamb from the priests' pens, and have it properly sacrificed. For obvious reasons," and a smile came in his eyes, "Jesus, even though you are firstborn in your family, I think it is better if you stay away from that place. Who wants to go for us?"

Leah and two of the Galileans jumped up from the ground where they had been sitting, saying in chorus, "We'd like to do that. We'll go."

"Fine," Jesus said. Turning toward Judas, he said, "Judas, as firstborn in your family, why don't you go with them."

Judas looked at Jesus quizzically, thought for a moment, then said, "I'd rather stay here, but if you want me to go, I will."

"I think it fitting, Judas, that you go with them to arrange for our paschal lamb," Jesus answered. "I know you'll make a good selection."

Later that afternoon, as the sun slid toward the horizon, Andrew began to round up the friends of Jesus. "Let's get ready to enter the city for our supper. Judas and Leah are back with our lamb. We can now go into the city to Mark's house for the meal. Leah will lead the way."

Within a few minutes the group started ambling down the hill that just ahead began to rise up toward the Tadi Gate and entry into Jerusalem. Though James, the Marys, and others of those closest to Jesus remained somewhat subdued by his conversation from the evening before, they were still caught up in the historical drama as thousands of their fellow believers converged on the City of David for their individual rituals and dinners. At its heart a solemn festival, over the centuries Passover had evolved into a happy occasion as families and friends came together for another of the great feasts that framed their religion.

Jesus labored to laugh and joke and keep a festive air about himself, struggling with the dark foreboding that lurked at the forefront of his mind. Were he, Cephas, and the others being watched? The temple officer had left a bit too nonchalantly the other night to suit Jesus. Joses, he had reluctantly concluded, was indeed directly involved in the plot to kill Caiaphas and Pilate. It was only a matter of time before the authorities began to put the pieces of the puzzle together, connecting them to his wounded brother and the attempted assassination. He dreaded the thought of what would happen to Joses if he were caught. Under torture and threat of reprisals on his family, Joses would most certainly admit his complicity. Within a matter of minutes, he would be on a cross! Oh, not another cross in his family! Please, Adonai, not another cross!

He shuddered when he remembered Joseph's agony, fresh and painful, as if it happened yesterday rather than nearly twenty years ago.

Mary broke into this inwardness. "You're having a hard time," she interposed quietly.

"Does it show that much?" he winced.

"Only to me, and maybe to your mother," she answered with a knowing smile and a pat on his arm.

His mother saw the two of them walking hand in hand. Pangs of memory stabbed at her. Most days she moved along without thinking too much of Joseph. Tonight, seeing Jesus and Mary walking like this, holding hands as she and her Joseph used to do, sensing the powerful love that flowed between them, rekindled feelings of the happy days she and Joseph had known. Her mind reached back to caress that other Passover all those years ago when she and Joseph had brought their ebullient young family to Jerusalem. Despair, longing, a palpable hunger to touch Joseph one more time nearly made her stumble. And Jesus's words last night only made her more anxious. She loved him no more or less than her other children, of this she was sure. James, the second son, so adored by Joseph; Joses, until recently so dependable; Judah, the boy who chose to stay completely out of the limelight; Simon, the youngest son, a fervent supporter of Jesus. The two girls, Miriam and Zipporah, in Nazareth with Judah watching over them. How she longed to see all three of them right now.

Still, Jesus, she more fully understood now more than ever, possessed and was possessed by the extraordinary. She could not fathom his differentness, though she was sure it came from a powerful, overarching, dramatic connection between himself and Adonai. Surely Adonai would not allow one so splendid, so gifted, so wonderful, generous, wise, and giving as Jesus to come to harm. No! Definitely not!

Jesus's little group flowed along with the river of pilgrims streaming in from the hillsides, surging through the Tadi Gate and the other yawning openings in the walls of the sacred city. Once inside, the river of humanity spread like a mighty pulsating delta spilling in every direction for rendezvous with friends and families. The people, so bent on their own celebrations, paid no attention to anyone else beyond themselves—that is, except the officer of the temple and his two troopers back in the crowd who kept their eyes on Jesus.

—

Nicodemus had finally made it back home, slipped into the small room that served as his private office, and dropped down into his favorite chair after a long day tending to his duties as chief comptroller of foreign currency exchange for the temple treasurer. Festivals were incredibly demanding, with thousands of transactions to handle. He had not been in touch with Caiaphas and others on his staff since the assassination attempt. He breathed a sigh of relief at the high priest's narrow escape. Caiaphas was not Nicodemus's true vision of a spiritual leader. He had to admit ruefully that Caiaphas and Annas had provided welcome stability to the Jewish religion and temple enterprise for several years. A sudden change, particularly one precipitated by murder, would be extremely complicated. Such attacks were so stupid. Inevitably, time and Adonai took care of bad rulers and poor government.

A loud knock at the outer door followed by a babble of voices in the courtyard snatched Nicodemus from his reverie.

"Master," Janna, his first servant, announced, bustling into the study, "my lord Jared says he has urgent news for you."

Now abruptly standing rigidly in front of his easy chair, Nicodemus ignored Janna and called out to his friend and colleague in the financial office of the temple, "Jared, I'm here in my room. Come in, quickly. What is your urgent news?"

Not waiting for the servant to leave and close the door to the room, Jared exclaimed, "Nicodemus, it's that man Jesus, the one you were so impressed with, the friend of Lazarus! You've talked about him often since you met him a few days ago."

"Yes, yes, Jared. He was powerful. Catch your breath. What about Jesus?" Nicodemus wanted to know, trying not to seem too alarmed.

"He's in very serious trouble. He's been implicated in the assassination attempt!"

"No!" Nicodemus exploded, stumbling backward. "That's impossible. He'd never do anything like that. Such violence is abhorrent to him. He's a teacher, a healer."

"That's not what they're saying at the high priest's palace. I was just there a short time ago paying wages to some of Caiaphas's freedmen and heard the whole thing."

"Tell, me, Jared. Tell me quickly!" Nicodemus demanded.

"They're not saying he actually took part. They're not even saying he had anything to do with the planning. They're saying he knows who did," Jared explained, his words tumbling over one another.

"But how?" Nicodemus asked, crestfallen at this terrible, totally unexpected news.

"I am not sure how the high priest learned of Jesus's involvement. Something about a friend of Jesus's saying Jesus had information, but I'm not clear on that point. I only know they plan to arrest him later tonight, after the city is asleep," Jared reported.

"Tonight? Where?" Nicodemus pleaded as he began to pace back and forth.

"I don't know that either, Nicodemus. The captain of the temple seemed to be making his plans on solid information, though," Jared anxiously explained.

"Do you know where Jesus is now, Jared?"

"No," his friend shrugged, "I have no idea."

"Who does?" Nicodemus queried.

"The captain knows, but he'll never tell."

In the next moment, catching a disturbing drift from Nicodemus, his highly esteemed, highly placed, and influential friend, Jared, now fully alarmed, said, "Wait a minute, Nicodemus. If you're thinking what I think you're thinking, you'd better get a hold of yourself."

"I don't know what you're talking about, Jared," Nicodemus answered coldly, looking away from his friend.

"I'm leaving here right now. Nicodemus," stark terror in his voice, "we never had this conversation. I was never here at your house tonight. Do you understand!"

"Jared, you have my word. I've not seen you in days."

Two hours later, Nicodemus, shrouded in a large cloak, the hood pulled over his head, walked casually so as not to suggest to the patrols he was anything but a pilgrim on his way to Passover. Finally, he found Mark's house. He had twisted around in the maze of streets, become lost a half-dozen times trying to follow the directions he bribed from the chief aide to the captain of the temple.

He knocked discreetly.

In reality he wanted to bang on the door and shout for Jesus to come out this instant!

An older man answered the door.

"I am a friend of Jesus," Nicodemus explained, his breath coming in short gasps despite his best efforts. "I understand he's here. Is that correct?"

The man looked closely at Nicodemus and said, "Jesus did not tell me anyone else was coming to Passover. Is he expecting you?"

It took all of Nicodemus's control not to scream at the man, shove him out of the way, and barge in. Instead, he replied, "No, Jesus is not expecting me. I am interrupting. But I come with news of an impending crisis. Please ask him to come to the door, or let me come in so I may speak with him."

"May I give him your name?" the man, apparently the owner of the house, said.

"No. I assure you Jesus knows me. Please, man, valuable time is wasting. I must speak to him."

"Just a moment," Mark said, closing and locking the door.

For what seemed an eternity, Nicodemus waited, swaying back in forth in his great anxiety, resisting the temptation to wring his hands or jump in through a window.

The door opened halfway, not to Jesus, but to a large, rugged man with warm features, half a head taller than Nicodemus.

In a heavy Galilean accent, the commanding man asked, "You say you need to see Jesus? I am Cephas, his friend. He's in the middle of Passover with his family and friends. Can your business wait?"

"No, my business cannot wait." In exasperation, glancing around to make sure no one was looking, he said, "Tell your master Nicodemus is at the door."

In the next moment the door swung wide open with Jesus urging, "Nicodemus, please come in. Forgive us. My friends are only trying to be helpful."

"As am I, Jesus," Nicodemus said, stepping briskly into the small courtyard with an air of urgency. "Jesus, you are in great danger. You must leave right now. The Romans and the high priest intend to arrest you this very night!"

Surprised, fear flashing across his face, Jesus said, "Why, Nicodemus, whatever do you mean? I have done nothing warranting arrest."

"Listen, Jesus, Romans and the high priest's people have implicated you in the assassination attempt. Apparently, someone you know told the high priest you have information," Nicodemus almost shouted at him.

"That's ridiculous! I knew nothing of the attempt" Jesus replied incredulously.

"It does not matter," Nicodemus spluttered, now pacing around the tiny courtyard. "They're determined to arrest someone. You are well known. You've been under surveillance for some time. Your teachings about not putting new wine in old wineskins have made some of the officials here nervous. You had that trouble in the temple. You are supposed to have made harsh statements about destroying the temple."

"I can explain all that," Jesus insisted irritably. "Any suggestion by the temple rulers of criminal intent, any notion I was trying to be subversive, is absurd.

"No one cares what you meant. Caiaphas's people are beyond plausible explanations," Nicodemus admitted, shrugging his shoulders in a gesture of futility. "For your own sake, for the work you are trying to do, Jesus, you've got to leave right now. I can sneak you out of town. For all I know, the guards are already on their way here. We must leave right now!"

To Nicodemus's amazement, the fear that had gripped Jesus a moment ago left him. "If your information is correct, and if someone told you how to find me, all of us are probably being watched right now," Jesus said. "I could not escape if I wanted to. I certainly do not want you to be in trouble. Nicodemus, I cannot run away, no matter how grave the threat."

"But you must. Your life depends on it," Nicodemus pleaded.

"That's probably true. Far more may depend on my staying," he answered with firm resolve.

Taking a cue from Jesus's attitude, calming down, Nicodemus averred, "Caiaphas is strong. He's not evil. Convince him you have no implicating information and he will let you go. I'll help by vouching for you."

"That's just it, Nicodemus. Though I had nothing to do with the attempts, I may have information I can never divulge," he admitted.

Jesus's straightforward admission hit Nicodemus with a thud. "Jesus, you are in serious trouble."

"Most likely," Jesus agreed without emotion. He smiled, "For now, good and brave friend, we are about to have our Passover celebration. You are cordially invited to join us."

"Are you going to proceed with a Passover supper when your very life hangs in the balance?" he asked, stunned.

"Our lives always hang in the balance, mine, yours," Jesus declared. "We are constantly participating in our own dying. You've put a great deal of your own life on the scales just by coming here. You decided to put what you felt was right ahead of everything else in your life for the moment. I have to do the same thing. And, yes, we are going to proceed with our dinner and would be honored to have one of your stature among our people. Join us."

The high priest's council member sighed. Jesus was right, of course. He probably had forever altered his life simply by coming to this house. He looked around the plain room, envisioned the mansion in which he and his wife lived, knew she would be worried about him, patted Jesus on his back, and said, "I should be pleased to accept your invitation."

"Everyone," Jesus announced as he and the highly positioned official entered the upper room, "you will remember Nicodemus. We met him a few days ago during our visit to the home of Lazarus. He serves Caiaphas on the Sanhedrin. He has decided to join us for our celebration."

Extending his arms to Nicodemus, Jesus said, "We welcome you as a brother to this supper. All who walk in the ways of Adonai will long remember what you have done tonight. You follow in the long line of people like Moses, blessed be his memory, willing to risk much and pay high prices to liberate people held captive."

Jesus, as the eldest son in his family, led his group through the ancient ritual of the Feast of Passover.

When they had finished the Passover, Jesus said to the small group, "Before we leave, I want to say that I am seeing more plainly Adonai's plans for me. I do not want to alarm you unduly, but my time may be even shorter than I had anticipated. As Joshua of old told the Israelites as they prepared to cross over the Jordan and enter new lands, *Be strong and of good courage. Do not be afraid, neither be dismayed, for the Lord your Adonai is with you wherever you go.* If I am taken, your temptation will be to scatter. I hope you stay together, either here or back in Capernaum, until your future gets clearer. You will face fear and danger. I tell you frankly, I am afraid. Still, by the power of Adonai, we will not be ruled by our fears."

"What are you talking about?" Cephas demanded. "Is someone about to hurt you?"

"Probably, Cephas," he answered.

"I will not let it happen!" the big man vehemently declared.

"You cannot stop it," Jesus said, gripping Cephas by the shoulder.

"But how?" James wanted to know.

"It appears someone who knows us well has given themselves over to Beelzebub," Jesus said without a trace of incrimination or hint he had any knowledge who might have gone to the authorities.

Shocked, each fearfully looked from one to another around the table. Judas, in a dark corner of the room at the far end of the table, shrank even further into the shadows. As Jesus spoke, to his acute irritation Judas's hands began to tremble. Perspiration popped out on his forehead and poured down his back.

"Listen," Jesus said, attempting to calm them, "nothing that happens to us is beyond Adonai's reach. You and I understand this. I do not have special knowledge of what these next hours hold. I do know that it's all in the hands of Adonai as Abba, that it is all part of his grand plan for you and me. Together, we will face what we face out there."

To dispel the pall that had settled over the room, Jesus motioned to them and said, "Let's leave. Mark needs to clean up and get some rest. He's surely been gracious to open his home to us and provide a memorable meal. Let's begin to head back to our encampment."

After a moment's reflection Jesus suggested to Nicodemus, "You probably should remain here until we are well out of the way. No need to endanger yourself further. Besides, we may need your counsel in the days and weeks ahead."

"I am not afraid," he assured Jesus.

To his own amazement, it was true. In a flash, the many possible ramifications of this encounter with Jesus tumbled through his head. He was just not afraid. It was a good feeling.

Taking a deep breath, fully expecting to encounter a troop of temple or Roman soldiers in battle gear, Jesus and his friends opened the door and looked up and down the darkened lane. To their vast relief the street was practically deserted.

As they began to file out, Mark reached out to Jesus and Cephas. "As you leave for whatever awaits you, I want you to know that this has been the most important night of my entire life. These hours with you, Jesus, feeling your spirit, catching your vision for all of us, seeing your courage, have forever changed me. If need be, I will sell my house and become one of your people here or anywhere you say." The three embraced, their hearts singing while their eyes cried.

"Thank you, Mark," Jesus replied. "I count you as a friend. Stay alert. Adonai has just begun his new work in us."

As the three of them separated, with Mark still standing in the door, Cephas whispered to Jesus, "Do we go right back to our camp?"

"I'd like to go somewhere to think and pray," Jesus replied softly. "I don't know where to go."

Mark spoke up. "There's a grove of ancient olive trees out on the hillside near Gethsemane. Probably no one will be there this time of night."

Jesus and Cephas looked at each other and nodded. "Again, thank you, Mark. I've seen the grove. I'll go there."

To Cephas, Jesus said, "I can be quiet there for a while, pray and collect my thoughts. None of you need to go with me. I'll be along soon."

"Not on your life," Cephas sputtered loudly, tossing caution to the wind, his voice echoing through the nearly empty street. Immediately, controlling himself again, he whispered, "James can take your mother, the Galileans, and Mary to the camp outside the city. I'm staying with you."

After a moment's hushed consultation in the street, it was agreed that James would, indeed, guide the women and the Galileans to the camp while Cephas, Andrew, John, and Simon would go with Jesus. Judas, visibly agitated, blurted, "I'm going with Jesus." In the flurry of everyone leaving, it flashed through Cephas's mind, "What's wrong with Judas?"

While James escorted his charges toward their camp, Jesus made his way through the darkness toward the grove of ancient, gnarled olive trees. None of those with Jesus noticed the three hooded men who hung back watching their movements. When it became clear the general direction in which Jesus was going, one of the men peeled away from the others, scurrying back into the city with the air of one bent on a serious mission.

As Jesus had hoped, the densely overgrown grove was free of other pilgrims.

"Cephas, keep your eyes and ears open for a while. I am going a bit further up the hill to pray. I know you're all tired. Try to stay awake. I will not be too long."

"You can count on me, Jesus," Cephas assured him resolutely.

An hour later Jesus returned to the group to find them all asleep, Cephas included. He smiled. How he loved these men, even troublesome Judas. Could it be Judas who had gone to the authorities? No! Judas would not do that. Judas had his share of personal conflicts, but nothing, Jesus was sure, could prompt him to betray his friends and family.

Let the sleeping men alone, he told himself. Everyone would have the opportunity soon enough to show their mettle. For his own feeling of security, he started to awaken Cephas, decided to let him sleep, and trudged back up the hill into the olive grove thicket.

He had been praying for another hour or so when he thought he heard the sound of tramping boots. He stopped, caught his breath, the better to hear. Nothing. He was jumpy. Nicodemus's news was frightening, he had to admit. Calm down, he told himself.

He climbed further up the hill, quite steep now. The exertion felt good.

There! The noise again. It was indeed the sound of men, several of them. The temple guards had indeed come for him!

So this was how it would happen. Arrested like a criminal in the middle of the night. In his worst nightmare he had not envisioned this. How would he fare? Would he disgrace himself, bring dishonor on his family, shame to the Holy One he had served for these years? O Abba, do you have to do this to me? Could you not have found a better way? I have served you faithfully. Do you now turn your back on me? Of course not. I know you will not. As we have been faithful to one another in good times and bad, we will remain steadfast now.

Wait, maybe they are not coming for me. Perhaps this is a big mistake. I may have to answer questions, but I know nothing about the murder attempts.

It's so dark. Where are my friends? Surely they're not still asleep.

As if in a bad dream, he threaded down the pitch-black hill toward the sounds, now growing louder. There, through the thick branches he could see burning brands bobbing like fireflies in the night. Was that Cephas bellowing above the din? But where were the others?

Coming on the scene, now flickeringly illuminated by smokey torches held aloft by heavily armed temple guards, it would have been comic had it not been so terrifying. Uniformed men bumped into one another, thrashing around in the near darkness, branches from the ancient olive trees tearing at faces and bare arms, swords drawn, held ready, posing far more of a threat to each other than to Jesus. True to form, before Jesus could interfere, Cephas flattened two of the guards. He grabbed up the sword of one of the fallen men and began flailing it back and forth in the murkiness.

"Cephas, stop!" Jesus shouted above the noise. "Drop that sword before you hurt someone or get hurt."

In the sudden stillness generated by Jesus's sharp order, the officer in charge looked at the man in deep shadows at his elbow who, without saying a word, nodded his head.

"He's the one," the officer called out to his men, pointing toward Jesus.

Immediately, Jesus was surrounded by a squad of temple guards whose drawn swords and pointed spears came menacingly close to his body. "Wait," the officer shouted, "we have strict orders to bring him in alive."

From within the circle of nervous young guards, Jesus said with amazing calm, "You have nothing to fear from me. I am not armed."

Ignoring his willingness to accompany the contingent without resistance, the officer called out harshly, "Take no chances. Tie him up!"

Rough hands began to wrap a heavy rope around Jesus from shoulders to waist, pinning his arms tightly by his side.

"Now, let's go," the officer commanded.

With a jerk of the dangling end of the rope, a hardened veteran yanked Jesus forward, causing him to fall into the tangle of rocks and tree roots. When Cephas instinctively reached to steady Jesus, two guards clubbed him unconscious with the butts of their spears.

Barely able to keep his footing, Jesus came upon Judas, whose panic-stricken face was momentarily illuminated by a wavering torch. "Jesus," he called out, "they'll not hurt you. Tell about the killer. They promised!"

"Judas, I love you. It's all right," was as much as Jesus could get out of his mouth before, once again, he was yanked through the grove.

—

Simon, Andrew, and John raced into the encampment, panting for breath, shouting at the same time, their words falling over each other, "They've arrested Jesus. The temple guards came charging into the grove and grabbed him. Cephas told us to run and tell you. He's doing what he can to help Jesus."

Both Marys, who had not closed their eyes since lying down, nearly tore down their small tent getting out of it at the sound of the men. James and the Galileans jumped up from where they lay, all terrified for Jesus, and, yes, for themselves.

"Wait," James pleaded. "Slow down! One at a time."

With Mary at her side, Jesus's mother slumped to the ground as the men poured out their story.

"Oh, my son, my son," she wept. Thrusting her arms to the star-studded night sky, she pleaded, "Adonai, please do not let anything happen to my son! He's your special gift to us all."

Looking up from the ground as she cradled Jesus's mother, Mary said to James, "What do we do?"

"I'll try to get into the city. Maybe I can find out something. With the gates shut, that'll be hard," he said, despair and helplessness in his voice.

After a few minutes, when the initial shock began to wear off, Leah asked, "Where's Judas?"

—

With no mercy, the guards dragged Jesus down the hill, across the Kidron Valley, in through the city's Shepherd's Gate that was narrowly opened for them and then promptly slammed shut and bolted. Jesus kept trying to say to his captors, "I'll walk! Let me walk! You don't have to drag me. I can't stay on my feet!"

They paid him no attention whatsoever. This rangy Galilean was no more or less special or threatening than countless other fugitives they had captured, trussed, and delivered, alive yet invariably bowed and bloodied for disposition by whichever temple or Roman officer drew the duty.

—

Cephas came to in time to see the darting, flickering torches trailing each other down the hill toward the city. His head throbbing, he labored to tell himself if only he could catch up with the guards, blend into their number without being detected, he might be able to slip into the city with them when the gates swung open. Exerting more strength than he knew he had, the fisherman pulled himself up from the ground, shook his head, and by sheer force of will compelled himself to trot after the guards. Gasping, about to blackout again, he nonetheless managed to catch up and make it into the city with the guards undetected. Though he hardly knew the city, he decided the guards were headed for the captain's quarters. Cephas dropped back enough to reduce the odds of capture while still keeping the weaving line of troops in sight. Sure enough, shortly, the squad, their officer, and the prisoner came to the imposing structure that served the captain as residence and headquarters.

If Cephas had any hope of getting inside that place, they were dashed when he saw six armed men standing guard before its heavy double oak doors. Nothing to do now but wait. What was this all about anyway? Then it dawned on him. Joses. Somehow the authorities had learned of Jesus's connection with the assassin. But how? Who? No one really knew anything about the wounded brother but Jesus and himself.

Still dizzy, as he began to look around in the shadows for a place to sit down close enough to the captain's house to keep an eye on the door, he noticed that a man, oddly familiar, appeared out of the darkness at the door and said something to one of the guards. After a couple sharp raps at the doors, one swung open to admit the hunched figure. As the man started to enter, he hesitated a split second and took a quick look around before disappearing into the house. That pause was all Cephas needed to recognize the face despite the poor light offered by one burning torch stuck in a niche in the wall of the house. Judas!

———

Waiting for the captain to enter the room, a battered Jesus determined to maintain his composure. He stood up straight, ignoring the way his entire body ached and bled.

When the captain entered, he said to the guard, "Untie the prisoner. From the way he looks, I don't think he will run far should he get away."

"Am I prisoner?" Jesus asked the captain, fixing him with a steady gaze. "Of what crime am I charged? Do I not retain any rights as a member of our Jewish nation?"

"A prisoner?" the captain responded mockingly. "Why, Nazarene, of course you are a prisoner. Charges? You are charged with the crime of conspiracy to murder the high priest and the Roman prefect. I can think of no higher crimes, can you?"

"I know nothing of these crimes except to deplore them."

"That's not the information I have," the captain answered.

"The information you have then, my lord captain, is false," Jesus replied.

"Let me put it this way, Galilean," the captain sneered. "Do you know anyone who might have taken part in the crime?"

"I have no certain knowledge of anyone who had anything to do with this crime," Jesus stated without blinking an eye.

"Ah, you are the clever one, Jesus of Nazareth. You could have been a lawyer." Leaning over in his chair, the captain said to the aide standing at his elbow, "No 'certain knowledge,' the man says. That's good, really good."

Jesus did not answer. Neither did he flinch.

"Did you recently treat a man who was seriously injured?" the captain demanded, mental jousting aside, his mood becoming decidedly more sour.

"Yes, I did," Jesus answered.

"You will tell me who that person is," the captain said.

"No, I will not tell you who that person is," Jesus replied.

"I have reason to believe that man had something to do with the crime," the captain declared. "If you do not tell me who he is, I can only assume you are harboring a criminal, that you are in a conspiracy to harm national leaders."

"You will be making false assumptions, my lord captain," Jesus answered.

A flick of the captain's eyebrow toward one of the guards and the man backhanded Jesus across the face with all the force he could exert. Jesus spun from the blow. Blood spurted from his mouth and nose. His knees buckled back, but he caught himself before actually falling to the floor.

"You will tell me about the man you treated!" the captain demanded menacingly, rising abruptly from his chair.

"I will never tell you who he is," Jesus answered defiantly, with a force that surprised the Jewish leader.

"You are a strong man, Jesus of Nazareth," the captain said, glowering at the prisoner. "We have broken far stronger. Before we are through with you, you'll give us the name of the man you're protecting."

When Jesus said nothing, the captain dismissively said to the big guard, "Flog him. Don't kill him. Make him talk. While you work on him, I'm going to take a nap."

Before Jesus knew what was happening, the guards had stripped him of his clothing, tied his arms around one of the room's supporting pillars, and laid a biting lash across his shoulders. Never had he thought anything could hurt like that. Silence. A snatch of Scripture flashed through his brain: *Like a lamb to the slaughter, he did not open his mouth.*

An hour later, his back hardly more than pulp, the captain returned. Without looking at Jesus, he said to the guard with the lash, "Well?"

"Nothing, my lord," he answered apologetically.

"Douse his back with vinegar. Maybe that will cool his head and clarify his thinking," ordered the captain.

Jesus's blood-curdling scream echoed throughout the large house. Judas, pacing in an anteroom, recognized the cry as coming from Jesus. Before anyone could stop him, he crashed into the room. Seeing Jesus's bloody back sagging, already nearly dead, Judas flung himself down before the captain. He cried out, "You said you would not hurt him! He had only to help you! You broke your word to me!"

"You sniveling traitor," the captain spat out at Judas. "You stupid fishmonger, your friend here refuses to help me. Besides, did you think I owe you anything beyond the money I have already paid you to finger this man? Get out of here before I have you strapped to one of these pillars and give you a dose of what we've already given him."

When Judas did not move, transfixed as he was on the broken form of Jesus, the captain ordered one of the guards, "Drag that piece of trash out of here. I never want to see him again."

"No, no!" Judas yelled. "You can't do this to Jesus. He's the best man I've ever known. He's only done good. You can't. I beg you, don't hurt him anymore."

With a lunge, Judas broke loose from the guard and ran toward the captain, holding his arms out beseechingly. With one swift movement of the guard's sword arm, Judas was dead on the spot, his blood drenching the polished stone floor.

"Judas, oh Judas," Jesus cried as he saw the hapless young man splayed in death.

Servants sprang from nowhere, it seemed, quickly wrapped Judas's body in a sheet, and hauled it out. Others of the captain's house staff rushed to clean up the floor. Within moments it was as if Judas had never existed. All traces of his young life were gone, vanished like morning mist when the sun comes out.

Looking at Jesus, the captain said, "It appears you are not going to tell us what we need to know. You leave me only one choice: You are hereby charged with conspiracy to assassinate the high priest and the prefect. In keeping with our laws, I will convene a court so that the charges may be fairly and honestly considered."

Within an hour, several members of the Sanhedrin had been roused from their beds and hurriedly escorted to the chamber. The guards had indifferently bandaged Jesus's back and redressed him in his tattered clothing.

The captain began by saying to the councilors, "His lordship, the high priest is too ill from the attempted murder to conduct this trail himself. As his second in command, I am authorized to hear the evidence and assist you in rendering a fair and impartial verdict."

To his clerk the captain said, "Read the charges."

In a monotone, the clerk read from a hastily prepared scroll. "Jesus of Nazareth is charged with conspiracy to murder our high priest and the personal representative of the emperor. He is further charged with threatening to destroy our sacred temple. And more, he is accused of having himself declared king of the Jews."

The temple treasury official was the first to testify. "With my own ears I heard him threaten to tear the temple down. He said if he were not able to tear it down, it would collapse of its own evil."

"Do you deny making that statement, Jesus of Nazareth?" the captain queried in his most magisterial voice.

Jesus shook his head. He would have tried to explain what he meant but knew any defense was useless.

Another witness testified, "I was standing at the Water Gate a few days ago when this man and his friends came marching in putting on airs. You would've thought it was the emperor himself. Several of his followers, jumping and cavorting around, hailed him as their new king. He made no effort to hush them. In fact, some of his people spread their coats on the ground for him to walk on like we do the high priest when he goes to the temple."

Before the captain could say anything to the accused, Jesus numbly nodded his head.

To substantiate the charge of conspiracy, the captain rose from his chair, glowered at Jesus, and intoned, "Unfortunately, the man from the Nazarene's camp who pointed at him as having knowledge of one or more of the killers died a few hours ago in an attempt to kill me. Yesterday, before me and witnesses, Judas, he called himself, swore Jesus slipped away from their camp in the night. This Jesus, Judas swore, used magic, not medicine, to cure one of the killers who had been wounded in the crime. Jesus has refused to identify the criminal. This Galilean, then, leaves me no option but to urge you to find him guilty of conspiracy to commit high treason and murder."

Looking at the half a dozen members of the Sanhedrin, some of whom were nodding off to sleep after having been snatched from their beds, the captain said, "Honored leaders of the Jewish people, what is your verdict on Jesus of Nazareth?"

"Guilty," they said in chorus.

"And what is the punishment?" the captain asked.

"Death," the sleepy men mumbled as they rose from the bench on which they had been sitting and shuffled out of the room.

—

Cephas tried to remain hidden in the shadows. The longer Jesus remained inside the captain's house, the more fearful he became. What could they possibly be doing to his friend? He was innocent of any complicity in the murder attempts. Surely they would not hold him simply because he could possibly know someone who might have been involved! And where was Judas?

He had been twisting and turning, agonizing, sweating, halting between the wisdom of waiting and his natural propensity to charge the doors when, through the dim light of the single torch, he saw the doors began to open. Two household slaves came out with a shrouded body on a stretcher.

Oh no, Cephas cried to himself. Not Jesus! Please, Adonai, not Jesus!

Judas? Could it be Judas? That didn't make sense. Judas had become an ally in this evil drama that was being played out.

Cephas had to know who lay under that sheet. Finding out put him in grave danger himself. What to do?

The stretcher bearers were walking directly toward him, though they could not see him hidden in his niche in the wall. As they came abreast of him, Cephas stepped out of the shadows in front of the slaves, his mouth dry as a stone.

"Who's dead so early in the morning?" he asked, conveying, he hoped, no more than idle curiosity.

Startled, immediately defensive, the slaves halted, glancing over their shoulders at the guards before the doors. Their uneasiness and the proximity of the guards were not lost on Cephas.

"What's it to you?" one of the slaves wanted to know, a mixture of alarm and warning in his voice.

Thinking fast, Cephas decided a measure of honesty might work. "I was supposed to meet my cousin here last night. He had business with the captain. He hasn't showed up. I'm getting nervous."

Glancing at one another, the slaves hesitated a moment, one nodding at the other. "This man had business with the captain. Didn't work out like he planned."

Both slaves smirked, letting Cephas know that, like all household help, they knew everything that went on in the master's house.

The other slave nodded at the shroud, "Take a look, but hurry. We've got more work to do after we dump this fellow in the ground."

Cephas, for all his strength, thought he would collapse as he reached his trembling fingers toward the sheet covering the corpse's face. Judas. Indeed, his cousin Judas. The pain he felt was mitigated only by his relief that it was not Jesus.

The look on Cephas's face gave him away

"Your cousin?" one of the slaves asked.

"No!" Cephas gulped, lying.

"This one's lucky, whoever he is," the other slave added with no emotion.

Snatched from his despair, Cephas asked, "How so?"

"The one this man snitched on," nodding at Judas, "why, he's going to the cross as sure as the sun will be up in a couple hours."

Cephas caught himself as he reeled back toward the wall.

"You know the other one too, Jesus the Nazarene, don't you!" the slave at the foot of the stretcher insisted.

For the rest of his life, Cephas would regret that next instant. Panic, sheer terror, overtook him as visions of the horrors of himself on a cross swept away love and courage.

"No! I don't know what you're talking about," he asserted so loudly that the guards at the door strained to peer into the street's shadows.

"Whatever you say," the slave at the head smirked. "It's nothing to us."

The other slave laughed. "Whoever knows him better get used to being without him. He's a goner, and today's the day."

The two slaves shuffled off into the dark, winding street, headed, Cephas would later realize, toward the pauper's cemetery outside the walls where Judas would be dumped, nameless, into a shallow grave dug by yet another pair of anonymous hands.

Shame, fear, pain, screaming grief drove Cephas from his shadows. Why had he denied knowing the best, most honorable, most generous, Adonai-like person he had ever known, ever to walk on the earth as far as Cephas was concerned? He groped his way through predawn Jerusalem with no idea what to do.

The execution had to be stopped. But how? Who? That man who came to the Passover last night. Was that only last night? It had to be a hundred years ago. Nicodemus. That's his name. He was impressed with Jesus. He's got power. He can do something. Where to find him? Who to ask? He dared not go back near the captain's house, especially asking questions.

Maybe someone up at the temple could tell him. But who? That was his best bet.

As he started toward the temple, another huge set of problems stopped him in his tracks. The group out on the hillside. They had to be told what had happened. Glancing up at the sky, it was still dark. No one would be at the temple until dawn. He would have time to rush to the camp, tell them the horrible news, then get to the temple. He could not waste a moment on indecision. Fortunately, the guards at the gate did not question him closely about the emergency family situation that required him to get out of the city before the gates were officially opened for the day.

A half-hour's frantic run brought Cephas to the camp. No one slept. They huddled around a small fire, talking in hushed tones, first one then another peering into the darkness toward the city.

Cephas burst into their midst, trying to talk, gasping for air. "Judas is dead. He betrayed Jesus!" Cephas spat out.

"Jesus? What of Jesus?" James demanded, his voice ringing out through the predawn stillness.

Holding up his hands for patience while he got his breath, he sputtered, "I'll tell. Give me a second."

With choking despair, he told them what he knew, including the slave's dire prediction.

"No, please, not Jesus! Not a cross!" Jesus's mother pleaded, wringing her hands, collapsing into James's arms.

Mary Magdala pulled her cloak around herself tightly and walked off into the breaking dawn.

Cephas, James, and the others huddled into a frantic strategy session. After several minutes tossing ideas back and forth, James began issuing orders: "Cephas, you alone know where Joses is. He needs to be told what's happening. There's nothing he can do. He needs to know. Go to him, and then come back here.

"Andrew, you and Simon try to find Nicodemus. See what he can do," James ordered.

Leah, who had been listening to the men from a respectful distance, spoke up, "My uncle might know how to find Nicodemus. He's always lived here."

"Good idea, Leah," James gulped. "Take a couple of the Galileans. Let's try every angle."

Just as the men and Leah started to dash away on their dreadful missions, both Marys, supporting each other, strode into the circle.

"We have also reached a decision," Mary Magdala said resolutely, choking back her tears. "We're going into Jerusalem. James and John, you're coming with us. We will plead with someone for his life. The captain. The high priest. The Romans. Someone! Anyone!"

Jesus's mother, in a voice full of steely determination, said, "We will be near him whatever happens." No one argued with her.

None dared ask, "What next?" The moment was far too full and portentous to snatch even a glance at the future.

—

While Caiaphas ate breakfast in his private chambers, the captain gave him the morning's confidential, off-the-record briefing on the previous night's events.

"We had to deal with some drunken Roman soldiers. They made a run at the temple just to cause trouble. Our guards were able to stop them. The priests from Samaria came into town late yesterday afternoon wanting to see you. We told them you still were not well. They unfortunately decided to remain in town for a few more days until you are fit. They are still complaining that too much money comes to us and not enough for them."

"The Samaritans have been upset for how long now, six hundred, seven hundred years? I'll talk with them. They'll leave as mad as when they came, but it's good for relations," the high priest groused as he continued eating fresh, warm bread right out of the oven, topped with a hefty slab of the cheese he relished.

"All in all, it was a fairly quiet night," the captain reported. Then he recalled, "Well, we did have one messy incident. That Nazarene, you know, Jesus."

"I remember," the high priest said involuntarily gingerly and touching his still painful side. "Did he tell you what you needed to know?"

"As a matter of fact, no. We used all the normal means of persuasion. He did not give an inch. Actually, he held his own quite well. Better than most I've seen go through the same ordeal."

"What did you do with him?" the high priest asked as he decorously wiped his mouth with a napkin of soft Egyptian cotton.

"I decided it was better to go ahead and get him out of the way. Better now than later. His popularity will only grow," the captain informed his superior.

"Do you believe he had anything to do with the attempt?" Caiaphas wanted to know, now looking with interest at his chief adviser, unfeeling hatchetman.

"No, my lord, he had nothing to do with it," the captain admitted. "He knows who did. He just will not tell us. May be a kinsman. The man did cause trouble in the temple the other day. For the last couple years, as Annas has told us, he has made some scurrilous statements about the temple."

"Is that enough to warrant executing him?" Caiaphas asked, his interest in the case rising. "We do not want any unnecessary trouble."

"I've thought of that, my lord. Some of his people, actually the poorest of the poor from up in Galilee, have been touting him as their 'new king,' Calling him 'Son of Man,' 'Son of God.' You've heard that sort of drivel before. The king part is sufficient to get him handed over to Pilate. If that's not enough, when

I tell Pilate my conviction that he's at least withholding information about the crime, he'll go along with us."

Picking up the captain's train of thought, the high priest chimed in, "And if the Romans do the executing, that puts the blame for the whole affair on them in the minds of the people. Good thinking, Captain."

Taking a sip of tea, the high priest said dismissively, "See to it. By the way, before you leave, would you please cut me another piece of that delicious bread?" he asked, pointing to the particular loaf he preferred. "Have a slice if you like."

"Thank you, my lord. I believe I will." Munching on the dark bread, he left the chamber to attend to the day's responsibilities.

—

Pilate was putting himself through the physical rigors to which he subjected himself every morning at dawn. He loathed the exercises, even after thirty years of such discipline. He had to convince himself every morning that this is what he must do. He hated flab anywhere on his body more than the exercise, so no matter where he was, he never failed to pull himself from sleep and sweat for an hour. The other inviolate rule was that he tolerated no disturbance, no interference short of a missive from the emperor, during his regimen.

Caiaphas and the captain, after years of dealing with the difficult prefect, followed the protocol. They had also learned that the surest way to get a quick decision from him was to catch him immediately after his morning program by having their envoy waiting at the door as he finished. With the sweat pouring from his well-toned body, while a slave stood nearby with a cool drink, the Jewish rulers could usually get their way.

As Pilate finished his exercises, he noticed Saruch, from the captain's staff, waiting for him at the edge of the small workout yard he had developed within the walls of his official residence.

He muttered to himself, *What do those priests want from me this morning?* Every day was something new with these people. How much longer before he could leave this despicable land so riven with petty quarrels over nearly nothing! These religious leaders spent so much time keeping up with rules and rituals that they hardly had time to enjoy the mounds of money they extracted from the ignorant worshipers of their Adonai. He, on the other hand, would enjoy the wealth he had stashed away, money he had accumulated any way he could. A couple more years, he calculated, and he could petition the emperor for retirement and live out his days in comfortable circumstances.

"What do you want so early in the morning?" he snapped at the envoy before the man could open his mouth.

"Their lordships have sent me, first of all, to wish you a pleasant day," he began.

"Bilge! Their lordships care nothing for my day nor my health! What do you want?" he growled.

Used to dealing with Pilate, the envoy did not flinch. "The captain has arrested a man, a Galilean, who is implicated in the assassination attempts. He and our court have found the man guilty of treason. Since the attack was also on you, they feel you might want to interview him and pass your own sentence."

"Why don't they handle him as they do other bothersome Jews?" Pilate sneered. "You people make noises about not being able to inflict the death sentence. Jews who give trouble disappear every day."

Feigning ignorance, Saruch entreated, "Why, my lord Pilate, what a terrible accusation to make against men who are followers of the Holy One!"

"Stop!" barked Pilate, taking a drink of the water the slave handed him. "I don't have time to talk about some crazed fanatic. Tell me, quickly, what the captain has come up with."

Ah, Pilate was again following the high priest's script. Saruch sketched the charges, concluding with the recitation that Jesus refused to tell what he knew, hence the charge of conspiracy.

"What else, Saruch? I know they've got more," Pilate insisted.

"Well," the envoy hesitated.

"Come on, man! I do not have all day."

"This Jesus has spent the last few years preaching against the temple. He's trying to persuade the people, primarily the Galileans who are already on the fringes of the faith, that they don't have to give money to the temple to keep the favor of Adonai."

Smiling for the first time, Pilate opined, "I'd say the man's pretty smart."

Ignoring the prefect's sarcasm, Saruch added, "There's more, my lord Pilate. He caused a riot in the temple the other day. The captain's police were barely able to quell it."

"Strange, I didn't hear about it," Pilate noted skeptically.

"Our people moved quickly to keep it under control," the envoy assured him, looking uneasily toward the ground.

"Or it amounted to nothing," Pilate interjected.

Again ignoring the prefect, Saruch went on, "And, a few days ago, a very large crowd of Jesus's followers hailed him as 'king of the Jews' when he came into town for Passover."

Now he had Pilate's attention. "King of the Jews," he repeated. Narrowing his eyes at the envoy, he queried, "How serious were those declarations? How many followers? Speak up, man!"

"Your lordship," Saruch confessed, "I was not there, mind you. But I have it on the highest authority that the crowd was quite large and they were very serious in declaring him their king."

Pilate paced back and forth for a moment. "Your leaders and I may have a problem on our hands."

"Yes, my lord," Saruch answered, already anticipating the approbation he would receive from the captain for a job well done.

To Saruch's vast relief, Pilate said, "Send the man to Antonio Tower. I'll alert today's crucifixion detail. We've got a couple more men who are on their way to the cross. One more's no problem."

—

Herod Antipas and Herodias raged at Boethus, their chief of staff, to no avail. "My lord, my lady," he pleaded, trying to camouflage the anger at them he felt, "we're doing everything possible to repair my ladies' wardrobe wagon. It's unheard of for an axle and a wheel to break at the same time. We've got an extra wheel, but we have no spare axle. We finally located a carpenter to make what we need. But it takes time."

"We'll miss the temple processional," pouted Herodias. "And I've had a new dress made for it."

"Me too," whined Salome, her beautiful, bratty daughter.

Cautiously, Boethus offered, "We could go ahead without the wardrobe wagon."

The withering look of incredulous fury on Herodias's face persuaded the man to drop that proposal, concentrating instead on getting the cumbersome wagon repaired as quickly as possible.

The local carpenter, while eager for the money he might earn by repairing the wagon, took fiendish delight in the tetrarch's problems. "Let 'em suffer for a while," the craftsman snickered to his sons.

Antipas and his entourage did not reach Jerusalem until the day after the processional.

"It's just as well," he tried to assuage his wife who did not get to wear her new dress. "I might have been attacked like Caiaphas and Pilate. I could be lying in the grave as we speak."

Herodias did not want him dead. Where would she and her daughter be without his position? She was not, however, about to let him off that easily.

"Oh, Herod, don't be so dramatic. As inept as the killers were, they would have missed. At any rate, the next time we travel, I do hope you will make sure we've got everything we need. Really, it's ridiculous that we missed the biggest event of the season for the lack of an axle, a piece of wood, and a wheel," she complained while she and Salome applied another round of the latest Egyptian makeup to their faces and arms.

The following morning, Boethus hurried to the royals' apartment excitedly. "My lord," he began, "I have news of some interest to you. You remember Jesus of Nazareth, the carpenter who embarrassed you after the Sepphoris fire and, later, snubbed you while he was out preaching?"

"Of course I remember him, Boethus. What about him?" Antipas wanted to know impatiently.

With a gleam in his eyes, Boethus said, "He's under arrest. Actually, under a sentence of death. The high priest and Pilate are accusing him of complicity in the assassination attempts!"

His interest immediately piqued, Antipas fairly shouted, "Come on, man, tell me what you know!"

When Boethus had given Antipas the details he had gleaned from the gossip mills, the tetrarch paused, thought for a moment, then said, "I want him brought before me. I knew all along a peasant like that so taken with himself would come to a sorry end. Let's see how clever he is now."

—

Andrew and Simon ran frantically toward the city, shoved their way through the crowds at the Tadi Gate, winding their way toward the steps that led to the temple compound. Bursting in through the arch that took them into the Court of the Gentiles, they stopped, grateful to see that, thanks to the early hour, the crowd of worshipers was not yet so large. This would perhaps make it easier to talk with a priest or a guard, someone who might help them find the Jewish leader.

Simon, struggling for breath, confronted an officer of the temple guard. "I must find a man named Nicodemus," he sputtered.

"Never heard of him," the officer replied brusquely, hastening on by the apparently half-crazed Galilean.

"Please, Father," Andrew pleaded with a priest between gasps, "it's a matter of life and death that I locate a member of the Sanhedrin named Nicodemus."

The priest merely shrugged.

Several more attempts brought them nothing. Undaunted by their lack of success, the men asked everyone who looked remotely official the whereabouts of Nicodemus. After what seemed like forever, Andrew queried yet another priest, this one vaguely familiar.

"Father," he begged, "please help me locate an official named Nicodemus."

The priest eyed Andrew a moment, cocked his head from one side to another, apparently trying to recall the man before him, then said, "You are with Jesus the Galilean, the one who caused me trouble the other day," the priest snapped.

With no time to waste on fruitless defenses, Andrew nodded, "My lord, I apologize for Jesus, for all of us. We meant no harm."

"What's the ruckus now?" Jediael wanted to know, softening his tone somewhat.

"Jesus, the best man you'll ever meet, is in serious trouble. Falsely accused. We're trying to find a man named Nicodemus who might be able to help him," Andrew exploded, waving his arms and pacing wildly back and forth.

Jediael looked closely at Andrew, then replied thoughtfully, his irritation assuaged, "Your friend, Jesus, made me stop and think the other day. That's good."

Trying desperately not to sound impatient, Andrew said, "Jesus would be pleased he was helpful. For now, you can help him. Do you know Nicodemus?"

"No, I do not."

Andrew's face fell.

"But," Jediael went on, "he has an office up here on temple mount. You might find him there in that section of the colonnade." Jadiael pointed to a section of the marble colonnade that surrounded the entire temple complex.

Darting in that direction, Andrew shouted back over his shoulder, "Thank you!"

Grabbing a surprised Simon by the sleeve, Andrew yelled, "Let's go. I may have found Nicodemus."

"Who wants to know, and why?" the clerk demanded officiously. "My lord, Nicodemus, does not meet people without appointments. He's too busy."

"Please," both men entreated. "It's a matter of life and death. A friend of his is in serious trouble. They were together at Passover only last night."

Convinced of their genuineness and the urgency of their mission, the clerk motioned for them to wait and disappeared into the small cubicle off the larger room.

Almost immediately, he reappeared. "My lord Nicodemus has not arrived."

Crushed, still determined, Simon pleaded, "Will you tell me where he lives? We will go to his house."

"I really should not," the clerk hesitated.

"You simply must," Andrew entreated.

A few seconds later, directions to Nicodemus's house in mind, the two bounded back down the steps into the city. The sun, by then, was well up.

—

As Pilate was about to sign the execution order for Jesus, Plancus, his chief of staff, stepped into the room. "Your excellency," he called out to Pilate, "an emissary from Herod Antipas is here and insists on seeing you."

Putting down the stylus, Pilate was tempted to refuse to see the messenger on such short notice, thought better, and nodded to have him admitted.

"Your excellency," the emissary intoned, "my lord Herod Antipas understands you have one of his subjects under a sentence of death, one Jesus of Nazareth."

"So?" Pilate responded irritably.

"Because the man is a Galilean, my lord believes he too should be involved in the investigation and should at least be consulted if the man is to die."

"Since when do I have to ask permission from the tetrarch or anyone else before I condemn a traitor to death?" Pilate imperiously wanted to know.

Braced for Pilate's arrogance, the emissary replied, "Your Excellency, my lord Antipas is not questioning your judgment. Believe me, he has no love for this man. Jesus has insulted the tetrarch on several occasions. Since Antipas is in the city, he merely wants to participate in the process whereby a troublemaker is brought to justice."

Glancing at Plancus, who gave an imperceptible nod, Pilate said, "I see no harm in Herod Antipas's request. Only for a short time, though. My men have work to do and cannot be tied up too long with unnecessary traipsing around."

As the emissary left, Pilate offhandedly said to his chief of staff, "When Antipas is done with the Nazarene, bring him here before you crucify him. These fanatics always intrigue me."

—

Shortly, Jesus was shoved into an audience room in Herod Antipas's quarters.

Swaying, trying to keep his balance, Jesus caught his breath, then nodded at the tetrarch. Even that slight motion made his head swim. He would have given anything to lie down on the floor, just crumple. Never had he been so unutterably tired, so near collapse. At the same time, he found resolve, strength to stand. And not only to stand, to meet unflinchingly the eyes of the pompous man in the large chair.

"Well, Jesus," Antipas smirked at Jesus, "we meet again. It has been a long time since you had the gall to question my integrity, and that over a few pieces of furniture."

"Yes, my lord," Jesus was able to reply.

Leaning to Boethus at his side while keeping his eyes on Jesus, Antipas said, trying to sound profound, "This," motioning toward Jesus, "is what happens to peasants who defy the power of Rome and of the Herods."

"And you, my lord," Jesus replied softly with effort, speaking, though he had not been invited to speak, "are what happens to anyone who ignores the ways of Adonai."

In a flash, Boethus sprang at the prisoner, backhanding him across the face with such surprising force that Jesus dropped to his knees. Blood once again streaming from a wicked slap, Jesus struggled to rise, all the while keeping his eyes on Herod.

Beginning to feel uncomfortable under the Galilean's steady gaze, a look that emitted neither anger nor fear, Antipas announced, "Jesus of Nazareth, you are about to die for your crimes."

With a shake of his head, Jesus slurred, again unbidden, "No crimes, my lord. You know that."

"Conspiracy is a crime," Antipas pontificated, the slightest hint of defensiveness in his voice.

All but depleting his store of energy, Jesus replied, "If conspiracy is refusing to betray someone dear, I am guilty, my lord."

To the several courtiers who clustered about the room, some amused, others bemused, still others loathing the spectacle, Antipas intoned, "See, he has admitted his guilt."

"Not guilt. Love, my lord," Jesus croaked.

"Well, it's stupid. Love, as you say, is going to cost you your life, Galilean," Antipas pronounced.

Again, from a deep wellspring of strength, Jesus quoted, *No greater love than to lay down your life for a friend.*

A moment of candor, one of the few in his life, came over Antipas. "No one would do that for me," the tetrarch declared, looking at the battered man standing before him.

"I'm doing it, my lord," Jesus replied, so quietly that Antipas and Boethus alone could make out his words.

"You mean that, Jesus of Nazareth. You really mean that," Antipas whispered with a misty look in his eyes. Quickly collecting himself, Herod Antipas rose from his chair, looked at Jesus, lifted his eyes to the courtiers, and declared, "I concur with the judgment rendered by the Sanhedrin and His Excellency Pontius Pilate. This man," he pointed his finger at Jesus, "is deserving of death. He is guilty of conspiracy. No one is safe until he is dead."

To the Roman soldiers who had hustled him into the audience room, the tetrarch called out, "Take him away!"

As the soldiers advanced on him, Jesus looked again into Antipas's eyes, in the same moment peering into the ruler's soul. "Antipas," Jesus murmured, "I lay down my life for my friend and for you."

Antipas in private moments would never be certain if Jesus had said those words or whether he *felt* that was what the Galilean said as the guards dragged him from the purple-draped room.

—

"Hurry," Leah's uncle Mark replied immediately when they breathlessly described the crisis with Jesus. "I don't know where Nicodemus lives. I just met him last night. I know a man who does. Come on, fast!"

Within a few minutes Leah, Mark, and the Galileans had the directions and were running through the still largely deserted early morning streets of Jerusalem. Leah, the girl from Magdala, determined to keep up with the men, hitched up her dress and dashed with them on their way to the great man's house.

Forever, it seemed to Leah, they ran, her feet and legs beginning to scream from the abuse she was inflicting on them. She wanted to stop, just for a second. She would not, though. The mission was too urgent. What's more, she had proven to herself she could run with the men. Despite her fears for Jesus's safety, she was the men's equal. She liked the feeling.

At Nicodemus's house at last, decorum tossed aside, Mark banged on the outer gate, calling, "Nicodemus, my lord Nicodemus! An emergency. Please open up!"

In a moment Nicodemus and his first servant were at the gate simultane-ously. Before the servant could protest, Nicodemus recognized Mark.

"What is it, Mark?" He demanded. "It's Jesus, isn't it? They've got him! Oh no!" he groaned out loud. He muttered angrily, "I knew they would. I warned him. Quick, give me the details."

He ran back into his house, threw on some street clothes, and rushed out through the front door into the street, calling to Mark and the others, "Follow me. They'll be trying him at the captain's house, I'm guessing."

Nicodemus's household had hardly collected itself after the bruising wakeup when another insistent rapping was heard at the gate. At least, Janna thought to himself as he opened the door, these two men are not quite as agitated as those other people were.

"Please," one of the men entreated, "we must see his excellency Nicodemus. A man's life hangs in the balance."

"He is not here," Janna informed the two men.

"Where?" they both exploded at the same time.

"He left a few minutes ago," Janna answered, playing to the hilt the role of protective and respectful first servant.

All pretense of respect gone, one of the men got in Janna's face and said through clenched teeth, "Listen, our friend's life is in grave danger. Nicodemus might be able to help. Tell me where he's gone. Now!"

"Another group of people came with a similar story. My lord Nicodemus left in great haste with them. He looked positively frightful. Did not take the time properly to..."

"Which way did he go?" Andrew almost shouted. "You've got to help us. We're wasting valuable time."

"I overheard my lord say something about the captain's house." he replied.

"Give us directions," Simon demanded.

With but the vaguest notion of where they were going, thanks to Jenna's pompous way of giving directions, Andrew and Simon raced down the streets now filling up with the people of the city.

—

"Ah, the 'king of the Jews,' they called you," Pilate snickered. "Are you the king of the Jews?" Pilate asked Jesus, his voice full of mockery.

"I am, I am the way to the king," Jesus mumbled, slowly sinking away into an exhausted torpor. His lacerated back hurt so fiercely that the pain hardly registered. He was barefoot. His only clothing was a tattered shift. His hair and beard were matted with sweat and blood. He reeked. He desperately needed to relieve himself. No respite was in sight.

"Who or what are you to cause such a stir?" Pilate demanded.

Jesus did not have the energy to answer.

Looking more closely at Jesus, Pilate sneered, "Tell you what, king of the Jews, we're going to let you wear a crown to your cross."

To his chief of staff, Pilate called out derisively "Plancus, have someone around here make his majesty, king of the Jews, a crown!"

Caught short by the order, Plancus replied, "My lord, where, out of what?"

"I don't care out of what, Plancus," he roared, "vines, grass, weeds. Just make it, and be damn quick about it!"

In a few minutes, during which Jesus stood silently swaying and Pilate paced, a slave girl of about fifteen was ushered into Pilate's office.

Over his shoulder he barked at her, "You are Jewish, aren't you?"

"Yes, my lord," she whispered, eyes fixed on the floor.

"Do you have a crown?" he demanded.

Terrified, she mumbled, "Yes, my lord. I made it out of weeds and sticks in the courtyard."

"Then crown your king!"

For a moment she did not know what he meant. When she hesitated, he snatched her by the arm and shoved her toward Jesus. "Go on, you stupid girl, crown him!"

Staring into Jesus's eyes, she placed the weed crown on his head, then backed away. Later, she would say she felt she had indeed crowned a king.

"No, you ninny," Pilate bellowed, now rising to the game, "you did not put it on firmly enough. It might fall off in his royal processional on the way to his coronation."

Pilate strode up to Jesus and crammed the crown of weeds and prickly vines down on his head. Protruding short, stubby, dried sticks scratched the skin on Jesus's scalp, drawing trickles of blood.

"Now, off with you, Your Majesty!" Peals of crude laughter rang out from the procurator. He did not notice, nor would he have cared, that he alone found the situation funny.

—

"Captain," Nicodemus implored in a voice shrill with demand, imprecation, and pleading, "you and Lord Caiaphas simply cannot go through with this execution."

"And, Councilor Nicodemus, to which execution do you refer?" the captain replied, feigning confusion.

"You know the one I'm talking about! Jesus, the Galilean. He's no more guilty of attempted assassination than you or I," Nicodemus insisted in fierce, measured tones, eyeing the captain for any sign of backing down. Nothing.

Raising his eyebrows questioningly, "My lord, Nicodemus," the captain now wanted to know, getting up from his desk, striding irritably toward the financier, "what, may I ask, is your interest in the Galilean, this person we have every reason to suspect is a co-conspirator in the assassination attempt?"

Without a moment's hesitation, he answered, "I met him at a mutual friend's house a few days ago. This 'person,' as you say, has a mind and spirit beyond anyone our nation has ever produced."

"Are you one of his followers?" the captain wanted to know, now more curious than defensive.

"Follower? I don't know that he is collecting a following. My conversation with him revealed a man who has no notion of going anywhere. He doesn't need followers," Nicodemus averred. "To answer your question specifically, and so your clerk hiding behind the drape over there making notes can get it down correctly, I am not a follower. I am an admirer. More, I stand in awe of him. You are trampling justice here."

The captain mentally stumbled a second, his mind entertaining its slightest semblance of hesitation, caught himself, then intoned to Nicodemus, "What's done is done. Besides, it's out of my hands. Pilate is in charge now."

"Oh, Captain," Nicodemus replied, unfathomed sadness in his eyes and voice, "with all due respect to you and Caiaphas, if Jesus dies today, it will be one of the darkest days in our long history of dark days."

Nicodemus studied the hard face of the captain for an instant longer. Shaking his head in despair, the council member said, "I am going to Pilate. Pray it's not too late."

Returning to his desk piled with documents to examine and make decisions about, the captain picked up his stylus, dipped its point into the ink cup, started to write, looked out the window at the morning fully come. Hmmm. A Galilean, the greatest man we've ever produced? That is saying a lot. And from Nicodemus, the hard-headed, utterly dependable banker. He's enthralled with the Galilean? Interesting. Maybe he and Caiaphas made something of a misstep handling the case so precipitously. No. Shaking his head. No. Starting again to write. Just another troublemaker. Perhaps smart. Probably not evil. But no! Better he's out of the way. Put an end to this problem before it gets out of hand.

—

Cephas, exercising every caution lest he be followed, took much longer than he had planned to get to the house. When he entered the tiny, dark room, stuffy with the smell of sickness, Joses lay propped up on a cot eating from a bowl with the assistance of a young girl.

Struggling for composure, Cephas greeted his friend's younger brother warmly, "Well, Joses, how are you feeling today? You look stronger."

"Why, Cephas, thank you for coming. You should not, though. It's dangerous," Joses replied, clearly but still weak. "I'm stronger. I would have to be. Otherwise, I'd be dead. Jesus is one great physician."

Looking again at Cephas, suspicions suddenly flaring, "Speaking of Jesus," Joses said, now trying to keep his voice level, "where is he? Why did you come alone?"

For an instant Cephas thought to put the wounded man off. Then, "Joses, there's been trouble."

Sitting upright on the cot, ignoring the searing pain in his stomach and side, Joses demanded, "What kind of trouble? It's not Jesus, is it?"

"Yes, it is Jesus. He's been arrested."

"Arrested? Why," Joses demanded, "why have they taken him? He's done nothing wrong."

"Judas," Cephas explained succinctly, "one of our men from Capernaum, told the high priest that Jesus knew some people who were involved in the assassination attempt. The temple police arrested Jesus last night after Passover."

"When are they letting him go?" Joses wanted to know, fearing already that he knew the answer.

"They're not. Some slaves from the captain's house told me Jesus," big Cephas began crying, "has been condemned to the cross."

"No!" Joses choked. "No. That cannot happen! I've got to get to the captain. Tell him what happened. If anybody's to die, it's me."

"Joses," Cephas, startled at Joses's response, wiping his eyes with his sleeve, stammered, "no, that won't do. You're too sick to move. It will not do any good. Only get you killed along with Jesus. There's nothing any of us can do."

"Damn," Joses swore. "Help me get out of this bed. Hand me some clothes. I'm going to try if it takes my last breath."

"But!" Cephas protested.

"No," Joses yelled through clenched teeth, "I'm going. Help me, or I'll do it by myself!"

"Here, Cephas," Joses muttered through biting pain, "wrap these strips of cloth around me tight so I won't start bleeding again."

Without a word Cephas complied, trying not to look closely at the bright red gashes in Joses's body. The wounds were healing. Any untoward movement could pull them open again.

"Let's go," Joses grunted.

"Here, lean on me," Cephas offered. "If you are determined to make this crazy effort, at least let me help you."

The daughter of the householder pointed them to Golgotha, a killing field outside the walls everyone in Jerusalem, lamentably, knew. "That's probably where they are," she told the men. "It's a bad place," she whispered fearfully as they left the tiny house.

———

"Pilate left for Caesarea about an hour ago," explained the Roman officer in charge of the small detail that guarded the prefect's house when he was not in residence. "He's gone. He's got some dispatches for Rome to tend to before a ship sails in the next few days. Nothing short of a call from the emperor himself will turn him back."

"But you fail to understand," Nicodemus started to explain again, "that a great man has been falsely accused and is on his way to the cross."

"Look," the officer said, glancing around to make sure no one was

listening, "if you're talking about that Jesus fellow, I agree. He should not die. There's no stopping it. Only Pilate can rescind the order. He's gone. He would not change his mind anyway. Not under any circumstances."

Refusing to give up, Nicodemus made one more try, "Please, you've got to help us," holding out his arms to include the young girl and the four men standing at the door with him.

"My lord," the officer said, "Pilate's wife even tried to intercede for the Galilean. She had some kind of dream that gave her bad feelings. Nothing! 'See to it,' the governor told the corporal of the execution details. They dragged your friend away."

Shaking his head in dismay, the officer, closing the door on Nicodemus and the others, said with finality, "There is nothing else you can do. All I can say is that as beat up as he was, he probably will not last too long on the cross. It's over for your friend. Too bad. He seemed like the kind of man I would have liked."

As Nicodemus started dejectedly down the steps, ineffably sad, the door swung open with the officer motioning for Nicodemus to come back. Hope? "My lord," the officer said in a low voice, "I will make one concession. When the man dies, you can have his body for burial. No need to let him hang there and rot on the cross like usually happens. I'll take care of it. I promise." The door closed again.

—

"Another one?" the corporal complained. "We've already got two strung up out on the hill. No problem, though. We'll handle it. We've got half a dozen uprights in place. Load up the prisoner with his beam. Let's get started."

To himself the corporal mumbled, *I signed up to fight for Rome, not kill crazy peasants. Oh well, duty is duty.*

In a moment, as the corporal collected rope, spikes, and a hammer from the supply room, the prisoner, prodded by a guard, came stumbling through the door into the courtyard. His hands were free so he could carry the beam. The guards had shackled his ankles with irons and a chain, as if a man in his condition could run even if given the chance.

"Where to?" one of the soldiers asked the corporal.

"That hill on the outside of the walls. The one that looks like a skull. 'Golgotha,' the Jews call it," the corporal said.

Making sure he had the gruesome supplies he needed for the morning's work, the corporal got the tragic little processional in line. Place of the skull. It fits, I guess.

"Load him up," the corporal ordered.

Two of the guards swung the five-foot, four-inch by six-inch beam onto Jesus's shoulder.

The weight of the cross beam the guards dropped on Jesus's shoulders was more than his straining bladder could stand. Urine soaked his tattered shift, splashing on the courtyard's cobblestones.

Jesus had no strength for a comment. He did not wince at the mess he had made of himself. Another Isaiah word flashed, *He was despised and held of no accord.* Conserve what strength he had for what lay ahead. For a fleeting second, memories of Joseph's killing field gripped his mind. My time now, he realized. Papa and Adonai, help me through this.

The butt of a spear jabbed in his back signaled the beginning of the end.

—

"Your Excellency," Saruch announced to the captain, "some Galileans are at the front door. Two men. Two women. They are kinspeople of Jesus, the man who was sentenced to death. They are pleading to see you. What do you want me to do with them?"

With a dismissive wave of his hand, hardly looking up from his paperwork, the captain said absently, "Send them away. It's over."

"My lord," interrupting one more time, "they said if you would not see them, they asked if you would tell them where Jesus is."

With a sarcastic laugh, this time not even looking up, the captain said, "Try Antonia Fortress or Golgotha."

—

For the first time since Jesus's death march began, the corporal looked at the haggard prisoner. Doing a double-take, the Roman soldier thought he had seen this man before. Hard to tell, though. He looked so bad. No, just another Jewish rebel. Powerful face and eyes, despite the beating he had endured.

"Which way do we go?" one of the guards asked the corporal. "Long way or short way?"

"Our orders are to take him the long way. Pilate wanted everyone in town to get a long look at their king," the corporal answered. Looking more closely at Jesus, the young Roman tried again to place the man. In his five years in Judea, he had had dealings with thousands of forgettable Jews. This man was different, very different. But who was he?

As they left Antonia Fortress, a veteran teased one of the new recruits, "From the looks of this man, you may have to carry the beam part of the way. He's not going to make it."

"Not me," the young soldier growled. "If he falls, we'll take a 'volunteer' from the street." He laughed at his own cruel joke about a volunteer. No one would volunteer to take another man's cross.

—

Jesus's mother, James, John, and Mary Magdala rushed as much as they could through the crowded Jerusalem's streets. The man at the captain's house had slammed the door in their faces before they could get directions to Antonia Fortress, and the guards at the door refused to talk with them, lest they be accused of inattention to their security duties. At first they could find no one in the street who would stop long enough to offer assistance.

"We're not making any headway," James fumed as they trudged in what they hoped was the general direction of the tower.

Jesus's mother saw an alert, intelligent-looking woman coming their way. Even though women did not normally talk to anyone in public, much less a stranger, Mary was desperate.

"Please," Mary stopped the woman passerby, "my son is in terrible trouble with the Romans. I've got to get to Antonio Fortress. I'm lost." She did not falter despite the tears that flowed.

The woman wanted to pass on by. Mary's obvious fear and the woman's aversion to the Romans prompted her to supply the necessary information.

Within a few minutes, guided by the woman's directions, the four of them arrived at the tall stone tower on the northwest corner of the temple complex. "There it is," John declared. "Hard to believe we had such a hard time finding something that big."

"What do we do now?" Mary Magdalene wanted to know.

"We find out what's happening," Jesus's mother answered with grim determination.

"I'll ask," John offered nervously.

He started up the stone steps of the tower.

"John!" someone shouted above the street noises. "John!"

Craning his neck to see who was calling him, John saw Leah, followed by Nicodemus and the Galileans, rushing through the crowded streets.

The small company of comrades in grief embraced one another.

Before they could recap the morning's panicked activities, the double doors of the Antonia Fortress swung open. The Roman sentries lowered their spears toward the small group that happened to be at the fortress at that moment, forcing everyone to give way for the military detail that emerged. A young soldier, hardly more than a boy, led the detail beating a small, round drum in solemn cadence. Behind him marched a corporal leading a square of eight unblinking Roman soldiers formed in a box formation surrounding a tall, lean, bloodied, weed-crowned figure who stumbled and struggled under the weight of a beam of weathered oak. Spike holes were visible at either end of the heavy timber, grisly memoirs of previous macabre episodes.

Jesus's mother wanted to faint, run away, lift the beam from her son's shoulders. Instead, she gripped Mary of Magdala's hand so tightly that the younger woman winced. Both Marys looked intently at the condemned man, son, lover, friend, hope, future embodied in that splendid human being uniquely endowed by Adonai, destined, they had been convinced, to change their world. Now, step by inexorable step, he was dying. And what a terrible, ignominious death! The worst devised by fellow human beings, inspired by their darkest, most demonically possessed nature.

Though their mouths emitted not a word, the minds of both women screamed, "How could this be!" Not Jesus. Please, not Jesus. Yet there he labored under the weight of the beam, under the weight of his brother's guilt, under the weight of the collective evil that surrounded him. Dying because of the sins of his torn and fragmented world. *Wounded by our transgressions...bruised by our iniquities.* The passion of his brief years had been to open men and women to the best within themselves, to connect them with the living Adonai. Now, today, as the morning sun bore down on the City of David, those very people for whom he had poured himself out had turned on him with a carelessness of staggering proportions, his great goodness crushed by their overarching evil.

James and John instinctively rushed to help Jesus. With machine-like precision, three spear-bearing guards lowered and pointed their weapons, stopping the men in their tracks. One more step by either of Jesus's friends would have meant instant death.

Nicodemus confronted the corporal, holding up his hands to halt the detail. "I am Nicodemus, a member of the Jewish Sanhedrin," he announced to the young Roman corporal in near-perfect Latin, a facility that startled the soldier, so unused was he to hearing his native language spoken by the Jews. "This execution is illegal!"

The corporal did not know this Jewish man. He did have the political good sense to appreciate the man's rank. He raised his arm into the air and called out to the detail, "Halt!"

"My lord," the corporal replied in a reasonable tone of voice, speaking halting Greek, "only out of respect for your office do I stop. Do not interfere with my orders. You may not like this execution, but it is completely legal. Now," he said, glowering at the older Jew, "get out of my way."

"Wait, you don't understand," Nicodemus interjected before the corporal shoved him aside while calling out to his men, "Forward!"

In his pain and stupor, Jesus had not yet seen his family and friends. The brief stop gave him an instant to look around. The sight of his devastated mother, grieving Mary, stricken and thwarted brothers and friends brought a spasm of pain, but also served to provide him with a new surge of strength, resolve, perhaps even a sense of purpose. They had not deserted him. Embracing them with one look as the detail began to move again, he gasped loudly enough for them to hear him, "It's all right. It's all right."

Later, his gasped blessing would become another source of comfort and clarity to those who picked up the pieces of his life, cut so short. They heard in his simple words the assurance that, indeed, this unmitigated tragedy had not completely leaped the bounds of sanity or holy purpose. Adonai would yet make right this monumental wrong, open minds to the embracing dimensions of Jesus's life and death and beyond. At that moment Jesus's words only intensified their searing pain as they were about to lose the man who, in his life and now in his death agony, reached out to everyone around him.

This was not the first time the corporal had waded through keening grief as he led convicted criminals to their deaths. He himself had a mother, brothers, and sisters, friends back in Rome who would have carried on like these people if he were similarly condemned. As much as he wanted not to hear and feel with these mourning Jesus, he could not entirely remove himself from the tragedy of the moment. Orders were orders. He would not falter. He would not allow anyone or anything to impede him. It was unsettling to him, a soldier, to let himself feel these people's hurt.

With the waning measure of awareness that Jesus still possessed, his body screamed from head to toe. His scalp, his shoulders, his back, legs, and feet were on fire, especially right now his feet. Oh, how his feet hurt! The soles were gnashed from being dragged from the olive grove through the streets to the captain's house and now beyond. He called up every ounce of strength he could garner simply to put one mutilated foot in front of the other. Where would this madness end? How long before he could stop? Then he knew he could not stop, would not be allowed to stop. He'd seen Joseph die on his cross. Others also. No! This could not be happening to him. He had never raised a hand against another human being. His years had been to make life better. He and Adonai had become so close, even one. Now this!

He would have to stand up straighter, regardless of his weakness. If he had no idea the meaning of his death throes in the larger scheme of the Holy One, he would at least show strength. Ending like this. He'd just started. Failure? No, his spirit resoundingly answered. Not failure. Too many people connected with the Holy One!

He pushed himself taller. With his dearest friends in the world nearby, he would go as far and as well as humanly possible and then some.

If Pilate had thought the people in the street would jeer at the weed-crowned figure stumbling under the cross, he was wrong. Other than the handful of friends who now grimly threaded along behind this melancholy parade, none along Jerusalem's streets knew him. They certainly did not ridicule the poor man. No one, they realized, no matter his crimes, deserves this torture. Instead of derision, they felt pity. And fear. In their world of swift, heartless, invariably unfair judgment, for the poor, the weeds, any of them could be in the same predicament within a matter of hours, minutes. Few implicated their religious leaders in this spectacle. The Romans were the killers.

Jesus crumpled. A guard lashed at him with a whip, shredding his bloody shirt to ribbons, more bright blood splattered.

*Got to get up*, Jesus screamed at himself. He tried. Oh, how he tried. His battered feet, trembling legs, and bleeding back simply would not respond to his mind's commands.

Furious, the corporal ordered the guard, "Hit him again! He's got to get up. We've got to get this over!"

Jesus did not fall prostrate. He remained on his knees. The beam teetered on his shoulder. He just could not rise.

As the corporal, in grim determination to get the execution accomplished, scanned the spectators for someone to take up the beam, a giant of a man edged his way through the crowd.

In a dialect that marked him as a Samaritan, Boaz announced in a booming voice, "I'll take it."

"Boaz!" Mary Magdala exclaimed, brightening, if but for a moment. "Boaz!"

Hefting the beam onto his shoulders, he who until so recently had lived in the grip of demonic anger, his eyes pouring tears, his booming voice choking with grief, answered simply, "Yes, it's me. Adonai sent me to Jerusalem last night. I thought for Passover. No, for Jesus."

"Move!" the corporal impatiently ordered. "If you're going to take the cross, let's go. Now!"

Relieved of the crushing weight, Jesus stood up, shook his head, pushed the matted hair out of his eyes, and started walking again. Everything spun. Still, he walked, his head now high, his eyes, while seeing nothing, looking ahead.

After nearly an hour of circuitous marching, the corporal, soldiers, their victim, and his friends exited the city through one of the smaller gates. A hundred yards beyond the walls, a small hill rose up on which a dozen men and women had collected to agonize around two young men already crucified. Mothers, fathers, and young wives wailed their grief. Four Roman soldiers kept the anguished bystanders away from their tortured loved ones. As the young girl had told Cephas, it was indeed a bad place.

Within minutes upon their arrival at Golgotha, Jesus lay on the ground, stripped of his tattered shirt, his arms outstretched held firmly in place on the beam Boaz had deposited as ordered by the corporal. A guard nonchalantly pulled a long spike from a bag held out to him by the corporal. Expertly, he placed the spike against Jesus's wrist and, with three strokes, drove it through the flesh deep into the beam. Jesus screamed and fainted. Before he could come to, the guard had nailed the other wrist.

Rolling dark clouds curtained the morning sun, which just a few minutes ago was shining clearly. It began to rain a steady, soaking downpour. The cold rain revived Jesus.

Four guards now stood Jesus on his feet, propping him up lest he again crumple to the rocky earth.

Using sturdy poles made for the purpose, the guards hoisted the beam with Jesus hanging suspended by the spikes into position on the upright. By fitting the middle of the beam over the notch in the upright, the cross was complete. There, Jesus hung, his feet almost touching the ground, though for all the good they did him, they could have been in the heavens.

"Bind his feet and legs to the upright," the corporal ordered.

"Do we make a seat for him?" a guard asked.

"No," the corporal answered through the rain, softening somewhat now that his job was almost done. "He's not going to last long. A seat only makes it worse in the long run. Let him die as soon as he can."

By the time Jesus was on the cross, any concern for his nakedness disappeared. *He had no form or majesty that one should look at him.* Suffering chewed his entire being, all his pain-crazed mind could confront. Push up on his tortured, maddeningly cramped feet and legs, grab a breath, then sag again against his spiked wrists. Staying alive was one labored breath at a time. That's all that mattered. Another breath. Or was that all that mattered? If only he could stop breathing, he could find the relief he craved. But life was too strong in this man to give up to death without a fierce struggle.

The women could not bear to look at him; neither could they look away. Their bones screamed like his. Their hearts threatened to burst like his. Their lungs labored for air like his. Every breath might be his last. They had to help him, to nurture him in dying as they had in living. When he stopped breathing, so did they. When he gasped again, so did they.

At one point Simon lifted his arms toward Jesus, calling out pitiably to his brother, "Jesus, save yourself like you have so many others."

—

Cephas and the limping Joses wound their way through the city as fast as they could on their way to the gate that would take them out to Golgotha. Joses, determined as he was to get to his brother, nonetheless had to rest every few minutes. He endured the pain made worse by terrible weakness. More than a few hundred yards at a time left him dizzy, an enveloping blackness threatening to lay him low.

The temple police guard under the shelter at the gate was talking amiably with passersby who came and went his way, ducking out of the rain. His job had placed him at this gate for several years, so he knew by face and name hundreds of Jerusalemites who used his gate regularly. He rarely gave anyone trouble, primarily because they rarely gave him trouble. His easygoing air, however, covered a surprisingly quick mind when it came to doing his duty. He could perk up instantly if something did not seem right. In all his years, he had rarely been hoodwinked and never reprimanded for carelessness at his post. Festivals increased the possibility of trouble. They also made him more alert. What with the attempt on the lives of the high priest and Pilate, he made sure he noticed everyone while still keeping up his banter.

When the corporal and his grisly detail had come through, the sun was bright, the sky clear, a light breeze blowing. Why make himself feel sad by looking over there at the killing field? And now, with the dark skies and the downpour, he certainly did not look in the direction of Golgotha. No need to make himself feel glum. The weather would do that for him.

Cephas and Joses almost made it through the gate unnoticed by the guard. As the two men approached the gate, the guard was talking with a pretty young woman who sometimes brought cakes to him and his partners at their post. He knew she felt special toward him, loved to tease with him. He certainly enjoyed her company.

As Jews, Cephas and Joses had no reason to slow down going through the gate. They had to present no passes or other documentation. In fact, they were so intent on getting to Golgotha, they hardly noticed the guard. Just as Cephas and Joses came up to the gate, Cephas turned his foot on a slippery rock, bumping into Joses, almost knocking him to the ground. The pain of the sudden movement caused Joses to cry out involuntarily in pain. This little episode caught the guard's attention.

"Do I know you men?" he inquired.

Recovering, the two men immediately sensed danger. "No," Cephas answered cautiously. "We are pilgrims returning home after the festival."

"Galileans?" the guard wanted to know.

"From where?" he asked.

"Capernaum," Cephas replied.

Looking at Joses, noticing for the first time how pale and wasted he looked, the guard asked, "Are you from Capernaum also?"

"No, I am from Nazareth. We have mutual friends. That's why we are together," Joses explained, deciding quickly in the moment to be as truthful as he dared.

"You don't look so good," the guard suggested.

"I got sick while I was here. Bad food I guess," Joses lied, he prayed convincingly.

"When your friend here," motioning toward Cephas, "fell up against you a minute ago, you yelped like he'd stepped on you. Like you've been hurt and he bumped your wound."

"My side is sore from throwing up. Maybe even broke a rib. I was mighty sick," Joses lied again. "He bumped into me, and it hurt."

Not wanting to create a stir with his suspicions aroused just enough to make him extra cautious, the guard said politely, motioning toward a stone bench just inside the walls, "Would you men have a seat over there for a few minutes? When the crowd clears out, I might want to talk with you just a bit more." He pointed them to a bench out of the rain in a niche in the wall.

Thinking fast, Cephas answered, "Sure, but we need to get to our homes. My friend wants to get back to Nazareth as soon as he can in case he gets sick again."

"Oh, Cephas," Joses grimaced, "that guard's uneasy with us. He's probably been told to be on the lookout for an injured man, especially one from Galilee."

"We'll have to pray that he doesn't look at us too closely," Cephas agreed anxiously. He had no doubt he could take the guard, but there were others on duty. Besides, that would just cause a riot. Even though the minutes were flying by, the two men had no choice but to wait.

—

The corporal had been keeping his distance from the three men agonizing on their crosses. He had been here before. It was always a sorry duty. At sundown he could leave, stationing a couple guards to remain on duty lest family members try to get their people down from their crosses. Drawing from his experience as an executioner, he could predict within a few hours when the men would die. The two younger men, hardly more than boys, would linger for a couple days. They had been scourged prior to crucifixion, but they were not too badly beaten. This other fellow was another issue. He already looked near death. Fine enough specimen of a man, he reasoned. From the looks of his body, no stranger to work. Still, the treatment he had received during the night had all but done him in. He probably would not make it much past sundown.

At midday another corporal came out from Pilate's office to make a routine inspection. He also carried with him a written order from the officer in charge of the Jerusalem garrison. "When Jesus the Galilean dies, Nicodemus of the Sanhedrin can claim his body for burial."

This man Jesus was special! But who was he? The corporal wracked his brain. Then it came like a flash. This was the healer Latvias had sent for to cure his little girl. Poor Latvias. Dead, murdered by Galilean assassins. And the little girl, she did not make it either. Now it all came back. He and Jesus had made the trip from the River Jordan camp of that man John to Phasaelis, where he and Latvias were stationed at the time. Why, that's been four or five years ago. Even though the little girl died, Latvias and his wife had never stopped singing the praises of the healer. Seems this man had helped the very sick child ease her way into death without fear and pain.

The corporal began to recall the time he had with this Jesus. Particularly on the return trip when it was just the two of them, Jesus had learned all about the soldier's own family, what his life as a boy in Rome was like, why he joined the army, what he hoped to accomplish. Never had the corporal felt the freedom to talk about himself as he did with the Galilean. The healer had discussed the life of the spirit in ways that made complete sense to the Roman. Funny, he had not thought much about the spirit until now. How could he have forgotten this man! Then, ruefully, looking into the face of the man on the cross, the corporal had to admit this man and the other one hardly resembled one another, except in spirit. Ah, the spirit *was* the same.

Instinctively, the corporal strode to the cross, looked up into the tortured face, and said quietly in Latin, not knowing if Jesus could even understand him, "Jesus, you're the healer. You tried to cure Latvias's daughter. Finally, I remember." Now looking away in embarrassment, an emotion all but alien to the corporal, the soldier muttered, "I am sorry this has happened to you. You don't deserve it. There's nothing I can do, but you don't deserve this."

To his utter amazement the corporal heard Jesus choke out in Latin through parched lips, "Forgiven."

—

The morning hours eased by. The sky remained dark, and the rain continued. Midday approached. Cephas and Joses by now were about to jump out of their skins. "We've got to do something," Cephas said under his breath. "This is driving me mad."

"Me too," Joses moaned, terribly distressed.

Cephas went to the guard. "We've been waiting here for a long time. Do you think we could be on our way?"

"I almost forgot you. I apologize. I will be with you in a few minutes."

In reality, moments after asking the two Galileans to wait, the guard had told one of his subordinates, "Go to the captain's house. Tell one of the officers I have a couple Galileans here. One looks like he might have been hurt. Could be one of the killers. I'll keep them here. Hurry."

The guard did not hurry. He stopped at a bazaar for a cake. He chatted with friends on the way. By the time he reached the captain's house, the officers he needed to see had left. Not having any sense of urgency about his mission, he talked to one of the captain's aides, who likewise picked up no feeling of haste.

"Go back to your post," the aide advised after a while. "Tell the guard to send the two men here with an escort. Sometime this afternoon, one of the officers will see them and make a judgment."

By the time the guard dawdled his way back to the gate, it was afternoon. His message infuriated the cautious veteran. "Look, if no one in the captain's house has any more concern than that, I'm going to let these two men go their way. The pale one may be one of the killers. If he is, so be it."

Free at last, Cephas and Joses left the city, hurrying as fast as they could through the drenching rain toward Golgotha.

From a distance of several hundred yards, Cephas and Joses could feel the silence that blanketed the small hilltop. Jesus's mother and Mary clung to one another, Leah helplessly at their side. James, John, Nicodemus, Simon, and the Galileans stood vacantly like statues. Boaz swayed, fighting grief and anger. Jesus hung limply from his cross.

Joses, sobbing, broke and ran toward his brother's cross, ignoring the frightful pain in his own body. Dropping to his knees, he embraced his brother's lifeless legs, stroking them, kissing his twisted, battered feet. Through paroxysms of tears, the younger brother keened, "I should have been on that cross. Not him. He died for me! He died for me!"

Cornelius, the corporal standing nearby, exclaimed from somewhere in the depths of his Roman soul, "We all belonged on that cross, not him. No! He died because of all of us."

Nicodemus, looking in the still, now serene face of Jesus, said simply, "*tetelestai*." The rain stopped. The late afternoon sun began to come from behind the dark clouds.

—

*to be continued*

CPSIA information can be obtained
at www.ICGtesting.com
Printed in the USA
BVHW070946090820
585898BV00004B/13

9 781635 281149